Easter

Michael Arditti was born in Cheshire and lives in London. He is the author of two highly acclaimed novels, *The Celibate* and *Pagan and her Parents*.

The Celibate

'An ambitious first novel, which traces the liberation of a human soul through a gradual revelation of the meaning of passion and the Passion' – *Independent on Sunday*

'An exceptional book: at its core it combines the sexual with the spiritual' – *Sunday Times*

'The author's anger, conviction and sharp observation hold the reader's attention throughout. An exciting début' – *The Times*

'It is unusual to find an English first novel of such unflinching moral seriousness . . . a varied and involving read' – *Times Literary Supplement*

Pagan and her Parents

'A subtle and complex reflection on the wider nature of love and attachment' – *Sunday Telegraph*

'A novel whose shining virtue is its undemonstrative moral cleanliness. Unputdownable' – *The Times*

'Arditti is a literary Hogarth, savaging modern England on many levels. An astonishingly intelligent, funny and touching book' – *The Scotsman*

'A moving novel about the survival of a modern family in the grip of death and the dead hand of convention' – *New Yorker*

MICHAEL ARDITTI

Easter

 ARCADIA BOOKS
LONDON

Arcadia Books Ltd
15–16 Nassau Street
London WIN 7RE

www.arcadiabooks.co.uk

First published in Great Britain 2000
Copyright © Michael Arditti 2000

A catalogue record for this book is available
from the British Library.

ISBN 1–900850–34–6

Designed and Typeset in FF Scala and Scala Sans by
Discript, London WC2N 4BL
Printed in England by Cromwell Press, Trowbridge, Wiltshire

Arcadia Books distributors are as follows:
in the UK and elsewhere in Europe:
Turnaround Publishers Services
Unit 3, Olympia Trading Estate
Coburg Road
London N22 6TZ

in the USA and Canada:
Consortium Book Sales and Distribution, Inc.
1045 Westgate Drive
St Paul, MN 55114–1065

in Australia:
Tower Books
PO Box 213
Brookvale, NSW 2100

in New Zealand:
Addenda
Box 78224
Grey Lynn
Auckland

in South Africa:
Peter Hyde Associates (Pty) Ltd
PO Box 2856
Cape Town 8000

For my father

'Now bless thyself: thou met'st with things dying, I with things new-born.'

Shakespeare, *The Winter's Tale*

'I love your Christ, but I hate your Christians. They are so unlike him.'

Mahatma Gandhi

'When you make the two one and when you make the inner as the outer and the outer as the inner and the upper as the lower, and when you make the male and the female into a single one, so that the male is not male and the female not female, when you make eyes in place of an eye, and a hand in place of a hand, and a foot in place of a foot, an image in place of an image, then you shall enter the Kingdom.'

Jesus Christ, The Gospel of Thomas

THE PARISH OF ST MARY-IN-THE-VALE

Huxley Grieve	*the vicar*
Jessica Grieve	*his wife*
Blair Ashley	*the curate*
Terry Holt	*the organist*
Judith Shellard	*a churchwarden*
Rosemary Trott	*a sidesman*
Lyndon Brooks	*the head server*
Willy Jeavons	*a server*
Hugh Snape	*a buildings inspector*
Petula Snape	*his wife, a nurse*
Russell Snape	*their son*
Laura Snape	*Russell's wife*
Lloyd Snape	*their baby son*
Myrna Timson	*Petula's mother*
Trudy England	*a retired secretary*
Julian Blaikie	*a doctor*
Eleanor Blaikie	*Julian's mother*
Edith Sadler	*her companion*
Lennox Hayward	*a retired doctor*
Femi Olaofe	*a former teacher*
Cherish Akarolo	*her niece*
Alice Leighton	*a painter*
Dora Leighton	*her baby daughter*
Dee Lawrence	*a computer programmer*
Joe Beatty	*a librarian*
Winifred Metcalfe	
Nancy Hewitt	*members of the Parochial Church Council*
Sophie Record	
Bertha Mallot	*a parishioner*

VISITORS TO THE PARISH

Jeffrey Finch-Buller	*managing director, Grafton Holdings*
Thea Finch-Buller	*his wife*
Maureen Beatty	*Joe's mother*
Dave Beatty	*her husband*
Damian Froy	*Joe's best man*
Lionel Potter	*a homeless man*
Ted Bishop	*the Bishop of London*
Esther Bishop	*his wife*
Alfred Courtney	*the Archdeacon of Highgate*
Henrietta Courtney	*his mother*
Ronan Hopkins	*an unemployed youth*
Broderick Loftus	*Eleanor Blaikie's brother*
Helena Grainger	*Eleanor Blaikie's daughter*
Massimo Scannelli	*Julian Blaikie's nurse*
Nick Grant	*Julian Blaikie's buddy*
Colin Brooks	*Lyndon Brooks' father*
David Stafford	*chairman, Grafton Holdings*
Sylvia Stafford	*his wife*
Julia Longman	*friends of Dee Lawrence*
Patricia Torrance	
Oliver Lambert	*an organ repairer*
Brandon Lynch	*a doctor*

PART ONE

ORDER OF SERVICES

SUNDAY
    10.30 a.m.   Blessing and Procession of Palms and High Mass.
    6.30 p.m.   Stations of the Cross.

MONDAY
    10.30 a.m.   Holy Communion.
    7.00 p.m.   Meeting of the Parochial Church Council.

TUESDAY
    2.00 p.m.   Solemnization of Holy Matrimony.

WEDNESDAY
    3.00 p.m.   Funeral Service.

THURSDAY
    10.30 a.m.   Eucharist with the Blessing of the Oils.
    11.00 a.m.   Office for the Royal Maundy.
    6.30 p.m.   Mass of the Lord's Supper.

FRIDAY
    12 noon   Celebration of the Lord's Passion.

SATURDAY
    7.30 p.m.   Order of the Seder.
    8.00 p.m.   Easter Vigil.

Blessing and Procession
of Palms and High Mass

Sunday 10.30 a.m.
St Mary-in-the-Vale, Hampstead

The Curate straightens his alb, kisses his stole and strides out to meet the donkey.

'Break a leg,' shouts Terry, the organist, who doubles as director of the Hampstead Amateur Light Operatic Society.

Blair winces and smiles. He is as sensitive to a theatrical reference as a right-wing pundit to a mention of his radical past.

He hurries down the churchyard path to greet the director of the City Farm who is waiting at the gate. He turns his attention to the donkey, whose demeanour as it leaves the van displays little awareness of the symbolic burden it is to bear.

'You won't try to ride him, will you? Only he has a weak back. We had some trouble with the Methodists last year.'

'Don't worry. I'm not Christ.'

'He likes you.'

The donkey's tongue tickles the hairs on Blair's wrist. He pulls a carrot from his cassock.

'May I?'

'Sure. But whatever you do, no sugar-lumps. He's diabetic.'

The Vicar prays with the servers and choir.

Huxley Grieve stares across the sacristy and searches for God. Eleven bowed heads mock him with the ease of their reverence. He reminds himself that it is the start of the most important week in the Church year. He dissects himself for an emotion to fit the occasion, but all he finds are words ... second-hand words which he has spoken for twenty-eight years running.

The fault doesn't lie in the words. He has kept his love for the poetry of Cranmer's prayer-book even when the mysteries behind it have seemed false. He sometimes fears that its resonant phrases have become not only the shape but the substance of his faith, as they roll like soft-centred chocolates on his tongue.

The problem lies rather in the practicalities. He has to approach the services more like a choreographer than a priest, ensuring that the servers have rehearsed the unfamiliar routines and that the Pascal Candle is ordered, trying to second-guess the number of worshippers so as not to over-consecrate. He has heard it said of art that God exists in the details; the opposite is true of church. He is as tied to a checklist as a mother of the bride.

Is this the true sacrifice of priesthood: that his mission to bring the love of Christ to his congregation, particularly in this Holy Week celebration of His Passion and Resurrection, is precisely what prevents him from sharing it? Administration alienates him from the very sacraments that sustain his faith.

If that were so, it would at least give him some hope, like Beethoven writing music he could never hear. But he fears that the truth is less benign. He is obsessed by a dream that he had on Friday night. He was preaching from the top board at a swimming baths. As he spoke, people plunged in all around him. His words inspired them to ever more dangerous dives. But there was no water in the pool and they fell flat onto their bloody, broken faces. They lay on the bottom in supermarket piles, until the only ones left listening to him were children too young to dive.

The Curate returns to the sacristy.

'I'm sorry I took so long,' Blair explains. 'I had to see a man about a donkey.'

The people gather by Whitestone pond. The sidesman hands out orders of service.

Hugh Snape gazes at his fellow worshippers blinking in the sunlight. Away from the pillars and pews, they seem to lack conviction, like conscripts to the Salvation Army. Theirs is a world of private prayer not of standing up and being counted on street corners. Their only other outdoor service is on Remembrance Sunday, and that is almost secular, more Queen and Country than God.

He watches the steady stream of cars flowing north, some to token family lunches, others to beat the queues at B&Q. The indifference of the motorists threatens him. One van does stop and a long-haired youth shouts a question. Rosemary Trott rushes up to explain. 'I'm the sidesman,' she declares with her tweed-skirted diction. He wonders whether, were the word the more neutral 'usher', she would be so insistent about its use.

An irritating giggle alerts him to the group of young men gathered by the boarded-up hamburger stall. They would do better in a Roman Catholic church with regular confession. He shudders to think of their backlog of sins.

The sidesman hands out palm crosses.

'I've brought my own,' says Eleanor Blaikie, waving Rosemary aside with a large frond cut from her conservatory. Stevenson, the parrot perched on her shoulder, squawks at the sudden swing. 'I see no reason I should make do with a miniature simply because I'm not in the choir.'

> The procession approaches, led by the Crucifer. The Acolytes follow, then the choir, the Curate with the donkey, the Thurifer and the Vicar. A policeman brings up the rear.

The donkey is greeted with enthusiasm by the children and wariness by the adults.

'Drawing attention to himself,' Eleanor says to her companion Edith. 'We'll be having cattle at the carol service next.'

'It would never have happened in Father Heathcote's day,' Edith agrees.

'Why can't that boy hold the cross up straight?' Jeffrey Finch-Buller asks his wife Thea. 'It's quivering like a juggler's pole.'

'Well of course; it's a circus,' Thea replies. 'Even the Vicar's in red.'

'It's all too high for me,' Myrna Timson says to her daughter Petula, while pulling her grey felt hat over her ears.

'I wonder what it cost,' Hugh says to his wife Petula. 'I hope it hasn't come out of church funds.'

'Sh-sh,' Petula says to both of them. 'The choir can hardly make themselves heard.'

> The choir sings:
> *Hosanna to the Son of David,*
> *the King of Israel.*
> *Blessed is he who comes*
> *in the name of the Lord.*
> *Hosanna in the highest.*

Thea inspects the women of the congregation, neatly dividing the lambswool from the angora. She envelops herself in her fur coat with the defiance of one who still serves British beef. If anyone had told her that she would spend Sunday morning on a traffic island by Hampstead Heath, she would have laughed. She is sorely tempted to hail one of the cabs cruising past, until she remembers her grandson. Lloyd is to be christened in St Mary's on Saturday and she has a duty to ensure that the church is sound. So far the signs are not good. The Vicar can't be blamed for the limp crosses, car-horn accompaniment or even the Thurifer's losing battle with exhaust fumes, but he should have anticipated the donkey.

Couldn't they have found one who would be less susceptible to the children's stroking? Its reactions would cause a riot on Brighton beach. Perhaps they thought that the sacredness of the occasion would tame its animal nature. If her own is anything to go by, there is little chance.

She weighs up the danger of the donkey attacking a toddler. The little black girl with the glass beads is uncomfortably close. She cannot believe that she, alone, is alert to its arousal. If they all want to play the innocent, so be it. Besides whom would she tell? The fearsome-looking woman with the dead fox around her neck and live parrot on her shoulder? The woman who handed out service-sheets as if she were giving them prep? Hugh? Petula? And let them attempt to make intimacy out of innuendo? Worst of all would be Jeffrey who might interpret it as a request.

The Vicar delivers his homily.

'I wonder if, before I start, I might ask you all to move in a little closer. I know that you like to keep your distance, to "preserve your own space", as it were.' Huxley fears that his tone, designed to ingratiate, simply grates. 'But it would hardly do for me to lose my voice at the beginning of Holy Week, would it?'

The only reply comes from the rattle of drills as workmen, their white chests attesting to their recent release from winter vests, take advantage of the Sunday lull to dig up the road.

'Come on now. No one's going to bite you.' He watches the compromise shuffle of a congregation which prefers to love its neighbour by proxy. Only Myrna Timson seems grateful for his licence and clasps her daughter's hand. She looks set to do the same to her son-in-law but ends up brushing the back of his anorak with her sleeve. The rest put up barriers as solid as pews. He is filled with despair. They have reduced the body of Christ to a pile of uncoordinated limbs. Gone is all sense of community. *Noli Me Tangere* might be the crux of the creed.

He is seized by an urge to tear up his notes and to preach on the text 'Beloved, if God so loved us, we ought also to love one another', but he resists. Instead, he clears his throat, more of frustration than phlegm, and begins.

'Once again I stand before you at the start of Holy Week, the week that is for Christians – and, indeed, for the whole world, did it but know – the most important of the year. In the events of this

week lie the clearest answer any of us will ever find to the mystery
of life. This is the week in which God enters into human suffering.
Our task is to offer an adequate response.'

The response of the drills is relentless, like drums accompanying
a tumbril, drowning the victim's last words.

'We now go to take part in the Passion story ourselves. As we
make our way back down the hill – and, indeed, in all our services
this week – let us remember that the liturgy is not a commemora-
tion but a re-enactment. Christ's crucifixion and redemption are
taking place every day. It's an eternal cycle which Holy Week en-
ables us to experience as a single moment. We may be living many
centuries after AD 33 but we all play roles in the story. Which one
are you? Judas? Peter? Veronica? Pilate? The informer? The liar?
The comforter? The washer of hands? Let us reflect on it as we
walk to the church, singing the processional hymn.'

> Ride on! ride on in majesty!
> Hark! all the tribes Hosanna cry!

Thea has earmarked her role as ruthlessly as an actress owed a
favour. Her choice is Mary who massaged Christ's feet with her hair.
Since they met when He was on His way to Jerusalem, it fits tempo-
rally as well as temperamentally. The thought of the hot oil dripping
from His toes onto her scalp is so overwhelming that she stops to
draw breath, only to find herself next to the Anoraks, her private
name for Petula and Hugh Snape, the aptness of which is doubly
apparent today. Worse, there is Petula's mother Myrna – Moaner
behind her back and sometimes to her face if she is caught off guard
– with her threadbare hair and doughy features, trundling along on
her thigh-thick ankles. She would make even the Red Sea smack of
Blackpool. Suddenly Palestine looks a less enticing prospect.

It seems hard that she should be connected – she refuses even to
think 'related' – to these people by marriage. She has never discussed Russell with Laura, in spite of enjoying the sort of intimacy
with her daughter only possible for a mother who regains her figure straight after giving birth. That may be the problem. If she had
huffed and puffed and talked disinheritance, she might have dissuaded her from this tradesman's-entrance wedding. Christ's is not
the only story to be repeated every day.

Seeing Petula poised to speak, she strides forward, only to be
attacked on a second front.

'Are you regular?'

'I beg your pardon?' For a moment she is back with Nanny and
syrup of figs.

'At the church.' A moon-faced woman beams at her.

'No. My husband and I have come because our grandson is to be christened here next week.'

'Same with us. Father and I are down for our son Joe's wedding.'

She decides to play dumb. 'Your father?'

'Oh no, that's just what I call him. He's Dave; I'm Maureen...'

I bet you are, she thinks.

'We've come down from Rochdale.'

'How brave.' And, displaying the form that conquers all in the winter-sales sweep-stake, she breaks free.

> Ride on! ride on in majesty!
> In lowly pomp ride on to die.

Myrna has no doubt of her role in the Passion story: she is one of the lame, cramming the streets of Jerusalem desperate for a touch of Jesus' hem. Ever since the onset of phlebitis, she feels as though she has been walking on stilts. Nevertheless, she strains to keep pace with her family, dismissing Petula's offer of a moment's rest. She must demonstrate her stamina; she must prove that she will not hold them back.

> Ride on! ride on in majesty!
> The last and fiercest strife is nigh.

Resolute to the last, Rosemary refuses to restrict herself to one of the weeping and wailing women of Jerusalem. Her shoulders are as broad as any man's. She might choose Simon of Cyrene, if it weren't for his colour. Blackness would be going too far. On which note, she frowns at the sight of the Vicar's wife walking with Femi Olaofe. Trust Mrs Political Correctness to make a point. What's more, she seems to have picked up a tramp with every intention of taking him into church. Has she no consideration for those who have worked for two days on the Easter spring-clean? And Rosemary knows that she is fated to be Veronica after all.

> The procession reaches the church. The choir sings the
> antiphon:
> As the Lord was entering into the holy city, the children of
> the Hebrews foretold the resurrection of life. With branches
> of palm trees, they cried out: 'Hosanna in the highest'.

Hosannas turn to hopelessness as Jessica Grieve approaches the church. She rallies by adopting its own tactic of hating the sin but loving the sinner. Who would not love this particular sinner? St Mary-in-the-Vale stands before her in all its mock-Gothic splendour:

the turreted tower topped with the double bellcote, the twisting bands of yellow, red and black brick, like the pages of a geology textbook come to life, as if the building itself were an answer to those Victorian fundamentalists who wanted to squeeze fourteen billion years of creation into a single week.

She reserves her hatred for the capital 'C', the Church that has blighted her life for thirty years, that has given her nothing to call her own, not even her husband. Huxley laughed when she called him a bigamist, but his marriage to the Church is far more than a metaphor. It is the essence of his being. Another woman she could handle; but how can anyone compete with God?

The early days were the worst. While Huxley stood golden-robed at the altar, she was left with the church-mice – only poorer – in a tumbledown vicarage that they could not afford to heat, living on the breadline which ran through the house like the mismatched carpet. For years while the children were small, they survived on charity. And it was given so grudgingly: a few pounds here, from the Friends of the Clergy for school uniforms; a few there, from the Corporation of Sons of the Clergy for family holidays. Even then there was a catch; after all, vicars can't be choosers. What good was praying 'lead us not into temptation' and then going abroad? So they sat in a windswept beachhut in Sidmouth, nursing sodden dreams of sunny Spain.

She is dismayed by the depth of her bitterness. She sounds like an ageing back-bencher or jilted bride. God – rhetorical device not Supreme Being – save her from joining the ranks of the wreckers, undermining other peoples' faith because she has none herself. Then, as she watches the congregation streaming into the porch, she realizes why she still comes to church after fifty years of a message so bland that it might as well be in Esperanto. Others have faith in God; she has faith in Huxley. Their means is her end. Just the sight of him standing head and shoulders above the crowd, his white hair and whiskers as distinguished as his nineteenth century namesake's, fills her with love.

> The procession moves up the nave. The Curate leads
> the donkey around the church. It takes fright at the
> cloud of incense and defecates by the font.

Thea gazes at the gorgeously gaudy interior and feels underdressed. A vision of opulence opens up before her. Arcades of angels draw her eyes to the chancel screen, as delicately illuminated as a letter in a mediaeval manuscript. Above her head, a midnight blue roof sends out shooting stars along golden ribbing. Beneath her feet, a mosaic floor throws up fragmentary faces from childhood tales. A rose window casts a kaleidoscope pattern from saint-filled petals, while zigzags of zebra-striped tiles encircle the walls. The burnished glow and musky scent imbue her with a deep sense of belonging. In a flash, she is transported to the Room of Luxury at Harrods. And, although there is nothing on sale but candles, she is at peace.

Before taking her seat, she moves to inspect the font. One glimpse of its alabaster base and panels of inlaid marble assures her that she can entrust Lloyd to its waters as confidently as to the family christening-robe. She makes to follow Jeffrey only to find that her foot is caught. But it is not a rut; it is shit. And, when she tries to shake it off, the shoe sticks to the floor. She casts a venomous glance at the donkey, ambling down the aisle with an insouciant toss of its tail. Hugh Snape, walking a step behind, proves to be an unexpected Prince Charming, retrieving the shoe, wiping it on his service-sheet, and handing it to her with a flourish. Mustering her shattered dignity, she hobbles up the nave, while the hymn-book woman runs across with a shovel.

'Gangway,' she cries lustily. 'I was a land-girl during the war.'

> The Curate leads the donkey through the Lady Chapel, past the organ and out through the sacristy.

'Never act with children and animals, eh Father?' says Terry from the look-out post of his loft. Blair responds with a watery smile.

> The congregation takes its seats.

Trudy England makes her way to the centre of the church. Too far forward and she might draw attention to herself; too far back and she might be left on her own. The middle-ground has been her life-long preference and, at sixty-seven, she is too old to change.

Her immediate concern is to avoid the angels which, in her view, should be left to rest invisibly on peoples' shoulders, and not hung in an all too vivid flight path above their heads. Her weekly prayers are regularly interspersed with thoughts of rusty nails, rotten wood and falls as fatal as Lucifer's. But her search for a secluded spot only leads to a new danger.

'Why won't any of you sit beside me? Is it because you think I've got no money?'

Her next concern is to avoid Bertha whom she has regarded as a witch ever since she told her that there was an age-old curse on her house and a plague-pit underneath it. Her suspicions are reinforced by Bertha's clothing – why else would she wear a rain-hat indoors and an apron outside her coat? – and, above all, by her eyebrows, which bulge like two tadpoles on the verge of becoming frogs. Judging that it would be unwise to offend her, she tentatively squeezes into the pew.

'Don't crowd me, dear,' Bertha says, as soon as she is settled. 'There's the whole church for you to sit in.'

She slides away, making sure to stay smiling, while Bertha unwraps a sweet.

> The Vicar announces Hymn 98.
> *All glory, laud and honour*
> *To thee, Redeemer King.*

Lionel hesitates at the porch; the woman who suggested the meal has gone inside with no word as to whether he is supposed to follow. A rumble in his stomach convinces him to take a chance. He steps inside and squints as though it were summer. His eyes need time to accustom themselves to the glow. He stares at the stony faces, both sculpted and human. Only the angels seem happy, hanging from the pillars like swimmers preparing to dive. They make him want to laugh but he thinks better of it. He takes off his cap for the first time in weeks and starts to cough. Then he cups some water from the basin and tries to wipe the dirt from his face. His skin sticks to his fingers. He feels as if he is back at school and waits for someone to tell him where to go. Sure enough a woman comes towards him.

> A member of the congregation reads the Old Testament lesson.

Rosemary intercepts the tramp at the holy-water stoup. 'Here you are,' she says, handing him two hymn-books, a prayer-book and the Easter leaflet, which he holds as if with a broken arm. 'You sit at the back with me,' she says, sacrificing personal comfort to the general good. As he gapes at the church, she makes sure to keep the collection box in constant view.

> The Curate reads the epistle.

Huxley listens to the music of Blair's voice, while the words float past, as sonorously superfluous as opera. He struggles to concentrate, willing the familiar cadences to restore his faith like a long-lost memory at the sight of home. But they mock him like the doorway of a dream.

His gaze drifts over the double-edged beauty of the church, which now appeals more to lovers of the Gothic than of God. It

survives as a relic of a bygone age when the parish and the community were one and an artist's vision extended beyond posterity. He
has care of its treasures if not of its souls. He looks at the gloomy
picture in the gilded frame and entitles it 'Study in brown hats and
blue rinses'. He does not ask for a larger congregation – he has
long lost faith in miracles – simply a more representative one.
Christ's message is universal; why has his become so restricted?
No priest could feel more like St Francis, as the shrill voices peck
at the prayers and warble the hymns.

Watching Blair walk back to his seat, his heart is full of envy.
There is a man who can cross the Eden mosaic on the chancel floor
and count himself truly in paradise. He can stand at the altar and
be both himself and Christ. He can elevate the cup and hear the
wind whistling through the empty tomb. Meanwhile others (no
names, no pronouns) search vainly for body-snatchers in the
crowd.

What went wrong? Where is the man who, thirty years ago, to
the horror of family and friends, threw up medicine in order to
dedicate himself to God? The body is much the same. The hair
grows white but it grows. Even the face remains itself. It is as if the
survival of the surface mocks the inner decay. Somewhere a faith
has been locked in an attic. How is he to rescue it? He scours
books, only to turn assertions into arguments. He takes the
Sacrament, but his spirit is left parched. If the way to God is found
in prayer, why is he walking backwards?

And yet, as he moves to the transept, he knows that the answer
belies the question. His last hope, like his first, lies in grace.

The Vicar reads the notices.

'As we come to the altar today, let us do so with thanksgiving to
God for all His mercies and with praise to the One who makes,
saves and sanctifies us. Amen.

'At six o'clock this evening, we will pray at the Stations of the
Cross. The Bishop will be joining us and I hope that as many of
you as possible will be present to greet him on his first visit to the
parish. Tomorrow night, the PCC will meet in the crypt at seven.
On Tuesday and Wednesday evenings, Father Blair will lead read-
ings from the works of Kenneth Leech after the six thirty mass.
Other midweek services are as usual.

'Would anyone wishing to make their confession, please check
the times in the Easter leaflet; if none of these are convenient, do
ring me at the vicarage.

'I have to apologize for the most unfortunate misprint in last month's leaflet. Father Blair will – I stress – be *walking* on behalf of Christian Aid in a fortnight's time. The error, which I know one among us has blamed on satanic influence but which I feel sure we can attribute to a more mundane case of printer's devils, may explain why there has so far been such a dispiriting response to so worthy a cause.

'If anyone would like to dedicate Easter flowers in a loved one's memory, please speak to Judith Shellard, who will be happy to take donations after mass.

'I would ask you to pray for Daisy Lawrence and Joseph Beatty, both members of this congregation, who are to be married in church next Tuesday, and for Myrna Timson who, I'm sure, will take with her the thoughts of us all when she goes to Westminster Abbey on Thursday to receive the Maundy from Her Majesty the Queen.

'Let us remember in love and tenderness all the sick, especially Susan Devenish, Iris Sage, Wallace Leyland, David Fern-Bassett (priest), Julian Blaikie and Cherish Akarolo. And, of your love, please pray for the souls of the faithful departed, especially Sophia Winterton who was laid to her rest last week. On her, and on all Christian souls, may our Lord Jesus Christ have mercy.'

The Vicar leads the prayers of intercession.

'So, what's the verdict?' Thea whispers to Jeffrey.

'Sh-sh.'

'No one can hear.'

'No complaints about the church. I'm less sold on the Vicar. There's rather too much of the "first shall be last" about him for my liking.'

'I think he's sweet.'

'Don't be taken in by the whiskers. He's a closet red. God bless the homeless; the unemployed; the single mothers. Not a word about the poor sods who put themselves on the line every day, creating the wealth to keep them in giros.'

'You'll reap your reward in Heaven.'

'Not according to him. Anyone on the top rate of tax is destined straight for the other place. I'm not asking for special treatment: no "God bless the property-developers" – fat chance! Just a modicum of respect: an acknowledgement that it's our names on the envelopes; our cheques on which all the rest depends.'

'Quite right,' she replies, with her tongue only half in cheek. For, beneath the mockery, she finds his attitude reassuring. Not once in twenty-five years has he disappointed her in the boardroom. Her

family considered him beyond the pale – a man from a public
school so minor that he never even wore the tie, who was so pathe-
tically eager to curry favour that he tried to befriend the servants.
Cousins scorned him openly; but she didn't care. She knew that he
would make more of himself than any of them; and he has.

'It would never happen in the country.' Jeffrey warms to his
theme. 'There, parsons preach Christ, not Christian Aid. We should
have insisted that Lloyd' – his disappointment at the lack of a third-
generation Jeffrey is dispelled by the bankroll of a name – 'was
christened in Suffolk.'

'And have to put up all the Anoraks' relations?' She shudders.
'And that ghastly mother! I only hope the Queen takes precautions.
Every time she comes near me, I itch.' She proclaims a propitiative
'Lord have mercy'. Jeffrey adds a loud 'Amen'.

> The Vicar proclaims the peace.

If there's one element in the service that Trudy would like to leave
out, it's the Peace. Only recently, she asked Blair why it was there.
He smiled and said that it was for all the people who hadn't been
touched during the week; by which she supposed he meant her.
He was wrong. The whole point of living in London is that you
don't have to touch people. You may brush against them in the
tube or stumble over them on a doorstep, but you never have to feel
anything. Except in church. And now, while everyone else is greeting family and friends, she's left to clasp the hand of a hateful old
woman with a papery skin and a peppery smell.

'Peace be with you, Bertha,' she says, mapping her fears on the
lumpy palm.

'Thank you dear,' she replies, all take and no give, leaving her
less at peace than before.

> *The peace of the Lord be always with you.*

The Peace is Myrna's favourite part of the service. It allows her the
freedom to embrace her family without any danger of overstepping
the mark. She kisses Petula whose lips make her think of pillows
and Hugh who hasn't shaved. She kisses Russell who wriggles and
Laura who presents her cheek like a passport. She bends to kiss
baby Lloyd, but Laura pulls him away as though he were something wicked in a fairy-tale. 'We mustn't wake our Sleeping
Beauty,' she says in that fleecy voice which she applies equally to
both ends of the age-scale. Myrna looks for reassurance and holds
out her hand to the row behind, only to let it sink on the pew as
Thea Finch-Buller's face proves to be as forbidding as her name.

The peace of the Lord be always with you.

Petula feels uneasy in Thea's presence. She never knows quite how
to address her. It's like her manager at the hospital. Is he the Bob
that's written on his lapel or the Mr Breeze that's written on his
face? Still, she takes her courage in her hands and holds out her
hand like a peace offering. Thea skims it as though she had wet
nails, purses her lips, and wishes her something that sounds like
Piss.

She is tempted to return the compliment enhanced by a simple
preposition. She has made the gesture and it has been rejected,
fuelling the sense of grievance that has been growing in her ever
since Thea dropped into her life like a catalogue for jewellery she
can't afford. She loathes everything about her, from the bottle-
blond hair and icing-sugar smile to the snub nose which looks as if
the tip had been trapped while she was listening at a door. She
suspects that she only added her Finch to Jeffrey's Buller in order
to have separate names for each of her two faces. Above all, she
resents her enslavement of Hugh, who is currently clasping her
hand, making the most of the church's licence like a schoolboy
with an art-gallery nude.

She feels no equivalent attraction to Jeffrey, in spite of his oily
certainty that no woman can resist him. To be blunt, he repels her,
what with the thicket of curls in the nape of his neck (as if his hair
hasn't receded so much as slipped), the laugh like a cartoon cad,
and the display of dentistry that shows him clinging to his youth by
the caps of his teeth. Even his car offends her: every time she sees
the numberplate JEF 1, she sees him lighting a cigar with a bank-
note. She is wary of the influence he exerts on Hugh. Watching
them exchange a sign of peace that looks more like a masonic
handshake, she recalls that it was on this very day that Christ threw
the businessmen out of the temple. She prays for a similar purge
of the church.

The peace of the Lord be always with you.

Jessica stands at the front of the nave in the pew formerly reserved
for the vicar's servants and now occupied by his wife. She sighs as
Judith Shellard greets her with a pinched 'Peace' and a dry handshake. She would gladly forgo the verbal promise for a practical
manifestation, say an embargo on phone calls to the vicarage between the hours of twelve and two and seven and nine, along with
the simpering 'Oh, I'm sorry, have I disturbed you while you're
eating? Mealtimes are such a movable feast when one lives alone.'

Then, just for once, she might not have to put the food back in the oven, while Huxley succumbs to the latest ploy to get him on his own. If they were living in a sit-com ('if'!), then 'Just popping out to see Judith' would be his catch-phrase.

'And here's a little something I prepared earlier,' would be Judith's, coupled with the claim that, having ruined his dinner, the least she can do is to offer him some of her own humble (spelt humbug) meal. And, when he insists on going back to his wife's casserole, she commiserates with him on her plain cooking ('but then, as everyone knows, she has so many other talents'). She wants to scream – a permanent breach of the peace – at the injustice. It is precisely because of the threat of interruptions that she has made the one thing which can be kept warm. If Huxley had stayed in medicine, she might have been a cordon bleu. She giggles at the fantasy, prompting Judith to withdraw her hand.

She exchanges a perfunctory 'Peace' with Winifred Metcalfe, who woke them at two last Thursday morning to tell them that she had just had a phone call from Jesus announcing the end of the world. Winifred's vacant smile makes it clear that the memory has vanished with the whisky. With luck, her coolness will help to bring it back. She moves on to Nancy Hewitt, who takes advantage of her outstretched hand to inspect her fingernails. The illwill is so blatant as to be almost funny. She sometimes wonders which these women would prefer: a single vicar so that they can legitimize their fantasies or a married one so that they can criticize his wife.

Their constant scheming makes her feel more like the wife of a cabinet minister. She is sure that Macchiavelli must have been a church-warden. They may give the vicar the freehold of the parish, but from then on he – and his ox and his ass and his wife, but especially the latter – belong to them. It is not out of deference that they place her in this prominent pew, but to keep her in their sights. Everything that she does comes in for censure, from her reluctance to allow meetings in her living room (to them, the unofficial church hall) to her refusal to rattle boxes for causes in which she does not believe. They pick at her clothes like a pack of fashion editors. When two of them called her aside on an urgent matter that turned out to be the button missing from Huxley's cassock, she was convinced that they'd finally driven her mad.

'I don't know about a camel finding it hard to get through the eye of a needle,' she said. 'I can hardly manage a thread.'

Neither of them laughed ... Fuck them, she thinks with a sense of daring; let them sew it on themselves.

She sidesteps Sophie Record, who holds out her hand to conceal her heart, and approaches Lennox Hayward in a genuine spirit of peace.

The peace of the Lord be always with you.

Rosemary sees the tramp looking bemused and sends him waves of peaceful thoughts, while keeping her hands fixed firmly to her sides. It is not that she is either squeamish or standoffish – after all, she touched far worse than him on the soup run – but, in a few moments, she will be taking communion: she will be holding Christ in her hands. She must be as pure in body as in mind.

The Vicar announces the Offertory hymn:
My song is love unknown.

The busybody who has been shoving hymnbooks at him now thrusts a plate of money at Lionel's chest. He is beginning to understand. This must be the reward for sitting through the service. It beats any meal. He checks the woman's face for confirmation. It gives nothing away. But there can be no other reason for her standing here so long. He does not want to take too much and wishes he had had a better view of other people ... that's the trouble with sitting at the back. He decides to play safe with one of the lucky-dip envelopes. But, just as he slips in his fingers, she whips the plate away.

'Well really,' she says. 'That's the limit!'
He should have picked a coin.

The Vicar invites the people to take communion.

Huxley watches the congregation mill forward in its usual confusion over whether to start from the front or the back. There was something to be said for the old days when Lady Blaikie took the lead, claiming the precedence of a grandfather who had been Bishop of Bath and Wells. Now she claims the privilege of age and arthritis and waits for the sacrament to be delivered like a pizza to her seat.

His flippancy repels him and he envies the poise of the communicants who, no matter how many times they have done so before, still approach the rail with reverence. Years of disappointment, as intense as any alchemist's, when the wine has proved no thicker than water and the bread no more nutritious than a stone, cannot rob them of the hope that today may be the day of transformation, when their sense of taste will transcend all others to reveal the presence of God. And yet the sight of their prayer-worn faces fills him with pity. What once seemed the conviction of true believers now looks like the addiction of inveterate losers, squandering their meagre resources on weekly lottery cards.

Their hearts cry out for a sign – his own hears a distant echo. But, as rational people, they would shrink from anything grand or Bernadettish ... Who can trust writing in the sky that has become the province of Coca Cola or a pillar of flames that burns with the fallout of the bomb? They ask rather for internal evidence, a burning conviction that will consume them as they consume the sacrament, suffusing the sweetness of the wine with the saltiness of blood.

The rattle of the ciborium in his hand warns him to restrain himself. But his thoughts escape unbidden and their tenor is un-surprising. For, while the others wait for the sacrament, he has already received it, a spiritual food as insubstantial as a weight-watcher's mid-morning snack.

The body of Christ keep you in eternal life.

Jeffrey feels queasy. There is something disconcerting about accept-ing food so directly from the hands of another man, especially when – he catches sight of the near-naked figure above the altar at just the wrong moment – that food is a third man's flesh. It may only be a symbol, but it still makes him gag. The wine, however, causes him no such qualms; he is used to the taste of blood.

The blood of Christ keep you in eternal life.

Since completing her Twelve Step Programme, Thea looks forward to the sip of wine with nunlike relish. The sense of sanctified sin-ning is the closest she ever comes to a black mass. But, today, that pleasure must be denied. After spotting the haircuts of the two young men on her right, she decides to intinct her wafer; Sunday morning is no guarantee against Saturday night. As she waits for the Curate, she catches sight of Myrna, absolved by age from kneel-ing, standing arms down, mouth open, obliging the Vicar to place the host straight onto her tongue, like a zookeeper tossing a sardine to a seal. Her revulsion is so great that she forgets to save the wafer, compelling her, after all, to risk the cup.

The blood of Christ keep you in eternal life.

For fifty years, Trudy has never once stood at the rail without won-dering whether this will be the day when God strikes her down. If He looks into her heart, as Jesus promised, then she has nothing to fear; but, if He looks into her blood, then she is doomed. Shaking like a bigamist at the banns, she swallows the wafer. When nothing happens, she starts to relax. She waits for the wine. Then, as Blair lifts it to her lips, a lie-detector detonates around her. It rings in her ears and her brain and her stomach. She chokes and retches. Sacrilege is averted only by Blair's deft removal of the cup.

The blast continues for so long that she begins to gain hope. A noise like this can only be all or nothing; it is too much for one old woman, like a gasworks built for a single Jew. She looks up to find the whole rail reeling. The choir breaks off its motet. Myrna, on her right, is so shocked that she ransacks her handbag for pills. Then she pulls out an accident-alarm, and the mystery is solved. Her son-in-law seizes it and presses the switch. Silence hits them like a powercut. Hugh and Petula fuss over Myrna, while Trudy trembles. It is at times like these that she most misses a family. But the nice young man from the library takes her arm and escorts her to her seat. Her secret is safe for another week.

> The Vicar and Curate retire to the sacristy, returning at
> the close of the final hymn.

'Back for the curtain call, eh Father?' Terry leans down from the organ loft and smiles.

> The Vicar and Curate take their leave of the congrega-
> tion at the West Door.

'How are you today, Bertha?' Huxley asks, as she shoots out, first as always, pulling her shapeless hat over her no less shapeless face.

'Fat lot you care. Why am I never on the sick list? You pray for everyone else.'

'You look to me to be in excellent health.'

'You only say that so's you won't have to visit me. You'd be round in a flash if I had scones. That's all you clergy care about: scones. Don't smile at me, young man.' She rounds on Blair. 'I shall write to the Bishop.'

She stamps down the path, as Eleanor Blaikie sweeps through the porch.

Blair turns to address her. 'We weren't sure we'd see you. I was at the hospital last night. Things aren't looking too bright.'

'Nonsense,' she snaps. 'The doctor assured me that it's just a hiccup.'

'He was asking after you.'

'Julian wasn't alone in having a bad day, yesterday. We were in Bath for my great-niece's wedding. The train was worse than Cairo. We had to travel working-class.'

She sails down the path, as indomitable as one of her late husband's battleships.

Myrna hobbles up to Huxley, followed by Petula and Hugh.

'I'm so ashamed, Vicar. I was sure I'd switched it off.'

'Not to worry. These things happen.' Huxley pats Myrna's hand. 'It's a big day on Thursday. You're bound to have a lot on your mind.'

'Oh yes,' she says. 'I've had so much excitement lately. I went to the dentist for some new teeth. Then I went to the audio clinic; that's for ears.'

Petula and Hugh lead Myrna down the path. Huxley continues his dismissals. Moments later, a young man leaps out of the bushes and runs towards him hurling abuse.

'You're as bad as all the rest – say you'll do something and then you never. Why bother to get us that money if you just piss all over us? Fucking hypocrite! Someone should set a match to this place – with you inside.'

Stations of the Cross

Sunday 6.30 p.m.
St Mary-in-the-Vale, Hampstead

> The Archdeacon moves out into the porch, where the
> Vicar and Curate await the arrival of the Bishop.

'Still no sign of our revered prelate?' Alfred addresses himself exclusively to Huxley.

'Not a whisper. This would coincide with Terry – our organist – defecting to *The Desert Song*.'

'Far be it from me to propose myself as a substitute: the Bishop's shoes are much too august for my humble feet.' Alfred points a pair of highly polished Church's. 'But, should you wish to spare your long-suffering congregation, I shall do my best to oblige.'

'Thank you, Archdeacon. But I think perhaps we should give him another five minutes.'

'Whatever you say.'

'Action stations,' Rosemary calls from her look-out post at the gate. 'Target sighted.'

'What a relief,' Huxley says.

'Quite,' Alfred says with less enthusiasm.

'There you are, Archdeacon,' Blair says jauntily. 'Your size twelves are safe after all.'

Alfred almost forgets his resolve and replies.

> The Bishop's car arrives at the gate.

Ted steps out of the car, lovingly clasping his mitre. He is a short man and his longheld aversion to vestments is tempered by gratitude for the extra height.

'A thousand apologies. I was held up at the prison. An inmate ran amok before the service. I could have left early but I didn't want to disappoint them. They look forward to my visits so much.'

Alfred affects an expression of discreet disbelief.

'Welcome to St Mary-in-the-Vale, Bishop . . . I'm Huxley Grieve.'

'Ted Bishop,' he says, holding out his hand, ever-hopeful that someone will suppose him dyslexic. 'Bishop by name, bishop by calling.'

'Shouldn't that be "by selection", Bishop?' Alfred asks, still see-thing at the blunder of the Crown Appointments Commission.

'Ah, the Venerable Alf!' Alfred squirms beneath the impact of the breezeblock vowels. 'I didn't see you in the shadows.'

Alfred draws himself up to his full height as if to refute any charge of inconspicuousness.

'This is Brian, my driver.' Ted effects a quick introduction as he takes his retractable crozier. 'And this is my lady-wife, Esther ... named after the only book in the Bible in which God doesn't ap-pear. That's just my little joke. There's not enough laughter in church, wouldn't you agree?'

Alfred watches with distaste as Huxley shakes Esther's hand. This dowdy creature in her catalogue clothes is, he is sure, the sole reason for Ted's emergence from the well-deserved anonymity of the Isle of Man. He and his two-up-two-down morality have been brought into London House as the antithesis of his predecessor. To suit some inane equation of marriage and respectability, an inade-quate such as Bishop Ted is raised up while a celibate such as himself is passed over. The Church is as subject to fashion as any-thing else, but there are limits, and, in his view, Esther Bishop is one of them.

'Lead on then, Vicar,' Ted urges. 'I presume you want me to give the final blessing, but I'll take my cue from you. This is a leap in the dark for me.'

'But one which I trust you'll find illuminating. We're very fortu-nate at St Mary's in numbering Alice Leighton among our congre-gation.' Huxley waits for a sign of recognition. 'You may have seen her work at the Whitechapel last year.'

'One of the many things I'm saving for my retirement.'

'Of course.' Huxley suspects a snub. 'It isn't easy in a church as ornate as this to incorporate new visual elements, but I think you'll find that Alice has succeeded triumphantly. She's created a series of Stations that puts the *via dolorosa* right at the heart of twentieth-century experience.'

> The congregation gathers at the first station.
> Jesus is condemned to death.

Trudy looks at the face of Christ as at a human parchment. She sees her history written in His expression. Etched on His features are those of her father and uncles. Echoing from His sentence is the death-knell of her youth. She wants to escape, not from the horror of the image but from the invasion of her past. Church should be a place of sanctuary, as much from memories as from people. This picture makes it dangerous; the figures so clearly drawn from her childhood that she suspects Alice of having stolen a photograph album from her flat.

The court has been transposed from Jerusalem to Vienna. The judges are no longer high priests but petty functionaries. Christ is not dressed in a robe but a singlet and shorts. She looks at the bruised lips and unshaven cheeks that bear witness to the brutality of His arrest. She searches for the reassurance of a halo in the torch that they are shining in His face. His soiled underwear leaves Him doubly exposed to the taunts of His tormentors. Set against their immaculate suits, His scruffiness is itself a crime. He has become the 'filthy Jew' of popular myth.

Then she recalls the little shops in the *Judenviertel* and realizes that it is Christ the clothier who is on trial. He has pinned the memory of His measurements on their bodies. He has left the taint of His tailoring on their skin. That is the outrage which they can never forgive.

She surveys the crowd for a face that will support Him, but its studied indifference allows her no hope. All she can see are men and women who wash their hands of Him as though they were freshening up before dinner. Her father used to say that people who ate together shared a bond. He placed as much faith in the fellowship of food as she has in the security of the English Channel. But, in that, as in so much else, Solomon Engelstein proved to have been misnamed. For the guests who once sat at his table now strip him of his citizenship as casually as if they were helping him off with his coat.

> The congregation moves to the second station.
> Jesus receives His Cross.

Trudy approaches the second station in the hope that Alice might be spreading the suffering among various victims. But it is not to be. The first thing that she notices is the crown of thorns – or rather words: brutal, bloody anti-Jewish slogans that eat into His skull, and, the next, that the Cross is not made of the usual wood but of a pile of holy relics. It towers as high as the Christmas tree in the *Rathausplatz*, a symbol both of His oppressors' faith and His own shame. As they strap the bar onto His back, it sinks like a working man's load on a leisured man's shoulders. He buckles under the burden of hatred, inhumanity and despair.

> The congregation moves to the third station.
> Jesus falls for the first time.

Trudy keeps her face hidden in case anyone is spying. On this of all weeks, she knows that she must take care. For, whatever the Vicar may tell them, the moral of the Passion is not to be found on Good Friday or Easter Sunday but at the Last Supper, where Jesus learnt that no one can be trusted, not even His friends.

She squints through bleary eyes as He crawls forward, crippled by the Cross and forced onto all fours like an animal. His back is bent double as if the bar were the beam of an attic in which He has to hide. And, while the rest of the congregation fix their eyes on the road, she gazes into the shadowy houses beyond. There, she sees families confined to the rafters like unwanted furniture, and old friends, converted to strangers by the strain of silence, struggling to make sense of the footsteps below. Meanwhile, a thousand miles away, a young girl weeps with laughter as Robinson Crusoe fails to make sense of Man Friday's footsteps in the sand.

Her life is a pantomime while theirs is a nightmare. At last, she can enjoy a Christmas without compromise; unlike the friends she has left behind, who suffer the whiplash of *Krampus* all year long. Crouched among splintery crates, I-spy is reduced to I-remember and hide-and-seek to hide-and-hide. As she sings *Three Blind Mice* and watches *Mickey* and *Minnie*, they sit poised with gagging hands for fear that the sight of a mouse will give them away. The rest of the world may picture them as Anne Frank, but, to her, they are Rosel, Sara and Marta, her former future-bridesmaids, and Ernst, at six years old, her one and only groom.

> The congregation moves to the fourth station.
> Jesus meets His mother.

Trudy is amazed that Jesus and Mary make no contact. They show no sign of recognition, only a fleeting family resemblance in their Munch-like expressions of pain. The road to Calvary has grown lonelier in the twentieth century. In the gospel, Mary set out to support her son on his final journey. Here, she appears to have come across Him by chance as He is being led away. Jesus fixes His eyes on the ground as though it means more to Him than His mother. Even on His death-march, His first thought is to protect her. The guards move Him on. Now they will never meet again, and Judas's will be the last lips to touch His cheek.

The more she stares at Mary, the more her face looks familiar. She watches a mother emerge like a memory from the paint. She is waving her daughter goodbye as if she were sending her off for a weekend, parting from her forever with an indifference more loving than a kiss. She offers her no explanation because she supposes her too young to understand. How she longs for her to realize that no one is ever too young to feel guilt. For sixty years, she has tried to make sense of this abandonment; at first, wondering why her parents hated her, and then, when horror recreated her life in the image of a newsreel, why they believed her unworthy to share their deaths.

> The congregation moves to the fifth station.
> Simon of Cyrene helps Jesus carry His Cross.

Trudy looks at Jesus and Simon, their bodies contrasted as sharply as chessmen. Negroes were also condemned by the Nazis; although not because they were short-sighted and soft-bellied like Jews. On the contrary, it was as if Hitler were jealous of men who could be strong without uniforms ... men like the athlete who had run off with the prizes at the Berlin Olympics, his medals hanging like a black cloud over the master-race. She was six years old at the time, but she still remembers clapping when she heard the news. She could not understand why her father did not share her pleasure. He called them *schwarzes* dismissively, as if they were nothing but their skin ... She instinctively blows her nose ... It was only later that she realized that people with shared enemies were not always friends.

There were very few Simons in Vienna. It was seeing them in London after the war that taught her that even an English hand-shake could be deceptive. But bus-queue prejudice, however cruel, was reassuring. It showed her that, if the butchery were ever to resume and people were to be snuffed out like Friday-night candles, then the Jews would no longer be first in line. Blood was less conspicuous than skin. Later still, when the carnage moved from Europe to Africa, she was amazed to discover that there were Ethiopian Jews. Never before had she felt so suspicious of God. How could He hate people so much as to make them both blacks and Jews?

> The congregation moves to the sixth station.
> Veronica wipes the face of Jesus.

Trudy supposes that Alice has painted Veronica as a nun as a sign that, although the hierarchy of the Church may have turned away from Christ's cattle-truck, individuals risked their lives to offer comfort. She knows that one of her friends, Hanna, found shelter with the sisters and went on to take vows herself, since she wrote to her when she was sent by her Order to England after the war. But she never replied.

Her own stay in a convent was less inspiring. She still feels the taste of fear in her mouth, as distinctive as that of 'evacuated milk', a confusion of word and sensation from the time when she was sent into a second exile to escape the London Blitz. At the age of ten, she was terrified of the nuns: the black-and-whiteness of them, the starchiness of their habits, the amount of space that they filled. She remembered her cousin Heinrich's stories of their eating Jewish babies. It was not until she saw *The Sound of Music* more than a quarter of a century later that she realized nuns were allowed to smile.

Even more terrifying than the nuns were the girls. She can still hear the entire form shouting at her as she walked into the classroom – 'Jew, Jew, Jew,' – cruelty uniting them like the creed. She clung to her desk as the world spun more quickly than it ever did in science. 'I am not a Jew,' she insisted. 'My father was a socialist like Mr Attlee. That's why I came to England. They send socialist children to camps.' But they continued to chant and there was nothing that she could say to convince them. It was only later, in the sanatorium, that she learnt that they had not unearthed her secret but were referring to her meanness in refusing to share a cake with a friend.

> The congregation moves to the seventh station.
> Jesus falls for the second time.

Trudy sees that the Cross is now constructed of newsprint but, rather than making it lighter, it seems to weigh Jesus down even more. Her eyes are so wet that it is hard to tell if He is staggering under the burden of prejudice or pulling the sheets around Himself to keep warm. She smiles to think that the double meaning doesn't work in German. Then she frowns in case anyone should suppose that she is smiling at His pain.

She knows what it is to sleep in newspapers now that Vienna has come to London. Since she can no longer feel secure in her bed – the first place that anyone looks – she makes a nest for herself on the living-room floor. But, last week, she received a visit from the Camden Health and Safety Department (English words but German meanings). The young man wore smart shoes which left marks like jackboots. He refused to take off his coat in case she saw what he was wearing underneath. He said that they were worried that her newspapers were a fire-risk. She wanted to know how they found out about them. She never opens the door after six o'clock, so no one could have seen inside. It is as if they can read her as easily as the headlines, or else the newsprint has rubbed off on her face.

The congregation moves to the eighth station.
Jesus meets the women of Jerusalem.

Trudy looks at the women who follow Jesus's journey, watching while His name becomes a number and the number grows to infinity. They stand on the road with their eyes fixed on the procession, as if they have a sacred duty to bear witness, fearful to turn away in case they should lose count. These are the women whom she used to see in the streets around Swiss Cottage, victims of their own survival, with memories as livid as scars. They walked down the Finchley Road as if it were the *Kartnerstrasse*, filling the cafés with the scent of Vienna – the violet-scented soap that put her in mind of her mother. And she remembers what she has read about soap and imagines that scent on another woman's skin.

A place called Swiss Cottage should be neutral but they made it a source of danger, wearing their over-elaborate clothes and over-emphatic jewels like an act of defiance, adding inches to their height with hair so stiffened that it hurt. She never spoke to them – that would suggest they had something in common – but she longed to point out that, even in London, they were making themselves a target. They should take their cue from her. She arrived as a girl of eight in 1938. Ten years later, she Anglicized both her name and her nationality. Trudi became Trudy, a lifetime of security in a single letter, and Engelstein England, a name that meant even more than a passport because they could never take it away. It was her permanent identification with the one country in the world that was not just an address but a state of mind.

'An Englishman's home is his castle' is as much a part of her heritage as 'innocent until proved guilty' and 'God save the Queen'. But is it the same when that castle is a flat? What happens when the tenant has lived in it at a protected rent for thirty years, long after all her former neighbours have gone, and she is left on her own with young people who barely say hello and bound up the stairs as if any time not spent in a room is wasted? The landlord wants her to leave. His agent came round; he lit a cigarette without asking, as if to emphasize his power. He offered her a room in sheltered housing in Hendon. He told her that there was a warden who could be there at the push of a button the moment that anything happened to her. He made it sound like a threat.

Things have already started to happen, things of a kind that the women in the picture would recognize. First, they changed the springs on the front door so that it was too heavy for her to open. She had to stand on the steps, like a beggar, waiting for one of the young people to come home. Then, they pushed a ladder through her window and patched the hole with wood. Next, they made late-night phone calls, full of breaths – breaths that seemed much closer than voices and far more menacing than words. Now, they are sending men to follow her home so that she dare not go out in the evening, not even to see Madge, her only friend, whom she worked alongside for twenty-five years. Madge insists that she is imagining things. But then imagination is a luxury to someone who owns a maisonette in Willesden, with a husband like a hammer in her bed.

She looks away from the painting but the women's eyes seem to be following her instead of Christ.

> The congregation moves to the ninth station.
> Jesus falls for the third time.

Trudy is relieved by the absence of Christ which absolves her of the need to take the picture so personally. It is as if Alice has decided that, at this stage, viewers should be spared the sight of His suffering and so she has painted the Cross from behind. Christ's face and body are hidden, apart from the agonized fingertips clasping the bar which prevent it from crushing Him into the ground. But this very impersonality creates new dangers. The identification of man and Cross is as absolute as the identification of Jew and race. Christ seems to be suffering the fate of a man who is nothing but an accident of birth.

She longs to give Jesus a face, albeit one that keeps Him at a distance. But then she remembers the faraway faces of Hollywood: all the flawless blond men with cloudless complexions who did to the imagination what the Nazis did in fact. Evenings spent at *King of Kings* and *The Greatest Story Ever Told* offered a far more invidious form of escapism than any spent at *Pillow Talk* or *Breakfast at Tiffany's*. For they were an attempt to escape from history ... if Christ were not a Jew, then there was no reason for the Nazis to kill the Jews; in which case, the Holocaust could not have happened. And the nightmare disappeared in the logic of a dream. When she learnt later that most film-producers were Jewish, she began to understand.

She studies the faces in the crowd. Their complicity is all too clear. Pin-striped pen-pushers whose spotless hands are seeped in invisible ink brush up against close-cropped thugs. Doctors whose scalpels are as well-worn as cutlery rub shoulders with a Pope who turned public protest into private prayer. Photographers capture a record as reliable as the Turin Shroud. Meanwhile, standing discreetly in the background is a couple less familiar than the others but instantly identifiable as the ubiquitous Herr and Frau Muller. As they vie for the perfect view of each passing atrocity – be it old men whose beards are chopped off like boy actors' or women who have never washed dishes being forced to scrub streets – they take care to keep out of the camera's eye.

> The congregation moves to the tenth station.
> Jesus is stripped of His garments.

Trudy sees Christ being stripped of His clothes as He enters the concentration camp. In return, He is given a uniform which strips Him of His identity. With its loose fit and prominent stripes, it looks like pyjamas; but pyjamas are warming only in bed. All gold and valuables are wrenched from His fingers and pockets and – she prays that He has yet to realize – from His mouth. His face wears a look of incredulity, which will not be seen again until the Allied troops roll in in armoured triumph to confront humanity's defeat.

She steals surreptitious looks at her fellow worshippers and wonders how much they can understand. To them, this is just another step on a symbolic journey. The horror of horrors, like the holy of holies, is a place too terrible to enter. For her, however, it is real. This is not just Jesus's journey but her mother's, her father's and her Eva's – her five-years-older sister who stayed behind in Vienna because her parents were determined not to disrupt her schooling. She wants to howl in protest when she thinks of the lessons which she must have learnt. And yet she stays silent. For she is not Trudi Engelstein but Trudy England. It is a warm April evening in London. None of this has any connection with her.

> The congregation moves to the eleventh station.
> Jesus is nailed to the Cross.

Trudy looks at Christ's limp body pleading for mercy even as His lips are too agonized to speak and she sees a man being subjected to a premature autopsy at Auschwitz. Doctors pump Him with pain in the name of science. One man suffers for the sake of humanity as if in some grotesque misreading of the Crucifixion. And yet, as they hang on their respective crosses, Jesus Christ has one advantage over Jesus Cohen. He, at least, is not a twin.

She is riddled with guilt at her own survival. It makes no sense that six million died and yet she has been spared. She knows that such feelings are commonplace; doctors who fled from Vienna on the same train as her will have given them a name ... even as the ones who remained behind compound them. But that offers little comfort. For, although she escaped the gas on the continent and the bombs in London, she is left to endure the blitz of her emotions and the cruel illusion of life which, like an amputee's lost limbs, mocks her with the sensation of what used to be.

To the guilt of her survival is added the heavier guilt of how little she has to show for it ... forty years as a secretary, thirty of them in the same office, twenty-six of them at the same desk, until the computers arrived to make her obsolete. Her boss explained that they would cut out all the donkey-work, and she suddenly realized how he had thought of her all those years. She failed to master the basic keyboard, but he kept her on until retirement, even though, some days, she did nothing more than open the mail. When he called it an act of charity, she pictured a donkey-sanctuary and laughed. It was small justification for being the only Engelstein left, at least in name – no, not even that. It should have been Eva. Eva would have lived a life full enough for four, rather than barely enough for one. She would have given her parents grandchildren, to scatter seeds on their unmarked graves.

> The congregation moves to the twelfth station.
> Jesus dies on the Cross.

Trudy stops short. In her journey round the church, she has come to a precipice. She cannot tell whether it is in response to the familiarity of the Crucifixion or to the impossibility of representing the Holocaust – which would require a canvas six million pieces long – but Alice offers no body, no background, not even any paint. The sequence is shattered. All that remains is an empty plastic bag, its very malleability a mocking reminder of human frailty, pinned to a small wooden cross which stands in a pool of blood.

The Passion has been reduced to its most basic element. What counts is not its pressure – whether it is high or low or any of the other things that doctors look for – but simply whether it is pure. A single grandparent will infect the supply like a virus. She looks to the top of the Cross, where Pilate wrote INRI, and, although she is too far off to see without squinting, she is sure that Alice has written JUDE, to make the association clear. To her surprise, she is starting to be grateful for the recognition of her feelings and for their setting at the heart of the church. At the same time, she is deeply confused. Christ's blood is supposed to be pure, so much so that a single sip ensures entry to Heaven and yet, here, it is presented as the opposite, as if it is not only Christ the victim but Christ the saviour who resembles her. And that cannot be true.

The congregation moves to the thirteenth station.
Jesus is taken down from the Cross.

Trudy watches the broken body being removed from the Cross by men in masks. Two figures follow their progress, an older woman and a younger man – who may be mother and son – in clothes that mark them out as modern tourists. They are visiting the concentration camp in its new incarnation as Holocaust museum ... she expects that by now it is billed as the Auschwitz Experience. Her pain is intense. The buildings should be razed to the ground. The memorial is superfluous, since it is something that no one forgets. Some people deny and others remember too clearly. But no one forgets.

In fifty years, she has enjoyed a single moment of oblivion. The war was over. She had a rotten tooth which required extraction. Every conventional fear was swept aside when the dentist said that he would have to use gas. At a stroke, his surgery became a shower-room. She shrieked; she sweated; she tried to run out but her legs rebelled. Confused by her reaction, he misjudged the dose and she started to laugh. She laughed and laughed while the drill tickled like a feather-duster and her memory was removed along with the tooth. But, when the effects of the gas wore off, the ache in her mouth was obscured by the ache in her heart. Her laughter echoed with her parents' screams.

She doesn't need to visit any camp. Auschwitz is part of her; her parents are buried within her breast. She has no more desire to see where they died than to return to where they lived. She had the chance. When she retired, the company gave her a special present, not Sheila's clock nor Madge's video, but a plane-ticket to Vienna and a weekend in the *Astoria* hotel. She broke down at the presentation ... but her gratitude was grief. How could she go? She has not left the country once in sixty years in case she should be refused re-entry. She has never even applied for a passport for fear that someone will steal it to use in a crime for which she will be expelled.

She donated the ticket to the church raffle. She expected that it would be the star prize but Lady Blaikie gave an old rug. The trip was won by the organist. He sent her a postcard of a white horse.

The congregation moves to the fourteenth station.
Jesus is laid in the sepulchre.

Trudy looks on as Christ's body is tossed into a pit of jumbled limbs and tangled torsos, which lie like mannequins in a shop window after a sale. Indignity is heaped on indignity like corpse on corpse. Identity disappears, since even dental records have been wiped out by the savagery of His treatment. The only mark of distinction is the crude, tattooed number on His rapidly rotting skin. His life as a man is complete as He festers with His fellow victims. The anger that she felt as a child on hearing of Mozart's pauper's grave is as nothing compared to her outrage in the face of this barbarism.

These are bodies that expose a nakedness way beyond mere lack of clothes. These are bodies that make the most serious-minded nude look like a pose from a men's magazine. These are bodies that cry out for all flesh to be covered up or painted over or placed on the gallery's equivalent of the newsagent's top shelf, not because of any harm that they might do to the viewer but because of the harm that the viewer might do to them. These are bodies that mock the word-made-flesh with the rattle of skin and bone.

She has reached the end of the road and exhausted her reserves. It is for the others to move on; she must go home. Preparing for bed takes much longer when the bed has to be made up from scratch.

She slips away from church as the congregation joins in the final prayer.

> O Saviour of the World, who by your Cross and precious
> Blood has redeemed us.
> Save us and help us we humbly beseech you O Lord.

Jessica waits in the vicarage to receive her guests. The parish Marthas have taken over the kitchen. 'We'd better scrub out the oven before cooking the sausage rolls,' Judith says, putting on rubber gloves like protective clothing. 'We don't want the Bishop coming down with botulism.' Similar clinical concern no doubt lies behind the invitation to 'Clean me' left on the sideboard in letters of dust. She would be the first to admit that, in this depository of congregational cast-offs, she has few incentives for housework; even so, she is taken aback by the exchange that she overhears from the stairs.

'I think I'll just go and pay a visit,' Winifred Metcalfe is saying.

'Are you sure that's wise?' Nancy Hewitt asks. 'I made certain that I went before I came. Anyone who believes that cleanliness is next to godliness can't have seen their downstairs loo.'

'We should entertain more,' Huxley declared in that maddeningly vague way he has, as if the action were contained in the verb. What he meant was that he should entertain, while she cooked and laid and served and smiled and washed and dried and screamed in silence. 'The Lord will provide', however admirable a principle, is less persuasive on an empty plate. She defies anyone to try to live with someone so unworldly. And yet, when she pictures him cycling through the night from Hampstead to Barnes because a baby he baptized had suffered a cot-death, kissing her without reproach after she refused to drive him, and hoping, without irony, on his red-eyed return that the call did not disturb her, she knows why she has stayed.

The visitors file into the house. She is introduced to the Bishop, a surprisingly small, bullet-headed, barrel-chested man with hair greased over his baldness. 'I apologize if we kept you away from the service,' he says.

'Oh me, I'm a heathen,' she replies, grateful to be fed such an easy line.

'My wife means in the original sense of "heath-dweller",' Huxley adds quickly.

She wonders if it's the Bishop's etymology or his sense of humour that is in doubt.

She guides people into the sitting-room. The Bishop and Archdeacon hold court at either end. She finds their rivalry contemptible. At least the women have the excuse of a lifetime of subservience. But these men have ruled the Church just as they rule the world. Why are they so inflexible? So the Bishop finds God in the pages of the Bible like a lazy schoolboy cribbing for an exam: so the Archdeacon finds God in a ritual meal the way that primitive warriors ate their dead chiefs: surely what counts is what they do with Him? And neither does much to impress her. The Bishop is so bigoted that, on a recent visit to a catholic church, he mistook a stuffed owl, strategically placed to ward off bats, for evidence of satanic practice. And the Archdeacon is so pharisaical that, only last week, she saw him furtively storing his sweetner in a pyx.

She acts the perfect consort, chatting to Mrs Bishop ... as convenient a mnemonic as Jones the milk. Esther – think Easter and it should be equally easy – is a chintzy woman draped in a shawl like an antimacassar. The dimple on her chin is so pronounced that it resembles a cedilla on her lower lip. She would make an ideal contestant on a daytime quiz-show, were it not for the fear in her eyes. Their constant movement unnerves her; but her children come to her rescue. She picks their photographs, one by one, off the table: her younger daughter, Angela, at Oxford; her younger son, Luke, in the Alps; her elder daughter, Lucy, on her wedding-day ... but when she reaches her elder son, Toby, on the bridge in

Kenya, she remembers why she no longer believes in God.

Esther puts a mother's hand on her arm, but she has outgrown sympathy. She takes her guest to meet the parishioners, starting with Hugh and Petula Snape, one of the love her/hate him couples so prevalent in her address-book. They, in turn, introduce her to their in-laws, something or other double-barrelled, a woman with a smile like a fluorescent light and a man who maintains a constant chorus of jangled change in his pocket, as if to keep a grip on what is real. She moves away to liaise with Judith, who assures her, in her best Mary Poppins tones, that everyone is eating. Then, at the moment of maximum embarrassment, the Bishop announces grace.

> We thank you for this food, O Lord, that we are about to share.
> We pray that you will use it for the nourishment of our bodies,
> that we can use them for the service of Jesus.

'I trust you're doing justice to this splendid spread,' Ted descends on his wife, whose eyes dart even more wildly.

'It almost looks good enough to eat,' she replies, her confusion passing as wit.

'You've done us proud, Mrs ... Mrs, I'm sorry. I've no memory for names.'

'You must meet a great many people.' Jessica wishes that she had so compelling an excuse.

'That's true. Although I never forget a face.' He looks at Esther. 'Who are you?' He seizes on Jeffrey's laugh. 'Esther's used to my teasing, aren't you dear?'

She smiles.

'It's very good of you to join us,' Jessica hears her voice slide like a hostess trolley. 'Especially at Easter, when you must have so much on. Huxley always says that Holy Week leaves him wholly weak.' She laughs.

'Really?' Ted's tone checks her. 'It's different for a bishop. Everyone's too busy in their own churches to want to see me. If there are any emergencies – parishes without pastors – I'll stand in. You Anglo-Catholics are the easiest. It's like sticking a mitre on a donkey. "Bless it, Bishop; swing it, Bishop; shake it, Bishop." Isn't that so, Alf?'

Alfred looks embarrassed. Ted has caught him with a particularly large lump of cheese in his throat.

'That's right! You make the most of the Good Lord's bounty.'

Jessica wonders if she should open another bag of crisps.

'Friend Alf likes his food. Not for him any crocodile tears over third-world famine. "How many will there be at the diocesan lunch?" my lady-wife asks me. "Nine," I tell her. "But since one of them's the Archdeacon, you'd better cater for ten."'

Alfred's eyes roll; his cheeks swell and he starts to choke.

'Are you all right, Alf? Somebody give him a good slap.'

Thea obliges with almost indecent haste. Alfred splutters crumbs, one of which lands in Esther's humous.

'You're cracking up, chum,' Ted continues. 'There are too many unfit clergy in this diocese – not your husband, Mrs ... Mrs ... yes (he's an example to us all), but others whose blushes I shall spare. God has no use for an empty vessel, but He certainly doesn't want one that's too heavy to lift. It's time to get off your knees. Run.'

'Run?' Alfred echoes incredulously.

'Some walk in the light of the Lord; I run. I'm up at six every weekday morning. Isn't that so, Esther?'

'Oh yes.'

'Everywhere I go, they recognize the purple tracksuit. They shout out that they'll see me in the marathon; I shout back that I'll see them in church.' Alfred reels. 'Then, by seven thirty, I'm at my desk, ready for whatever the day has in store. Most people sleep too much. Think what you could do with an extra two hours. Take Mrs Thatcher.'

Jeffrey nods in approval. Jessica shudders. There is a swearbox in the sideboard exclusively reserved for mention of the former prime minister; but she judges that now might not be the time to bring it out.

'You certainly look fit,' Thea gushes. Jessica suspects that he is about to roll up his cassock in a show of muscle.

'The body is the temple of the Lord. It must be treated with respect.' Ted directs both words and gaze at Alfred.

'I shall bear it in mind,' Alfred says. 'Now, if you'll all be so kind as to excuse me. This temple is reserved for private prayer.' He makes a slight bow and walks out.

'A great character,' Ted says, 'one of the old school. You can't help liking him for all that.' He turns to Thea. 'Are you a parishioner?'

'No, not at all. We live in Stockwell. In a converted primary school.' Thea relishes the combination of fashionable house and unfashionable area. 'Though we have a small place in Suffolk for weekends.'

'Quite a large place, actually,' Jeffrey says, reluctant to undersell himself to a stranger. 'Our grandson is being christened here next week, so we thought we'd come on a recce. Make sure the Vicar was up to scratch. You hear such stories these days. Jeffrey Finch-Buller, Grafton Holdings, my lord.' He holds out his hand and hopes that he has hit on the correct form of address. 'And this is my wife, Theodora.'

'Oh don't bother the Bishop with names,' she says. 'You heard. He can never remember them.'

'I shall make a special effort with yours.'

Thea simpers.

'I gather that you know my chairman, David Stafford,' Jeffrey continues.

'Yes of course. We meet in the House. Imagine old Ted Bishop in the Lords. They keep you on your toes there. No recycling last year's sermons. Not that anyone here has ever done that. Oh no, no, no, no, no. David and I have become good mates. At first, he was surprised to see me side with the government. They expect the Lords Spiritual to vote with the Opposition.'

'It's a disgrace,' Jeffrey fumes. 'The Church should be above politics. I'm glad to see you set an example.'

Much to Jeffrey's annoyance, they are interrupted as the Vicar introduces his curate to the Bishop.

'I've heard about you,' Ted tells Blair, who starts. 'You're supposed to be brainy. Brains aren't always an asset in a parish. You don't need brains to minister to people. Just a stout heart, a pure soul and a good pair of lungs to preach the word of the Lord.'

'I try to have those too.'

'I must say it does a man good to hear you.' Jeffrey refuses to be sidelined. 'There's so much cant spouted from pulpits today. And it's so selective. What about "And did those feet in ancient times"? When do you ever hear about that? But the idea of Jesus coming to this green and pleasant land is anathema ... the story of the crown of thorns sprouting at Glastonbury is a legend. It's high time the Church of England lived up to its name.'

'Darling,' Thea says, 'you sound like an old fogey.'

'Some might think that it's time for the Church to live up to its message,' Blair says. 'Standing up – no, shouting out – against poverty and injustice.' He breaks off before he confirms the Bishop's suspicions.

'I'm sorry,' Jeffrey says, 'but the moment you use those words, I switch off. I know where they're going to lead. And, to be frank, I resent it. I subscribe to charities. My wife's on the board of several.'

'Please Jeffrey,' Thea says, 'it's not something I care to broadcast.'

'There's far too much mawkishness in the Church about poverty,' Ted says. 'It's quite taken over at Christmas. Fortunately,
Easter isn't a no-room-at-the-inn time. Spiritual poverty is what we
should be tackling. Believe me, I know. I'm not one of your nam-
by-pamby young men wearing out their Oxford bags praying
"Please God, send me somewhere they drop their aitches". My
father was on the railways.' He turns to Thea. 'Your father would
have had me horsewhipped if I'd so much as walked up his drive.'

'Surely not?' She tries not to sound excited.

'But one man – the local curate – had faith in me. He was no do-
gooding intellectual. He taught me to box . . . to use my fists . . . to
fight the good fight for the Lord. And look where it's led. From
sleeping top to toe with my two brothers, I now have a whole floor
of bedrooms I don't use.'

'There's an old Russian proverb,' Blair says. '"It's better to have a
hundred friends than a hundred rooms".'

'Communist propaganda,' Jeffrey snorts.

'I trust you're as familiar with the *Book of Proverbs*,' Ted says
coldly.

'How true!' Esther interjects. 'A hundred rooms just leave you
ninety-nine more to be alone in.'

'Please don't give my wife any more wine,' Ted says.

'I've had one glass, Ted.'

'"I do not permit a woman to teach or to have authority over a
man; she must be silent." 1 *Timothy* Chapter 2 Verse 12.' The
sharpness of Ted's tone shocks his listeners. He attempts to brush
it off. 'Right, I think we should leave these good people to themselves. You heard Mrs . . . Mrs . . . humph.' He coughs away his
confusion. 'The Vicar has a busy week ahead.'

Holy Communion

Monday 10.30 a.m.
Heath Lodge Residential Home

> The Vicar adjusts the case on his shoulder and opens
> the door.

As Huxley enters the home, he is struck by the familiar smell of
soiled stockings, stale breath, desiccated flesh and disinfectant. A
wispy old woman with folds of goose-skin polishes the bannister
with her cardigan.

'Good morning, Mrs Kente.' He hears himself as though on the
radio. 'I'm glad to see you're looking well.'

'I've no time to talk. There's still half the staircase to do. I have
my orders.'

He pictures a punishment regime.

'Oh no, are you the Inspector?' Her lower lips quivers.

'Molly pet, it's the Reverend,' Sister Baptista says. 'Don't you
want to say hello?'

'No time. If they find a speck of dust, the house'll be shut down
and they'll put us all in a home.'

'Molly never stops: dusting and polishing the whole day long.
Still, it keeps her busy. Not like the rest of the poor souls. You carry
on, pet. I want to see my face in it.'

'Who wants to see your ugly old face? You'll crack the wood.'
She gives a chesty chuckle.

As the Sister turns a threatened reproach into an embrace,
Huxley remembers the matrons at school whose show of friendli-
ness in his parents' presence fast evaporated behind their backs.
He fears that they may need an inspection after all.

> The Vicar puts on his alb and stole and enters the day-
> room.

Huxley walks through the room which resembles an ante-chamber
to death. The residents sit in armchairs and wheelchairs symmetri-
cally placed around the walls facing a gaping hole at the centre, an
arrangement which makes manifest the reality of their peripheral
lives. They are reduced to a world of greys and greens and browns,

the colours of their food and clothes and decoration. The only exception comes from the garish images of an overbright television,
which nobody watches. He presumes that it offers the daylight
equivalent of a night-light's reassurance: proof that life flickers on,
even as it passes them by.

He contains his disgust as he picks up their hands, trying to
squeeze without squashing. He is not sure which offends him
most: the warm damp palms which recall the people they once
were or the cold cracked ones which anticipate the corpses that they
must soon become. They barely register his presence as they slump
with fly-catcher mouths. Their bodies are as lumpy as their chairs;
their minds are as crinkled as their stockings. And yet they too are
made in God's image. So where is He? Or is this the true image of
God in the late twentieth century: not muscles stretched across the
Sistine ceiling but old, confused, neglected and unable to die;
humanity kept alive by puppeteer-nurses just as God is kept alive
by ventriloquist-priests, until an enlightened euthanasia sweeps
both away?

An old woman, curled over the arm of her chair, her legs splayed
like a wishbone, weeps silently into her sleeve. What comfort can
he bring to a grief which she cannot even name? What absolution?
For her, he is prepared to act the magician, his Amens as potent as
Abracadabras; but she fails to recognize the robe.

'Do you see who it is, Nora?' Sister Baptista asks.

'It's Jesus,' she answers slowly.

'Close.' The Sister laughs. 'It's the Reverend come to give you
communion.'

'It's Jesus.' Nora's eyes light up. 'Come to take me to heaven.' In
her attempt to rise, she flings herself onto the floor.

Huxley helps to lift her back, like a steeplejack determined to
conquer his fear of heights. His suspicions about the stickiness on
his hand are confirmed by the Sister's complaint. 'Now look what
you've done, you naughty girl. Jesus won't want you if you're wet,
will he, Reverend?' He smiles wanly. 'Oh no, Jesus will call to the
Devil and say "Devil, you come and fetch Nora. She's too dirty for
Heaven. We don't want any smellies up here."' No longer able to
condone her theology, he protests. She cuts him short. 'This is the
third time I've changed this pet today, Reverend. I call them pets, it
helps.' She leads Nora out.

Huxley moves to Mr Mayhew in the next chair, one of only two
men in Heath Lodge, as much in a minority in his old age as in
the dancing classes of his youth. 'You must take me away, Doctor,'
he wheezes.

'I'm not the Doctor; I'm the Vicar. Don't you remember? I visit every month.'

'The people here are dangerous. They come down in the middle of the night with no skirts on and hatch plots.' He points to the returning Sister. 'She's the worst. She puts on special scent.'

Huxley pats his hand and pulls himself away. He continues past a group of women known as 'the three Graces', which he assumed to be a particularly tasteless joke until he discovered that they did indeed share the name but, since none of them was able to remember it, it never caused confusion. He moves on to Mafeking, who was born on the night of the lifting of the siege and whose life has declined in parallel with the Empire. 'I'm so glad to see you Vicar,' she trills, offering a sign of recognition that makes him equally grateful. 'I've come to visit my friend Marjorie. But, if you'd be so kind as to call us a taxi, I'll take her away. I'm sure that this isn't the best place for her. Everyone's quite mad.' She starts to cry.

'Come now pet, there's no need for that,' Sister Baptista says; but Mafeking, as ever, shuns anyone black.

Huxley is deeply embarrassed. The Sister, however, refuses to take offence and points out with a wry smile that 'This place used to be a guest house. Last year we found a mouldy sign they must have hung in the window "No blacks or Irish". Stick to that now and you'd be in real trouble. All you nice white English people would have to look after your old folks yourselves.'

'Yes,' he agrees; while imagining hordes of pensioners thrown out onto the streets. He pictures his own parents, both eminent scientists in their eighties, their world a system of soluble problems. Any thought of that system failing fills him with dismay. They despise his faith as feeble-minded. His mother, a retired osteopath, still thinks that he abandoned medicine in order to spite her. His father, a palaeontologist, with little interest in anything – including his son – less than 64 million years old was quieter in his condemnation but equally cutting in his scorn. They blamed his apostasy on Jessica, in spite of all his protestations that, having grown up in a vicarage, she had vowed that the very last man she would marry was a priest. He can hardly expect her to devote herself to a mother-in-law whose first words on introduction were 'she has an interesting misalignment of the lower jaw' and who has behaved as if that were her main point of interest ever since.

He feels a desperate need to escape and tells the Sister that they should start the service. As she goes to fetch two of her colleagues, he switches off the television to the accompaniment of a harrowing groan.

The Vicar sets up the altar on a rickety card-table. He
hands out hymn-books, wedging them in the folds of
rugs, balancing them on bony knees.

'If you'll turn to Hymn 289,' Huxley says, 'we'll sing "O happy
band of pilgrims".' He winces as Nurse Bridget plays enough false
notes to make even the most steadfast pilgrim stumble. And yet it
appears to be a one-man band. No anchorite could feel lonelier as
he listens to his solo baritone. To his relief, he is joined in the
second verse by Sister Baptista, whose cheer-leading contralto spurs
a few of the livelier residents to wave their hands and drool. Then
Lily comes into her own. The familiar tune penetrates the torpor
and takes her back sixty years to her days as a star on the
Temperance Hall circuit. But the purity of her voice is not reflected
in her choice of words.
  'O happy if ye labour
  As Jesus did for men!
  O happy if ye bugger
  As Jesus buggered them!'
  'Stop it, Lily,' Sister Baptista says, 'you bad girl.'
  'If I'm bad, you're mad,
  And I've songs that'll make your hair curl.'
  Huxley shudders at the use of rhyme that has already taught him
never to address any word to her that ends in 'unt' or 'uck'. 'Let's
skip to the last verse,' he says quickly; but Lily is into her stride
and the pilgrim band is assailed by calls to 'roll me over in the
clover'. He turns with gratitude to the Prayer of Consecration,
which proceeds undisturbed until one of the Graces decides to take
a walk.
  'What's the matter, love?' Nurse Dympna asks.
  'You won't help,' she replies.
  'Try me.'
  Huxley over-enunciates the prayer.
  'My dress. I want my dress,' Grace bleats. 'My mother's bought
me a beautiful white dress. She wants me to wear it for church.'
The Nurse is soothing her when Lily bursts in with a cackle.
  'Silly old bitch,
  Out without a stitch,
  Look at all the curtains twitch.'
  Sister Baptista moves to Lily. 'Right. Come on you, out! You're
in disgrace.'
  'In disgrace; in disgrace,
  Lipstick on her lips and powder on her face.'

Sister Baptista and Nurse Dympna bundle her off on her bandy legs.

Huxley intervenes: 'Can't she have one last chance?'

'One last chance pulled down her pants –'

'I said that was enough, Lily,' the Sister shouts, whereupon Lily shifts the mood as swiftly as a cinematic storm, with a verse of 'I know that my redeemer liveth'. The nurses stand still. Grace's sobbing stops.

> The Vicar takes the paten and moves along the line of chairs, offering the Host to the people.

Huxley moves to Mrs Sylvester, a woman whose son is dead and whose daughter-in-law hires an actor to ring her once a week at the home.

'It's your son,' the nurses say.

'When are you coming to see me?' she cries into the phone.

'I came last week; have you forgotten?'

'He says he came last week.' She turns to the nurses in confusion.

'But of course he did. You've just been drinking too much milk of amnesia,' they reply with a laugh. And it is a deception practised with the best of intentions because, if she ever discovered the truth, Mrs Sylvester would lose what few wits she has left; but the effect is to leave her even more disorientated than before. As he places the wafer on her tongue with a 'Take and eat this in remembrance that Christ died for thee,' he feels as if he is perpetuating a similar fraud. It is not Christ's death that is at issue, but his own attempts to peddle them false hope.

How can he keep faith with his faith or his function as a nurse prises open the mouth of a crow-footed crone to receive the wafer, which she resists for fear that it is medicine? He has always refused to regard the sacrament as medicine to the soul; its effect depends on engagement. But this is the seed falling on stony ground . . . parched, dust-swept, eroded ground. He wonders if they take, literally, a crumb of comfort. So why is he here rather than out in the factories and pubs? Why isn't he talking to people who might answer back, people who will measure God against the reality of their lives rather than use Him to make up for the lack of it? Is the answer not that he reassures them but that they reassure him? They remind him of a time when a priest had a definite role, doubts were the province of the agnostic, and the mystery of the world could be contained in a handful of words: 'The body of Christ'.

He offers the Host to Lily.

'Rum-ti-tum-ti-tum,

Stick it up your bum.'

He waves away the nurses' intervention.

'It's the body of Christ, Lily.'

'My name's Lily,

I'm not silly

And I bet you've got a big willy.' She clutches his crotch.

Watching Lily whimper as the Sister smacks away her hand, he reflects that she is merely giving shape to his more refined parishioners' desires. He has lost count of the number of good church ladies who have wanted to help him break the Seventh Commandment, as if the Adulterous Bible were the Authorized Version in NW3. Lily, at least, has the excuse of senility. Hers is the unkindest fate of all, left teetering on the edge of time, no lifeline but her libido. Nevertheless, he has finally found the role that has eluded him: sex symbol to frustrated gentlewomen. If the *Church Times* or *The Lady* ever wish to boost circulation, they have only to introduce a new feature ... Readers' Curates or Page Three Priests.

'Roll me over in the clover,

Roll me over, lay me down, and do it again.'

The Vicar pronounces the blessing and leaves the room.

As Huxley is walking through the hall, an old lady is being hustled into the lift. Catching sight of him, she calls 'Did you get my Christmas card?'

'It's Easter, Connie,' Sister Baptista says.

'I decided not to send any this year, but I was afraid people would think I was dead.' She enters the lift. 'Are you coming? This one goes to Venice.'

'Thank you, but it's only one flight; I'll walk.'

'The flight's fully booked; you must take the lift.' The gates close like a curtain across her mind. Huxley strides up the stairs and down a corridor thick with the fug of foetid bodies and fuddled brains. He knocks on Laura's door.

'Come in,' a nurse shouts. He enters to find Laura sitting on the commode.

'I beg your pardon; I'll come back.'

'Don't you be worrying now, Father,' the Nurse says. 'We've just been doing our number twos. Let's give ourselves a little wipe now, shall we?' He tells himself that the pronoun signifies closeness rather than condescension. 'There now. Here's Father come to bring you the Holy Mass.' She tucks the old lady like a bedwarmer between the sheets. 'Poor darling, she can't be telling one day from the next. We'll be giving them a hot cross bun but, to her, it's just bread with currants.' He wishes that she would be less expansive with the potty. 'Every night, I pray to Our Lady that she'll be taking her to her mercy. Frank says I'm after doing myself out of a job. But it's a terrible waste of a life: a body nothing but a bladder. See here, Father.' She waves the evidence under his nose. 'It makes you think.'

It makes him think that he should never have given up medicine. Then, at least, he would have been able to pre-empt the Virgin with sleeping pills. 'I'm afraid I don't have much time.'

'Aren't I the one, Father? Frank says that if they ever put a tax on talk, he'll be off ... to be sure, he's an awful tease. Still, I'd best put this out of the way. We don't want our Lord looking down on Laura's doings.'

He concludes that there is more respect for life in a mortuary. There, they plug any leaking orifice; they don't hold up bodily wastes for public inspection. He is repulsed by a vision of humanity stripped to its essence: mere reflex with no means of reflection. He finds a new rationale for church burial: to restore the dignity that has been removed in old age.

The Nurse props up her patient on the pillow as Huxley speaks a short prayer. He holds out the Host and, as he utters the words 'the body of Christ', he is amazed to see Laura raising her hand. She lifts the wafer very slowly to her mouth and laboriously chews. He offers her the cup. She sips and sinks back. His fear that the effort has killed her is quelled by the gentle billowing of her chest.

'There now, darling,' the Nurse says. 'Don't you look the peaceful one?'

'She raised her hand. I thought you said that she couldn't move anything for herself – that you had to feed her.'

'And that's God's honest truth. But it's a glorious thing. Somewhere deep inside, she knows that this is Our Lord's blessed body.'

'But how? Do you think that she knows it in her mind or just in her memory – like a nursery rhyme?'

'She takes no notice of anything else. Try to get her to open her mouth with a "one for mammy" and you'll be wasting your breath.'

'So it's only for communion?'

'I've seen it over and over, Father; faith's the very last thing to go.'

'But why? Is it simply a case of conditioning: the fear of God drummed into her as a child? Or is it something intrinsic to her very nature, something she – like all the rest of us – was born with, as basic as the capacity for speech ... more basic than the capacity for speech, since it survives when speech, and everything else, has failed?'

'You'll be talking now of conscience?'

'No, something far more fundamental. God made us in His image and imbued us with the need to respond, so that, all our lives, we feel a nostalgia for our origins like exiles yearning for home. We're always taught about the wisdom of old age – this is it.' He sees her looking dubiously at Laura. 'All outward signs to the contrary. It shows that religion isn't an imposed system but our most essential human faculty – not an attempt to explain the world but the inherent explanation. The irony is that our eyes are so clouded and our lives so cluttered that it's not until everything else has been swept away that we're able to see.'

Meeting of the
Parochial Church Council

Monday 7.00 p.m.
St Mary-in-the-Vale, Hampstead

> The members of the Parochial Church Council take their seats in the crypt.

Huxley studies the nursery-school visions of heaven dotting the walls: 'It will have the biggest football pitch ever ... We won't have to eat veg ... There will be lots of churches ... It will be full of vicars.' He wishes that he felt so sure.

He watches the PCC members taking their places, determined to make the most of the only authority that most of them will ever wield. Their air of self-importance is somewhat deflated by the seating which, apart from two teachers' chairs, is scaled to the children who use the crypt by day. Myrna is allotted one of the full-sized chairs by virtue of age, while Nancy Hewitt is made an honorary octogenarian on the grounds of bulk. Rosemary invokes the spirit of wartime improvisation to a sceptical Winifred Metcalfe, while Judith admits to Trudy and Sophie Record that the arrangement has a certain Alice-in-Wonderland charm. Hugh Snape snorts at her in disbelief as he squats with his bottom scraping the floor.

> *Almighty God,*
> *you have built your Church upon the foundation*
> *of the apostles and prophets*
> *with Jesus Christ himself as the chief corner-stone.*
> *So join us together in unity of spirit by their doctrine,*
> *that we may be made a holy temple acceptable to you;*
> *through Jesus Christ our Lord.*

Hugh listens to the prayer in intense irritation. It is not just the furniture that leaves him feeling like Gulliver among the Lilliputians. As the only man on the council – the only lay man that is, but then the clergy don't count – it is up to him to keep the meeting on track. Women are far too fond of detours (he has had thirty years of Petula's scenic routes). So he taps his watch as if cocking a starting-pistol. Huxley takes his meaning and coughs.

Petula, as secretary, offers apologies for absence from Cynthia

Charteris, Gill Levington and Alice Leighton, who is busy with preparations for tomorrow's wedding.

'I think it's safe to assume,' Huxley says, 'that Lady Blaikie won't be coming after her recent bereavement.'

'When? Who? Did Julian die?' Nancy asks.

'Yes. I'm afraid so. Late last night. Blair was with him.'

Blair sees the company turn to him. Their faces express sympathy but their eyes entreat reassurance. He says nothing. Rosemary pats his hand. Her ring scratches.

'What did he die of? He was so young.'

'Thirty-seven,' Blair says flatly.

'Legionnaire's Disease,' Huxley replies. 'He caught it in Naples.'

'He should never have gone abroad,' Nancy says. 'It's the water.'

'But you're not safe anywhere nowadays,' Judith says. 'Last summer, we had to boil the water in Torquay.'

'Ladies, ladies,' Hugh says. 'I think we're straying from the point.'

'On the contrary,' Rosemary says. 'Since we're dealing with apologies for absence, this is very much to the point. I think, Vicar, that we would all appreciate it if you said a short prayer.'

'Do you really?' Huxley seems as taken aback as if she had asked him to tap-dance. 'Yes, of course.' They bow their heads: the women in prayer; Hugh in frustration. Rosemary slips to her knees, a gesture that the coconut matting makes her instantly regret.

The Secretary reads the minutes of the last meeting.

After signing the minutes, Huxley turns to 'matters arising'. Judith asks whether there has been any progress on Dr Hayward's rent increase.

'It's not looking hopeful,' Huxley says.

'You did write to the Palace?' Blair asks.

'Yes. And I was directed back to the Crown Commissioners.'

'Surprise, surprise!'

'His GP and Social Services both made representations. Glenda Jackson took up the case. But no joy.'

'Then ought we to interfere?' Judith asks.

'He's ninety-three,' Blair says. 'For sixty years, he worked among the poor of St Pancras. Is he now to be chucked on the streets because he can't pay the rent?'

'Landlords no longer care,' Trudy says. 'Mine has hidden cameras in my room. Everything I do is on video. He wants to find evidence of men. I tell you he will find nothing!' Her screech is met by an embarrassed silence.

'But you have a private landlord, Trudy. Dr Hayward is living in Crown property.'

'We've tried everything,' Huxley says. 'We explained that, given his age, it was unlikely that the shortfall would last too long.'

'Nonsense,' Winifred says. 'He'll outlive us all. Why, in seven years time, he'll be getting his telegram from the...' She looks at her shoes.

'You can't expect Her Majesty to concern herself with individual tenants,' Rosemary says. 'It'll be in the hands of agents.'

'They'll still report to her,' Blair says. 'She's the one setting the agenda.'

Petula is writing as furiously as a Japanese student.

'I don't think we need to minute that last exchange,' Huxley says. 'We'd do well to remember Our Lord's injunction to render unto Caesar –'

'Dr Hayward's been rendering unto Caesar for sixty years,' Blair says. 'And now she's kicking him out.'

'Fortunately, he's been found a very pleasant flat in Spencer House, where he'll be among friends.' Huxley smiles at Nancy and Sophie. 'We'll just have to make sure we all keep a close eye on him. Perhaps Sophie, you might arrange a rota.'

Blair groans. On the Day of Judgement – if there is a Day of Judgement – Huxley will still be arranging rotas.

'Believe me,' Myrna says to Blair. 'Dr Hayward won't hear a word against the Royal Family. He told me that Maundy Thursday would be the most exciting day of my life. Then he offered me a biscuit from a Silver Jubilee tin.'

The Finance and Buildings Officer's Report.

Hugh adopts a Churchillian stance.

'Well, there's both good and bad news. St Mary's finances are, I'm afraid, in a very shaky state. If we were a business –'

'Which we're not,' Blair interjects.

'If we were, we'd be bankrupt. Our overdraft amounts to nearly £60,000.' The women all look shocked, apart from Trudy who finds the figure reassuringly unreal. 'On top of that, the bank is no longer willing to treat us as a special case. They intend to levy the full charges.'

'How much will that amount to?' Huxley asks. 'In layman's terms, as it were.'

'About £7,200 a year.'

'Daylight robbery,' Blair says.

'Commercial practice,' Hugh says.

'Precisely.'

'If we might return to the real world,' Hugh says, determined to keep his feelings in check. 'We're also faced with major expenditure. Ever since, I've been on this PCC ... how long is that now, Madam Secretary?'

'Eight years,' his wife dutifully replies.

'We've been putting off essential repair-work. Believe me, everyone who walks through the doors is at risk. The wiring system is lethal; it desperately needs replacing.'

'About how much will that cost?' Huxley asks, adding 'very roughly' for fear that too accurate an estimate would put him on the spot.

'£25,000.'

'Is that off the top of your head?' Blair asks, 'or do you speak with authority?'

'I am an authority!' Hugh barely contains his anger. 'I deal with these things every day.'

'We're fortunate to have such an expert among our number,' Huxley says.

'There's more. The blockage in the guttering has caused water to seep into the walls. There's considerable discolouration over the Moses window. Finally – and it's by no means a comprehensive list – the church is infested with mice.'

Huxley at last identifies the pet-shop scent in the air.

'I've had an estimate from Rentokil, who would want to come about eight times a year at £200 a visit.'

The women grow less happy at their proximity to the ground.

'I'll have to win the lottery,' Nancy says. 'Oh, you don't disapprove, do you, Father?'

'I wouldn't like to commit myself either way.'

'I have a far less controversial scheme,' Hugh says. 'I ask you all to listen carefully. We're very lucky at St Mary's to have a valuable asset. I'm talking of the old clergy-house.'

'Which we've earmarked as a hostel for the homeless,' Blair says. 'We've applied for grants.'

'And we've been turned down. So which is to be our priority: the church or the hostel? You heard what the Bishop said yesterday: "it's only a Church that's lost sight of itself that fills its time with soup kitchens".'

'And you've heard what Christ says every day: "Feed my sheep".'

'It's far from certain we'd get permission for the change of use.'

'And what would it do to house prices?' Nancy asks. 'It's no use putting on your widow's-mite face, Blair. I am a widow; I have to think of these things.'

'We're straying from the point again,' Hugh says. 'We simply can't afford the hostel. There are serious structural defects: hairline cracks indicating subsidence, external walls built without a damp course. The roof requires extensive repairs and, as we're in a conservation area, we'd have to replace it with the original lead. Then we'd need to upgrade the safety system; which means escape routes, fire doors, fire walls, smoke detectors and smoke alarms. And, as if that wasn't enough, there are the new *Construction Design Management Regulations*, which pose a real risk of our being prosecuted should anything go wrong on site.'

'Would that be to the whole PCC or just the Vicar?' Rosemary asks. 'I mean we may as well be wise virgins.'

'What?' Judith asks, startled.

'Putting oil in our lamps,' she says smugly. 'Who hasn't been reading her gospels lately?'

'Aren't surveys often subjective?' Blair asks.

'Are you questioning my judgement?'

'Not at all. I'm just suggesting that another surveyor might paint a rosier picture.'

'Go ahead then, ask someone else. I really don't know why I bother. For eight years, all that's stood between this church and collapse has been me. You come here and, after five minutes, you want to pull everything down.'

'I was simply wondering –'

'An outside surveyor would have charged a minimum of £600. I gave my services free: gratis: for nothing.'

'I want to propose a vote of thanks to Hugh for all his hard work,' Huxley interjects. 'Please minute it.'

'You look down on me because I lack a few letters after my name – because I've come up on the tools rather than from a fancy college. I know my job. I've sweated over buildings that all those collar-and-tie men have just wandered through.'

'Hugh please,' Petula says. 'You're shouting.'

'Right. Well, is there anyone else who wants to question my motives or my competence?'

Petula bites her tongue and continues to write.

'Definitely not,' Huxley says. 'But there's one point I fail to understand. What you began by calling a "valuable asset" now sounds like a liability.'

'If we retain it, yes, but not if we sell. I propose we put the building in the hands of a developer.'

'Not an estate agent?' Nancy asks.

'And pay them ten or twenty per cent? Now that would be a sin. My way cuts out the middleman. All I need do is call up my contacts from the Council: find out which companies are sniffing around. Then we can approach them, while keeping the upper hand.'

Blair snorts.

'Do you have a better idea? Like this, we can maximize the return to the church, see to all the repairs, invest the remainder and,' he throws a sop to Blair, 'even make a substantial donation to charity.'

'Splendid,' Huxley says. 'It sounds like the answer to all our prayers. But are you sure you'll have the time, Hugh? Petula said you were up to your eyes.'

'For the church, I'll make time.'

'Really splendid. Now, does anyone have anything to add or should we take a vote on Hugh's proposal?' He assesses the silence. 'Right then, all those in favour of pursuing a property deal, please raise your hands.'

Hugh, Myrna, Rosemary, Nancy and Huxley himself raise their hands.

'All those against.'

Blair, Trudy, Judith, Winifred and Sophie raise their hands.

'Mine is more of a let's-have-another-think vote than an absolute no,' Sophie says.

'Mine too,' Winifred says.

Judith applies her principle of never taking the same side as Rosemary.

'Five all. Oh dear; does this mean I have to use my casting vote?'

'Yes,' Hugh says. 'It has to be settled.'

'Petula dear,' her mother says, 'you haven't voted.'

'I've been so busy writing, I've not had time to think.'

'Don't you want the scheme to go ahead?' Hugh entreats her. 'You, of all people, know the benefits.'

Yes, she knows the benefits. They have become his nightly pillow-talk. He has given her a vantage point in the District Surveyor's office from which to watch his fellow workers lining their pockets, while his own remain frayed and bare. He has shown her planning officers with privately planned pensions, solicitors driving secretly solicited cars, and estate agents paying for country cottages in small-denomination notes. He has explained how honesty is so far from being the best policy that it is counter-productive. People either take him for a fool or assume that he must be covering even murkier tracks than their own.

Fifteen years at the same desk have filled him with resentment. Younger men have been promoted and retirement is within view. Decades of dreams have vanished along with the value of his pension. Now he has a chance to revive them. The clergy-house site seems like a godsend. It will make the perfect access road to Jeffrey's new development (increasing his profit by an estimated three million pounds). And, although even Jeffrey is unable to bulldoze through the conservation order, it is amazing how fast a building falls derelict when vandals strip lead off the roof or arsonists break in through an unlocked door.

She stares at Hugh's fervid face. By contrast, she feels quite calm. She cannot blame him; he has been corrupted by association. It is hard to resist temptation in the plausible shape of Jeffrey Finch-Buller – only the snake-skin belt gives him away. He has offered Hugh £250,000 for brokering the deal. Hugh, in turn, insists that no one will lose. The church will receive far more than it would have done without Jeffrey's interest, while they will secure their place in the sun: early retirement to an olive grove in Spain.

The no-losers clause is invalidated by a single glance at her mother. She has voted with Hugh out of loyalty rather than principle ... except that, to her, loyalty is a principle. But then she has never known the pull of divided loyalties. She has never been forced to choose between a parent who moved down from Yorkshire to live with her family and a husband who delivers deadly 'over-my-dead-body' prohibitions. She has never owned a spare room filled with filial guilt.

'Petula,' Huxley calls. 'Are you with us? You look miles away.'

She calculates that she is hovering somewhere above the Pyrenees.

'We need to make a decision,' Hugh says. 'Just say you agree.'

'I can't, Hugh; I'm sorry. I vote against.'

'What?'

'Are you sure?' Huxley asks in surprise.

'Quite sure.'

'In which case, the motion is defeated by six votes to five. I'm afraid we'll have to think up another scheme to raise cash. What does anyone say to a summer fair?'

'What are you trying to do to me?' Hugh asks Petula.

The others shrink from any public recrimination.

'I was thinking of the church. Isn't that why we're here?'

'Once again, Hugh, I want to thank you for all you've done. I'm sure your report will prove invaluable as we consider alternatives.'

'Excuse me,' Hugh says. 'I must have some air.'

'Would you like me to come with you?' Petula asks.

'No. Stay with your minutes. Clearly, they take priority.' As he jumps up, his chair sticks to him. He shoves and squirms but is unable to shake it off. He grows increasingly frenzied, like a doctored dog chasing its wound. Finally breaking free, he flings the chair against the wall, cracking its leg, and storms from the room.

'Oh dear,' Huxley says, 'I think it's time to turn to "any other business".'

Solemnization of
Holy Matrimony

Tuesday 2.00 p.m.
St Mary-in-the-Vale, Hampstead

The Vicar addresses the people:
Dearly beloved, we are gathered together here in the sight of God, and in the face of this Congregation, to join together this man and this woman in holy Matrimony.

Maureen Beatty sits in the front pew and purrs. She has never been a church person, either by choice or by childhood. She prefers to be holy at home. She listens loyally to the morning service on the radio and always tries to switch to something contemplative like dusting or chopping vegetables rather than vacuuming or changing sheets. She hums to her favourite hymns from the *BBC Hymnbook* . . . even the name has a reassuring ring. Last summer, she went to her local church – the price of tea with the Vicar – and found it full of hot-faced men and women in sweet-wrapper dresses, all clapping and swaying and praising the Lord on tambourines. She felt like the dot on a domino. The next time the Vicar invited her, she gave him some home-made chutney instead.

She is glad to find that St Mary's is a church of a very different colour. The paintings and statues and flying angels are as good as any in a guidebook. The windows cast a rosy glow over an already auspicious day. But then it would be hard not to be moved by the occasion. As a girl, she wanted every service to be Christmas carols; now she would like them all to be weddings: complete with flowers and hats and warm, summer tears.

'You're not starting already; they've only just walked in,' her husband David (full Christian name in church) says, as she takes out a handkerchief.

'It's just a precaution,' she hisses back, refusing to let him spoil her big day. She blinks her eyes and wrinkles her nose as he sits by her side in a suit smelling of must and mothballs, his lapel dwarfed by his flower like the cocktails they were given in Greece.

The Vicar's voice resounds through the church as he expounds the purpose of marriage.
First, It was ordained for the procreation of children, to be

brought up in the fear and nurture of the Lord, and to the
praise of his holy Name.

Maureen agrees with God. Children are what make – and make up
for – a marriage. A wave of tenderness flows over her as she turns
to her son standing calmly – too calmly – at the altar. When he
rang them with news of the wedding, her first thought was that
Daisy must be pregnant. Nothing else could explain such a hurried
ceremony to a fiancée they had yet to meet. She found it hard to
disguise her disappointment at his denial. Although she would
never admit it even to Dave (a mere monosyllable at home), she felt
as frustrated by Joseph's restraint as she was mystified by his
choice of bride. And yet, however unsatisfactory Daisy may be in
other respects, there is hope in her hips.

Secondly, It was ordained for a remedy against sin, and to
avoid fornication.

Maureen has no wish to argue with the prayer-book, especially
since, if she remembers rightly, it was written by King James I, but
it seems to express an unduly negative view of human nature, even
of men. She can only speak for herself – that is for Dave – and the
dirty-linen side of things is well in the past, but he always had a
perfectly healthy sexual appetite (the sort that eats whatever is put
in front of it without asking for seconds). She cannot believe that
he needed her as a safeguard against sin.

As for herself, she followed her mother's advice to grin and bear
it (or, at least, bear it; in the dark, the grin was optional). She put
up with the indignity: the rustling of her nightie when all that she
wanted to do was sleep; the beery, blistery breath on her cheeks;
the heaviness on her hips which was supposed to engender passion; then the lying awake on the damp sheet, curbing every urge
to swab herself down in case he should take it as a criticism. In
time, he lost interest, just as he had in the ice-skating which had
also been a weekly event when they first married. His last attempt
was on the Queen Mother's ninetieth birthday. They had been invited to a slap-up do at the British Legion and, when they returned
home, one thing led to another, except that it did not lead far
enough. Dave took it badly and he has never bothered her since.
Still, she has no plans to switch to twin beds. There must always be
room for an impromptu hug.

The Vicar calls on the Bride and Groom to make their
vows.

As one who sets great store by names, Maureen finds Daisy's unfortunate. She is far too much of the Ox-eye daisy for her liking ...
less delicate little petals than a great thick stalk. Nevertheless, it's a
relief to hear the name used at all. She half-expected the diminutive
Dee, which Joseph has repeatedly urged on her, in spite of her
polite – but firm – refusal.

'But Mum, Dee wants to be called Dee; it's her choice.'

'If everyone chose their own names, what would be the point of
parents?'

'People call me Joe.'

'That's different; it's expected. Joe DiMaggio. Joe Kennedy.'

'Uncle Joe Stalin,' Dave interjects.

'He was a communist. They shorten everything.'

'You can call me whatever you like, Mrs Beatty.'

'Why thank you, Daisy. And you can call me Mother. You're one
of the family now.'

'It takes time, mum,' Joe says. 'Dee's only just met you.'

She refrains from pointing out that he is the one who has kept
them apart for the past eighteen months. Meanwhile, Daisy effects
her own compromise by referring to her as Mother Beatty, which
may be the custom in New Zealand but leaves her feeling like
something out of a pageant.

She is determined to be the perfect mother-in-law, but it would
help if Daisy were just a little more womanly – silly word but no
other will do. It is all very well being a computer programmer, but
that does not stop her learning to cook. Take Maureen Lipman: she
acts, runs a home, has children and manages to write a column
about it in *Good Housekeeping*. But, when she asked Daisy what her
specialities were, she laughed and said 'Take-away pizza and micro-
wave curry'.

'I shall cook, Mum; I enjoy it,' Joe said, which gave her a twinge
of discomfort, even though she knew that all the most fashionable
chefs were men.

> The Bride takes the Groom by the hand and repeats her
> vow after the Vicar.

Maureen knew it was too much to hope that she would promise to
obey. She may not mean it – what woman does? – but it would be
a gesture. On which note, she can think of several others that
would not go amiss ... her eyebrows would look none the worse
for a pair of tweezers nor her hair for an old-fashioned perm.
But her offer to accompany her to the salon was refused point-
blank. She was taken aback. She could understand if it was Mrs

Wainwright's daughter – the one who went out to pick oranges – being made to have a bath in the synagogue in front of her future husband's relations. But all she was suggesting was a shampoo and set.

She determined to say nothing – not even when she saw the wedding-dress or what she was told was the wedding-dress, since nothing in the colour, cut or material gave any hint. She said nothing about the lack of bridesmaids. She even said nothing when she heard that, in the absence of Daisy's father, a woman was going to give her away. Daisy wasn't to blame for her parents being on the other side of the world – although in her view (which, of course, she kept to herself) it showed a shocking want of family feeling – but were there no men for her to ask? Joseph told her that the Church allowed it. But then the Church seemed to say 'anything goes' as often as Amen nowadays. This was on a par with the people who called God, Her, and the Queen, Elizabeth Windsor. Nevertheless, she resolved not to interfere.

> The Vicar wraps the couple's hands in his stole.
> *Those whom God hath joined together let no man put asunder.*

Maureen is disappointed by the chaste kiss that Joseph plants on Daisy's cheek. Ordinarily, she disapproves of public displays of affection, but this is an exception. Footballers show more enthusiasm after scoring a goal – and some of them score hat tricks, whereas you only marry once ... at least in theory ... at least in church. Joseph has warned her that the ceremony will be very low-key (which, no doubt, explains his bride's make-up). They aren't even taking a honeymoon, owing to pressure of work. It's hard to credit that a librarian and a computer-programmer are engaged on matters of such importance that they can't be spared for a fortnight. The real reason must be their apprehension at being alone. What they fail to realize is that, however disagreeable at the time, the experience will mellow in the memory. Memories are as important as any pension-plan to secure their old age.

> *Forasmuch as Joseph and Daisy have consented together in holy wedlock, and have witnessed the same before God and this company, and thereto have given and pledged their troth either to other, and have declared the same by giving and receiving of a ring, and by joining of hands; I pronounce that they be man and wife together, In the Name of the Father and of the Son, and of the Holy Ghost. Amen.*

The Bride and Groom, the Best Man and the – Maureen does not know how to describe the female father-figure – move out to sign the register. By rights, she and David should have been asked, but she has never been one to push herself forward. She takes the opportunity to examine the congregation. It is disconcertingly small. She hopes that the cameraman, whose pony-tail has been bobbing irreverently in her line of vision, will be careful to disguise the gaps. The secret lies in a strategic use of pillars. She has sat through so many dull videos that she longs for one with a difference – something arty with angles, which will impress those friends who have never been to a London wedding, the sort of film that might be shown late-night with subtitles on Channel Four ... not too late-night, she thinks with a jolt, as she remembers one recent screening. It was enough to give insomnia a bad name.

The choir are whooping, almost gargling, through the chorale. Her sister, sitting in the row behind, taps her on the back.

'They're a bit flat, aren't they?'

'No, they're Maori – the songs, that is. Daisy's from New Zealand. I expect it reminds her of home.'

'How much more is there?'

'How should I know? It's a medley of traditional melodies. I find it very soothing.' She fears that even a white lie turns black in church. 'Prince Charles and Princess Diana had Kiri te Kanawa at their wedding. She's Maori.' Her pleasure at the connection turns to alarm at the precedent, and she leans forward before Susan has a chance to point it out. She feels a jab on her shoulder.

'I gather we're not eating till eight o'clock.'

'So as people have time to get there.' Maureen is fast losing patience. 'Joseph and Daisy's friends work. They're not like your Bernie: one plastic kneecap, and the rest of his life on benefits.'

'At least Bernie and Sandra were married on a Saturday, as is right and proper.'

'Stop clacking, you two,' Dave says. 'We're in church.'

'It's all right; it's like the adverts. We're allowed.'

'I understand you're upset,' Susan presses her advantage. 'Your only son gets married and half the women turn up in jeans.'

'They're emaciated women ... I don't see what's so funny about that.'

'I just wish you'd told me it was informal. I'd never have bought a hat.'

'If money's a problem, Susan, send us the bill. David and I wouldn't want you to go short.'

She sits back, ignoring Susan's prodding until it threatens to bruise.

'What is it now?'

'There!' She points to a young woman breastfeeding beside a statue of Mary. 'I suppose you're in favour of that too – you and your "emaciated" friends.'

Maureen prays – in a non-religious sense – for the Vicar to emerge and continue the service.

'She should learn a little respect. Thrusting her nipple –' Susan mouths the taboo – 'right in the Virgin's face.'

> The bridal party return from the sacristy. The Vicar
> mounts the pulpit.

'I would like to welcome you all to St Mary's on this very happy occasion of the marriage between Daisy and Joseph ... Joseph and Daisy. I don't intend to take up too much of your time.'

'That'll be the day,' Dave mutters. Maureen kicks him.

'But I would like to say a few words about what this occasion means to me and, I hope, to them. Joseph has been a valued member of our congregation for many years. We think particularly of his sterling work on the parish newsletter and his transformation of the church garden. Daisy is, of course, a more recent addition to our lives. She has blown in from the Antipodes like a breath of fresh air.' Try as she will, Maureen finds it hard to think of her as a breath; a gust, more like, or a gale. 'Indeed, I like to think that their romance blossomed as they pasted together the newsletter – sticky fingers brushing inky hands (speaking of which, should any visitor care to take a copy, they are available in the porch as you leave). For myself, I view it as not so much losing an editor as gaining a desk-top publisher.'

Maureen laughs to fill the gap.

'The English language is rich in double meanings but, to my mind, none is more resonant than the verb "to marry". As a priest, I feel far closer to those I marry than a mere facilitator; I consider myself part of the ceremony in a very intimate way.' Maureen shifts in her seat. 'I must have married several hundred people during my ministry. But, before you run for either the police or the Guinness Book of Records, I would like to assure you that, for the past thirty years, I have been very happily married to Jessica. So, when I speak of the joys of marriage, I know what I mean. ·

'Daisy and Joseph were determined to make their commitment in church. This makes them something of an anomaly in an age when, as the pundits tell us, fewer and fewer people are choosing to marry and more and more marriages end in divorce. In my view, the Church itself is much to blame for this disenchantment since, behind the dresses and the anthems and the celebration (and may I take this opportunity to ask you, please, not to throw confetti in the churchyard), it perpetuates an essentially negative concept of marriage. Take "the causes for which Matrimony was ordained", which I read at the beginning of the service. The first was "the procreation of children", which sounds uncomfortably like Hitler's plan to populate the Reich. The second was "a remedy against sin": a lifelong equivalent of that strange one-piece undergarment which the Mormons wear ... But then the Church has never felt at ease with sex. I remember, before Jessica and I were married, the priest, an old-style celibate, attempted to enlighten us on the act of love. He likened it to clearing our throats. "You feel this irrepressible urge to cough," he said; "then you do and you bring up some sputum."' Really, Maureen thinks; this is too much. '"And then you don't want to cough again for days." Was that any sort of encouragement to two young people to explore the joys of each other's bodies? However, if I may be allowed to adapt his analogy, I wish Daisy and Joseph a severe attack of bronchitis tonight.'

Maureen acknowledges the titter but fails to see the joke. She dislikes his harping on sex. Vicars today are as bad as agony aunts, preaching orgasms at every opportunity. What sort of message does it give to an old-fashioned couple like Joseph and Daisy – and, after all, it is their wedding – who have so far settled for a goodnight kiss? Still, she agrees with him on one thing. Now that they are man and wife, there's no point in waiting – better to plunge in and get it over with, so as to concentrate on the real joys of marriage: compatibility, companionship ... she stops as she looks at David. It's like the first dip in the sea at Southport; your body soon grows accustomed to the chill.

'Even the third of our matrimonial causes, the "mutual society, help, and comfort", although more positive, sounds unduly practical. It puts the balance-sheet – the household accounts side – of marriage, before the bedsheet – the love. For the essence of Christian marriage must be to place the love that two people have for one another – Daisy and Joseph, Joseph and Daisy – in the context of Christ's love for the world. Christ didn't marry, but the puritanical tradition of the Church has made far too much of this. In a sense – in a very real sense – He is married to every one of us. I don't mean that "mystical union that is betwixt Christ and his Church", which the prayer-book presents as an analogy, nor the compensatory "brides of Christ" of an order of nuns, but a genuine, physical intimacy. After all, He has become man; He has taken our flesh, yours and mine, just as husband and wife are one flesh with each other. Like them, He loves "for richer for poorer, in sickness and in health", although, in His case, there isn't the proviso of "till death us do part".

'Those of us (and I speak for myself), who know the blessing of a happy marriage, know that it is indeed a miracle. But that doesn't give us the right to disparage those who either cannot or have no wish to share our ideal. Remember, Jesus said "In my Father's house are many mansions". And, just as we all know people who lead worthy lives outside the Church, so we also know people who have loving relationships outside marriage. We – Jessica and Huxley, Daisy and Joseph, Maureen and David –' Maureen feels the same mixture of fear and excitement as when she calls House at Bingo. 'We are the fortunate ones; we must never become the complacent ones. We must reach out to those in other relationships just as the Church reaches out to those in other faiths, no longer trying to convert them but rather to discover our common ground. Marriage means breaking down the barriers of the self, not putting up the barriers of the couple.

'Daisy and Joseph, may the Lord grant you every blessing in the course of your future life together. In the name of the Father and of the Son and of the Holy Spirit. Amen.'

> The Vicar pronounces the blessing. The organist plays
> the wedding march. The Bride and Groom process
> down the aisle.

Maureen folds up her handkerchief, which has remained disappointingly dry. As she clasps David's arm to follow the newly-weds down the aisle, she feels herself enveloped in warmth as though she were trying on a fur coat. Then a terrible thought sends her at a near-gallop to the porch where Joseph and Daisy are already posing for pictures.

'You don't want to emigrate, do you?'

'What, mum?'

'Promise me, you're not going to live in New Zealand.'

'Whatever gave you that idea? Dee never wants to set eyes on the place again.'

'Oh Joseph, you've made me so happy.'

'We aim to please. Come here and give me a kiss.'

'It's Daisy you should be kissing,' she says without conviction.

'There's room for both.'

She plants a maternal kiss on his cheek. Then, watching Dave's paternal handshake, she thinks that, just this once, he might have dropped his reserve.

The photographer rounds them up like a sheepdog. All things considered, Maureen is not sorry that they picked a day which has made it impossible for the bulk of her family to attend. The north–south divide seems more marked in person ... she casts a hostile glance at two young women with rings through their noses like cattle. She will have far more control over the viewing of the video than she would ever have had in the flesh. She must corner the cameraman. There is no call to linger on any of the faces, including the Bride's. Daisy could be quite an attractive girl in the right lighting. She has a beautiful bone-structure underneath the fat.

Funeral Service

Wednesday 3.00 p.m.
St Mary-in-the-Vale, Hampstead

> The Vicar speaks the sentence over the coffin.
> *I am the resurrection and the life, saith the Lord: he that*
> *believeth in me, though he were dead, yet shall he live: and*
> *whosoever liveth and believeth in me shall never die.*

Huxley approaches the coffin in the knowledge that this is where
his own will stand, should he die in the parish; although, as a
priest, he will lie with his head, and not his feet, towards the altar,
the one exception to the equality of the shroud. Today, he finds the
anomaly particularly disturbing. Are they trying to insure for every
eventuality ... positioning him in case he feels the need to deliver
a last-minute homily? Or do they expect some transcendent wisdom to filter out the way that corpses of saints are said to exude an
odour of sanctity? His mockery rings hollow. After all, in death, for
the first time, he might have something worth hearing ... 'I am
the resurrection and the life saith the lord.' In death, for the first
time, he might have proof of what he proclaims.

He needs proof fast, not just for his own sake but for the sake of
his congregation. How can he hope to guide other people to Christ
when his own path is unsure? He would give all of Matthew, Mark,
Luke and John for the gospel according to Lazarus, the one account
which would replace speculation with material, immaterial facts.
Every other avenue is closed. He no longer finds an answer in
prayer; his desperation is as self-defeating as a lover's, sickening
God with self-pitying pleas. He touches the wood of the coffin and
begs Julian to act as intermediary. All he asks is a sign – nothing
Vincent Price (no 'one tap for yes, two for no'), but something
internal, eternal, and utterly convincing: a rush of returning faith.

He tries to focus on the service and feels like an actor in a badly
dubbed film, whose speech is at variance with his lips. It's not the
problem of the prayers. He acknowledges the power of the time-
honoured words to absorb the grief: words that speak of certainty
without pomposity or effort; words that were his sole support
when, four years earlier, he spoke them over Toby ... never has he

felt more of a priest than when conducting the funeral of his son. Since then, his beliefs have been subject to a gradual erosion. Like the prehistoric cave-paintings in Lascaux wrecked by the advent of modern tourists, his faith remained rock-hard in isolation only to crumble on exposure to the world.

> The Curate reads the sentence over the coffin.
> *We brought nothing into this world, and it is certain we can carry nothing out. The Lord gave, and the Lord hath taken away; blessed be the name of the Lord.*

Blair takes refuge in the past. It was funerals that first attracted him to the Church. Other services confused him, the prayers as impenetrable as the news, the sermon as hard work as homework. But funerals were different. The grim people and heavy hymns, even the uncomfortable seats and threadbare kneelers, so inappropriate to a God of Life, suited a God of Death. And he buried the white-robed, white-bearded man in the clouds soon after he buried his grandfather, replacing Him with an old-fashioned undertaker in a frock coat and top hat, straight out of his illustrated Dickens. The one colour that held no fears for him was black.

He longed to make the image real and follow in his heavenly father's footsteps. In a class full of would-be footballers and pop-stars, he was the sole future funeral director, an admission which labelled him first as a joker and then as a freak. Unabashed, he determined to put in some practice, but his do-it-yourself services for dead rodents – who were, after all, God's creatures – ended when his mother caught him using the spare-room cupboard as a makeshift morgue. Stung by her charge of morbidity (the disease-threat he laughed off) and his subsequent ban from woodwork, he decided to stick to church, scanning the announcements of death in the local paper and playing truant from school.

How he envied priests their privileged position – dominant yet detached ... a detachment which he longs for today, when he is only able to survive by filling the coffin with sand like that of a missing airman. And yet it was many years before he transferred his allegiance from undertaking, years which saw his gradual progress from the back of the nave to the main body of mourners. He would imagine himself the illegitimate son of the deceased – so much more resonant a word than dead – embellishing his Sunday suit with a black armband and tie.

The more he looked the part, the bolder he became, until one day he seized his chance and jumped into the last car in the cor-tège. He sat, squeezed between the scratchy, pin-striped knees and shiny, stockinged legs of people who already smelt of the cemetery. Their hostile glares spoke volumes, which were quickly translated into words. But he was so rapt by his own performance that he considered them the intruders and defensively insisted that he was the deceased's unknown son from Birmingham. It was only when one old lady burst into tears and another slapped his face that he learnt that his supposed father had died aged twenty-five.

They dismissed his story of mistaking the church and refused to let him out of the car even when he bawled that he still had to find the right one (his performance was now less convincing). They clasped him like a wreath and demanded that the driver call the police. The police, in turn, told his parents, who agreed to send him to a child psychologist. She gave him simple tests with ink blots in the shape of bats and tombstones and shrouds, before asking why he'd tried to make a mockery of the occasion. He replied that, on the contrary, he'd wanted to share it. Funerals were the one place that people were treated with respect.

She suggested that he might find a healthier outlet for his imagination in the school play. The conscript became a convert and, throughout adolescence, he encountered death legitimately on the stage. His parents, relieved at first, lost their enthusiasm when he chose to apply to drama school. 'Why must you always do things by extremes?' his father asked; although he was, in fact, doing them by halves. The other half remained in church ... gradually growing into the whole. Not that his theatrical training has been wasted. 'You make praying so easy,' Myrna said. 'Even when we're on our knees, every word carries.' But he remains actor enough to know that clarity is no substitute for truth, and he reflects, as he picks up the stoup, that funerals felt much less painful at the back.

> The Vicar and Curate circle the coffin, sprinkling it with
> holy water. The Vicar recites the thirty-ninth psalm.

Eleanor glances at the service-sheet and sees that the psalm is a long one. She tries to relax into a reverie, but her mind is racing. She is grateful that she and Julian had grown estranged, or else his death would be unbearable. As it is, it seems more like the final poste restante address. The real pain came many years ago when both he and his sister turned against her. She decided then not to mourn. They had their own lives; she was their mother not their trustee. And, at that moment, she too became free. Nothing that they did could hurt her again. She would not depend on them, nor on her need for them. They were just two of the people who formed the boundaries – who fortified the borders – of her world.

Poor Edith (the phrase is an apostrophe not an emotion), with her lending-library view of life, feels cheated by her composure. Having read some tract about the loss of a child being a parent's greatest tragedy, she is expecting her to turn into Sybil Thorndike. The idea is preposterous. In any case, death is neutral. There is no scale of significance: sparrow at the bottom, son at the top. She grieved more for her spaniel than she did for her husband ... which doesn't mean that she loved him more, simply that he was more lovable. The dog was faithful and affectionate; the Admiral quite the opposite. Death is like a child's crayoning-book, which takes on whatever colour you choose.

Stevenson sits with reassuring heaviness on her shoulder. He, at least, should not die on her, defying nature and all expectations of longevity. Edith's horror at his attendance is a further source of comfort. She thinks it an affectation – worse, an impiety; but she is wrong. Stevenson was closer to Julian than most of the people present – mere Christmas card names topped with Good Friday faces. Nor has he had to dress in borrowed plumes; he sports his black-and-white markings by right.

Gazing at the reredos, she feels an almost Mediterranean warmth towards the Virgin. And yet, for all her eminence, Mary remains a mysterious figure, who barely merits a mention in the gospels between the stable and the Cross. When she does appear, Jesus treats her coldly, insisting that His first loyalty lies with His friends, in exactly the same tone as Julian's. So be it. Mary certainly would not have moped around, endlessly reliving the glories of His childhood. Like her, she had a life of her own.

Jesus's friends can have been no more welcome to a mother than Julian's. Fishermen were one thing – salt of the earth – but Matthew was a publican ... to say nothing of Mary Magdalen and the rest of the breed who sinned for their suppers. Nevertheless, Mary swallowed her pride and stood alongside them at the Cross, just as she herself stood beside Julian's friends in hospital. And, just as Jesus told Mary to look on John as a second son (only a man could suppose that affections are so easily switched), so Julian urged her to rely on Blair. There, however, the similarity ends. Mary may have swooned in John's arms, but she is made of sterner stuff. There will be no unseemly show of grief. She will stand at the vault and shake peoples' hands and thank them for coming, and then never set eyes on any of them again.

Propriety is all that she has left. Morality is relative; it has changed so much in one lifetime. Sin has been downgraded; buggery is no bar to a bishopric nor divorce to the Royal Enclosure.

Propriety, however, remains absolute. That is the code by which she has lived and by which she is burying Julian. She will return him to his ancestors; he will be as much his father's son as he was at the font. Scorning Edith's cant, she gives thanks that she remains alive to take charge. Left to themselves, who knows how the Mary Magdalens would have memorialized him? But she, who gave him his name, will ensure his epitaph, walling him up in the impregnable silence of the family tomb.

The Curate reads the lesson from Revelation, Chapters 21 and 22.

Lennox Hayward lifts a rheumatic hand to a rheumy eye. And yet at his age (an age when every thought provokes that prefix), he has been bereaved so often that the funeral service has become as familiar as the Lord's Prayer. Grief is tinged with envy as he contemplates the coffin. Each night before falling asleep, he prays that the dream will never end and his sheet become his shroud, and each morning dawns on disappointment (thoughts which he diagnosed as morbid at forty feel quite healthy at ninety-three). What's worse, he still has all his faculties ... no life, but all his faculties. How he longs to lose his mind and become a burden on someone other than himself. As a boy, he believed that the luckiest man in history was the Wandering Jew, who, having cursed Christ, was condemned to live forever. Only now can he appreciate the full horror of such a fate.

He has refrained from cursing Christ, but he curses Nature. To a childless doctor, the death of a child he has delivered is the closest he comes to the death of a child of his own. Of all the hundreds of births that he has attended, Julian's remains clearest in his mind, on account of his mother's extraordinary reluctance to admit pain. Her face was as swollen as her belly; her skin was battered and bruised; and yet, in eight hours of flesh-rending labour, she barely raised her voice above a moan. He has never felt more scared for the scars left on both mother and baby. Now, as he watches her bury her son as impassively as she bore him, his emotions rise up like ghosts. Once again, he wants to take her hand and urge 'Scream, shout, rage against the world that has done this to you!' But, instead, he sits politely in his pew while Huxley mounts the pulpit steps.

The Vicar delivers the address.

'We are gathered together to bury the body of Julian Blaikie and to commit his soul to God. We all have our own memories of Julian, many of yours being far more intimate than mine, and I am anxious not to trespass on them. Besides, when Julian and I discussed this service in hospital, he was adamant that he did not want a eulogy of any kind. So I would like to use these few moments to set his death within the broader context that we in the Church experience as Holy Week.

'One of the strangest and most controversial events of the entire week – and one that exercises far more power over my own imagination than the familiar imagery of the cock-crow or the crown of thorns – occurs on the Monday. Jesus is making His way back to Jerusalem from Bethany. He feels hungry and, finding a barren fig tree by the roadside, curses it, whereupon it withers on the spot. At first, this seems completely out of character: Jesus, the life-giver, dealing out destruction and doing so in an apparent fit of pique. Successive scholars have attempted to explain away the story as symbolic, but I believe that it's vital to acknowledge an actual incident, expressing Our Lord's frustration. Which is where it relates to Julian – that is to us.

'Jesus is revealing His frustration, yes, and His anger – an anger every bit as real as He showed in the temple the previous day – that God's creation is not as perfect as He would wish it to be, that it has taken on a life of its own: a life in time. God exists outside time and the world exists in time. God's greatest gift to humanity is time, because time offers the possibility of change and redemption. But a world in time is a world away from God, so that, even as He gives us His greatest gift, He leaves us at our most vulnerable, subject to disease and devastation, despair and death.

'Jesus is rebelling against this. When He curses the fig tree, He is in a very real sense cursing God . . . and let's not forget that He is Himself on His way to being crushed and cursed on the Cross. It's a sentiment which you and I may well share. We may feel angry with God, not least on an occasion such as this. After all, we are made in the image of God; we partake of the divine simply by being human. And yet we, who have the seeds of perfection within us, know that we are not perfect: a fact of which death is a constant reminder. But, while acknowledging – and even indulging – our emotions, we must realize that, far from death making life meaningless (as is the thrust of so much materialist philosophy), it is precisely what gives it meaning, because it is the essence of the imperfection that connects us to the perfection of God.

'It's the arbitrariness of death which seems so cruel. And, believe me, it seems every bit as unjust to me as it does to you. My presence in this pulpit doesn't mean that I have all the answers – far from it – simply that I know how to frame the questions. And I have so many. Why, Lord? Why? Why? Why? Why? Why? Or am I like a man peering through the wrong end of a telescope: from earth to heaven rather than from heaven to earth?'

He looks around at the sound of an echo. In the front pew, Stevenson has picked up his words. 'Why? Why? Why? Why?' He shudders as he hears his soul-searching treated to the parrot's parody.

'Quiet!' Eleanor commands. But her decrees appear to have less effect on birds than they do on humans. He continues to squawk: 'Why? Why? Why?'

'Edith, take him out.' Eleanor turns to her companion. 'Quick. Don't dawdle.'

Huxley watches as Edith, blotched-faced and black-coated, hurries through the congregation, the parrot perched precariously on her upper arm. 'One lump or two?' he demands, as insistently as the man restored to speech in the gospel. 'One lump or two?' Huxley observes the mourners retreating gratefully into irreverence and knows that he must retrieve the initiative. He resists the urge to allude to the age-old conundrum of whether animals have souls and returns to his theme.

'How apt that it takes a not-so-dumb animal to throw my question back at me. After all, what logic lies behind our protests when someone dies young? It's imperative that we don't endorse the mentality of our secular world which appears to regard every death as an affront and early death as a failure. Nowadays, we readily accept the concept that time is relative; and yet, when it comes to the moment of death, we adopt a clockwork chronology. "Too soon", we cry, not selfishly but humanly, at anyone who fails to live out his biblical span. But the value of a life bears no relation to the length of it. The litany of great men and women who died in their prime is the proof.

'As some of you will be aware, my own son was killed four years ago, at the age of twenty-two, while working on an aid programme in Kenya. At the time, Julian was an immense solace to both my wife and myself. Not only did he pay for us to fly out to the camp the following summer (and I can't begin to tell you how much it meant to meet the people who'd worked alongside Toby), but he was also one of the rare people to talk to me about Christ.

'One of the hardest things about being a priest is how few people do talk to you about Him. It's almost like having a disreputable relative. Parishioners see you as the expert – you have the letters before and after your name. But everyone has Christ in his heart. And it was Julian who reminded me that Christ also died young and still accomplished more than any other man in history. At His death, He was of no more consequence than the two thieves who were crucified alongside Him. There was no reason to suppose that His teachings would last longer than those of any other itinerant preacher. But His friends kept His memory alive, just as we have kept Toby's and we will keep Julian's. So let us not mourn for a life prematurely lost but celebrate one fully lived, which will remain to help and to hearten us forever. In the name of the Father and of the Son and of the Holy Spirit. Amen.'

> The congregation sings the hymn
> *Love divine, all loves excelling.*

Lennox puts more faith in divine love than in human memory. He thinks of his wife buried in an oblivion far deeper than the soil of Highgate cemetery . . . a grave at which there is no one but himself left to mourn. He wonders how many people even know that he was married. He never refers to her; it only leads to either mawkishness or embarrassment. His former cleaner assumed that it made them partners in grief, giving her leave to involve him in every twist of her tea-cup tragedies. He felt that Emily was being cheapened by the connection and removed her photograph from display. The cleaner retired, but he never replaced the picture. He relied on the truer likeness in his heart.

Emily Furness Hayward . . . née Moss. Born 3rd June 1905. Died 11th November 1928. The maid is not dead, but sleepeth. No wonder that he mistrusts memory, when he can recall the words on her gravestone more clearly than the smile on her face. They had been married eighteen months when she was struck by Spanish flu. But, in spite of the Vicar's licence to rage against God (little different from Huxley's now), his only quarrel lay with himself. He was a recently qualified doctor; he believed in medicine not just as a palliative but as a panacea. And yet he could not even save his own wife.

Fifty years later, when he was asked by some young consultants to name the greatest medical development of the century, he answered 'Flu injections'. And, as they laughed at what they considered the parochialism of general practice, he felt as though Emily's epitaph had crumbled to dust.

> The pallbearers carry out the coffin through the church.

Eleanor fixes her eyes on the shimmer of sunlight in the doorway, like a pilgrim's on a cathedral spire. She walks through the nave on her brother's arm, flinching from the flabby touch that puts her in mind of nursery puddings.

'Bearing up old girl?' he asks, when they reach the porch.

'As you can see.'

'A1 for effort, I'd say. Difficult . . . delicate balance.'

'Quite.' She refuses to perform a post-mortem on the funeral.

'Strange birds, parsons. All that Why Why Whying. Not a word about Heaven.'

'There was no need, Broderick. It was understood.'

'Still, no harm in spelling it out. Padre at school always said it would be like a great feast. And, believe me, that meant something then. Kept the old nosebags so empty, we'd have sold our souls for a streak of bacon.' Discretion disguises a chuckle.

Eleanor stares at Edith sitting in the back of the car. 'Look at her,' she calls at her companion through the open window. 'Caring nothing for my loss, only her own comfort.'

'You're so cruel, Eleanor. I wanted to stay in church. You know how fond I was of Julian.'

'I know how you tried to ingratiate yourself with him.'

'He liked me.'

'He liked everyone. You are hardly significant enough to have counted as an exception.' She turns to her brother. 'You will have to travel behind, Broderick, with your niece.'

Broderick moves dutifully away, to be replaced by Rosemary.

'Beautiful service, Lady B.'

'I'm glad you enjoyed it.'

'I was wondering if you needed anything before we go to the . . . you know.'

'Yes, a moment of privacy. If you'll excuse me . . .' Eleanor closes the door and winds up the chatter-proof glass. 'Really, that woman! Lady B: as if I were a character in some cheap thriller! She mistakes abbreviation for intimacy and euphemism for tact.'

'She doesn't know what to say.'

'Then let her keep silent.'

'You can be so hard, Eleanor. I don't think you realize.'

'Don't you?'

Broderick climbs into the second car, alongside his niece, Helena, and Massimo, Julian's nurse.

'I only ever seem to see my family at weddings and funerals,' he says.

'Not much difference,' Helena replies.

'On the whole, I think I prefer funerals. You don't have to worry about the other lot.'

'I'm glad you've come, Brodders,' Helena says.

'So am I, my dear. Such short notice. It was touch and go.'

'So inconvenient for Mother, Julian dying in Holy Week. It was either unseemly haste or leaving it till after Easter, and you know how she detests delay.' She swallows a sob.

'How are you, my dear?' He pats her knee with avuncular impunity.

'I ache. It's like seeing the final door slammed on my childhood and then getting my finger trapped.'

'You're forty-two.'

'That only makes it worse.'

'Your mother seems to be coping.'

'Oh yes, she's a marvel. She could stand as a monument over Julian's grave.'

'You've still not made peace?'

'Uncle darling, you make peace after the little rifts: burning a house; stealing a husband; bankrupting a company. But a breach such as ours isn't so easily healed.'

> The Vicar and Curate take their places in the hearse.
> The Vicar sits in front, the Curate in a fold-down seat
> beside the coffin. The cortège drives slowly away.

Bertha stands outside the churchyard, watching Petula help Myrna into her car.

'Who's going to take me?' Bertha asks.

'I'm afraid I've already promised Trudy,' Petula says.

'It's a four-seater, isn't it? You won't know I'm here. Shall I go in front? I expect you two'll want to sit together.'

'Well, with my legs –' Myrna says.

'I'll push the seat forward.'

'Right then.' Petula sighs. 'It seems to be settled. Is everyone comfortable?'

Myrna yelps.

'That was me,' Bertha explains. 'I pushed the wrong way.'

'Are you all right, Mum? We don't want any mishaps before the big day.'

'Yes, I think so.'

'Would anyone care for a little something to warm the spirits?' Bertha takes out a hip-flask. Her offer is declined. 'You'll be sorry later. It's cold work standing at gravesides.'

'Do you go often?' Petula asks.

'Just paying my respects.'

'Do you want to be buried or cremated, Myrna?' Trudy asks.

'Do you think we could talk about something more cheerful?' Petula asks.

'But it's a funeral,' Bertha says.

'Oh cremated. Ever since I saw a programme about the Brontë sisters dying because their water was poisoned by a graveyard, I knew I couldn't take the risk.'

'Me too,' Trudy says. 'I've already paid for the niche. You have to think of that if you're on your own.'

'I'd never be burnt,' Bertha says. 'I read what happens. They put you in the oven and, after a while, your legs crack and bang against the lid of the coffin. Then the men all start to sing *Knees up, Mother Brown*.'

'Please!' Trudy says.

'Really, Bertha,' Petula says. 'Let's have some music.' She twists the dial.

'Then, when they put you in the urn, the ashes may not even be your own. They just rake up bits of bone like at the chippy. I'm going to have the full works. Oak coffin and all.'

'You'll have no one either,' Trudy says.

'I'll have the Vicar. Only now, as we came out of church, I told him "I want no one but you taking my funeral". And – who says vicars can't have a laugh? – you know what he answered? "My pleasure, Bertha. Shall we pencil it in for next week?"'

Eucharist with the
Blessing of the Oils

Thursday 10.30 a.m.
St Paul's Cathedral

The Bishop is robing in the Dean's Vestry. The Vicar
stands by the door.

A shaft of light accentuates the sweat on Ted's upper lip as he
struggles into his cope. Huxley contemplates lending a hand but
fears that he may give offence. He feels like a school prefect summoned by a new headmaster and unsure whether he is to be car-
peted or commended. Ted seems determined to maintain the
suspense.

'I have a strong sense of the changing-room whenever I come
here,' Ted says. 'The Balham Boys Club, class of 1957, where I first
found God. Of course, the smell is different ... embrocation replaced by beeswax and old brocade. But the anticipation is the
same. When I walk up into the pulpit, I feel as heady as when I
stepped out into the ring.'

'Did you box seriously ... that is professionally?' Huxley wonders
if the boxer-bishop is to be the scholar-bishop of a more brutal age.

'The first, yes; the second, no. I gave it up when I was asked to
lead a Bible Study Group. God knocked out Bruce Woodcock in the
opening round. But it's still a part of me. An eye for an eye and a
tooth for a tooth: that was a text that really spoke to me. Black eyes.
Lop-sided grins.'

'I'm more of a turn-the-other-cheek man myself.'

'No one can understand the desire for justice who has never had
the need to fight. I have ... I still do – against the cynics who claim
that I'm a flyweight in a heavyweight job, that I haven't got enough
here.' Huxley finds the position of Ted's hands, one on his head,
the other in his lap, ambiguous. 'Take today. Everyone's wondering
how I can bless the oils when I don't believe in blessing inanimate
objects. But I do believe in using oil for healing, so I shall bless
that. See what I mean. I'm going out there to win and not just on
points.'

Ted sits. Huxley's hopes of a balanced discussion are dashed by
the single chair.

'Conciliation: that's my watchword. After the controversies of my predecessor, people are looking to me to make peace. And I won't let anything stand in my way. The Church is bigger than any of us – evangelical or catholic. We must co-operate ... except at the expense of first principles. That's not conciliation; it's capitulation ... not turning the other cheek but lying down and letting them wipe their feet on you.'

Huxley's conviction that Ted must be seeking his opinion on his sermon is jolted by his next question. 'How would you describe your relations with your PCC?'

'Perfectly viable. May I ask why?'

'I've always set a lot of store by a vicar's handling of his PCC. If he can't control it, it doesn't bode well for his wider ministry.'

'I'd hardly call it control; we're a team.'

'You have charge of their souls. If that's not control, what is?'

'Souls rarely come into it. We generally deal with insurance and drainage and basic wear-and-tear.'

'And sale of church property? You look surprised. How is it that the private affairs of a small North London parish have come to my notice? I make it my business to know what goes on. And I can tell you that certain highly placed people are very interested in your clergy-house. They've asked me to have a word – only a word, mind you – in your ear.'

'Who are they? Conservationists?'

'Do you know David ... Lord Stafford?'

'No, thank Heavens. Though I feel as if I do. Every day, I see the fall-out of his policies on the streets.'

'That's all in the past. He's no longer in government. He's taken his talents to the City. Grafton Holdings. I gather they've made an offer on your clergy-house which has been rejected.'

'Nothing's been rejected.'

'I'm very glad to hear it.'

'That is we've decided not to sell the building. It was one of the options available. I don't understand why it should mean so much to Stafford. There are plenty of houses for sale in the area. Have they found oil in the garden?' Huxley laughs.

'I don't know why he's interested; but he is. And he expects me to deliver. It's my credibility on the line. Mine. I'm not asking this for my own sake, but, if I'm to speak with any authority on behalf of the Church – if the Church is to have a voice with the people who count – then I have to speak in a language which they can understand.'

'Surely, in God's eyes, everyone counts?'

'But, to do God's work, we can't always afford His scruples. There are powers of darkness in the land, Vicar, and they're growing. Satan is abroad. It's only with a strong Church – with the right people on our side – that we can defeat him.'

He is interrupted by a knock at the door.

'I've made my position clear; I trust you'll look to your own. Have a word with the churchwardens. Throw in my name if it helps. There's more at stake than the solvency of one parish. Come in!'

The Bishop's chaplain insinuates his head around the door.

'It's the Archdeacon of Highgate, Bishop.'

'Show him in.'

Alfred enters, robed for the service.

'Blessings to you, Alf. You know Huxley Grieve, of course.'

'Yes, but how extraordinary! He's precisely the man I came to talk about.'

'Really?' Huxley asks.

'For a vicar with such a small congregation,' Ted says, 'you're causing quite a stir.'

The Vicar and his wife take their seats for the service.

Jessica has never felt moved by St Paul's, finding its bulk vertiginous rather than awesome. There is something about its massive uniformity, along with the disproportionate number of war memorials, which makes it unique among the great cathedrals in speaking to her more of the temporal than of the sublime.

This morning, her misgivings are accentuated by the meagre turn-out. This is the one service to which she always accompanies Huxley. It is an occasion not just for the renewal of vows but for the reunion of old friends, as clergy come together from throughout the diocese in a welcome demonstration that the spiritual map of London transcends the physical. But ideology makes absentees of so many: evangelicals, who refuse to use oils except for healing – to which end they can apply any household brand; catholics who respect the oils but not the Bishop, whose hands bear the taint of women priests.

She softens her resentment as she thinks of the pressures which so many of them are under, alone by inclination or, more painfully, by default. She recently read an article about the psychological problems suffered by astronauts since their descent. The journalist, typically, saw the issue in terms of stardom: the where-do-they-go-from-here, there's-no-way-but-down syndrome. She, however, remains convinced that it was the effect of their exposure to the infinite on a scale beyond the scope of human capacity. And, the more she reflects, the more she equates it with Huxley, since this is what he and his fellow priests undergo every day, standing at the altar, as alone and insignificant as on a space-walk, confronting the infinite inaccessibility of God.

> The congregation sings the Introit Hymn, as the Bishop's procession enters from the Dean's aisle.

Huxley distrusts the choice of hymn. The tumultuous chords and triumphalist words heralding the Bishop's entrance are clearly intended to identify the little man in his mitre with the Holiest in the height. Having sampled his tactics in the vestry, he knows that nothing is left to chance. The room had bristled with hidden threat: if he does not bring his influence to bear on the PCC, then pressure will be brought to bear on him.

Would that be such a tragedy? Perhaps a push is just what he needs. He is fifty-two years old. It isn't too late to start afresh. After all the years of dithering, it might even force him into taking a stand. A swift glance at Jessica assures him that he won't lack support. He is overcome by a rush of love. What he would give to be a second Betjeman, able to dash off an ode to the beautiful woman singing at his side! It has to be Betjeman, not just on account of the setting but because there is nothing free-form or jagged about his passion for her. It is poised and polished and slightly old-fashioned and full of the most felicitous rhyme.

Any decision that he takes will depend on her. He looks across and wonders what she will feel. He knows what she will say – 'You must fight' – but what will she feel? The Church has provoked their sharpest disagreements ever since the irony of his vocation pre-empted her filial rebellion and ensured a seemingly effortless transition from vicar's daughter to vicar's wife. Her own spiritual journey, which has encompassed Buddhism, Shintoism and reincarnation, although sometimes too public to be politic (he will never forget her telling the old Bishop of Norwich that she was sure they had been milkmaids together in Regency Bristol), has never threatened his. And yet it is precisely because she has made such sacrifices for him that he has felt obliged to conceal from her the full extent of his doubts. Isolation is a lesser burden than ingratitude. It's not 'I told you so' that he fears so much as 'Why didn't you tell me this before?'

His creed has become a paradox: 'I doubt therefore I believe', the *cri de cœur* of twentieth-century liberalism. No wonder the evangelicals find it easy to pour scorn. How much simpler it must be to

locate salvation in the utilitarian prose of their New International
Bibles, to read myths as though they were history and history as
though they heard it on the news. Meanwhile, liberalism limps on,
as decimated in the Church as in politics: a weak third force trying
to hold its own between the two rival wings of doctrinaire catholi-
cism and fundamentalism. And yet it is far more than his personal
belief that is at stake, for liberalism has always been the quintessential English virtue – the philosophical equivalent of decency and fair
play.

The problem comes when the paradox becomes a mere contradiction, when doubt so dominates faith that it becomes the sole
theological question and so determines identity that priesthood itself is compromised, leaving nothing but words ... the words of
the 1662 Prayerbook, which he insists on retaining, as if to distance the sense in the sound. In this of all weeks, he must be able
to find a more honest solution. Today, he has come to renew his
vows. But how can he renew what he no longer affirms? His faith
is like a library book which, having been renewed for months by
phone, is finally recalled. As he walks up to the desk with the dog-
eared, dog-chewed volume, all he can think of is how, with so few
resources, he can afford to pay the fine.

> The Bishop mounts the pulpit. He lifts his eyes to the
> dome and prays *Lord God, may your written word be our
> rule, your Holy Spirit our teacher, your greater glory our
> supreme concern.*

'This is a very important occasion for me, as I hope it is for everyone here. It's my one opportunity to address my whole team in
what I like to think of as Head Office, as we all, bishops, priests
and deacons, prepare to play our parts in the great events at hand.
And we are a team, from the humblest curate to the most venerable
archdeacon, standing together to fight the good fight for the Lord.

'It's no secret that, in recent years, this diocese has had its share
of difficulties. While intending no slur on my distinguished predecessor – by the by, I know that his many friends will be happy to
hear that, according to the Abbot of St David's, he has now fully
adapted to life under the monastic rule – I'm sure we all pray that
my arrival will mark the start of a new era of reconciliation and
hope.

'It's customary to use this sermon to reflect on the nature and
duties of ministry. I trust you'll forgive me if, in all humility, I start
by saying rather more about myself ... not too much, since, after a
great deal of arm-twisting, I've agreed to let the BBC film a profile,

which is to be broadcast later in the year. Nevertheless, I'm aware
that there are many of you here whom I've yet to meet (although
I'm sure we'll soon be putting that to rights). I'm also aware that
some of you have expressed doubts concerning my lack of experience of parish ministry. But, believe me, that only gives me more
respect for those of you toiling away on the shop floor.

'I'd like to share with you something of my spiritual journey and
to pay tribute to my two very special guides. The first who, you
might say, gave me my ticket was a South London curate; the
second who, you might say, punched it was Billy Graham ... not a
name we hear nearly enough of in Church circles nowadays. I first
encountered him when he was on his Mission at Earl's Court. I
was taken along by a friend, and, believe me, at seventeen, I could
think of better ways of spending a Friday evening; but not for long.
Billy's message rang out loud and clear: "Come to someone who
will save you; give yourself up to Christ." And I took up that challenge. I was moved by the Spirit. I found my way to God.

'And God opened his arms to me. He helped me through night-
school to gain the qualifications I needed to free me from the fac-
tory. He helped me through Wycliffe and my curacy. He helped me
in my work as Secretary of the Scripture Union and as Diocesan
Education Adviser for London. And, finally, He called me to be a
bishop.'

Alfred is seized by a fit of coughing.

'All the while, I was blessed with the support of my dear lady-
wife. For I'd married the most charming woman as she was then
... and still is now, of course. And would you believe that, after
thirty-five years, we recently received an invitation addressed to
Bishop Edward Bishop and partner? I wrote back that there were
some households left where a man has a wife and not a partner.
But I digress ... or do I? For now that I've moved back to this
diocese, God has entrusted me with an even greater task: to purify
it; to purge it of pernicious liberalism.'

Huxley is shocked, as much by the timing as the task.

'Surely, I hear you ask, in the midst of so many other evils – the
godlessness, violence, impiety and impurity – that are rife in the
modern world, liberalism can't rank very high on the list? But I tell
you it's right at the top; because it's liberalism that allows all the
others to flourish. Liberalism is the flab on the body of Christ. It
saps the strength and the spirit. It's my job – our job – to put back
the muscle.

'Be in no doubt, we'll hear howls of rage from some quarters.
We face powerful enemies. Intellectuals prize liberalism because

they thrive on ambiguity. Artists prize liberalism because it allows them free rein. But the man in the street is crying out for a strong moral lead. And it's up to us to provide it.

'What's more, a liberal Christian is a contradiction in terms, because liberals believe in asking questions, to which Christians already have the answers. If you don't believe me, you haven't read your Bible. And if you don't read your Bible, then you've no business being a minister. The Thirty-nine Articles state – in black and white – that the Bible contains all things necessary for salvation. That is what you affirmed at your ordination: the Thirty-nine Articles. Not thirty-eight or thirty-seven, but thirty-nine. And, if you can't uphold the articles of the faith, then there's no place for you in the Church of England.'

A voice shouts Hallelujah. Alfred bridles as at a heckler.

'To liberals, the Bible is an embarrassment. They read the "Old" in Old Testament as obsolete; they read the "New" as new at the time. They treat Christ as a law-breaker rather than a law-maker; they treat Job as if he were King Lear. They define Hell as alienation from God rather than good, old-fashioned pain. They view the Bible as just another volume in their library, when it should be the central weapon in their armoury. Is it any wonder that Satan's banner is flying high, even in the shadow of the Church?

'But let's not despair. For, although Satan is strong ... and I feel him to be stronger in this diocese of London than in any other, the ministers of the Lord are stronger, with the Holy Bible as their sword and their shield. It's your role to raise that shield above your whole congregation. I used to regret that I wasn't born in Our Lord's lifetime. But, now, I believe the Church is due for such a revival that Peter, James and John will look down from heaven and wish that they were back on earth. Hallelujah!'

The word is returned like a mating call. Ted holds up a Bible.

'This is the witness of God. Amen.'

Office for the Royal Maundy

Thursday 11.00 a.m.
Westminster Abbey

> The Wandsmen, resplendent in black and red, escort
> the Maundy recipients through Dean's Yard.

Myrna's brain is tinkling with nursery rhymes. Every muscle in her body strains for reverence; she longs to make each moment last for the rest of her life. But she is being thwarted by a childhood demon.

> *Pussy-cat, pussy-cat, where have you been?*
> *I've been to London to visit the Queen . . .*

At her age, she is content to live in her memories. What is so unfair is that old memories are driving out new ones. The future is being paralysed by the past.

Hers has been a modest life: one man whom she loved and married and nursed (largely the latter); one daughter whom she nearly lost at birth and of whom she feels fonder than it seems safe to admit; thirty years spent cooking school dinners, trying to ensure that children had at least one chip-free meal a day.

She is relieved to find that the pussy-cat has been driven out of her head . . . but the rush of relief restores it:

> *Pussy-cat, pussy-cat, what did you there?*
> *I frightened a little mouse under her chair.*

The air ripples as she enters the cloisters, as though an order of ghostly monks was being summoned to prayer. She grips Blair's arm for both reassurance and support, as she stumbles over the ancient stones.

'Did you ever think of becoming a monk?' she asks.

'I beg your pardon?'

'When you thought of becoming a vicar.'

'That wasn't so much that I thought of it as that it thought of me. But the answer to your question is no. I'm not cut out to be a contemplative. Although I did once play one. Abelard, who fell in love with a nun and had to be cast . . . cast out.'

They pass the monument to Sir Francis Chichester. Myrna frowns. She dates all that is disrespectful in the modern world from the day when his wife wore a trouser-suit to meet the Queen.

'Listen to me, prattling,' she says. 'You'll be sorry you came.'

'I feel honoured.'

'It's an honour for me to be escorted by such a handsome young man.' She is grateful, nonetheless, that he is wearing a suit and not his usual black shirt and jeans. 'I feel like the cat that swallowed the cream.' Oh no ... shoo, pussy! 'Petula was all set to bring me, but Laura's baby-sitter cried off at the last minute and she had no one else to ask. She offered to rearrange her appointment at the hospital, but I wouldn't hear of it. With my legs, I know what it can be like. One man hasn't even come today because he's seeing a consultant. He was afraid he'd have to wait another year.'

'I suppose it depends on your priorities.' Blair feels the pull of the plaster on his arm.

'Still, to give up the chance to meet the Queen! I'd have come even if I was on a stretcher. Like the MPs. I haven't seen any wheelchairs. But the letter said they don't have to curtsey. Her Majesty won't be offended if you're disabled. She wants us all to enjoy this special day.'

'How kind.'

'I've always felt a closeness to royalty. I was born the day that King Edward VII died. My mother wanted to call me after the King, but she could never decide whether it should be Edwina or Georgina. So she called me Myrna after my great-aunt. Still, I'm not sorry. A name can be a lot to live up to. I wanted to call Petula after a flower, but Eric, my husband, said what if she turns out not to be a looker? So we settled on Petula after the singer. And I thought, with Petula, there'd always be a petal inside.'

A steward, wearing morning-dress and an embossed smile, directs them to the Undercroft entrance, where Blair leaves Myrna.

'I'd better go and find my seat.'

'You're supposed to be right behind me, so you should have a grand view.'

'I'm sure I will. Now remember, the important thing is to enjoy yourself.'

'All I can think of is what if she speaks to me.'

'You just say "yes ma'am, no ma'am, three bags full ma'am"; don't worry.'

She smiles wanly and shuffles down the steps. She knows that Blair is trying to help but wishes that he had chosen some other phrase. As she walks into a room that resembles a bowls club, she is assailed by a new nursery rhyme.

> *Baa, baa black sheep*
> *Have you any wool?*

Yes sir, yes sir,
Three bags full.

The Queen and the Duke of Edinburgh drive from
Buckingham Palace to Westminster Abbey.

Elizabeth unwraps a Callard and Bowser butterscotch and calculates that she should have just enough time to suck it before they
arrive ... it goes against all her principles to crunch. The great
virtue of holding the service in London is that it doesn't occupy the
entire day. For Ely or Exeter, she has to be up at dawn, but, in one
of her Abbey years, she can enjoy a long soak with Terry Wogan
and a leisurely breakfast, do her duty, and be back at BP in time for
lunch.

There are no delays *en route*, but then there never are. Long gone
are the days when she believed that every girl had her personal
policeman and her grandfather's head on stamps. It is not that she
regards an empty road as her due ... she lays no more claim to the
Queen's Highways in their current state of disrepair than to the
Queen's English as broadcast on the BBC. But, with her time more
rigorously regimented than any Gordonstoun schoolboy, it would
put out too many people if she were late.

She leans back, allowing the warmth of the sweet to spread from
the roof of her mouth to the tip of her tongue, and reflects on
simple pleasures. As she tries to ignore Philip's tone-deaf rendition
of *If I were a rich man*, she is hit by a wave of melancholy, which
the prospect of the ceremony ahead does little to dispel. In recent
years, she has found the Maundy Service increasingly irksome.
There is no surer reminder of her own mortality. She blames
Henry IV (among her least favourite monarchs) for his insistence
on relating the number of recipients to the sovereign's age. Each
spring, she is forced to watch the passage of time reflected in ever
more wizened faces. It makes a nonsense of the single candle on
her cake.

Philip breaks off his humming. 'So, it's the wrinklies, this morning, is it?'

'Senior citizens,' she reprimands. 'Remember we count as ones
ourselves.'

'Nonsense,' he replies gruffly. 'There's no such thing. You can't
be a citizen; you're the monarch. And they are subjects. Senior
subjects if you like, but nothing more. Precision is of the essence,
no matter whether you're running a country or a ship.'

She forbears to mention that he only captained his frigate for a few months, whereas she has been ruling the country for forty-five years. She trusts that he is not going to be difficult.

'It's such a waste of resources,' he adds. 'If you want to give them a bonus, why not put it on their giros like at Christmas? Most of them spend far more than they're given buying new clothes.'

'It's tradition, Philip.'

'Tradition or not, it's a bit bloody much to expect me to ponce down the nave with that bunch of flowers as though I were Rudolph Valentino.'

'I think you mean Nureyev.'

'Same thing. They were both wooftahs.'

She prorogues the discussion. Philip is always at his worst before anything religious. She blames it on his family. It can't have been easy to have a mother who founded an order of nuns and believed that Jerusalem was on a regular bus route from London. But then he seems to have considered the Church of England itself infra-dig ever since those South Sea Islanders made him a god.

His muffled cry of 'Battle stations' takes her by surprise and she recklessly swallows the final slither of butterscotch. As the Rolls pulls up outside the Abbey gate, her heart sinks at the display of dignified decrepitude from the Yeomen of the Guard. Must everyone around her be crumbling? What she wouldn't give for a few young Grenadier Guards! Nothing makes her bosom swell like the sight of their broad shoulders, manly chests and strapping thighs. Quashing her disappointment, she greets the Dean who escorts her to the group of faces and hands (there is no time to think of them as people) in the porch. She spreads out her clerical small talk as sparingly as the filling of a garden-party sandwich. Blandness is all. Ever since the never-to-be-exorcized dinner when she confused the politics of the Korean ambassador, she has stuck to the three 'w's: 'What do you do?' 'Where are you from?' and the Weather.

> Led by the Beadle, the Royal Procession moves slowly
> down the nave.

The opening chords of the hymn scatter the three blind mice which have been scampering across Myrna's mind. It is one of her old favourites from *Hymns Ancient and Modern*, not one of those new ones from a booklet. Vicars today are far too fond of booklets. People don't want hymns that they have to think about; they want ones which allow their hearts and voices to soar.

There again, singing in so large a congregation is as safe as singing in the bath. She would never have ventured that top E at St

Mary's. Her voice is as erratic as a thirteen year old boy's. As the children of the Chapel Royal pass by, resplendent in their gold-braided tunics, red breeches and black stockings, she has a stark sense of the pain of growing up, which the sight of their adult counterparts in their plainer cassocks and surplices fails to displace. The order of service states that they were present at the battle of Agincourt. She pictures them bravely singing as the arrows whistled overhead ... rather like the cockneys smiling through in the Underground in the Blitz.

The Royal Family was wonderful in the War. They could have gone to Canada, but they stayed in Buckingham Palace to share the hardship of their people. The King measured out his bathwater just like everyone else, and Princess Elizabeth served in the ATS. The young will never understand. Russell and Laura say that the monarchy is an anachronism (a word she hates almost as much as euthanasia). They probably think the same of her ... no, she mustn't make light of it. They claim that the Royal Family is the thing that keeps Britain (or rather 'the UK') in the past. What they fail to appreciate is that that is where a lot of people wish to remain.

She turns towards the door as blatantly as if the organ were playing *Here comes the Bride*. She peers past the white copes of the canons and the gilded cope of the Dean to pick out the Queen's pink hat. For one meteoric moment, they are standing together. If she stretches out her hand, they will touch. But, as she catches Her Majesty's eye, she can see that she was expecting someone different. She reads the accusation forming on her lips: this is the wrong Myrna Timson. Then the procession passes on and she realizes that it was a smile.

She observes her fellow recipients, the men white-haired and grey-suited, the women with hats perched as precariously as Lady Blaikie's parrot, and sees the multiple reflection of her own rapture. They know that they are taking part in history, not just in a ceremony that dates back to the Middle Ages but in a tradition as old as the gospel. For this is no ordinary honour, like a knighthood or the Order of the Garter; this is the Order of the Last Supper. She is standing in line for the Queen just as St Peter once did for Christ.

> The Precentor prays:
> *Lord Jesus Christ, who before instituting the Holy Sacrament at thy Last Supper, washed the feet of thine Apostles; teach us, by thine example, the grace of humility;*

and so cleanse us from all stain of sin that we may worthily
partake of thy holy mysteries.

While having no wish to emulate Marie-Antoinette in her dairy, Elizabeth always enjoys kneeling. It is good practice to be in the presence of a higher power, especially at a service such as this which is all about humility. There is, of course, a vast gap between humility and humiliation – as no one knows better than she – and she is grateful that her contribution is limited to the financial. It is bad enough rubbing noses with Maoris without having to wash peoples' feet – and old peoples' feet at that, all bunions and blisters and smells. Charles will probably revive the custom. It appeals to the Laurens-van-der-Post side of his nature, while his former wife (she refuses to use the D-word) would no doubt bathe them in *Body Shop* lotions from head to toe.

She shudders – which she trusts that any observer will attribute to the intensity of her devotions – and flips through her ancestry in an effort to remember which of them it was who actually went in for the foot-baths . . . Bloody Mary, of course – the name that always gave Margaret the giggles. If memory serves, she even used to crawl the length of the hall on her knees . . . like that frightful Filipino woman when she was acquitted of fraud in New York. It must be something in the Catholic temperament. Thank heavens for Elizabeth . . . the first, that is. She restored the royal dignity. A woman with all of her father's strengths and none of his appetites, she really was a 'chip off the old block', even if Crawfie did cross it out of her exercise-book as a 'most unfortunate phrase'.

It is hard to concentrate on prayer in a building chock-full of memories and memorials. She is moved by the presence of so many dead Queens. Only a few yards away, Elizabeth herself is buried along with her sister. Then there's Mary Queen of Scots and the Mary of 'William and', not to mention Queen Anne surrounded by all her dead children . . . a fate that no longer appears quite as tragic as it did. She takes heart from the richness of her family history, which makes up for the deficiencies of the present-day. People love calling her a Philistine – almost as much as they do a German – but she never tires of reading a good Georgette Heyer. Why is it that no one seems able to write a decent royal romance any more? She peers at Philip and frowns.

The Precentor prays:
O God, who dwellest above all heavens, yet hast respect unto
the offerings of the children of men; who also hast taught us
by thy blessed Son that works of mercy done unto our breth-

*ren find acceptance in thy sight; bless, we beseech thee, with
thy favour Our Sovereign Lady Queen Elizabeth.*

Elizabeth remains aloof from the intercession. Even after all these
years, she is unsure of the ethics, or the etiquette – which, to the
Crown, are first cousins – of praying for herself. At least at the
National Anthem, she can hum the tune.

Blanket prayers bring cold comfort. Who's to say what people
really think when their eyes are shut? Still, if she can rely on anyone, it is this congregation. They are the ones who sent their cloth-
ing-coupons for her wedding-dress and their pensions after the
Windsor Castle fire. They are the ones who ply her with tea and
cakes in their dreams. And yet, as the Precentor concludes to a
barrage of rusty Amens, she remains uneasy. She cannot help wondering why, if their sentiments are genuine, so many petitioners
should be having so little effect.

> The Queen, escorted by the Lord High Almoner, the
> sub-Almoner, and two Yeomen of the Guard carrying
> the Maundy, moves into the nave and begins the
> distribution.

Myrna has accepted that a perfect view of the choir-screen and a
partial one of the Queen are the price which she has to pay for
taking part. She discovered back in 1953, when she watched the
coronation, that, even in black-and-white, through the rain-lashed
glass of a television-shop window, she had a better perspective than
the aristocracy in the Abbey . . . which was the moment she realized
that the world had changed. Today, she has tried to focus on the
Yeoman of the Guard stationed at her elbow; even though, in the
flesh, he seems more ruritanian than royal. The Queen, by contrast, is a perfect mixture of ancient and modern, like an antique
chair that has been fully re-upholstered but in keeping with the
original design.

> The choir sings *Zadok the Priest*, as the Queen moves
> further down the nave.

Elizabeth finds it easier to dispense the Royal Maundy than the
royal smile. Despite years of experiment with differing degrees of
tooth, she has never yet found one which works to her satisfaction.
She always manages to look as if it belongs to someone else.
What's needed is a neat equivalent of the regal wave. But faces are
less compliant than hands, and people expect more of them . . .
such as emotion, the very thing which she was taught to conceal.

So she bows – metaphorically – to the Beauty Queens and the Queens of the May, who have nothing to lose but their dreams. As they compete for their catwalk crowns, they can afford sincerity: flashing smiles of ambition as naked as their flesh.

She walks down the endless line, thinking fondly of King Arthur's round table. Every so often she breaks the monotony with a few well-chosen words.

'Have you come far?' she inquires of an old man with medals (medals are always a good sign).

'Cricklewood, ma'am,' he replies.

'Cricklewood, really? How nice.' She moves on, pleased at having injected a personal note into the formality of the occasion.

'Keep them somewhere safe,' she tells an old lady, whose leafy hat inspires such levity.

'Yes of course, your majesty. I shall treasure them. And then, in my will, I've left them to my grandson. That's Peter – the same as yours. He collects coins. He's a numis ... a numis...'

'Yes, well they all are at that age.' Elizabeth walks on sharply. She does not know which she finds more taxing: the unpredictability of the young or the garrulousness of the old. Her life relies on the rubric; if only people would read it and take note how to behave. Still, lunch is only fifty pensioners away. She beams and moves on.

'This is for you, your majesty,' an old woman says, handing her a pot of jam in exchange for the purses.

'How kind,' she replies, startled by the reversal of roles.

'It's damson,' she adds. 'I made it myself.'

'Damson, really?' Even the word makes her queasy. She hands it to the Lord High Almoner and carries on. How much gratitude do they expect for a pot of jam? There was a time when monarchs were given real presents. Cardinal Wolsey gave Henry VIII Hampton Court; Disraeli gave Queen Victoria India ... and she gets jam.

She stops beside a dumpy woman, whose potato-shaped face is accentuated by its doughy dimples.

'Have you come far?'

'Archway, your majesty,' Myrna replies.

'Archway? Really? How interesting.'

The choir sings *Salvator Mundi*.

In the intensity of the encounter, Myrna perceives that all distinctions between public and private have been swept away. She finds herself thrust from the thrill of Maundy Thursday into the incredulity of Easter Sunday. The Queen's face is as familiar to her as her own, but no TV screen can prepare for her presence nor Christmas message convey the effect of her voice. She feels as if every vein is protruding from her body. She cannot tell if she has gone weak at the knees or if her legs have seized up in mid-curtsey. She is half-way through a Thankyou, when another voice – but not a nursery rhyme – booms from the back of her head.

'Liar! Sham! Hypocrite!' It is a deep voice, a man's voice, some-how recognizable and yet so improbable that she knows that it must be a dream. 'You offer what costs you nothing: the Monarch's mite!'

The choir continues to sing. No one stirs. The quivering vein in the Queen's throat is the only hint of disruption.

'You give with one hand and you take with the other: distribut-ing alms while evicting Lennox Hayward from his home.'

What is he saying? Why is he bringing in Dr Hayward? She feels that she should know, but all she can hear are the words . . . words now lost in the scraping and scuffling behind her. She turns to see that it is Blair . . . Blair being thrown to the ground, his mouth gaping like a goldfish. Three Yeomen of the Guard are pinning him down as in a scene from a comic opera. But nobody laughs. Two Ascot-looking men run up and drag him out towards Poet's Corner. She hears his bones bumping against the stones.

The choir carries on singing as though through a hail of arrows. The Lord High Almoner escorts the Queen back to the line, where she resumes the distribution, Everyone seems so determined to act as if nothing has happened that, after a few moments, Myrna be-gins to wonder whether anything did . . . although her relief at her reprieve is tempered by a fear that she may be going mad. Clutching the two damp purses like talismens, she decides to risk turning round for a glance at Blair. But, as she does, the full weight of irreversible reality hits her like a blow from the Yeoman's pike. In the packed ranks of the Abbey, she is faced with the one empty chair.

> As the service ends, the Dean conducts the Queen and
> the Duke of Edinburgh to a reception in the Jerusalem
> Chamber.

Elizabeth is losing patience with the Dean's litany of excuses. It is bad enough to have been insulted by a madman without having her intelligence insulted as well. Anyone would think that the Garter motto had been changed from *Honi Soit Qui Mal Y Pense* to *Courage Under Fire*.

Philip fumes, his male pride inflated by his marital position. 'Who the hell was it? One of yours by the look of the collar.'

The Dean feels his own collar tightening like a noose.

'I don't know, sir. It could be a crank.'

'Is there a difference?'

'I understand that the Clerk of Works has the matter in hand.'

'Fat lot of good that'll do. Vicars: they couldn't organize ablutions in a baptistery!'

Elizabeth decides to intervene. 'I thought that the rest of the service went splendidly. Such uplifting tunes. The psalm: who was it by? Sir Arthur Sullivan?'

'Samuel Wesley, I believe, ma'am.'

'Well, I was close, wouldn't you say? Nine out of ten for effort.'

'Certainly, ma'am. Practically full marks.'

'Young Trot!' Philip ignores the diversion. 'I'd put the whole lot on the first train to Siberia ... or, worse, Wales.'

'I can assure you, sir, that we shall conduct a full investigation.'

'What is unfair,' Elizabeth says, 'is to accuse me of lack of feeling. It may be Crown property, but I'm hardly a seaside landlady. The Crown is me and yet I am not the Crown.' She looks sharply at the Dean. 'One would hope that a clergyman well-versed in the Incarnation would be the first to understand.'

> The Wandsmen escort the recipients through the cloisters and into the Great Hall of Westminster School.

Myrna clutches her handbag close to her chest. Having listened to the Secretary's warning about the dealers who will be waiting by the gates, she half-expects an advance party to jump out from behind a pillar and prise the purses from her grasp. That they should come today of all days betrays a cynicism that exceeds even their behaviour at jumble-sales (elbowing their way to the books and the bric-a-brac without so much as a glance at the cakes). If they think that all old people are a soft touch, they are in for a shock. There are some things more precious than money. Besides, she has promised the coins to Russell and Laura as a christening present for Lloyd.

She doesn't know when she has ever felt so wretched. This is a day which she was supposed to remember for the rest of her life ... which was supposed to make up for the rest of her life. And now all that she wants is to hurry home and forget. But memory can't be switched on and off like a hearing-aid. She has to stay, since, according to her watch, it is half-past twelve and Russell is due to collect her at two. She suspects that his main concern is the coins ... but that is just the misery talking – or rather screaming – and she should know better than to pay attention. Nevertheless,

she can't leave early when he is taking time off work. The best
thing is to seek sanctuary in the Abbey, avoiding company and
trying to keep warm.

She sits in St George's Chapel. Although it says *Reserved for
Private Prayer*, she feels sure that no one will mind if she just rests.
Through the glass door, she gazes at the flickering flame on the
tomb of the Unknown Soldier. The world has changed so much so
fast that the modesty of her life no longer seems a virtue but a sign
of its insignificance. As she gazes at the battlefield banners and the
war heroes' plaques, all she can think is how little her life has been
and how little difference it has made.

At a quarter to two, she hobbles back to the archway where she
has arranged to meet Russell; by a quarter-past, she sees her fate
writ as large as the face of Big Ben. She is an eighty-six-year-old
orphan with no one to fetch her from school.

Only Petula can save her. She drags herself across the square to
a phone booth so plastered with prostitutes' cards that she can
barely see the glass. She wonders at their brazenness so close to
the Houses of Parliament. Then she notices a woman with a whip
offering 'personal services to naughty boys of all parties'. She drops
her coin on the filthy floor and stumbles into the street for air.

Too depressed to take a taxi, she trudges to the tube. Overruling
the pain in her knees, she limps down a flight of steep steps. At
the bottom sits a raggedly man, all grey and blue and brown, with
trousers bandaged like a soldier in the trenches and a hat like a
flower-pot on his head.

'Spare any change, lady?' he asks.

'I'm sorry?' she replies, to the question rather than to the
request.

'Just a few coppers for a bite to eat.'

'Yes, of course,' she says, opening her handbag and pulling out
her purse, which seems surprisingly supple. She hands him some
coins and makes her way to the train.

The beggar looks at the coins in bewilderment, which turns to
fury. 'Disney money. I'm worth more than fucking Disney money!'
And, in a flood of invective and a stream of spittle, he flings the gift
away.

Mass of the
Lord's Supper

Thursday 6.30 p.m.
St Mary-in-the-Vale, Hampstead

The Vicar kneels at a prie-dieu in the Lady Chapel.

Huxley tries to find a language of prayer which will avoid the contention of words. Words carry too much baggage, refugees from countless former thoughts and phrases. However much they may try to adapt, they never lose their links with the past.

The most loaded word of all is God: a word that carries the baggage of every exile since Adam and Eve were expelled from Eden. His God ... her God ... Moses's God ... St Paul's God (not to mention the Hindus' Brahma or Mohammed's Allah): a word so steeped in subjectivity as to be a miniature Tower of Babel. It is a word which he invokes a hundred times a day and yet its meaning still escapes him: a word that can barely contain the pain of its own vowel. But then how can anyone ever make sense of that which exists beyond language, which stands in the same relationship to it as a thunderclap to rain?

Christ sought to make sense of it. Christ has always sat easily on his tongue ... as a word as well as a sacrament. Christ made an abstract noun concrete as surely as He gave an invisible God a human face. He came as much to rescue us from the flaws of our concepts as to redeem us from the burden of our sin. And yet even His words have lost their power. 'This is my body' has become stale; 'this is my blood' has turned sour. They have been cheapened by the routine consensus of common prayer. And none has suffered more than the Lord's Prayer: Our Father reduced by repetition to the gibberish of a Dadaist collage.

Help comes from musicians, conjuring God in the blast of an organ, and from artists (he allows his eyes to flick open), enticing Him in through stained glass. But it remains secondary, a means to worship rather than the end. 'In the beginning was the Word': the Christian God does not dance or copulate; He writes the universe into being. In Eden, the first task which He gives to man is to name every living creature ... So why is it that, after all these years, His own remains elusive? God the Father? God the Judge? God the Clockmaker? ... God the Metaphor. Or is that the true price of the Fall: that the essence of God should stick like Adam's apple in his throat?

To make his torment worse, the precision that has deserted his faith has signed up with his despair. He takes some comfort from the richness of its expression the way that a dying man welcomes the confirmation that he can still feel pain. It bears witness to the once-potent presence of God as mockingly as an atheist's casual blasphemy. And yet it would be arrogant to presume that he feels the loss of his vocation any more than a nurse in a run-down hospital or a teacher from a closed-down school. He is just another sacrifice on the altar of rationalization ... even if, in his case, it is no economic metaphor but a spiritual fact.

Now, in the cruellest irony, he has to lead his congregation on a journey through Christ's agony in the Garden. His personal feeling will subvert his priestly function, making him too much the fellow sufferer, too little the guide. He prays, with Christ, that the cup might be taken from him. But, as he turns to the cross for solidarity, all he can see is the fragmented reflection of his own anguished face.

'I'm sorry to interrupt.'

He jumps, as Blair taps him on the shoulder.

'Don't worry. I'd finished ... to tell the truth, I'd barely begun.'

'I got your message.'

'I've been trying to find you everywhere. What's happening? I've got the Bishop on my back and half of Fleet Street in the garden. I was forced to lock the door.'

'I know. I had to run the photographic gauntlet. "This way, Blair," they shout, as though I were still on TV.'

'You are. Only this time, it's the news.'

'Believe me, I didn't plan it. How could I? You didn't ask me to go till last night. But when I saw the Queen distributing alms with one hand and signing a notice to quit with the other...'

'She didn't sign anything. She's just a symbol.'

'Fine. So I made a symbolic protest.'

'I blame myself. I should have told the Bishop that I had a prior engagement. I wish I had. I learnt a good deal this morning one way or another – certain services you've been holding behind my back.'

'What? Oh, you mean Tuesday?'

There is a loud knock at the door. Huxley spins round with the foreboding of one who has been thrust from the world of Father Brown into that of James Bond.

'The enemy is at the gate.'

'I think you'll find it's the congregation.'

'But it's only...' Huxley looks at his watch. 'Good Lord, it's six fifteen.' He leaves the Lady Chapel, reflexively genuflecting to the tabernacle, and hurries down the nave.

'Just one thing.' Blair is caught out by this sudden display of purpose. 'I was hoping that you might be able to do without me tonight.'

'But I'll be on my own!'

'You will be whether I'm here or not. The state I'm in now, I'd be more of a liability.'

'Yes, of course. Don't be so selfish, Huxley. I'll let you off – but on one condition.'

'Not the wet-sponge stall at the summer fête!'

'That you go out somewhere and unwind. Put all this to one side. See some friends.'

'The only friend I want to see is Julian. Don't worry. I haven't completely flipped. But, with everything so rushed this week, I've not had a chance to say goodbye. I need some time by his tomb.'

'Now?'

'Yes.'

'Won't the cemetery be locked?'

'There are ways.'

The knocking continues.

'One minute!' Huxley raises the tension by rattling his keys. 'Right then. You slip away. I won't go under. And neither will you. You're made of stronger stuff.'

'No, just softer stuff that's solidified.' He laughs sadly. 'Amber should be my middle name.'

Huxley opens the door to Hugh Snape, who strides straight over and shakes his fist at Blair.

'You've gone too far this time.'

'Calm yourself, Hugh,' Huxley says.

'He's insulted the monarchy!'

'An institution,' Blair replies, 'no longer taken seriously by any-one but gossip columnists and stamp collectors.'

'Do vows count for nothing any more? At your ordination, you swore to obey the Queen.'

'Christ withstood Herod. Am I to do any less?'

'I know your sort, always trying to make Our Lord into some kind of anarchist hero.'

'And I know yours, turning a humble Nazarene carpenter into a first-century Viscount Linley.'

'I really don't think anything is –'

'This is the man we have ministering to us,' Hugh cuts Huxley short. 'The man you intend to put in charge of the clergy-house.'

'Oh not that again!' Blair loses patience.

'You'll be giving him *carte* (he endows the word with two syllables) *blanche* to fill it up with anarchists and degenerates.'

'Yes, I gather you made your feelings very plain to the Archdeacon,' Huxley says.

'They're not feelings; they're facts.'

'If you had a problem, you should have come to me.'

'A fat lot of good that would have done. You think the sun shines out of his jacksie.'

'I can't listen to any more of this.' Blair marches out of the church.

'What about the service?' Hugh shouts after him.

'Father Blair was never due to assist tonight; I'm on my own. So, if you'll excuse me, I must go and vest.'

Huxley's departure is interrupted by the arrival of Rosemary, who rushes in, contriving to take off her scarf and cross herself in a single motion. 'What are all those reporters doing outside?' she asks.

'Didn't you watch the news?' Hugh asks.

'I've given up the box for Lent.'

'Then you missed seeing our curate attack the Queen.'

'I wouldn't say "attack",' Huxley says, 'it was more of a challenge.'

'Was he armed?' she asks.

'Heaven forbid! It was entirely verbal.'

'He should still be shot. That must be why they were asking about his sermons. Since they were trampling over the daffodils, the one which sprang to mind concerned the lilies of the field. But they didn't write it down.'

Winifred Metcalfe and Sophie Record come into church.

'I'd better report for sidesman duty,' Rosemary says, 'or the Vicar will be putting me on jankers.'

'And I must go and vest!'

> The Organist plays *Jesu, joy of man's desiring*. The acolytes light the candles on the high altar.

Lennox sits in the front row beside Jessica and looks in scorn at the journalists. The presence of the eight middle-aged men has done much to redress the sexual imbalance of the congregation but nothing to improve its ethics. They are bunched together in the St John the Evangelist chapel, beneath the great Burne-Jones window of Moses delivering the Tablets of Stone. He watches them prop their notepads in the pages of their prayer-books and jot down their first impressions. As the setting sun highlights the Ninth Commandment, he wonders if the effect is purely fortuitous or denotes a more providential conjunction of natural and moral law.

He had his first brush with the reporters earlier in the day, when he was woken from an afternoon nap by the entryphone wailing like an air-raid siren. Lost in the wartime world of his dream, he opened the door and invited three strangers into the flat. They had barely introduced themselves before they began asking questions. They treated him with clinical detachment, demanding his age as if they were counting the rings on a tree. He could not work out why they were interested. The words eviction and the Queen and Westminster Abbey failed to make sense either singly or together. He did not even realize that it was Thursday until after they'd gone.

The visit disorientated him and he needed to sit down. The next thing he knew, he was flat on the floor. A cup of tea which he must have overturned lay beside him, the cold liquid puddled on his chin. He picked himself up like a puppet, testing each limb as though he were straightening its strings. He could think of no one to call but Huxley. He was out, but Jessica hurried round and took him back to the vicarage. Over a slice of simnel-cake (shut away since Ash Wednesday), they pieced together a picture of the morning's events, which was later amended by the five o'clock news.

The amazement of hearing his own name in the context of Blair's protest was as nothing to seeing an interview with his great-nephew. Giles discussed him with a proprietary air which even the most partial observer (his mother) could hardly consider justified by the single visit he had paid him last year. Nevertheless, viewers throughout the country were informed that his uncle was stubbornly independent (but 'a great character') and had repeatedly resisted his family's attempts to persuade him to live with them. To his – no doubt, stubbornly independent – recollection, he had refused their one invitation for Christmas, on the grounds that 'You can't be alone at Christmas' might carry more weight had they shown the slightest concern that he was alone for every other day of the year.

Jessica insisted that he spend the night at the vicarage ... with the same solicitude that has led her, for many years, to include him in her own Christmas party. He surprised himself by the speed with which he accepted. She tried to persuade him not to venture out this evening as there were sure to be more journalists nosing around. But he was determined to stand firm. They had forced him out of his home; they would not ... they will not keep him out of his church.

> The Churchwarden moves to the chancel steps and announces that the service will be late in starting.

Judith considers punctuality to be as noble a virtue as patience. Nowhere is her timekeeping more rigorously applied than when approaching the eternal. She once proposed to hang a sign in the church porch 'Latecomers will not be admitted until a suitable break in the proceedings', a course from which she was only dissuaded by Huxley's detailed exegesis of the parable of the labourers in the vineyard. This evening, she is particularly anxious about the effect of any delay on the journalists. It is all the more important after Blair's outrage that they see St Mary's in a good light. One well-chosen sentence along the lines of 'this jewel of England's Gothic revival, nestling in Hampstead's historic Vale of Health' would repair a lot of damage. It might even be coupled with a mention of the charming churchwarden.

'Doesn't any service in this church start on time any more?'

Her hopes are dashed as Bertha follows her coarse inquiry with a raucous rendition of 'Why are we waiting' to the tune of *O Come, All Ye Faithful*. The reporters look round as she rushes over to silence her.

'Father has some highly important business, Bertha. He won't be long.'

'She does have a point.' Hugh Snape presses his advantage. 'Some of us have been hard at work all day.'

'What do you want me to do?' she asks. 'I can hardly take the service myself.' She smiles in the direction of the St John chapel, where her opposition to women priests might be less well-known.

'What are they doing here?' Bertha points across the nave at Joe and Dee who, happily, remain out of earshot. 'I thought that they got married this week.'

'They did.'

'Then why aren't they away on honeymoon?'

'Not all young people can afford a honeymoon these days; they have to work.' Nevertheless, and although she wouldn't dream of admitting it to Bertha, their decision to remain in the parish offends her most deeply held beliefs.

'I suppose they don't need one nowadays. The whole of life's a honeymoon. All sex, sex, sex.'

'Yes, very well, Bertha.'

'Sex, sex, sex.'

'I take your point. You don't need to repeat it.' She wishes that Terry would play a little louder.

'They must put it in the water. Look at that one.' She indicates Alice, who sits with Dora on her knee. 'Quite brazen. No father and no shame.'

'Careful. She'll hear you.'

She speaks *ex officio*, since she too disapproves of Alice and deplores the decision to baptize her baby at the Easter Vigil. But, when she raised the subject at the PCC, she was overruled. Blair even quoted the gospel about casting the first stone. It is not that she claims to be without sin – far from it; but, when it comes to sins of the flesh, she feels safe in picking up a pebble.

> The Organist plays selections from *The Desert Song* in the style of Bach.

Petula sits surrounded by her family, although the warmth implicit in that phrase is absent. She has barely spoken to Hugh since the clergy-house vote, but her initial irritation has been replaced by the fear that he is planning a fresh line of attack. Misgivings envelop her like the cold sheets of a single bed. Moreover, he seems to have taken against Alice as well as Blair. A casual remark about Lloyd's and Dora's christening provoked the furious response that 'that woman's child' would never be joining his grandson at the font. She was amazed; but, when pressed, he refused to elaborate, asking how, after Monday night, she could ever expect him to confide in her again.

She turns from her husband to her mother, sitting as still as a dormouse, her sparse hair curled like balls of marzipan, exposing the sugary scalp underneath. She finds her composure unnerving and longs for her to rage, if not against Blair – who is best left to his conscience – then at least against Russell – who no longer seems to possess such a faculty. He may be her son but she has exhausted her stock of excuses. Not only has he yet to express remorse for abandoning his grandmother, but he has contrived to suggest that the fault was all hers for failing to possess a mobile phone.

Even so, the selfishness of the son is nothing compared to the folly of the mother. None of this would have happened if she had not been so intent on proving her indispensability to Laura. Rather than agreeing to babysit, she should have told her to phone Thea, who, for once, must surely have cancelled the hairdresser, the manicurist, the remedial masseur, or whoever is the current favourite in the elusive quest to turn a lifestyle into a life. And yet so desperate is she to compete with a woman whose closeness to her in age is belied in every other respect, that she refuses to relinquish her only advantage. A non-starter in the glamorous granny stakes, she will at least carry off the dependability prize.

> The Organist plays selections from *The Desert Song* in the style of Handel.

'If it doesn't start soon,' Laura whispers, 'we'll have to go. Baby'll want his feed.'

Petula restrains herself from asking whether she is referring to Lloyd or Russell.

'Won't I be glad when Saturday's over,' Russell says, 'and we can get back to church as usual.'

'It's all my fault,' Myrna says.

'Do please stop that, Mother,' Petula says.

'The Vicar'll be dealing with Blair. It only happened because he came with me to the Abbey.'

'In which case, it's Laura's fault; it's Russell's fault; it's Hugh's fault; and, most of all, it's my fault. You're the last person to blame.'

'All right, Petula.' Hugh smirks. 'There's no need to take it out on your mother.'

She struggles to suppress a scream.

Trudy scurries in and selects a seat in front of Myrna. She unbuckles her belt and turns to her. 'My watch must be fast.'

'No,' Myrna replies flatly. 'The service is twenty minutes late.'

'You look flustered, Trudy.' Petula leans forward. 'Are you all right?'

'It's my drains.' Trudy's tone is so coy that Petula wonders if they are the Austrian equivalent of 'waterworks'. 'They're blocked. With concrete. The water comes up when you want it to go down.'

'Are you having problems with your drains, Russell?' Petula discards the euphemism.

'Not that I know of,' he replies, squirming.

There is something about the shape of her son's shoulders that always makes Petula think of slipping through the net.

'No, it's just me. They want me to go. They cut through my wires, so, for five days, I have to live with candles as if I'm in love ... I am not in love.'

'Did you say nothing to Russell? Russell, didn't you help?'

'We lent her a candle.'

'A special aromatherapy one,' Laura interjects. 'To rebalance her auras.'

Trudy kneels to pray. Petula refuses to let the matter drop. 'But the building belongs to Jeffrey. That's why the children are living there.' She leans across to Russell. 'Did he pour that concrete?'

'Shut up, mum!' He swivels round as if to shield his wife from her mother-in-law's suspicions. 'You should be careful what you say. Being in church doesn't give you immunity.'

'What's happened to you, Russell? Are you my son?'

'Listen!' he exclaims ... 'Listen,' he whispers. 'She should go down on her knees to us.' He breaks off at the sight of her praying. 'If it wasn't that his daughter lives in the building, Jeffrey would have brought in the Rastafarians.'

> The Organist changes chords abruptly and commences
> the Introit as the choir and servers enter.

'At last,' Bertha exclaims. 'Perhaps now, someone will wash my feet.'

> The Vicar delivers his sermon.

'Today, the pace of Holy Week quickens. On Maundy Thursday, a sense of danger enters into our narrative of the Lord's Passion. The focus of liturgy shifts from the temple in the heart of the Holy City to the refuse-ground outside the gates and from the priest at the altar to the scapegoat on the hill.'

Huxley shakes off an image of Blair praying in the cemetery, like a sacrifice waiting to happen.

'The change in mood is reflected in the way in which I appear before you. Immediately after the sermon, I shall take off my chasuble and put on the apron of humility in order to wash your feet. This is a very intimate as well as a very humbling act. We all know how St Peter tried to prevent Jesus washing his feet. He considered himself unworthy to be waited on by the Son of God. But might there have been another reason? Was he as wary of Jesus' humanity as of His divinity? Was he afraid to expose himself to another man's touch ... indeed to anyone's touch apart from his wife's? Here, as so often, St Peter speaks for us all. We wash the feet of the very young and the very old, but, for the rest, we shun such proximity. Jesus, on the other hand, encouraged it, just as He did when Mary wiped His feet with her hair. He wasn't afraid of intimacy either with women or with men.'

Huxley detects a flurry of interest in the St John chapel, as men whose only intimacy lies in their underpants, pick up their pens.

'Most of us are terrified of contact. See how you're sitting now, dotted in ones and twos throughout the nave. Some of you are with your families, some with a friend; but that's as far as it goes. Which makes me wonder what you're saying when you pray that "Though we are many, we are one body, because we all share in one bread". Is it just a form of words? The "How are you?" "Very well, thank you," of everyday greeting, which is recognized code for "Keep your distance". Those of you who took part in the Palm Sunday procession will remember my asking you to move closer for the sake of my voice. Well, now, I ask you to move closer for the sake of Christ.'

He watches while people weigh the metaphor against the deed.

'Is that the best you can manage? A half-hearted shuffle to humour the Vicar: a demonstration of intent which you hope will pass for the act? I'm not that gullible. So I ask you again – especially any newcomers – to come down to the front. There's no call to be shy.'

Silence adds force to his request. He waits as, with varying degrees of reluctance, the congregation moves forward. The journalists, however, sit firm.

'Thank you. I trust that that wasn't too painful. Believe me, it wasn't meant as an experiment in pulpit power but to make a crucial point. In an age when we define ourselves by the gaps – rather than the ties – between us: when individualism eats like a cancer into the body politic, it's essential to affirm the body of the Church.

'I sense a resistance from some of you already. I'm treading on dangerous ground – swapping the pulpit for the hustings. And, as we all know, vicars are supposed to remain above politics: to preach the Bible as if it were a set of homilies on a Victorian sampler, the ethical equivalent of *Home, Sweet Home*. The irony is that it's our very blandness – our Humphrey Dumpty-like neutrality – which makes us appear as cynical as politicians.

'To muzzle the clergy is to neuter Christ. His life is as political as Karl Marx's or Che Guevara's or Margaret Thatcher's. I don't just mean in His statements about the first becoming last and the meek inheriting the earth, or in His unorthodox choice of dinner companions, but rather in His lifelong challenge to our compromised humanity. In the sixties – those bad old days which some of us remember with affection – a popular slogan claimed that "Eating bacon is a political act", and, although that would have been anathema to a first century Jew, I mention it now to remind you that everything Christ said and did sprang from an integrated radical vision ... not least in the event we commemorate tonight, when, with breath-taking brevity, He laid down a new world-order: "That ye love one another, as I have loved you."

'That simple phrase should be the keystone of our morality and the brickwork of our politics (which, too often, seem to be built on greed and faced with self-interest). Morality can't be split, like tennis, into indoor and outdoor, however much the gurus of individualism try to dress up their dogmas in Scripture. Beware of ideologues bearing bibles! Stick to Jesus with His basin and towel.

'Which brings me, finally, to Father Blair. Most of you will have heard by now of what happened this morning in Westminster Abbey ... and I fear that we will hear a good deal more of it in the days to come. One of our number was a witness and, another, an unwitting accessory; to both, I extend my sympathy. I don't intend to make any further comment, except to say that, as a man and as a priest, Blair has my love, my support and my prayers ... as I hope he will have yours. Please bear in mind that, whatever its effect, he made his protest in the name of Christ. He chose to take on the mantle of Christ in the Temple; I choose to put on the apron of Christ in the Upper Room. But, in Christ, there is no divide between public and private. For, if we truly live our liturgy, can there be any event more damaging to received wisdom, more threatening to established order, than when Our Lord took a basin of water and washed His disciples' feet? If that's not "eating bacon", I don't know what is.

'"A new commandment I give you, That ye love one another; as I have loved you." In the name of the Father and of the Son and of the Holy Spirit. Amen.'

> The Vicar descends from the pulpit, takes off his chasuble and puts on an apron. He moves into the nave, accompanied by three servers, one holding an ewer, one a bowl, and one a towel. He kneels, washes, dries and kisses the feet of each recipient, while the choir sings the antiphon *Where charity and love are found, there is God.*

Jessica watches Huxley lay Sophie's feet in his lap and wash them as reverently as a nursing mother. He seems so much more at ease when handling the bodies of his congregation than when consecrating the body of Christ. And yet she wonders what he would say if he knew the true source of the smile on Sophie's face. To have retained his innocence at fifty-two is almost as unfair as to have retained his looks. He speaks of politics with the sincerity of someone whose only compromise has been to vote. It is time for a

change of roles: let him be the cynic for a while and her the ideal-
ist. Even her hippiest friends, who free-loved their way through the
sixties, sold out to the eighties. Huxley alone has kept faith. And
where is he now? On his knees.

She feels as pained as a boxer's wife seeing her husband take a
battering in the ring. The indignity continues as he kneels in front
of Bertha, three layers of sock and a support-stocking by her side,
her pallid calves waxy and veined like a supermarket stilton, thrusting out her leg as though for free chiropody. From her, he proceeds
to Joe, Alice and Dee, and then to Trudy, who is so panicked by his
touch that she inadvertently kicks him in the ribs. Recovering his
breath, he moves to Edith, who barely deigns to lift an ankle, treat-
ing him like a shoe-salesman. 'That's my husband,' she wants to
shout, 'he deserves your respect.' And yet, given the daily humiliation of life with Eleanor Blaikie, she can hardly be blamed for
savouring the one occasion when the boot is on – albeit off – the
other foot.

Following his path across the nave and into the St John chapel,
she hears Huxley urging the journalists to join in. 'It's not like
taking communion,' he says. 'There are no rules. Would you rather
be spectators at the Last Supper?' Better that, she thinks, than
spectres at the feast. She half-expects them to favour their traditional formula of 'I made my excuses and left'; but his gentle
persistence wins through and they remove their shoes and socks. A
moment later, she is struck by a smell as foul as a chemical fertili-
zer. Even Huxley seems shocked by such perceptible rankness, as
he struggles to maintain his poise.

Finally, he reaches her. She wonders, as he takes hold of her feet,
whether he does so as a husband or as a priest and whether he
feels any conflict of instinct. His touch is so tender that she refuses
to believe that it is impersonal. It is all she can do not to recipro-
cate. She does not want to share this man with anyone, not even
her own children. He gazes up at her and all the boundaries of her
flesh dissolve. Such rapture is enough to restore her faith in God.
And yet, as he dabs her toes with his towel, she is filled with the
spirit not of worship but of romance. She is Cinderella and he
Prince Charming: the glass slipper fits and he will spirit her off
into an enchanted future, not the glacial hereafter of heaven but
the glittering happily-ever-after of fairyland. He seals his intentions
with a kiss, before moving on to Femi and Cherish.

> The lights dim as the Sacrament is carried in proces-
> sion to the Altar of Repose. The bell tolls as the Vicar

changes his robes from white to purple. The sanctuary
is stripped of all adornment and the church plunged
into darkness.

Judith feels threatened by the lack of a dismissal. Like a play with
no curtain call, there is nothing to mark the transition between the
two worlds. The unease appears to be universal. No one wants to
be the first to leave in case it betrays a lack of endurance. The only
movement is guttural, as throats are cleared the length of the nave.
Eventually, the journalists shuffle out in a pack, without so much
as a genuflection. One of their number, groping in the dark, trips
over a pricket-stand and takes the Lord's name graphically in vain.
She decides to put the appeal-leaflets back in the box.

   She waits for the rest of the congregation to exit before helping
the sidesman to put away the prayer-books: a task compounded
less by the darkness itself than by the licence it gives to Rosemary's
reminiscences of the Blitz. As she looks towards Huxley, keeping
vigil alone at the Altar of Repose, she is overwhelmed by a feeling
of emptiness. She resolves to show her support and kneel alongside
him, until she realizes that the emptiness is as much in her
stomach as in her mind. So, with a backward glance at the length-
ening shadows, she ventures out into the gleamy night of the
churchyard, where she is struck by a phrase as deeply etched as an
epitaph. 'Then all the disciples forsook him, and fled.'

Celebration of the Lord's Passion

Friday 12 noon
St Mary-in-the-Vale, Hampstead

> The Vicar prostrates himself before the altar. The congregation kneels in silence.

Huxley lies prone on the chancel floor, his red robes flowing around him like pain. Stretched out on the stone, he feels less like an Anglican priest than the virgin sacrifice in a druidical rite.

> A member of the congregation reads the Old Testament lesson.

Huxley forsakes his worm's eye view of the world and tries to focus on the service. His face is numb from its encounter with the mosaic. His cheeks bear the imprint of humility. As he glances around the nave, he sees a congregation as bitter and bewildered as the crowd on the first Good Friday.

He watches Eleanor making her way to the lectern, her stick tapping as regularly as time. The clucks of approval which echo around the church are a clear endorsement of her fortitude in the face of Julian's death ... the last gasp of the 'Britain can take it' spirit on which the older generation were raised. To them, the golden eagle from which she reads stands as a fitting emblem of her courage; to him, it provides a fortuitous frame for her pretension. For, after a perfunctory nod to the altar, typical of her stiff-necked manner, she announces the lesson from Isaiah as though she were certifying that it was sound.

> The Vicar reads the notices.

'As we prepare to venerate the Cross, let us do so with thanksgiving to God for sending His son, Jesus Christ, to sacrifice His life for our sins. Amen.

'I'd like to welcome you all to this celebration of the Lord's Passion and to extend a particularly warm welcome to any visitors.'

A quick survey of the nave confirms that his greeting is uncompromised by reporters.

'The church will remain open for private prayer after the service,

so please feel free to return throughout the day. Tomorrow's Easter
Vigil will begin at eight o'clock and, weather permitting, we shall
gather around the fire in the churchyard. I hope that all of you –
especially the children – will remember to bring musical instruments: whistles, castanets, bells, cymbals, drums. So that we'll be
able to raise the roof with the good news that Christ has risen.

'On Easter Day, low mass will be at eight o'clock and high mass
at eleven. If there are any of you still waiting to make your confession, would you please see either myself or Father Blair ... would
you please see me after the service.

'I should like, if I may, to say a brief word on the subject of
Father Blair. As I expect most of you know, he is currently being
held in police custody. I was able to visit him for half an hour this
morning and was encouraged to find him in excellent spirits. I'm
sure that all of you will wish to join me in giving him every support
both in person and in your prayers.'

The barbed silence leaves him exposed.

'Let us remember in love and tenderness all the sick, especially
Susan Devenish, Iris Sage, Wallace Leyland, David Fern-Bassett
(priest), Cherish Akarolo and Lennox Hayward. And, of your love,
please pray for the souls of the faithful departed, especially Julian
Blaikie who was laid to his rest this week. On him, and on all
Christian souls, may our Lord Jesus Christ have mercy.

'Now, as we sing Hymn 111 "O sacred head, surrounded", would
the members of the Junior Church please make their way to the
crypt, where Miss Record is waiting to tell you about the Easter
story and why the church looks so different today.'

> O sacred head, surrounded
> By crown of piercing thorn!
> O bleeding head, so wounded,
> So shamed and put to scorn!

As Femi Olaofe leads her niece Cherish through the nave, she is
seized by a sense of dread. She hears the rustle of hymn-books as
adamant mothers resist their children's pleas. She turns to a trucu-
lent boy who is kicking against his pew.

'Are you going downstairs, Robin? Would you take Cherish? She
can't see very well on her own.'

'It's not fair. I'm not allowed.'

'But you always ... doesn't he always go?' She appeals to his
mother.

'Usually,' she admits, 'but, since it's Good Friday, I thought I'd
keep him here.'

'It's boring.'

'That makes two of you, darling. I told you that, if you're good, I'll take you to the Fair this afternoon.'

As Barbara Lowell turns back to the hymn, Femi is horrified to find herself alone in the aisle with Cherish, the focus of everyone's attention. She hurries to a second woman.

'Aren't your children going down to the crypt?'

'She won't let us,' her daughter complains with doll-beating emphasis.

'You know what it's like,' the mother apologizes. 'My husband's at home, waiting to drive to his parents. We may have to slip away before the end.'

> *Thy comeliness and vigour*
> *Is withered up and gone,*
> *And in they wasted figure*
> *I see death drawing on.*

Huxley moves down into the nave. 'Has everyone gone on strike? Miss Record will be wondering what's wrong.'

'I want to go,' Tristram Bentinck says.

'Then will you take Cherish?' Femi asks.

'No, I want to stay with you,' Cherish says, as frightened as in an airport lounge.

'I'm sorry for her,' Tristram's mother says. 'Truly, I am. But she's blind. What if she falls?'

'But she's always been blind,' Jessica says, swivelling in her seat to face her. 'What's different now?'

'It doesn't matter. Really, it doesn't,' Femi says, cursing herself for failing to register the change in circumstances. 'Come on, precious.' She leads Cherish back to their pew.

Huxley returns to the chancel.

'Is that what you call being a Christian?' Jessica asks Joyce Bentinck.

'I'm only trying to protect my kids. Is that so wrong? Yours are grown up. They can look after themselves.'

'Not all of them,' Jessica replies, brushing the leaves off Toby's grave.

The Vicar ascends the pulpit to deliver his sermon.

'May the words of my mouth and the meditations of all our hearts be acceptable unto you, O Lord, our strength and our redeemer.

'I'd like to start by asking you to gaze around the cheerless church, with its altars stripped and its statues covered, and accustom your minds to the gloom of Good Friday. I know that many of you find this disturbing. You'd like to skip today and jump straight to tomorrow evening, when the bells peal and the candles are lit and everything is back to normal. But there are those for whom this is normal. For them, Good Friday, with its agony and despair, is as good as it gets. The darkness that enveloped the earth at Christ's death has never lifted. The constant flood of pain has eroded the joy from their lives.

'We can all identify such people: the desperate, the depressed, the lonely, the loveless, those without jobs or prospects or self-respect. But, in naming the obvious candidates, it's easy to miss the countless others, whose misery is concealed behind family and friends and status and wealth. It's even easier to miss those whose faith is a public profession, who proclaim the Easter message while they are stuck in a Good Friday time-warp ... that is until one of you children who have been held back from Junior Church whispers to your mummy or daddy that the Vicar is standing naked in the pulpit. At which point, this delicate stole and sumptuous chasuble will be exposed as the Emperor's new clothes.

'What do you want from me ... except, of course, that I don't ask such embarrassing questions? Self-exposure is bad form, as alien to the British temperament as a Sacred Heart. But the answer is of vital concern to us all, because what you ask of your priest is a measure of what you ask of God. This week in the parish, I've officiated at weddings and funerals; I've celebrated mass and heard confession. And I've come to the conclusion that, far from looking for a dynamic relationship with God, most of you want to keep Him at a distance, in reserve for times of need. And your demands of me are equally pragmatic. If I put a cassock on a pole and placed it in the centre of the room, it would serve just as well ... Huxley Gummidge, the clerical scarecrow.'

He is startled by a child's laugh.

'On Tuesday, I visited a woman in a hospice. There's nothing unusual about that – quite the reverse – except that, this time, I was called in by someone I'd never met. And, as I sat by her bedside, holding her weightless hand and sharing the utmost intimacy, I felt such a fraud that it was all I could do to stop myself begging her forgiveness. The relationship had no reality. I'm aware, of course, that she was talking to the priest rather than to the man; but there has to be some connection between the two. My words of comfort seemed to be more a form of pain-relief, on a par with her daily morphine, than a genuine expression of God's love.

'Please don't misunderstand me, I can think of few worthier

occupations than to relieve someone's pain but, if that's to be the
extent of mine, I'd have done better to stick to medicine. A priest
has to offer something more. I used to silence any doubts by picturing myself as a spiritual conduit, the means by which God reached
you even if He bypassed me, like a painter or composer whose
messy private life did not sully the sublimity of his art. And yet that
now seems too pat. For, if God's love is all-powerful, then surely
someone who has devoted his life to His service . . . who comes into
daily contact with His mysteries, would have felt the effect in his
heart?

'Nor, if I'm honest – and is there any more shaming phrase? –
do I find much evidence of the Holy Spirit in many of you. In the
light of recent events, I find that taking the Sacrament means as
little to some people as swallowing an after-dinner mint. The
Church may be losing members, but it has no lack of hypocrisy,
subterfuge and denial. People jostle for position who would be
better suited to a bridge or a golf club . . . except that they'd never
be allowed through the doors. This week, I've lied on behalf of one
parishioner and been lied to, in turn, by others. Only a moment
ago, I saw the ostracizing of a child. Meanwhile, my curate – as
fine a man as I've ever known – has been vilified and locked up in
a police cell.

'I can no longer close my eyes to the truth. If God's message
isn't reaching us, it may say something about us, but it may also
say something about the message . . . and that's what frightens me.
If God intervened in human history, surely something should have
changed besides the calendar? In the two thousand years since
Christ died, I find no confirmation that His death has altered anything. There's not a single sign that the world is either a better or a
happier place. Technological and scientific achievement have not
been matched by moral progress. Electricity leads to the electric
chair and gas to Auschwitz. The main improvement has been in
the means of destruction; crucifixion is no longer considered to be
a cost-effective death.

'What is life but an inexorable cycle of birth, copulation, defeca-
tion and death? (I'm sorry but, if you wish for a not-in-front-of-the-
children sermon, then you shouldn't have kept them from Junior
Church). Is this a world transformed by the Resurrection? Disease,
despair and violence are so commonplace that merely to list them
risks banality. And yet, as this century above all others has shown,
evil is no less evil for being banal. Is this a world transformed by
the Resurrection? Theologians may argue that evil is a painful necessity, the grit in the shell of the oyster that allows us to exercise

our free will, but, even if that's true (and I remain to be convinced), its effect is disproportionate. The pearl of great price comes too dear.

'My question as to whether the world has been transformed by the Resurrection is not rhetorical. I yearn for your replies. Is it God who has abandoned us or we who have abandoned Him? Is He dead, as Nietzsche claimed, or merely locked up on trumped-up charges on Devil's Island? We need to know the answer if Easter Sunday is to be more than a date in the diary ... a chronological necessity and a theological blank, if Christ's screams of agony are to be converted into allelujahs and our prayers this Holy Week are to resonate from the empty tomb rather than to echo from the splintering Cross: My God, my God, why hast thou forsaken us?'

> The Vicar proclaims the solemn prayers; the congregation kneels.
> *Let us pray for the holy Church of God throughout the world: that God the Almighty Father will confirm it in faith, increase it in love, and preserve it in peace, so that we may worship Him in peace and tranquility.*

Judith distrusts nostalgia, not the emotion itself so much as its ubiquity. Now that people are nostalgic for everything from mint humbugs to steam engines, she is reluctant to admit her own longing for the liturgies of her youth. Chief among them is the three-hour Good Friday meditation, sacrificed on the altar of the so-called family service. It seems particularly perverse at St Mary's, where the congregation includes very few families ... at a rough glance, there are five (if you don't – and she won't – count Alice Leighton and her baby). Nevertheless, worship, like everything else, is run for their benefit. It's not just holidays which are subject to a single-person supplement; it can only be a matter of time before they charge one in church.

She brushes aside a strand of the rich hair which has gained her an erroneous reputation as a woman with a past. She has no past, at least in that sense. She is, as she defiantly asserts, a spinster, a word which sounds almost like a profession (unlike virgin, which feels as if someone is following her in the dark). She has never worked. After her mother's death, she kept house for her father, typing his translations and, when his sight failed, reading to him from the Bible (the King James version) and English poetry (the Oxford Standard Authors). Her favourites had their pages doubly titled ... Wyatt, Raleigh, Sidney, and even a bowdlerized Byron, their noble lineage a safeguard against ignoble lines.

Since her father's death, she has lived in a house which is far too big for her, surrounded by memories and cats ... her milkman calls her the Brigitte Bardot of Hampstead Heath. For human contact and divine worship, she relies on the Church, for which she ardently prays. Her faith has never faltered since her wartime confirmation in St Paul's. Pigeons nesting in the damaged roof circled the nave throughout the service and, as she knelt at the rail, one swooped down and defiled her dress. Some girls would have screamed – several giggled – but she soldiered on in an appropriate fashion. Then, as she returned to her seat and her mother fussed over the smirched satin, she remembered the dove at Jesus's baptism and the public humiliation was effaced by the private sign.

> *Let us pray for Edward, our Bishop: that like as the Lord our God hath appointed him to this office, so he may give him health and strength to guide and govern God's holy People.*

Jeffrey always finds difficulty with one-to-one communication, let alone one-to-three-in-one. He prefers to send memos: a method which, clearly, has no place with God. The ancient Greeks had the right idea: post a request to the Oracle, burn a goat, and wait for a reply. Quid pro quo: that is a system he understands. There's a lot of sense in a sacrifice. He has never been able to grasp why Luther raised such objections to Indulgences. Of course, they were open to abuse and no one could be an arbiter of the afterlife, but at least they promoted charity, while providing funds for the Church.

The key issue is the productive use of wealth. Jesus Christ, who was, by His own admission, no businessman, pointed the way with the parable of the talents. He himself has made a great deal of money without doing anything of which to be ashamed ... a few bent rules (and a few more bent people) but no broken ones. Boundaries are strictly maintained. Some of his employees may be less scrupulous (that is the price of delegation), but God understands. Is He responsible for everything that the Inquisition or the mullahs or Ian Paisley do in His name? People shouldn't always blame the top man ... Communication proves to be refreshingly easy when one speaks the same language as God.

Despite his initial reluctance (and the Vicar's heretical sermon), he is glad that he came. His deep-felt belief that a wife takes care of the Church side of life, along with family and friends and everything domestic, does not stem from any lack of faith. On the contrary, his is a very real, wash-behind-your-ears, Sunday-morning-chapel faith, as exhilarating as a touch-line, with row upon row of

ruddy-faced schoolboys hymning the Almighty as raucously as, the
day before, they were cheering on the first fifteen. Can there be any
finer model of Heaven than the mystical hierarchy, clean-limbed
energy and inviolable traditions of an English public school?

These are the schools which, for hundreds of years, forged the
builders of Empire; they still do, only now the empires are financial. The struggle remains as tough and the Church's role as crucial, which is why he prays intently for Edward, our Bishop. After
the Curate's most opportune disgrace, the Vicar will be susceptible
to the slightest pressure, and he is counting on Bishop Bishop to
apply it. Not that St Mary's will lose out. Even if he pays them less
than the property is worth to Grafton – and who's to say what that
is amid so many intangibles? – it will still be more than it's worth
to anyone else. And the hidden benefits are incalculable. The development will bring an influx of new parishioners. Vicars always say
that the church's true wealth lies in its people. He is giving them
something that money cannot buy.

> *Let us pray for all who are preparing for baptism: that God*
> *in his mercy may make them responsive to his love, forgive*
> *their sins through the waters of new birth, and give them*
> *new life in Jesus Christ Our Lord.*

Thea knows that God sees straight into her heart but she is sure
that He is not averse to an attractive exterior. She is equally convinced of the susceptibility of Christ. Her favourite moment in the
entire Bible occurs when Mary (why is it always Mary? They
might as well be in Ireland) pours oil on His feet and dries them
with her hair. She would defy anyone to find a more erotic encounter in the whole of literature ... it way outstrips Shirley
Conran and her goldfish. When her own hair was longer, she had
tried to reenact the scene with Jeffrey, but he squealed and claimed
that he was ticklish, his lack of adventure as obvious in bed as at
the table. For all his big talk, he is plainly a wham-bam-thankyou-
ma'am, meat-two-veg-and-sticky-pudding man, more roly-poly than
rumpy-pumpy.

She approaches God in much the same way as she did her
earthly father ... the nursery flirtation that contrives to keep just
on the right side of danger. Of course, she does not expect God to
fit so neatly around her little finger or to show the partiality which
so incensed her sisters. She sometimes wishes that He had more
in common with his comic-book cousin on Olympus, whose amor-
ous exploits, as recounted by a suitably god-like guide, formed the
highlight of her last trip to Greece. She was especially taken with

his metamorphosis into a golden shower . . . until Jeffrey spelt out the vulgar connotations of the phrase.

She smooths the creases of her simple jersey dress over the curves of her filigree figure. She has always taken trouble over her appearance; it's her own form of *noblesse oblige*. In the country, she vetoed the vicar's intention to bring forward the Sunday morning service because it would have allowed her less time to prepare. Even so, no amount of time would be enough for some people. She permits herself an uncharitable thought as she glances at Petula, who looks as though she has come straight from a bed-bath. The presence of good women no longer intimidates her. Thank God for Martha and Mary, the frump and the live-wire. There is a place for each.

She prays not only for those who are preparing for baptism but for those who are coming to watch. She is expecting quite a crowd. They are sure to be impressed by the church (she mentally unveils the statues). For all their faults, the Anoraks have the sense to worship near Petula's work rather than in their own parish. The one snag – and it's major – is that Lloyd is not the only baby being christened. No wonder Laura has tried to keep it quiet. The congregational mix will be worse than at her wedding where, at least, the bride's and the groom's sides were distinct. And it's all very well to cite the traditions of the Easter Vigil, but the family has traditions too. No Finch has ever been christened as a job-lot.

> *Almighty and everlasting God, who dost ever bless thy Church with new members; we beseech thee that thou wouldst increase the faith and understanding of those preparing for baptism.*

The moment that she prays for Lloyd, Petula feels her nipples tingle. She began to lactate the very day that Laura told her she was putting him on a bottle. Her initial shame at the anomaly turned to pride when she realized that Nature was using her to give him what he lacked from his mother. But, so far, she has been unable to fulfil the role. She is terrified that Russell or Laura may suspect and ban her from seeing him. So she cradles him in the crook of her arm, enthralled by his pink smell and pulsing body. But every time that she tries to lift him to her breast, guilt tracks her like a security camera and she quickly lays him down.

She prays with all the fervour of fear as she thinks of Lloyd's future. Society is being shattered and he will be left to crawl through the shards. Tomorrow, he is to be baptized in a ceremony which is little more than a prelude to his grandparents' party.

There, women with faces as hard as their jewels and men with the freshly powdered threat of boxing promoters will toast him from Thea's 'everyday champagne glasses' and offer the christening presents which count as valid business expenses. She is desperate to rescue him before it's too late, spiriting him abroad under an assumed name like the victim of a cult. But such subterfuge is not in her nature. And she is seized by a sense of hopelessness: a seeping sourness in her mouth and a curdling in her breast.

> Let us pray for the Queen and those set in public office or authority in this land, that God may guide their hearts and minds rightly to govern our nation.

In addition to praying for her, Myrna has been composing a letter of apology to the Queen. The final version must wait for paper less seasonal, but more appropriate, than her bunny rabbit notelets. After Blair's protest, it is vital to assert her loyalty. All last night, she lay awake in terror of soldiers bursting through the door.

Although never as staunch a royalist as her husband, who maintained that the Queen should dissolve Parliament and rule by divine right, who devoted his life to re-enacting Civil War battles, and who caught his death at a waterlogged reconstruction of Marston Moor, she shares his belief in the Queen as Defender of the Faith. It is a rare comfort, in an age of bishops who are obsessed with sex and don't believe in the Virgin Mary and vicars who would rather talk about Africa than Galilee, to feel that the Church is in the hands of someone who never speaks out of turn ... who never speaks out at all except at Christmas. Eric had a book which showed how the Queen was a direct descendant of Joseph of Arimathea from one of his trading-trips to England and, although the argument was too dense to follow, there was no denying the family tree.

> Let us pray for the Jewish people, the first to hear the word of God, that they may continue to grow in the love of his name and in faithfulness to his covenant.

Trudy never feels the pain of her Jewishness more acutely than on Good Friday. Her longing to miss the service is exceeded only by the fear that to do so might expose her to comment. She feels a complicity in murder as intimate as that of a woman on the anniversary of her abortion. It is the day from which she dates her loss of innocence, ever since a schoolfriend refused to talk to her in the park because she had killed the baby Jesus. At once, all her parents' hopes of assimilation were dashed. She realized that her difference from the blond, blue-eyed girls in her kindergarten was more than pigmentation. Her sallow skin and crinkly hair stood out like the mark of Cain.

Although she failed to recognize it until much later, Katrin was right. She did kill Jesus. All the Jews did, however much they may try to deny it. They cannot have it both ways. If they insist on tracing their identity back to the Old Testament, then they have to accept responsibility for what they did in the New. Their forefathers – the ones whom her father so revered – promised Pilate that 'his blood be on us and on our children'. She has felt that curse like the blood of the unborn babies trickling out between her legs.

Her life has been an attempt to atone for her guilt. She prays that her former co-religionists may follow suit. But they remain stubbornly unrepentant, congratulating themselves on a survival which is foolhardy rather than heroic. They cling to history like children to cot-blankets as if drawing comfort from the smell. They hoard traditions like black-market supplies. No rain-forest tribe lives deeper in the past. And yet they have been overtaken by events. They wait for the Messiah with all the misplaced zeal of Jacobites toasting *The King over the water*. Legitimacy is not the issue so much as power.

Under cover of contemplation, she checks that she remains unobserved. She is terrified that the intensity of her prayers may be revealing too much. She thanks God that He gave her a face which says hymn-book rather than Talmud. And yet even that solace has been shaken by the phone-call soliciting jumble for a Zionist charity. She protested that she was not Jewish; but the more she shrieked, the more she sounded Viennese or, worse, Swiss Cottage. She immediately requested a change of number, surprising herself by her graphic invention of obscene calls. But she is under no illusions that, having found her once, they will not be able to do so again. The parting threat that 'We will be in your area on Sunday' pierces her flesh like a tattooist's needle. She shivers as though someone were goose-stepping on her grave.

It is no wonder that people distrust the Jews, even those who claim otherwise. She looks down at the evidence in her hand. The Vicar's prayer is extempore; the words on the page are fixed, entreating God to 'deliver this people from the darkness of their ignorance'. Of course, Father Huxley does not say them. No doubt he finds the sentiments embarrassing and laments the lack of cash which makes them dependent on pre-war booklets. And yet it is these rather than the pleas for love and understanding which reflect the true attitudes of the Church and underpin the cruelty of the men who have been hounding her for months and who are moving closer every day.

There is no escape. She cannot go to the authorities since it would entail admitting who she is – was – is (past and present are as confused as they were sixty years ago) ... Trudi Engelstein is buried; the cemetery may have been desecrated but she will not allow the body to be exhumed. Nor can she seek sanctuary in a church which conceals its true thoughts like splinters in the pews. In despair, she stares at the wall only to confront the terrified face of Christ on His journey to the Cross. It tears her in two. She is condemned like Him and she is condemned for Him. There is nowhere to turn, no place to hide and no prayer to pray.

> *Let us pray that God the Almighty Father may heal the sick, comfort the dying, give safety to travellers, free those wrongly deprived of liberty and rid the world of falsehood, hunger and disease.*

Jessica prays for Lennox who is now in hospital, their early morning return to his flat having uncovered a scene of devastation: drawers rifled, cupboards ransacked and papers scattered like packaging. Shock, suspicion and the police followed in swift succession. The smug gleam of the silver seemed to rule out any ordinary burglary. Even at first glance, it was clear that valuables had been overlooked in favour of letters and photographs. Her instant identification of the culprits was matched by the officers' caution. So she retreated to her customary rite in the kitchen, only to be summoned back to find Lennox collapsed on the floor. Twenty minutes later, she accompanied him in the ambulance to the Royal Free, leaving the policemen to search for finger-prints which she felt sure would be, at least metaphorically, stained with ink.

Strapped to a stretcher and clutching an empty photo-frame like a shield, Lennox attempted to make himself heard above the screech of the siren. She put her ear to his lips to ease the strain. 'Emily died nearly seventy years ago,' he mumbled. 'I never looked at another woman. Now all that's left of her is this.' He held up the frame and gazed at the glass, crying the old man's tears she remembered from her father: stinging streams which flooded the furrows of his face. She took his scaly hand and willed him to sleep with a filial-maternal squeeze. 'Seventy years we've been together,' he repeated. 'With never a cross word.'

She saw him settled with a staff nurse whom she had once met with Petula. The personal connection offered some consolation in the anonymity of the hospital. As she gave them such details as she knew, she found herself repeating his age as though it were his single salient feature. It made him seem as vulnerable as the cluster of candles on his cake. Now, as she prayed for him, she couldn't tell whether she was asking the Universal Spirit to heal the sick or to comfort the dying. She was grateful to be spared the choice.

> *Let us commend ourselves and each other to the Lord our God, and pray for the grace of a holy life, that with all who have departed this world and have died in the peace of Christ and those whose faith is known to God alone, we may be accounted worthy to enter into the fullness of the joy of Our Lord and receive the crown of life in the day of resurrection.*

Bertha perks up at the word 'ourselves'. She has studiously avoided responding to any of the previous petitions from fear that, if she asks God to do too much for other people, He may be worn out when He reaches her ... like the time at school when, having offered sweets to all her friends, she was left with none for herself (even after fifty years, the memory rankles). She knows that it isn't quite the same with God, who has sweets and more to go round. But, since He fails to share them out equally, it makes sense to take care. So she prays for her mother who 'died in the peace of Christ' and for the sick as an insurance but, as for the rest of them, she won't waste her breath.

Besides, everyone prays for peace and the Bishop and the Queen; no one prays for Bertha. No one so much as talks to her unless she insists. Now that she has a bus pass, she travels around London during rush-hour so that people are forced to sit next to her. Then she starts conversations. She asks about their families if they are white or where they come from if they are black (to show that she makes no distinctions). They rarely reply. Some look through their newspapers, as if what's happening on the opposite side of the world matters more than what's happening in the next seat. Others take out a book, which obliges her to peer over their shoulder. They usually end up by snapping it shut, even if it's a library book, which is public property. Sometimes, her only satisfaction comes from watching them get off before their stop. At least she has left her mark on their lives.

> Two servers carry a large wooden cross, wrapped in hessian, from the west door to the sanctuary. At the chancel steps, the cloth is removed. The Vicar and the congregation venerate the Cross.

Eleanor moves forward, her thoughts fixed on Christ but tilting towards Huxley, who should have shown more consideration for her grief. No doubt he has justifiable complaints against some members of the congregation but none which can be levelled at her. A mere two days after Julian's funeral, she has returned to church, managing even to read the lesson. She might have expected some credit (a discreet reference in the notices) but, instead, she has been subjected to the general abuse. She will shame him by her composure. Ignoring her arthritis, she drops as deep a curtsey to the cross as a débutante's to the cake at Queen Charlotte's ball.

She is about to press her lips to the wood when an upward glance at the beam fills her with horror. Julian is hanging from it: a drip piercing his arm and a tube plunged in his chest. He catches her eye and winks, proffering a smile which sends a billow of bile sweeping down his chin. She wills the vision – the mockery of a vision – away. It is a drug-induced phantom, the after-effect of the sleeping pill to which, in a moment of weakness, she succumbed. She must not betray herself by so much as a tremor. With a wave of her hand, she summons Edith to help her unfold her concerti-naed limbs. Clasping her wrist, she returns to the pew.

'But I must go up to the cross,' Edith moans.

'Nonsense,' she replies. 'Christ always put the living before the dead.'

The choir sings the Reproaches.

Trudy watches the congregation filing up the nave, their devotion compromised by her presence. The resentful glances they are cast-ing at Huxley should be deflected onto her. She was the target of his sermon. It is her lies which have infected them. She has killed Christ twice over by profaning the spirit of His church. Suddenly, her course becomes clear. It is on this day – the anniversary of her greatest crime – that she must proclaim her guilt. She kneels at the foot of the cross but, instead of kissing the wood, she beats her breast.

'Jew! Jew! I am a Jew! I killed Christ and I am poisoning your church. I eat your bread and I drink your wine, but I am an impos-ter. I am a Jew! A Jew!'

She feels the cross shudder as her pain pounds through it, leav-ing the servers struggling to hold it straight. She backs away from further sacrilege. Huxley moves towards her but she squirms from his grasp. 'No, you mustn't touch me. I am a Jew!' She hides her face in her arms and sinks to the floor. But the throbbing, chatter-ing, seeping mass of her is soothed by a hand on her shoulder. She looks up to see Jessica smiling down on her: not a nothing-is-wrong smile but an all-will-be-right one. Trust floods into her like sunlight through a nursery window, and she allows herself to be led away.

The Organist plays the introduction to the *Crux Fidelis*.

In the absence of any cue from Huxley, Terry follows his guiding principle (drummed into three generations of stage-struck HALOS): the show must go on. He recognizes the same uncertainty in the congregation as in an audience after one of its members has collapsed. Real-life drama has eclipsed the liturgy. Those who remain feel diffident about their involvement. It is up to the cast to win them back.

> *Faithful Cross! above all other*
> *One and only noble tree!*
> *None in foliage, none in blossom,*
> *None in fruit thy peer may be.*

'Did you know about that?' Jeffrey leans over to Hugh.

'It's news to me.'

'She's clearly a head-case. There's no way she can stay on in that flat now; it's too great a risk.'

> *Sing, my tongue the glorious battle,*
> *Sing the ending of the fray;*
> *Now above the Cross, the trophy,*
> *Sound the loud triumphant lay.*

The words of the hymn filter into the sacristy, where Jessica is reviving Trudy with communion wine.

'What have I done?' Trudy asks.

'You'll feel better now. Lighter.'

'Lighter, yes, like an accident where they cut off your legs. How will I ever be able to stand?'

'We'll help you. That's why we're here.'

'You're here for Christians. It's a church.'

'It's a house of God. God isn't just for Christians.'

'No? He has been all the rest of my life ... my parents, my sister.'

'I've always thought you left Austria because your father was anti-Nazi.'

'My father wasn't anti-Nazi. My father would have been pro-Nazi if only the Nazis hadn't been anti-Jew. Oh no, please stop. You mustn't make me say these things.'

'But what about you, Trudy? Haven't you been saying them to yourself for fifty years?'

'It's so easy for you. Is there anyone in the world more fortunate than an English lady? With your gardens and your Fortnums and your fair play. You don't know what it's like to have the past like lead in your heart.'

'Were your parents sent to camps?'

'What else? I used to wonder why I'd escaped. Until I realized I never had. You can wake up every day; you can wash and dress and walk and talk. But don't be deceived that you're alive.'

'You must have hope.'

'You should try saying that at three in the morning to a girl of sixteen who's survived the war. But she hears rumours that Hitler isn't dead – that his body in the bunker is a Russian trick – he escaped, some say to South America and some to England, because that would be the last place anyone would expect. And he comes to her at night and leaves his moustache like a spider on her pillow. He explains that the doctors are making him a new face so that he can visit her whenever he wishes. And, from then on, she sees his teeth behind every plastic smile ... no, no, you understand nothing.' Jessica envelops her in a hollow hug. 'The one man I could trust was Jesus, who only touched women to heal them: Jesus, who forgave all His enemies, even the Jews.'

'It's for the Jews to forgive the Christians.'

'Why, when they can't forgive themselves?'

'What have you done that's so dreadful? You arrived here when you were a little girl.'

'I grew up quickly. I thought I could hide, as much from God as from anything. If I came to church every Sunday, He'd grow used to me. He'd forget that I'd ever been anything else. When I stood in line for Heaven, I wouldn't have to wear a yellow star.'

'Trudy, don't you know that the hardest thing in the world these last fifty years has been to believe in a God that could allow the Holocaust to happen? How can anyone believe in a repetition after death?'

'You're so wrong. You think you must respect other peoples' religions as if they were different coloured skins. But why? Religion is truth, not tolerance. God doesn't look at the outside; He looks within.'

'Yes. Into peoples' hearts ... what they believe, not what they profess.'

'It's all the fault of aeroplanes.'

Jessica is baffled.

'In the past, when people went on journeys, they took ideas with them ... they thought about them on the way; now they bring them back like souvenirs. They clutter up their minds like their mantelpieces. They forget who they are.'

She trembles so hard that Jessica fears she may have a seizure. She rubs her forehead and her wrists and, when that proves to be ineffectual, she rushes to a drawer and pulls out the first vestment she can find: Huxley's gold-and-white Easter chasuble, which she throws over Trudy's shoulders.

'Trudy, I must make something clear: I'm Huxley's wife; I'm not his twin. I don't know what I believe. You don't lose a child and keep the same ideas about God.' She remembers Huxley. 'At least you don't if you're me. I think – I say "think" not to hedge bets but for the sake of accuracy – that I believe in God. But I don't believe that Christ is the only expression of Him. He's one; but so are Buddha and Moses and Mohammed and you and me. Look at the enormous variety of people, all shapes and sizes, not to mention flowers and animals and insects and trees. The glory of life is its diversity. So, how can there be only one son of God?'

'There are lots of mountains but only one Everest. The perfect man: the highest peak.'

'That's assuming that men – people – are the pinnacle of creation. If I thought that, I'd despair. But I don't. Hope survives because, in a century when we've seen humanity at its worst, we've also seen it at its most insignificant. We've become aware that we're part of a universe containing millions of other solar systems. It's inconceivable that we're the only intelligent life-form. And, far from finding that a challenge to my faith, I believe that it offers a chance for renewal. If humanity is less crucial to creation, it gives me a lot more confidence in God.'

'You think we may be attacked by other planets?'

'Oh no, Trudy, no.' She kisses her. 'What I'm trying to explain – no doubt, badly – is that, if we believe both that we're the products of evolution and made in God's image, then we have to accept that that image will be very different in the different conditions of other worlds. And, if God appears in many forms across the universe, why should He only take one here on earth?'

'You're flying too fast, but now you're in a space-ship, bringing back rocks from the moon.'

'No, I'm standing still, but I'm studying a chart and a telescope as well as a bible. Christians believe that God is three-in-one, but I know that He is more. There are so many manifestations of the divine. The one you believe in is a choice, but it's not a choice like the colour of your curtains. The choice chooses you. The only crime is to deny the choice in your heart.'

> The Vicar fetches the Sacrament from the Altar of
> Repose and places it on the High Altar. He invites the
> congregation to come forward for communion.

Eleanor watches the last of the communicants return from the rail
and waits impatiently for Huxley to bring her the Host. An already
long and histrionic service is rendered intolerable by the delay. He
raises the wafer as if he expects her to respond. She pretends not to
understand. It is an outrage! He always offers her the Sacrament
in her seat. It's not a question of special treatment (although age
and rank used to count for something in the Church) but of sparing her legs. She made a heroic effort for the Veneration and nearly
collapsed. She steals a glance and finds that he has not moved a
muscle. In which case, neither will she.

Not since she was a schoolgirl has she known such public humiliation. Here is proof, if any were needed after the sermon, that he is
mounting an all-out attack on her. He must be mad, given the scandal of his curate, to risk alienating his most powerful parishioner.

She feels the intensity of the congregation's gaze on her back.
She is equal to any battle of wills, but the wafer in his hand is too
powerful a weapon. So, summoning all the dignity at her command, she hobbles the few feet to the chancel steps. There is no
meekness in her heart nor contemplation of the Mysteries, only the
solace of planning a suitable revenge. She refuses to kneel. Huxley
presses the wafer in her palm with the words 'the body of Christ'.
She turns back to the nave. She is determined to eat it as always in
her pew.

> The Vicar wipes the ciborium and consumes the
> crumbs.

Huxley trembles at his daring. He has struck a much-needed blow
for equality. If Myrna Timson and Nancy Hewitt manage to make
their way up to the rail, then so can Eleanor Blaikie. She occupies
her pew as if it were the royal box at Covent Garden. Well not any
more. He smiles. Self-assertion has brought him a double victory
over her arrogance and his own despair ... But the relief proves to
be short-lived, for she has moved back to her seat without consuming the Host. He has no doubt of her ability to commit sacrilege
out of spite. So he returns reluctantly to the offensive.

'Lady Blaikie, you still have the Host in your hand.'

'My mouth is dry; I can't swallow it.'

He wonders if she expects him to rewrite the liturgy and pour
her some wine.

'You must consume it now.'

'Do you wish me to choke?' she asks outraged.

'It's my duty to ensure that you have consumed the Host before you leave church. I must keep you here, by force if necessary.'

The tension around them reaches penalty pitch.

'Have you lost your mind?' She brushes away Edith's hand and stands to face him.

'Consecrated wafers are highly sought by satanists.' He does not care if he goes too far; she is a witch. Then, as he underlines his point with his finger, Stevenson leans across his mistress's shoulder and takes a bite. He howls. A child giggles.

Eleanor's grim smile flickers like an optical illusion on a rock. She swallows the wafer and smooths Stevenson's feathers. 'Are you satisfied? Come Edith,' she calls in ear-trumpet tones. 'Anti-Christ has taken up residence in this church. It's no longer any place for us.' She walks with an almost spring-like step to the door.

> The service concludes without the customary blessing.
>
> The Vicar goes straight to his office.

Huxley is surprised to find Jessica sitting at his desk, idly flicking through the parish register.

'What happened to Trudy? Is she all right? Did you call an ambulance?'

'Two in one morning and people might begin to talk. She's gone home. She wanted some time to think.'

'I'll go right over.'

'It's not us she needs. I thought I might ring the Waxes ... what's happened to your finger?'

'Lady Blaikie set her parrot on me.'

'Are you serious?'

'Half.'

'Did she take exception to something you said?'

'I made her come up to the rail for communion.'

'And the church is still standing?'

'I don't know what prompted me: whether it was for Blair or for Julian or just for Christ. Is that perverse? Now that I've lost faith in Him, I want to protect Him more.'

'You're not perverse, Huxley. But that cut needs a bandage. Where's the first-aid box?'

'In the cupboard on the left, behind the spare thurible.'

Jessica disinfects and bandages Huxley's finger. He holds it up.

'Do you suppose this is what's meant by sharing Christ's suffering?' he asks bitterly.

'That seems to me to be the least of it.'

'I no longer know what's real.' He clasps her close. 'Apart from you.' He traces her face with his fingers. 'This is real.' He flicks his hand through her hair. 'And this.'

'What about the body of Christ? The blood of Christ?'

'Too much of that comes from here.' He thumps his chest. 'Like a child playing a game. This bed is an island or this doll is a baby or this wine is blood. The Eucharistic prayer might as well begin "Let's pretend".'

'You never used to set such store by what you could touch.'

'Then I must have changed. When? How? I don't know. I believe in the Church. I believe in two thousand years of tradition, but I no longer believe in the Resurrection. I have a rational mind; I need a faith that respects reason.'

'Is it the business to do with Blair?'

'It must be connected, although I'm not sure quite how. I've always tried not to be swayed by personal considerations. I refused to abandon Christ when Toby died. My faith seemed all the stronger for flouting my feelings. It became impartial and inconvenient and to be trusted, like a life-long pacifist signing up for a just war.'

'And now you've been wounded in action?'

'Now I've defected to the enemy.'

'That's not true.'

'An enemy that has gradually battered its way into my beliefs, knocking out stone after stone until the whole edifice has collapsed.'

'To be rebuilt on firmer foundations.'

'Christ talked of the man who built his house on sand, but what about the billions who've built theirs on parchment? I used to be glad that the gospel accounts of the Resurrection weren't consistent. I thought them a guarantee of truth. After all, if you were planning a conspiracy, you'd co-ordinate your story better. And you'd find a more reliable witness than Mary Magdalen. But now I feel that it simply shows how much muddle existed from the start.'

'Can this be the same man who despised the idea of a faith which depended on historical evidence?'

'Certainly it can. Only he no longer adheres to a faith which flies in the face of all the evidence. Put Matthew, Mark and Luke, let alone John, in the witness box and they'd be laughed out of court. Would you please explain, St Luke, how Jesus could be born at a time when Herod was king and Quirinius was legate, when Quirinius didn't in fact become legate until after Herod's death...? A slip of the quill, I see. Then would any of you care to comment on a series of miracles which defy the laws of nature but conveniently – so conveniently – fulfill the Old Testament prophets... ? Coincidence, I see. And how about the likelihood of a Passover trial which contravenes the most sacred Jewish customs... ? No answer. I rest my case.'

'Since when have you laid so much emphasis on the Bible?'

'Since every other argument for God was exploded. We're told that we're living at the end of history; I think we've come to the end of faith.'

'I've yet to see the proof. On the contrary, the pull of religion has never been stronger. Everywhere you look, the fundamentalists are making strides, from Jerusalem to Tehran to Amritsar to Holy Trinity, Brompton.'

'Fundamentalism isn't faith, it's despair ... no, I'm serious. It's as much of a cry for help as a suicide. It's a flight from life, a denial of that human freedom which is the most precious gift of God. Fundamentalists leave their brains outside their churches the way that Moslems leave their shoes.'

'I'm relieved. Whatever else you've lost, at least it's not your passion. And, to quote my favourite priest, the opposite of faith isn't doubt, it's indifference.'

'I won't go through the motions. I shall ring London House and ask them to find someone else to take the remaining Easter services.'

'Are you sure that's wise? Particularly after Blair.'

'It's honest. That must count for something.'

'What you need is a holiday.'

'We're having one in six weeks' time ... the parish pilgrimage to the Holy Land.'

They both begin to laugh. Huxley takes off his chasuble.

'I meant something more restful than watching Rosemary Trott haggling over postcards in the Garden of Gethsamene, or assuring Judith Shellard that her virtue isn't at risk from every man with a beard.'

'What a farce! An apostate priest and his agnostic wife leading a tour of Bethlehem-on-Avon. But then, even if it were a genuine holiday, just you and me on a desert island –'

'Don't tempt me!'

'It wouldn't be enough. I'd still have to deal with all this when I came home. What I need is a sign, conclusive confirmation of the risen Christ. Don't look shocked; I'm hardly unique. Quite the reverse. I'm taking my place in a long line of sceptical clerics, an alternative Apostolic Succession that can be traced back to St Thomas.'

'What sort of a sign? Resinous madonnas that weep: porous statues that drink: plaster saints that quiver behind candles?'

'Now you're laughing at me.'

'No Huxley, I'm trying to help you to laugh at yourself.'

'It's too late. Besides, the sort of sign that I want would be far less contentious – one which convinced the critical as well as the credulous. I'm talking of nothing less than a total ban on suffering, imposed by a God who acknowledged that, if history is an experiment in human resilience, then He's gathered sufficient data.'

'Are evil and suffering so ubiquitous? What about the love and kindness we see around us every day? Where do they fit into your secular vision? It isn't cruelty that needs to be explained but compassion – all the more so now we know that we're just a mass of genes struggling for survival. There has to be something beyond matter: a Universal Spirit which lies behind the miracle of human goodness. It may not be the risen Christ but, for want of a better word . . . several better words, I'll call it God.'

Huxley contemplates her in silence.

'But I thought that you no longer believed in God.'

'Whether I do or don't isn't the issue. What counts is that I believe in you. I've watched the light inside you spread like the flame from a taper. And that's what gives me hope.'

Huxley gazes at the cross above his desk, the bronze arms of the Christ hanging tautly in an agonized Y, as the church clock strikes three.

THE ORDER OF THE SEDER

Saturday 7.30 p.m.
Rosecroft Avenue, Hampstead

> The family and friends gather around the dinner-table.
> The Mother blesses and lights the candles.

Trudy wears her black dress. 'All you need is one good black dress,' Madge used to say. 'A pendant here, and you're at a cocktail party; a scarf there, and you're at a funeral.' Trudy never goes to cocktail parties ... For this evening, she has added a white shawl pinned by a Celtic cross. The design may be inappropriate, but it is the only brooch that she has. She trusts that the shape and decoration will offset any offence. Its curved sides and artificial rubies bear as much resemblance to the austerity of the Crucifixion as she does to a lifelong Christian. There can be no more fitting relic of her ornamental faith.

She sits at the table, a licensed intruder, while children, who have been told not to stare at her, peep. Jessica Grieve has arranged for her to celebrate Passover with the family of a colleague from the Citizens' Advice Bureau. She feels that she is being slotted into other peoples' idea of a resolution, but she doesn't object. On the contrary, she puts herself in their hands as though they were doctors. 'You'll like the Waxes,' Jessica promised. 'They're reverent rather than religious. They observe all the traditions you knew as a child.'

She worries about her role in the ceremony. She is terrified of failing to respond or, worse, of anticipating a phrase, breaking the silence as embarrassingly as breaking wind. Her host hands her a prayer-book, written half in English, half in Hebrew. She prays (to herself) that they will stick to the former, as she opens the book at the front and then, prompted by an instinct which she believed lay buried alongside her parents, turns to the back. She has returned to the back-to-front world of her childhood, but it no longer seems odd. On the contrary, it has a logic and a magic reminiscent of the inverted words in the codes she invented with Eva. At the thought of her sister, her eyes fill with pain.

As a distraction, she directs her watery gaze around the company.

Ruth and Benjamin Wax have four children, two boys and two girls of a dark Semitic beauty, a rich, display-case sheen on their skin. The other guests are Benjamin's parents, whose white hair she attributes to age rather than background (brought up in England, they switched on the war on the wireless), two cousins visiting from Israel and two family friends. Any sense of belonging vanishes with the sudden realization that, because of her, they are thirteen at table. Not only has she destroyed the symmetry of the setting but she has brought them bad luck. She is wondering how best to restore them to their original dozen, when she recalls that the root of the superstition lies in Judas's presence at the Last Supper. Touching wood, she trusts that this is the last place where it will apply.

> The Father takes a sprig of parsley from the Seder plate, which he dips in salt water and distributes to the company. He holds up a piece of Matzah, saying *This is the bread of affliction which our fathers ate. Anyone who is poor, may he come to eat with us.*

Trudy feels as if she is back in church. She looks at her watch. Eight o'clock. Under normal circumstances, she would be attending the Easter Vigil. She uses *would* not *should* now that she is saving her *shoulds* for other things. As Benjamin lifts the Matzah, he seems uncannily like Huxley at the altar: 'This is the bread of affliction' for 'This is the body of Christ'. But then the Lord's Supper is really the Last Supper and the Last Supper a Passover Meal ... a connection emphasized by the current calendar. She is recovering the authenticity of her worship as well as of her past.

It would have been tactful for Benjamin to have cut out the words about welcoming the poor, the way that Huxley cut out the prayers about converting the Jews, or at any rate to have mumbled them into his beard ... He has such an attractive beard, not the patriarchal bush of Abraham but a neatly trimmed border, which speaks of masculinity at once cultivated and controlled. He is the kind of man she would have liked for a son ... no, that's too easy; he is the kind of man she would have liked for a husband. Sorrow overwhelms her as she measures her life in lost chances. Rallying, she rebukes herself for her qualms. Any invitation to a woman over sixty must be an act of charity ... or else of self-seeking, which is worse.

The white lace tablecloth, silver candlesticks and gilt goblet set aside for Elijah, guardian of Israel (she banishes the thought that he might have done the job better), along with the men in their silver-threaded skull-caps and the women in their Saturday Sunday-clothes, transport her back to Vienna and the heavily furnished dining-room of their flat in the *Neulinggasse*. That is, however, just a temporary stop on a longer journey. For, as she gazes at the food on the Seder plate – the Matzah, roasted egg, dried bone, parsley, lettuce and horseradish – she finds herself emerging from the dryness of the Red Sea with a nation which has escaped the wrath of Pharaoh. And she realizes that her childhood faith was not destroyed in Auschwitz, that its source lies much deeper and she is tapping into it once again. God's love is revealed as clearly at Passover as on the Cross.

No meal has ever meant so much to her, not even the food parcels sent from America during the war. She is back at the table she left in 1938 and to which she failed to return, even after the final All Clear. The ritual has resumed as if sixty years were a mere gap between courses. It is the same Passover supper that her parents served before organizing an egg hunt on Easter morning. But what they viewed as the best of both worlds, others held to be divided loyalties. Overnight, compromise became the most dangerous of principles. And, although he continued to dismiss the Nazi threat, her father dispatched her abroad, to an English associate of the bank.

Memories return, which she thought had been held back at the Austrian border. She feels again the horror of the train as she hurtled into the darkness, accompanied only by a maid who crammed their compartment with her seductions. Deference disappeared, to be replaced by a succession of young men who unbuttoned their trousers in front of her as if she was of no more consequence than a lavatory attendant. It was then that she knew that the world had changed. The maid who was due to take her on to London – she forgets her name, even though, in the cruellest irony, she is able to picture the mocking gash of her grin more vividly than her mother's gentle smile – left the train in Paris with one of her lovers ... she thinks that he was in uniform, but then, in her recollection, every blond man is in uniform, so she cannot be sure. Her final act was to steal her purse. At a stroke, the 'precious little Trudi', whose hair she had brushed a hundred times every evening, was transformed into a 'filthy little Jew'.

With her name and forwarding address scribbled on a label around her neck, the human baggage made her way to Calais and across the Channel. At Dover, the combination of her wide eyes and correct papers ensured entry, even though the only English phrase which she could remember was 'God Save The King'. She was asleep when they finally arrived at Victoria and woke up in a taxi with her head resting on a bosom which felt like a board.

Her initial fears proved to be groundless. Both Mrs Stafford (Aunt Lydia) and her husband (Uncle Giles) welcomed her warmly. The same could not be said of their children. At first, David and Vivien appeared to be fascinated by her exoticism and showed her off like a new pet. But later, when her ordinariness became apparent, they transferred their allegiance to a tortoise. She was useful to them to make up numbers, especially in games which required a Nazi, but, most of the time (and no matter how small she tried to make herself), she intruded on their space. All hope of friendship evaporated when she heard them begging their father to send her away. From his hushed reply, she knew that, even though the label had been detached, she was still a parcel to them.

She remained at the poste restante address for the next ten years, except for a temporary redirection to Norfolk, from which, bruised by exposure to a convent full of girls even sharper than Vivien, she returned, determined to change both her name and nationality. Uncle Giles, however, insisted that she wait until after the war, claiming that it would be deeply hurtful to her parents: an argument which might have carried more weight had he himself not buried any mention of them in a gaping silence. The most he would authorize was the switch from the 'i' to the 'y' of Trudy. Vivien retaliated with the monosyllabic Trude, while David, adding insult to an injury only he knew the truth of, amended it to Prude.

Six years later, when she made her official application, Uncle Giles and Aunt Lydia returned to the subject of names. From their fudging, it was clear that they half-expected/half-feared that she would choose Stafford. On that score at least, she was able to reassure them. She disdained the parochial. England ... she would be Trudy England. They were not amused. Although their words were equivocal, their looks accused her of a vulgarity as gross as ordering the most expensive dish on a menu. With less restraint, Vivien proposed that she should call herself Israel like Palestine. She remained undeterred. Seeking to appease them, she stressed the assonance: the echo of the old Engelstein; nevertheless, her true motive lay elsewhere. Like the traditional Butcher, Baker and Butler, the name was the key to an identity. She would wear it as proudly as any VE Day soldier draped in a Union Jack.

> The Father blesses and distributes the remaining items on the Seder plate, first Matzah, then a portion of

lettuce dipped in paste, and, finally, sandwiches of Matzah and horseradish.

'I'd like to propose a toast.' Benjamin raises his glass. 'To Trudy.'

'Trudy,' everyone repeats.

Trudy stares into her glass. She searches for a suitable response. 'Thank you,' she says. 'It's very good of you to invite me.'

'It's our privilege,' Ruth says. 'You've allowed us the opportunity of sharing.'

'Don't you have a family?' Reuben, the younger boy, asks.

'I'm afraid not,' she replies.

'Miss England's family was killed by the Germans,' his grandfather says.

'The Nazis, father,' Benjamin says, with the forgive-and-forgetfulness of a new European.

'I had two families: a family in Vienna who were taken from me and a family in London who took themselves away.'

Trudy feels the pain of this second loss as never before. Although she continued to visit Aunt Lydia and Uncle Giles until their deaths, all contact with Vivien and David ceased at their mother's funeral. After three years of unacknowledged Christmas cards, she could no longer blame the post. Her only news came from articles about David as he climbed the government ladder. As recently as last week, a report from the House of Lords caught her eye as she made up her bed.

'Don't you have any children?' the younger girl asks.

'No, I never married.'

'Were you too ugly?'

'Rebecca!' her mother reprimands. 'Anna, take away Becky's glass. She's had more than enough to drink.'

'Yes,' Trudy replies. 'But not on the outside.'

'I want my wine,' Rebecca says. 'I like it.'

'No, you don't,' Reuben says. 'You think it's sour.'

'I still want it.'

Trudy recalls her own relish for the bitter-sweet taste of growing-up.

'Ow!' Reuben screams. 'Becky kicked me.'

'Reuben . . . Rebecca,' their mother says, 'stop showing off. Don't forget, this is the meal where we thank God for keeping us together. Father, pour Trudy some more wine.'

She goes out into the kitchen.

'Where did you spend Passover before you came here?' Mark, the elder boy, asks Trudy.

'I didn't.'

'But you're Jewish.'

'Mark, that's enough questions,' his grandmother says. 'You're not at school now.'

'No,' Trudy says, 'let him ask. He has the right. I haven't celebrated Passover in nearly sixty years.'

'Trudy goes to St Mary's Church,' Benjamin explains. 'She's a friend of Jessica Grieve.'

'Are you a convert?' Mark asks.

'I wish I knew. I just went in one day and sat down.'

'Then you went back?'

'Part of me did. Not the brave part. But then I was using that simply to stay alive. You're very lucky to have a family who keep up the traditions.'

'I want to give my kids a sense of who they are,' Benjamin says. 'Assimilation's one thing; conformity's quite another. These two even support a football team from a city they barely know.'

'Man United!' the boys chant in unison.

'See what I mean?' their father says.

'They go to Jewish schools,' their grandfather says.

Trudy looks at the boys, the older on the verge of adolescence, danger darkening his upper lip. 'But aren't you frightened?'

'Of what?' Benjamin asks.

'To make them targets ... boys in blazers.' She utters the word as if it were on fire. 'Thugs will fight.'

'Thugs will always fight. This way if need be – and please God it won't – there'll be more of us to fight back.' He turns to his father. 'Do you remember, when I was Reuben's age, buying me a history of Britain called *The Island Race*?'

'I bought you so many books.'

'That's one that sticks in my mind. Because it was a lie, right down to the title. There's no island race. What counts is our diversity: that we haven't fallen for some nationalistic fantasy of flaxen-haired Saxons and copper-haired Celts. I want to acknowledge all the island races, from the Picts and Scots to the Bangladeshis and Bengalis, with particular reference to my own Jewish/Russian/Roumanian and my wife's Jewish/Armenian/Pole.'

Trudy watches as Ruth wheels in a trolley laden with food, which she starts to serve. She longs to leave while she still has a shred of identity intact. She feels as if she has fallen into a lake and emerged with all her contours showing. At sixty-seven years old, she has no use for new beginnings. Her one hope is to live out the rest of her life in what passes for peace. It is clear now that she must accept the developers' offer. She will move to an address where no one will find her. She will join the local church and fade into the pews like a Hiroshima shadow. In six months, it will be as though she has never lived anywhere else ... and, in ten years, it will be as though she has never lived at all.

Her resolve holds fast until she sees the eggs.

'I hate boiled eggs,' Rebecca says.

'So don't eat them,' Reuben taunts her.

'These ones are special,' their mother says, 'traditional at the Seder. They stand for new hope ... fertility.' Reuben giggles. 'You needn't laugh, Reuben; you came from an egg yourself.'

'Then I'm certainly not eating it,' Rebecca says.

'Are you all right, dear?' Benjamin's mother asks Trudy.

'Yes, it's just the eggs. It's so stupid. I see eggs every day. Why should these be any different? I'm sorry. You've been so kind. But I have a migraine. I really must go home.' She stands but is unable to move her feet. One of the children must have glued her shoes to the floor.

'Of course,' Benjamin's father says. 'Would you like me to drive you?'

'Not yet, Father,' says Ruth, who alone has heard Jessica's story. 'Please stay a little longer, Trudy. There's nothing to fear. You're among friends.'

'You wouldn't want me as a friend if you knew the truth. Believe me, I'm not worthy of your table. You invite me here as a Jew; but I am a Jew-killer.'

Rebecca starts to cry.

'Now look what I've done. I'm so sorry.'

'Who did she kill?' Rebecca asks.

'Nobody, darling,' her mother says. 'Trudy's talking figuratively. It's a way of saying "forgetting" – that is, not keeping peoples' memories alive.'

'If only you were right,' Trudy says. 'Very well, I'll tell you what I did. You can be the first to hear. What an honour! I've never told ... but then I've never needed to tell. I was sent to England in 1938 by my parents – my blind parents who glimpsed something blurry from the corner of their eyes. I had an older sister, Eva, whom I loved – I truly loved – but whom, at the same time, I resented ... You must treasure each other, children, believe me. The English family invited us both, but my parents refused to let Eva leave school. This was proof of what I'd always suspected: she was their favourite and they wanted to get rid of me. I was such a child!'

'You were a child,' Benjamin's cousin Leon says.

'I was a danger to children. I've barely begun ... So when Uncle Giles told me to beg my parents to reconsider and send Eva while there was still time, I never mentioned his offer. A few months later, he told me to write again. He insisted that it was her last chance ... a threat which to me meant early bedtime not death. No, there can be no excuse. He gave me his own letter to enclose; but I tore it up. In return, I told him that Eva had gone to France. And, for the next six years, there was no way of knowing. It wasn't until after the war that he and Aunt Lydia found out the truth. They never reproached me with it, but they put up their guard. They no longer talked of adopting me. When they'd seen how I behaved towards my own family, why would they invite me into theirs? And why should you?'

She breaks down. Benjamin's mother hugs her.

'You must have been so frightened.'

'I didn't want her here – prettier, cleverer, the favourite all over again – but I never wanted her to die.'

'It's a well-known fact that most murders happen within the family,' Mark says.

Trudy sobs louder.

'Thank you for that contribution, Mark,' his father says.

'I was trying to help,' he says, aggrieved.

'Did you drive the trucks? Did you run the camps? Did you light the ovens?' Leon asks Trudy. 'All you did was fail to send one letter.'

'Two letters.'

'Two letters which might not have reached them anyway ... which might have been withheld by the authorities.'

'Yes.' Trudy clutches at a straw. 'No.' She sinks backwards. 'All the others arrived.'

'Things were getting harder. News was blacked out. Stations were no longer places from which you could leave. What's more, it happened nearly sixty years ago. We let murderers out of prison after ten: we let mass-murderers live in luxury in Argentina; while you lock yourself up for a crime you didn't commit.' Leon holds out his hand. 'Do you see what I'm holding?'

Trudy looks at his empty palm. 'I see nothing.'

'That's because you're afraid to pick it up. Look closer. It's a key.'

'I don't understand.'

'This is your chance to set yourself free.'

'How can I ever be free without Eva's forgiveness? How can she forgive me when she's dead?'

'Can't we forgive you on her behalf?' Benjamin asks. 'We who are Jews invite you to share in our food, in our fellowship and our love.'

'Are you sure that it's Eva who can't forgive you?' Ruth asks.

'I've never been to their graves; they have no graves. I was the only one left and I didn't even say *Kaddish*.'

'It's natural that you wouldn't want to admit they were dead,' Ruth says.

'I've said so many prayers in churches, but they've all been in English. It's like talking to God through an interpreter when I want to talk to Him in my heart.'

'Talk to Him now,' Benjamin says.

'What?'

'Say *Kaddish* for your parents here.'

'How, when I don't know the words?'

'Then let me be your voice (I don't say your interpreter). I can speak it for you.'

'So can I,' Leon says.

'And me,' Mark says.

'What about your dinner? It's supposed to be a celebration.'

'That's right,' Ruth says. 'Now we can celebrate a double deliverance.'

'I don't know what I've done to deserve such kindness,' Trudy says. 'But yes. I thank you. I accept.'

Benjamin takes the carving-knife and moves around the table to Trudy. She stifles a scream as, without warning, he makes a two inch slit in her shawl, above her left breast. She feels as if she has been both wounded and made whole.

Everyone stands as the men recite the *Kaddish*. Listening to the unfamiliar resonance, Trudy imagines that the cut in her shawl has opened the way to her heart. A deep peace descends on her. She has recovered the faith beyond consciousness – and conversion – which is patterned in her blood. As she prays, she begins to bury her guilt and to breathe the true holiness of God.

THE EASTER VIGIL

Saturday 8.00 p.m.
St Mary-in-the-Vale, Hampstead

> The congregation gathers in the churchyard. The
> Bishop, robed in white and gold, attempts to light the
> Easter Fire.

Dressed in a grey suit and raincoat, his clerical collar the only con-
cession to his calling, Huxley stands uneasily among his parishioners, like a managing director at a works outing. Nobody meets
his eye, apart from Rosemary Trott who looks ready to spit in it.
She settles for a muttered 'skrimshanker' as she hands him his
service-sheet ... he is relieved not to find a white feather tucked
inside. He turns back to Ted, who is rearranging the kindling as
desperately as a priest of Baal in the battle with Elijah. But his
hopes of a burst of flames – a smoke-screen to cover his confusions
– soon fizzle out. As he watches the fire flare up, only to splutter
and fade in the wind, he sees the symbol of Christ's new life
become a symbol of his own flickering faith.

> The Bishop douses the wood in paraffin, sets a match
> to it, and blesses the fire.

Esther stands in her husband's shadow, transfixed by the hiss and
crackle of the flames. Sparks spit in all directions, as though the
wood were making one last attempt to escape its fate. As she listens
to the drone of Ted's voice, the monotone that has underscored
thirty-five years of marriage, she determines to add some new notes
– grace-notes – of her own. She is flushed with the possibilities of
resurrection, secure in the knowledge that no one will attribute it
to anything more than the heat of the fire. She moves to Huxley,
who is on his own at the edge of the congregational circle.

'You must find this strange.'

'I'll have to consult David Stafford on what it felt like to return to
the back benches. I can't be sure in this light, but I think I recognize the noble lord.'

'Yes. He came for dinner last week. Ted gave me a list of dishes
to serve and subjects to avoid.'

'Really?'

'Of course. He hates to leave anything to chance. Ask his mother. Three weeks after she was widowed, he bought her a book called *Cooking For One*. I don't see Jessica.'

'No, she's in Belsize Park. On a mission to rescue Blair.'

A fierce 'hush' from Bertha chastens them. They focus on the prayers.

'Ted's in his element,' Esther whispers.

'I'm surprised. Lighting the Paschal Candle is hardly your tradition.'

'I meant having to deal with an emergency. He always functions best under an SOS. He doesn't even mind that you're here.'

'I never thought he'd come himself. I imagined he'd send his chaplain or pull someone out of retirement.'

'You're lucky it wasn't yesterday. He stood in for a vicar with appendicitis in Bethnal Green. He used the example of the Penitent Thief to attack liberal sentencing policy.'

Huxley looks at her. 'That's very sharp.'

'You'll think me disloyal.'

'No, just unexpected. You're supposed to be Mrs Creamed Cheese and Crackers.'

'I'm supposed to be a lot of things I'm not any more.'

> The Bishop carves a cross into the Paschal Candle, marking it with the letters alpha and omega and the numerals of the year.

Thea has compromised between her need to attend to her guests and her need to pay attention to the Bishop by placing herself directly in front of the fire, where she can both see and be seen. While comfort might dictate a cooler coat, she is prepared to suffer the slight moistness down her spine for the sake of the effect ... the shimmering silver grey of the fox which subtly complements the powdery delicacy of her own complexion. But her attachment to fur is not just skin-deep. She wears it as a matter of principle: in protest against the anti-cruelty campaigners with their absurd claim that all species are equal. They might as well suggest that all people are equal, which is patent nonsense. She belongs to a very rare sub-species, *Bella Regina*, endangered but not extinct, domesticated but not tame. Besides, if men have given their lives for beautiful women, why shouldn't animals? She hugs herself as if to affirm the power of her flesh.

She shudders as Jeffrey's breath chafes her cheek.

'Everything in order?' he asks in his parade-ground whisper.

'Perfectly,' she replies. 'Except for the Bishop's carving. It's strange; I was sure he'd be good with his hands.'

'Where are the Anoraks?'

'Mr's over there with Laura and Russell. Mrs is coming straight from the hospital. She'll be in uniform. Hugh said he hoped we wouldn't mind.'

'What about Great-granny Anorak?'

'Her plebitis is playing her up.'

'Don't you mean phlebitis?'

'I know what I mean ... According to Hugh, she's in disgrace. Some story about having given her Maundy money to a beggar. Russell threw a fit and refused to accept the rest. So now she's writing to ask the Queen for replacements.'

'She's off her chump.'

'Anyway, it seems that Hugh has forgotten to pick her up.'

'You mean the old duck's still standing in the hall?'

'Not standing, Jeffrey. There'll be chairs.'

> The Bishop inserts five grains of incense into the candle.

'I wish he didn't look so miserable with that candle,' Jeffrey says. 'Oh, there's David. I must have a word.'

He moves off and bangs into Bertha.

'Ow! Watch where you're going. There's metal in that leg.'

> The Bishop lights the candle from the fire, saying *May the light of Christ rising in glory, dispel the darkness of our hearts and minds.*

A shift in the circle brings Thea side by side with Sylvia Stafford – Lady Stafford to give her her due, which Thea rarely does. Never has 'she's no lady; she's a life-peer's wife' sounded so apt.

'Darling, the coat!' Sylvia exclaims. 'It's heaven!'

'Oh this old thing.' Thea purrs modestly.

'Even so. So few of us have the nerve to wear our old things any more. I've had my mink made into a lining for my Burberry.'

'Dear Sylvia, always so practical. You're an inspiration to us all.'

They smile at each other warily in the gloom. As Sylvia deliberates how, short of dropping it, to draw Thea's attention to her new ring, her gaze drifts across the flickering figures ... Chanel chic cheek by jowl with charity-shop bargains.

'Who are all these extraordinary people? They look like protestors at a road-site.'

'They belong to the other baby being christened.' Thea is deter-mined not to lose face. 'Aren't they sweet? So fresh and unspoilt.'

Sylvia stares at her in disbelief.

> The Bishop holds up the candle, saying *Christ our light.*
> The people answer *Thanks be to God.*

'No one but you,' Sylvia says to Thea.

'No one but me what?' She is unable to suppress a note of irritation.

'Such a coup to get the Bishop ... and then not to say a word.'

'Oh that,' she says casually. 'It's only London, not Canterbury.' She forgets whether guardian angels are canonical, but she is hap-py to give them the credit tonight.

'David was quite amazed when we saw the mitre. They're col-leagues in the House.'

'I know,' she sighs.

'David thinks very highly of him. Says he's a rough diamond.' She seizes her chance to flash the ring, but Thea fails to respond. 'The wife's a wash-out. We had dinner there last week. David says she doesn't have a word to say for herself, just echoes her husband. Clergy wives are often like that, David says.'

Thea tries to establish a mother-of-the-bride precedence as the congregation moves towards the porch. Meanwhile, Sylvia returns to her theme.

'Angela Hutchison only managed the Dean of Windsor for her grandson.'

'Was that the spina bifida?'

'Yes, poor little mite.'

'It hardly seems worth it.'

'Thea really!'

'Don't come all holier-than-thou with me. It's one of my chari-ties. I've danced for it, auctioned for it, even sat next to Fergie for it. No one can say I've not done my bit for spina bifida.'

> The people light their candles from the Paschal Candle.

Entering the porch, Thea smiles graciously at the youth who hands her a candle. She holds it at arm's length like a child with a spark-ler. Waiting to proceed to her pew, she edges away from Sylvia. It is as well to remove temptation out of the range of dripping wax.

> The people stand with lighted candles, as a chorister
> sings the *Exultet.*

Petula slips into church and makes for her family at the front of the nave. First, she has to brave the ranks of Thea's and Jeffrey's friends, who stare at her as if from the pages of magazines she might read at the dentist's. Less fearsome, if only because more familiar, are Thea and Jeffrey themselves ... indeed, Jeffrey even prompts her to smile with his vain attempts to keep his candle alight. Quickly looking away, she is delighted to see Alice and her companions, standing firm against Hugh's threats. But as she takes her place, the vague sense of apprehension which has accompanied her all day assumes a definite shape.

'Where's Mum?' she asks Hugh.

'She couldn't come,' he whispers back. 'I'll explain after.'

'Where is she?' she insists, ignoring the injunction to rejoice.

'She's at home.'

'Is she ill?'

'Just tired. She wasn't up to all the standing.'

'Nonsense! I rang her from the ward at five o'clock.'

'Mum ... Dad, sh-sh!' Russell leans across. 'Save your rows for later.'

Petula faces the altar. She tries to lift up her heart as the hymn demands, but fear weighs it down. All at once the truth becomes clear. 'You never went for her, did you?' she hisses at Hugh.

'Never went where?'

'To fetch my mother.' His evasion is answer enough. 'Car keys!' She thrusts out her hand.

'Not now, Pet. You won't have time.'

'Car keys!' She leaves her hand outstretched.

'You know how you hate to drive at night.'

'Yes, but there are other things I hate more. I'll be fifteen minutes. Now give me the car keys, or do you want me to shout?'

Hugh gropes for the keys in a pocket heavy with coins and passes them to Petula with a shrug which suggests that he has withheld them for her own good. She strides down the aisle as if after a stretcher.

'What's wrong with Mum?' Russell asks his father.

'She's gone to fetch your grandmother.'

'Well done!'

'What else could I do?'

'You're a man, aren't you? You shouldn't let your wife walk all over you.' He smiles wanly at Laura, who walks over him with the expertise of a Thai masseuse.

> The people extinguish their candles as the *Exultet* ends.
> The Bishop reads an Old Testament lesson.

As Ted raises his arms in blessing, the sides of his cope spread out like wings and he pictures himself hovering protectively over the shepherdless flock. He looks with suspicion at the gilded eagle which crowns the lectern. His brush with the owl at Holy Innocents has left him chary of any combination of Anglo-Catholics and birds. And yet, after a series of rituals as alien to his background as a public school code, it comes as a relief to reach a part of the service to which he can fully respond. As he proclaims the clear, no-nonsense truths of the *New International Version*, he hears the church resound with the authentic voice of God.

> The church bells are rung. The altar candles are lit. The choir sings the Gloria.

In the organ loft, Terry surrenders to the ecstasy of Easter. This is where Saturday night and Sunday morning become one. He pounds the pedals as if he were performing a tap-dance at the Palladium. He fires off chords like the cannons in the *1812 Overture* at the Albert Hall. Then he twists around to observe the congregation, only to find the Bishop looking up at him with a face like Lent.

> The Acolyte leads the congregation in procession to the font, where the Bishop blesses the baptismal water.

In spite of Thea's innuendo, Jeffrey fails to find Ted's plunging the Paschal Candle into the font remotely erotic. Nor can he raise a smile when she whispers that the Wicked Fairy has arrived. For Myrna has been reduced to a minor irritant now that he has identified the mother of the other baby to be baptized. It is the woman who painted ... designed ... daubed – he resists any fine art terms for such foul artefacts – the Stations of the Cross. It is the woman who has brought politics and blood and sickness into the church. It is the woman whom Hugh claimed to have seen at the wedding and whom, with his usual empty assurance, he insisted that he would have banned.

He should have known better than to trust a man who could not even persuade his own wife to vote for him on a matter of mutual profit. He will have to take action himself. It is not that he advocates a witch-hunt. His motto has always been 'live and let live', so long as it is in the privacy of one's own home ... or, in special cases (he thinks of Janine), one's office. But such license stops well short of church. Some places must be kept sacred. Christ's love may be all-forgiving, but this isn't just the church of

Christ; it's the Church of England. To baptize that woman's child
would be to endorse an England without values: without decency:
without backbone. It would turn the font into a sewer.

> The Bishop asks the parents and god-parents to come
> forward.

Ted has never been good at arithmetic. He affects indifference,
claiming that the greatest mathematician in the world cannot solve
the equation of the Trinity. But even he can spot the discrepancy in
the figures in front of him. On his left is a full complement of
parents and godparents, including, to his delight, his friend David
Stafford. On his right is an amorphous trio: a plump man in a suit,
a young woman in a velvet dress and workman's boots, and an
older woman (presumably the mother), whose hair is a bizarre
mixture of bands and braids. He is not prepared to ask them
whether they affirm the faith and renounce evil until he has settled
a more basic question. He turns to the man.

'Are you the child's father?'

'I'm her godfather.'

'Then where's her father?'

'He can't be here today,' the woman with the hair says. 'He's
disappeared.'

'Disappeared?'

'I can vouch that they've prepared themselves fully for baptism,'
Huxley interjects.

Ted remains unconvinced but, having recognized two reporters,
he is loath to expose any further irregularities in this scandal-riven
church. 'Very well,' he says in a tone which suggests quite the
opposite. 'Shall we proceed?'

> The Bishop addresses the godparents of the children to
> be baptized: *Dost thou, in the name of these children,
> renounce the devil and all his works, the vain pomp and
> glory of the world, with all covetous desires of the same, and
> the carnal desires of the flesh, so that thou wilt not follow
> nor be led by them?*
> The godparents reply *I renounce them all.*

'No,' Jeffrey shouts, to the general amazement. 'You can't baptize
that child.'

'Jeffrey, what's the matter?' Thea asks, visualizing a team of
caterers standing idly by a groaning buffet.

'She is.' Jeffrey points at Alice. 'You ask where the father is,
Bishop. I'll tell you. In some recycled yoghurt-pot or jamjar.'

'What is it?' Thea puts her hand to his forehead. He brushes it aside.

'I don't want to spell it out. There are certain words that shouldn't be spoken in church.'

'Like what?' Alice asks. 'Love, truth, tolerance?'

'Like deviance, like perversion,' Jeffrey replies. 'I won't have my grandson dipped in the same water as her child.'

Lloyd's howl conveys the general horror.

'We're here to welcome this child into the Christian family. What sort of family is that?' Jeffrey points to Alice and Dora.

'My sort,' Alice says. 'The sort which doesn't spring straight from a Persil ad.'

'Would you all please return to your seats,' Ted asks. No one responds.

'You must do something,' Esther says to Huxley. 'They're your parishioners.'

'They lied to me,' Huxley says. 'They made a mockery of their vows.'

'Look at her,' Jeffrey says. 'Look at her friends. Look at her pictures.' He indicates the Stations of the Cross. 'Look at her Christ.'

'Yes, my Christ. Mine as much as yours.'

'He isn't even human.' Jeffrey grabs hold of the Twelfth Station. 'Just an empty colostomy bag full of blood!' He pulls the picture off the wall and staggers under its unexpected weight.

'Put that back!' Alice shouts.

'Order!' David Stafford shouts in a momentary return to the Commons.

'You should respect the house of God,' Huxley says to Jeffrey.

'That's rich, coming from a man who, only yesterday, preached a sermon denying His very existence.'

'If you think that, then you seriously misunderstood.'

'Will somebody please explain to me what's been going on in this church?' Ted asks.

Judith begins to sob.

'I was expressing doubts ... uncertainties concerning the Resurrection.'

'On Good Friday?' Ted asks.

'Precisely,' Huxley replies.

Petula tries to steady her thoughts while the men's voices storm around her. She pushes her way to the front. 'Would you all please listen to me for a moment. Please!'

'Petula,' Hugh pleads.

'Yes, that's my name. Pet ... Petal. Not any more.' She points at

Jeffrey. 'This man has no right to condemn anyone. He has a scheme along with my husband – only I think it's called a scam – to buy the clergy-house. Hugh has fiddled the survey –'

Hugh grabs her and presses his hand over her mouth.

'She's tired. They're short-staffed on the ward. I'll take her home.'

He pulls her arm. She clings onto the font as if seeking sanctuary. 'I'm sorry, Hugh,' she splutters. 'But I can't keep quiet. The idea – it must be obvious now – was that Hugh would make out that the building was in a far worse state than it is. But, by chance, he knew a developer who'd take it off our hands. And then Jeffrey would make the most of the knock-down price to knock it down for good.'

'But it's a listed building,' Rosemary says.

'Was that a "but"? In Jeffrey's world, there are no "but"s, only "and"s.'

'This is slander,' Jeffrey says. 'I have witnesses.'

'So do I, as God's my witness ... And, of all the millions he stood to gain from his new access road, Jeffrey was going to give a quarter of a million to Hugh.'

'Pounds?' Rosemary asks in amazement.

'Yes,' Petula says. 'Try not to think too badly of us. I say "us", because it was me as much as Hugh. You've no idea how plausible Jeffey can be.'

Thea feels as though she is watching daytime TV. 'Wonderful!' she says. 'We come for a christening and land up with a confession.' She turns expectantly to Ted. If the baptism fails to take place, it won't just be Lloyd who is left in limbo. She wonders whether, for insurance purposes, a cancelled service counts as an act of God.

Ted looks at them, aghast. 'Is this how you celebrate Easter?' he asks. 'Is this how you greet the risen Lord?'

'It's my wife,' Hugh says desperately. 'She's got the wrong end of the stick entirely.'

'You dare to tell me that I have no place in the church!' Alice upbraids Jeffrey. 'You're the one who wants to defraud it.'

'You defile it,' Jeffrey says.

'I try to live a Christian life.' She ignores his hollow laugh. 'With love and creativity.'

'Creativity: this?' He lifts up the Twelfth Station.

'Yes.'

He drops it. The glass shatters. Alice shrieks.

'You bastard!'

'It's blasphemy, not art.'

He hurls himself at the wall and wrenches off another picture, throwing it onto the floor. He makes a lunge for a third but is held back by three of his friends. Alice keens over her damaged pictures, her room for revenge restricted by Dora. As blood from the Crucifixion trickles onto the tiles, Dee tries to prevent anyone touching it. 'No, please, leave it to us!'

Both babies are bawling, resistant to their mother's reassurance. Two children are crying. Judith and Rosemary are arguing over who should fetch a cloth. Ted sinks to his knees.

'This is the Devil's work. I feel his presence among us. His breath is burning the back of my neck. I ask you to pray with me – all you who hope for salvation – that we may cast the spirit of Satan from this church.'

Esther turns to Huxley. 'You must take over.'

'I can't.'

'Then at least ask your organist to play something . . . a hymn to bring us together. *Jesus Christ is risen today!*'

'Is He? I don't believe that I'll ever know the risen Christ again.'

PART TWO

I refuse to bargain with God ... to offer up my abstinence like a nun at the altar in return for the assurance that the lumps on my palms are mere bruises and the catch on my chest just a cough. I refute any moral dimension to either condition or cure. The whole structure of my belief rests on the apparent paradox that, while eternal justice is infinite, human misfortune is arbitrary. The laws of nature are not the laws of God. The inner treachery of disease, the mocking protuberance of famine, the mass slaughter of earthquake and drought are not punishments for our wrongdoing but the price of free existence in a world which is imperfect because it is separate from God.

I refuse to compromise with Christ ... to use my prayers like a stockbroker's insider-dealing, begging Him to relieve my suffering, when He suffers for me till the end of time. Like a father who tells a fallen child to squeeze his hand and let the pain pass to him, so He takes on the pain of the world. The whole thrust of my practice lies in the apparent paradox that, while Christ has risen from the tomb, He remains forever nailed to the Cross. Easter Sunday may supercede Good Friday on earth but, eternally, the two days coexist. He has vanquished evil, and yet, hanging hurt and humiliated, His blood mixed with His torturers' spittle, He endures all the torments of Hell. As a priest, I am charged with bringing people into communion with that sacrifice. Now I must bring myself.

The intention comes easier than the act. I walk into the clinic, brimming with the confidence of a full congregation singing a familiar hymn, only to feel it drift away in the confusion of an omitted verse. The atmosphere has radically changed in the twelve years since my last – and only previous – visit when, as a young actor, I made the dark descent through the bowels of the building and into a waiting room which, with its single pot plant and rows of green plastic chairs, appeared deliberately designed to deny hope.

Now that despair prevails without any help from the décor, there seems to have been a compensatory effort to soften the surroundings. Running along one wall is an aquarium, where goldfish drift aimlessly back and forth like prisoners in a recreation yard, turning intermittently to the glass and gulping kisses as if in mockery of the other occupants of the room. Elsewhere stand a hot-drinks dispenser, a television (mercifully silent) and piles of magazines, a bizarre combination of out-of-date glossies and free gay weeklies featuring half-naked coverboys whose flesh is further cheapened by the badly smudged print. But the cosy informality is belied by the bleakness of the posters. Twelve years ago, the notice-board was dominated by a pregnant man, as though that were the most shocking image to which male sexuality could be subject. Today, there are notices of bereavement groups and benefit agencies and a stark reminder of the importance of making a will.

I proceed to the reception-desk. In place of the sour-faced harridan, whose cabbage breath still haunts me from my previous visit, stands a snub-nosed young man whose cropped hair, white T-shirt, black jeans and red ribbon are intended to give him the shorthand appeal of a uniform. I whisper my name – or rather my pseudonym – and add that it is my first appointment. He holds out a form and asks me which clinic I went to before. Receiving the reply 'nowhere', he looks both surprised and faintly disapproving, as if to suggest that regular check-ups are the base-line of a sexually responsible life. I pull my scarf even tighter around my collar as I take the designated seat.

To my surprise, I find five fellow patients. By coming at nine o'clock, I had expected to beat the rush. I feel as if I am waiting outside a Post Office on dole day behind men whose sole remaining ambition is to be first in line. We sit in silence in accordance with an unspoken code. I relieve the tedium with an adult version of a child's game: I spy with my little eye something beginning with A-I-D-S. But all that I see are the bleary eyes and rough chins of an alarm call. One man returns my gaze with a glimmer of recognition. I detect a former fan of *Locums* and shrug off the don't-I-know-you-from-somewhere leer.

My fear of identification extends from my face to my neck. My collar bites into me like a brace. The room exudes a cloying heat as distinct from genuine warmth as an air-freshener is from a woodland glade, and yet I dare not remove my scarf. I improvise an elaborate scenario in which I'm a hospital chaplain on a pastoral visit to a patient too terrified to take the test. Jumping into character like a getaway car, I prove my instincts to be as sharp as ever ... but my reactions remain rusty. 'Nigel,' the receptionist calls. 'Nigel Clarke,' he repeats. It is only when five faces stare at me suspiciously that I recollect my alias. 'Dr Lynch will see you now. Down the corridor. Room Seven.' I exit quickly stage left.

The door is ajar, so I cough ... which sounds like a symptom. Brandon looks up, his amazement magnified by his granny-glasses. His hand falls from his chin to reveal a wisp of a beard which seems to be searching for its roots.

'I was expecting a Nigel Clarke.'

'My nom-de-clinic.'

He fails to smile.

'You can't just barge in. This is my surgery. I'm seeing patients.'

'I am a patient ... a potential patient. I want to take the HIV test.'

'Why come to me? There are other clinics in London. There are other doctors at this clinic.'

'I trust you. Whatever your opinion of me, I know you won't let it cloud your judgement.'

'Don't be so sure. You'd better sit down.'

As I take a seat, my eyes are drawn to the tub of condoms at the front of his desk. With a pang, I remember the tin of sweets that our family doctor used to keep for after injections and measure the distance which I have travelled since then. Brandon takes out a form and asks me for details of my sexual history with all the clinical bravado of a staff nurse discussing bowels.

'Roughly how many partners would you say you've had over the past year?'

'None.'

'None!'

I can't tell whether I have strained his credulity or challenged his doctrine of guiltless orgasm ... a prescription as universal as Prozac.

'And last year?'

'None.'

'Blair, why are you wasting my time? You may not have noticed but there's an epidemic out there. I'm a busy man.'

'I've been celibate for four years, ever since I split up with Julian.' He perks up like a scoutmaster at a coded confession of masturbation. I fail to add that, most nights, I've prayed myself to sleep so as to avoid the loneliness that weighs heavier on my chest than any bedfellow or to mention the teddy bear dusted down from my parents' loft and propped on the adjoining pillow, a child's consolation disguised as an adult joke.

'So what makes you think you may be infected?'

'Have you forgotten the cemetery yesterday, when I showed you the lumps on my hands?' I hold them out as if for alms.

'How long have they been like this?'

'A little over two months.'

'So why have you left it till now?'

'Mainly because of Julian. Given what he was going through, my own fears seemed self-indulgent. Also, I have another lump on my side. I'm ashamed to admit it, but I thought I'd been singled out.'

'I don't follow.'

'To receive the stigmata.'

'Oh Christ!' He sounds as though he has stepped in vomit. 'The life peerage of the Church's honours list. Why must your God always make you suffer?'

'If you intend to carry on where you left off yesterday, then I think I would prefer to see one of your colleagues. Besides, I'm due at Westminster Abbey in an hour. A parishioner is receiving the Maundy.'

'So why make this appointment?'

'She only asked me to accompany her last night. And tomorrow's Good Friday. I couldn't bear to have it hanging over me all weekend.'

'Then we'd better get to work.'

Having exhausted my sexual partners, he turns to my sexual practices. The most extreme activity becomes commonplace when designated by a tick or a cross in a box. The reciprocity of love is reduced to the either/or of active or passive partner. As he asks the questions, I grow aware that he is picturing me with Julian in an intimacy which, as Julian's best friend, he always resented. His hostility was so marked that I used to speculate on a secret passion, in spite of the seeming security of his ten-year relationship with Neil. I am no longer convinced that the assurance of his expertise is worth the intrusion. He reaches the end of the form and a space for any other comments which, to my alarm, he begins to fill.

'I take it you imagine you were infected by Julian.'

'For what it's worth, yes. I've had no other partner in almost ten years.'

He takes off his glasses and stares at me.

'You're entitled to believe what you like. But I'd say it was you who infected Julian.'

'What?'

'I'm not blaming you. Unlike the Church, we don't deal in guilt-trips. There's only one Commandment in force here, "Thou shalt not kill", and it's easily kept.' He points to the tub on his desk.

'Of course. The new morality. Anything goes so long as it's wearing a condom. If Moses were alive today, the tablets of stone would be made out of latex.'

'Religion is to morality what a portrait is to a person. I'm faced every day with the one real moral issue: how to keep people alive.'

'That isn't a moral issue; it's a medical one.'

'Not if you hold that the ultimate value lies in human life.'

'Which is where we differ. I also set a value on death.'

'You don't need to tell me. I tried to give Julian life, whereas you gave him death. Congratulations! You won.'

'I'm struggling to make sense of the metaphor.'

'Don't strain yourself. You gave him hypocrisy; you gave him denial; you gave him AIDS.'

The extravagence of his accusations cannot offset my guilt. Julian bore the brunt of both my professions. First, he endured the humiliation of my soap-opera celebrity, reading interviews in which I talked of seeing someone special: name withheld but pronouns fraudulently supplied. Then he suffered the subterfuge of my curacy – not just the need to keep our relationship secret from the world at large but to keep it perfect for those in the know. The pressure of being part of a model couple, whose lives were all hearts and flowers (but no glands), for the sake of the middle-aged ladies who called us 'the boys' and invited us to tea and doilies, was what drove him to rebel. When that rebellion took the form of other men, I asked him to leave.

'Do you think that you could take my blood now? We're both running late.'

'First things first. I'd like to examine you.'

'Is that necessary?'

'If you'd rather see another doctor ... ?'

'After going through all this? Please, just do what you must.'

He directs me to the couch, where he examines my throat, pressing down my tongue with a force which he failed to apply to my arguments. He rubs a swab against the roof of my mouth.

'Did you ever wonder why I decided to specialize in STDs?'

'No,' I croak, trying to protect my throat and to prevent his reading my suspicions.

'All my friends who weren't going into general practice chose to specialize in cancer or paediatrics. But I came here. And it wasn't such a glamorous field twenty years ago. Not at all. But I was exorcizing my upbringing: the novitiate I was sent to at seventeen – is there any worse fate than to be a poor boy in rural Ireland? – where the brothers wanted our balls as ruthlessly as their predecessors did the castrati's.'

'Ow! That hurts.' I fear that I may swallow the swab.

'It certainly did.' He refuses to be deflected. 'We used to sing a

hymn about Christ washing us in His blood. Only it wasn't our
bodies He washed but our brains. He washed our brains so much
that we hated our bodies. They were dirty ... disgusting and had to
be repressed. But why? How can we be so foul if we're made in
God's image? Or did His hand slip at the crucial moment, so that,
when it came to "down there", we Saturday creations are really
Friday afternoon models?'

'You can't dismiss an entire religion on account of one bad
experience.'

'Flip through the breviary,' he says. 'Check out the number of
saints who are adolescent, even pre-pubescent, and who died rather
than submit to any sort of sexual contact. Or look at the contrast
between the Mother Goddesses of the East and Mary – the Virgin –
whose vagina is so taboo that she's said to have conceived her son
through her ear.'

'I recognize the voice of a lapsed Catholic.'

'Not lapsed – ex. Ex!' His eyes blaze with affront. 'That's the
Catholic Church's masterstroke. They don't even allow us the dignity of disavowal. We're just erring sheep ready to be welcomed
back into the fold. But not me; I broke free. And, ever since, I've
been determined to help people enjoy their bodies ... to remove
not only the shame from sexuality but also the mysticism, to present it as a natural urge, no more nor less meaningful than eating
a bar of chocolate.'

'I've never met such a hedonist.' I find it hard to make my objections felt while his hand grazes my nipple.

'The word's pronounced *humanist*. Drop your pants.'

'I beg your pardon.'

'Your pants. We don't have all day. I have other patients and you
have Westminster Abbey.'

I feel both shy and suspicious. I console myself with the thought
that, to him, my genitals are as bloodless as those on a civic statue.

'Pleasure is crucial.' I would rather he weren't saying that while
squeezing my testicles. 'Now, with this bloody virus hanging over
us, it's more so than ever. That's something Christians never seem
to understand. You walk into a church and what do you see? A
man nailed to a cross. But, unless you're into S & M, you're unlikely to be attracted by it. That said, there's an awful lot of maso-
chism in Christian belief: the desire to be beaten, restrained,
humiliated and mastered. Bend over.'

'What?'

'I need to conduct a rectal examination.'

He takes out a pair of rubber gloves, which he stretches onto his fingers with an ominous squelch. I am determined not to flinch. The slightest hesitation will allow him to dismiss my views as a morbid fear of penetration. As I submit to the indignity, I have a clear vision of Christ in the hands of His tormentors. I am afraid that I may be about to choke.

He asks whether I intend to spend my life on the *via dolorosa*, but I cannot make any serious response while his finger remains inside me. He withdraws it with a 'plop', which I pray is an air bubble. He peels off the gloves and throws them into a box marked Contaminated. I have a strong suspicion that the entire procedure has been an exercise in revenge.

'Now would you roll up your sleeve.'

I turn away from the needle, my squeamishness compounded by his reference to 'a little prick'.

'We usually insist that anyone taking a test sees a counsellor first but, in your case, I'll make an exception. You're not going to do anything stupid. After all, you have your God to keep you warm.'

'That's right.' I shiver. 'What time do you want me back?'

'We should have the lab results at about three-thirty.' He looks at his file. 'Which fits in nicely as I have a gap at four.'

'I'll be here.'

I return to the waiting room. The empty chairs have been filled. Piped music, too generic to be identifiable, tranquillizes the air. The receptionist calls 'See ya, Nige,' as I struggle with the automatic door. I still fail to recognize my name.

I ease my way into the street as though I were returning from a month's retreat. The city has changed in my absence. The colours are sharper; the noises louder; and the faces more frenzied. I watch the pedestrians streaming past. A mother pushes her shopping in a push-chair while her daughter waddles by her side. A young man, pressing a ghetto-blaster to his ear, weaves through the crowd on roller-skates, as if in practice for more powerful wheels. A cyclist, exercising his dog, tangles the lead in his spokes and narrowly averts an accident. A middle-aged woman dangles a designer shopping-bag, the monstrance of her 'more is better' creed. I long to approach like a missionary and ask what Maundy Thursday means to them. What stage are they at on their Holy Week journey? Or are they still waiting to pack?

Easter is an embarrassment, the memory of a crime which haunts us all. 'What did you do on Good Friday, Daddy?' 'I brayed for Barabas; I jeered at Jesus; I went home and roasted an ox.' 'But I meant last week, Daddy, not two thousand years ago. Or are you really that old?' 'No, children. But Good Friday is that young. It happens every year: every day: every minute. It's the connection between God's time and ours. You'll understand it better when you're grown-up.' Will they? Or will they be betrayed by the trappings? Guess the weight of the Easter Egg in the window. A pound to buy a ticket and the closest estimate wins. 'Come on, missus. It's for charity. Christ died to save us. Surely you can afford one pound?'

'The trouble with Easter,' a parishioner once told me, 'is that there's so little in it for the children.' No amount of egg-hunts can compete with Christmas lights and trees. Nor are there any easy Easter stories. How different things might have been if Dickens had written *A Paschal Carol.* As I walk down into the Underground, I speculate on a possible plot. Tiny Tim (ironically nicknamed on account of his obesity) would be an ordinary fun-loving schoolboy, and Scrooge a killjoy vicar, who ruins Easter, which as everyone knows is a festival devoted to the consumption of chocolate, by alluding to crucifixion and sacrifice. He disobeys the directive to preach only the upbeat parts of the gospel ... the feeding of the Five Thousand, the healing of the sick, the Parable of the Good Samaritan (with the initial mugging expunged). But, after a visionary encounter with the spirit of Easter-yet-to-come, a giant, genetically-engineered rabbit, he promises to make no further mention of Christ's 'terminal event' on the Cross.

Irony is a congenial companion and passes the time until I emerge at Westminster, where a beggar on the steps lifts his arms towards me in supplication. In an age of knife-edge penury, he appears almost too mangy. His jacket is ragged and stained and his trousers bandaged. The tongue of his boot sticks out in disdain and, on his head, sits a battered bowler with a flower in the brim.

'Talk to me,' he says as he pockets my change. I am startled. I expect the usual gratitude, the 'God-bless-you-sir' that warms the hearts of the well-to-do while worming their consciences. 'Don't just walk away. Talk.'

My concern is taunted by a tinkling Sunday School hymn which transforms itself into 'the rich man in his vestry; the poor man in his crate'. I realize that his need to make contact is as desperate as his need for food. Checking my humanity against my watch, I squat by his side ... an impulse I instantly regret on exposure to the blast of ammoniacal air from his gummy mouth. My usual 'There but for the grace of God go I' is lost in the prospect of my own decline.

I assert my current health by sprinting across Parliament Square to meet Myrna in Dean's Yard. She wears a felt hat and coat which

accentuate her stoutness, while her face is so heavily made up that
it seems to be embalmed.

'I do appreciate you coming, dear,' she says, 'at such short notice.
And in the middle of Holy Week.'

I am embarrassed by her effusion of gratitude at the grandson-
duty which is so basic a part of a curate's life.

We walk through the cowl-cool air of the cloisters. I leave her at
the entrance to the Undercroft and make my way into the abbey
church of the one English monarch who might have been justified
in distributing the Maundy, St Edward the Confessor. The most
that his successors could achieve was saintliness by association as
they jostled to position their monuments around his tomb. I feel
my customary sense of intimidation at the anyone-who-was-anyone
aspect of the Abbey: the rival queens and politicians; the aristocrats
and abbots; the soldiers and scientists; and, above all, the novelists
and poets, whose overcrowded Corner shames me with the thought
of how much I have still to read.

I take my assigned seat in the nave, where the chairs have been
set out to face each other, a significant reorientation from Cross
to Crown. Doddering on their dignity, the recipients file in like a
parody of a children's crocodile, all shiny heads and shoes,
brooches and medals, their false teeth fixed in heartfelt smiles at
the sight of their companions. Myrna takes her place directly in
front of me and basks in the reassurance of the perfect procedure.
Only the solitary straggler at the rear of the procession spoils the
effect, an abandonment of the two-by-two principle which reflects
the true hierarchy of the 1990s, as one old man rates a visit to
his hospital consultant more highly than presentation to the
Queen.

'Hail to the Lord's Anointed' rings through the nave, as if to
create a deliberate confusion between 'great David's greater son'
and King George's elder daughter. As she makes her regal progress
down the aisle, wearing a dress in a pink so shocking that viewers
at home must be adjusting their sets, I gaze at the panoply of
Church and State assembling in the sanctuary, propping each other
up like two drunks at the fag-end of a party. This is the side of the
Church I love that I hate. There can be no stronger proof that its
foundations rest not on Peter's rock but on Anne Boleyn's pillow.
It was moulded to a monarch's convenience and so it has remained, with Passion sacrificed to pageantry and compassion to
ceremonial.

Exposure to the Abbey's history-book inspires me to turn the
pages of my own. I feel like a schoolboy who longs to punctuate

the pomp with the cry that, when I was twelve, I wrote out the Lord's Prayer twice on the Queen's backside ... but the joke is as ancient as a Penny Black. I try to escape such irreverence on my knees, only to find myself plunged into deeper turmoil when the Precentor calls down blessings on 'Our Sovereign Lady Queen Elizabeth'. My head fills with the image of a ninety-three year-old doctor forced to vacate Crown property, while my heart fills with a Christ-like fury on behalf of the oppressed.

I watch the Queen parade down the aisle as though preparing to unveil a plaque, while the recipients clutch their bags of fool's gold, and I see that I must represent Christ in the nave as well as at the altar. Just as He refused to keep silent when He saw the Temple occupied by the money-lenders, so I must speak out against its appropriation by the Queen. I must expose the hypocrisy that makes a public show of charity while forcing a lifelong tenant out of his home.

She approaches within spitting distance of me. Myrna's curtsey leaves us momentarily face to face. 'Liar! Sham! Hypocrite!' I shout. 'You offer what costs you nothing: the Monarch's mite!' She stands stock-still, her sole reaction a flicker of distaste as if she had been forced to sit through a display of native dancing. 'You give with one hand and you take with the other: distributing alms while evicting Lennox Hayward from his home.' I hear a scuffle, but it is only when my arms are pinioned that I realize it involves me. I am pushed to my knees. 'You are a false Christ ... an anti-Christ!' The words continue to pour from my mouth like a charismatic's, although the intervention of *Zadok the Priest* drowns them from all but my immediate neighbours. Myrna turns around, her pasty face frozen in pained astonishment, while three Yeomen of the Guard press me to the floor. As they drag me out past shoes and stockings, a well-polished brogue aims a kick at my kidneys. I am grateful to be lugged into the relative safety of Poet's Corner, where I am bumped over Byron, Auden and Henry James.

The final view as I gaze back at the nave is of the Queen proceeding with the distribution. There can be no surer sign that this is England, where protocol reigns and any breach will be brushed into the shadows. I hear a key scraping in a lock and, a few moments later, renew my contact with the ground as I am dragged down some steps into the Chapter-house. The grey of the stone dissolves into blackness as my head hits a wall.

Colour and consciousness return as I find myself in a small, stuffy office dominated by a mortuary-sized filing cabinet. Behind a desk sits an ascetic-looking man in morning-dress. To his side stand two marshalls in blood-red gowns, who exude the traditional NCO's air of barely suppressed violence. Looming over my chair are two Yeomen of the Guard, medals gleaming on their chests. In cadences which speak of a lifetime's translation from the classics, the man at the desk quizzes me about the purpose of my protest. I explain that, as a priest, I could not stand by and watch Christ's example being abused.

'The Royal Maundy has been distributed since the Middle Ages. Do you think that the present queen is less fitted to the task than, say, King John?'

'I deal in absolutes, not comparisons.'

'So, to satisfy yourself, you disrupt one of the great occasions of state.'

'Her Majesty reacted superbly,' one of the Marshalls says.

'The Monarch is magnificent under stress,' his companion replies.

'But that's precisely my point. It shouldn't be a great occasion of state; it should reflect the humility of Christ.'

'So you, with a few years of theology behind you, choose to argue with centuries of tradition. You upset all the recipients – decent, honest men and women (nominated I might add by their local churches) – for whom this marks the recognition of a lifetime of service to the community.'

'Then give them the MBE.'

He looks at me aghast. 'I have the MBE!' I say nothing as he continues. 'The service was being televised. Gone are the days when the BBC would fade to a stained-glass window at the first sign of trouble; now they positively seek it out. Do you think it helps in an age of dwindling respect for authority that millions of ordinary men and women should see a curate' – I wonder how he knows my rank – 'attacking the Supreme Governor of his Church?'

'Respect isn't unconditional; it has to be earned.'

'You talk like an American. You may fancy you're upholding the individual conscience but, in practice, you're supporting mob rule. How would you like it if I came along to St Mary-in-the-Vale and heckled one of your sermons?'

'If you had reason to believe I was speaking in bad faith, then you'd have every right.'

'Or if, when you were acting, I'd booed you off the stage?'

I stare at him in astonishment. 'How on earth did you know that?'

'Do you suppose that Abbey security is as archaic as its drains?' He reads the short account of my life which is set out in green and white in front of him. 'I fear that you may regret ever having quit the boards.'

'What does that mean? Are you charging me?'

'Is that what you want? A martyr's crown – preferably made out of thorns? No. There are other options open to us. We saw what you did. We know who you are. Now you may go.'

'Just like that?'

'Just like that. Or would you prefer an escort?' As he speaks, the two Yeomen formally cross pikes. The clang echoes through my head. 'The exits are clearly marked.' His mouth creases almost imperceptibly. 'Indeed, you may find all of your exits more clearly marked than you think. Good day.'

He returns his attention to his computer. Neither the marshalls nor the Yeomen stir. I make a tentative move and, when nobody checks me, walk to the door. From the corridor, I look back at the room to find my gaze met by indifference. As I hurry down the stairs, each step reinforces my conviction that the authorities are playing some kind of cat-and-mouse game and, as soon as I reach the bottom, there'll be a guard to lead me back. But the hall is empty, and I stumble aching and blinking into Dean's Yard. I am all set to search for Myrna when I see, to my surprise, that it's already two-thirty; she'll have left long ago. I'll just have to kill time until I'm due at the clinic ... I am struck by the irony that I may soon be praying for time to stand still.

Crossing Parliament Square, I assume that every hoot is a reaction to my outburst. I award myself 'most hated man in Britain' status from the jostling crowds. Even the tourists look hostile. Once in the tube, I try to occupy my mind but, with nothing to read, not even an order of service, I am left to speculate on my two companions: an overweight woman with BAD optimistically stretched across her bosom and an olive-skinned youth superfluously reading *The Joy of Sex*.

In the person of Nigel, I return to the clinic. The receptionist greets me like an old friend, which, far from putting me at my ease, confirms my sense of running out of time. I take a chair between a rangy man with bed-sit skin, who sits in a world of his own which he appears to have occupied since the sixties, and a young woman in a sari as rich as a Bombay movie, who stares intently at the aquarium, her limpid eyes ringed with fear.

I distract myself by reviewing events in the Abbey. I'm answering questions in the Clerk of Works' office, when I look up to find Brandon standing at the door. 'Nigel Clarke.' He spits out the name like an insult. 'Would you come this way?'

I walk in the wake of his disapproval. He ushers me into the room and closes the door. He looks at me with bemusement. 'Are you hurt? Your ear's grazed and you have some sort of lump on the back of your head.'

'I slipped. Don't worry, it's not a lesion. At least not yet.' My casualness fools neither of us.

'Please take a seat.' His offer sends my *Richter* reading soaring. Bad news ... sit down; good news ... remain standing: the positions are as fixed as on a barometer. I stoop over the back of the chair as if to keep my options open. He picks up a file but, just as he is removing a sheet of paper, the telephone rings. He speaks quickly. 'I'll be down in ten minutes. I've a few odds and sods to clear up here first.' I wonder into which of the categories I fall.

He focuses his attention on me. 'I now have the result of your HIV test and, I'm afraid to say, it's come back positive.'

The acid pain in the pit of my stomach seeps sourly up into my throat. The words twist into me like a Chinese burn.

'This is bound to come as a shock.'

'No, not really. After all I've had my suspicions.' I hold out my palms with a smile. But my composure is crumbling even as I try to reassure him. The past has returned with a vengeance, like a long-lost child in a melodrama.

'You're taking it very calmly,' he says. 'But then I wouldn't have expected otherwise.'

I slump forward; the chair swivels round and knocks me off balance.

'Are you sure you don't want to sit down?'

This time, I accept the offer. I am surprised at how hollow my chest feels. My voice emerges in gusts of air. I experience a wild conflict of sensations, like the survivor of a bomb-blast who discovers, as the nurse draws the curtains, that he has lost his legs.

'As I'm sure you know,' he says (although I'm no longer sure of anything), 'a positive result doesn't mean that you have the virus, simply that you've been in contact with it. Your T4 cell count is high and there are no signs of current viral activity. Now is there anything you want to ask me?'

I would like to look at the results myself. It might help to see them printed out in front of me. But he replaces them quickly in the folder, as though they might reveal something which is better kept back.

'So you have no questions?'

I try to concoct one for form's sake, but all I can think of is to ask whether his clock is showing the correct time. He looks baffled and checks against his wristwatch.

'No, it's a few minutes fast.'

'That figures.'

To my surprise, I find myself in tears. I try to sniff them back. 'I'm sorry. I don't know what's come over me.'

'Go ahead, cry. Tears are human.'

His hostility amazes me.

'Well, at least I've made one person happy. Yesterday, you said this was just what you wanted for me.'

'I wouldn't wish it on my worst enemy.'

'So what does that make me?'

'I'll pass on that one for now. We'll see how a taste of the real thing transforms your gospel of suffering.'

'I've visited dozens of people with AIDS in hospitals ... in the hospice.'

'Visiting's easy. Visiting's "I've got to go now, but I'll be back tomorrow; is there anything you'd like me to bring?" It's very different when you're the one stretched out in bed, desperate to appease the pain.'

'At least I'll know that the pain has a purpose. I only hope I shall prove myself worthy.'

'It's incredible.'

'What?'

'You've not been diagnosed five minutes and you're revelling in it already. Look Lord, I'm suffering too!'

I am stung by his cruelty.

'Since you know so well how I feel, perhaps you'll suggest how I can celebrate Easter when all that I see is the Cross?'

'What's the problem? You have a script. Now there's one last thing and it's crucial. You must give me your word that you'll tell no one about this before you see me again next week. Too often, patients have confided in people who've let them down badly. Understand?'

Having obtained my assurance, he shows me out. I walk down the corridor, taking carefree steps aimed at convincing myself as much as the nurses and patients visible through the half-open doors. My heart is pounding at the cage of my chest and I need a moment's solitude. I slip into a lavatory, redolent of the previous occupant. I retch but, in place of the basinful of vomit which would attest to my inner turmoil, all I produce is a slither of phlegm.

My one thought is to head for home. The tube trundles northwards, too slowly for my raging blood. I reach Hampstead and make my way up to the Vale of Health ... the name chastens me. But I take heart from the anonymous rows of suburban villas, all privet borders and bourgeois privilege, which show not a curtain-twitch of interest in the indiscretions of a curate. So I am quite unprepared, as I turn the corner to my own house, to meet a pack of journalists clicking cameras and firing questions. I long to know how they have discovered my diagnosis. It's only when I catch the words Maundy and Abbey that I realize their concern is with the Queen.

I dash to the front door which, to my surprise, is open. I wander through the house like an actor in a film, only without the comfort of technicians to keep the terror at bay. I make myself a mug of tea and curl up on the sofa, which has never looked a duller shade of boarding-house brown. I lay out pictures of Julian around me like lilies on a coffin. I open the letters which remind me of the past ... which remind me that I have a past. I trace my finger across the 'I love you's, which move me as deeply as when they first slipped off his pen. I trust that that love, which sustained me through years of estrangement, will do so across an eternity of death.

The silence works on me like a call to prayer, and yet I am unable to respond. I either deny the fear which dominates my mind or turn devotion into a letter to Father Christmas ... please may I have a bicycle and a Scalextric, oh yes, and a cure for AIDS. I long to talk to a friend, but Brandon's prohibition works as powerfully as a disconnected phone. I make do with the messages on my machine. To my relief, none of them mentions the Maundy. The first three are routine parish business. The fourth is a cryptic summons from Huxley. The fifth is from my mother to say that, if I'm doing nothing special over the holiday, I might care to come home.

Funnily enough, Mum, I am doing something special. I'm celebrating the resurrection of Christ.

Returning her call, I am taken back to a world where the dour industrial landscape is matched by the drab domestic interior. I enter the hall, its shelves filled with souvenirs of other peoples' holidays, its windows frosted with disapproval, and my nerve fails. Nevertheless, it's important to warn her about the Abbey. Now that the journalists have tracked me down, they are bound to make their way to Hanley. I picture my mother putting on her Sunday voice and handing out family history along with the best Wedgwood ('My husband's in Rejects'), before passing round evidence of my early exhibitionism by the paddling pool and my tarnished promise on the athletics track.

'So many cups. He always came first. We never thought that he'd turn out . . . well, you know.'

I dial a number, which is as much a part of me as my multiplication tables and dates from the same era. My father answers with a wariness which lingers long after he hears who it is. 'How are you son' he asks, the 'son' designed to convince himself of a relationship which is distanced as much by vowels as by miles. At least face to face, he has the comfort of his own reflection: the same high cheekbones, wide mouth and cleft chin . . . even if my slate-grey eyes, my best feature according to my former agent, come from my mother. I too rely on formula with a 'well' and 'busy' which pre-empt any further discussion. After thanking him for the invitation, I explain that I will be unable to take it up as I am needed in church.

'We thought that they might give you this year off.'

'It doesn't work like that.'

'Sheila's Bob has to work Saturdays, but they give him one in four.'

'Another weekend.'

'Do that. Your mother misses you.'

I take no offence because I know that, ever since I grew too old for a father's kiss, mother has been a synonym for parent. Conversation peters out and I shrink from introducing the Abbey. I put down the phone with a 'God bless' which divides us more sharply than any goodbye. Guilt seeps over me as I acknowledge how much I've disappointed him. I should have had a father like Brandon's, who longed for his son to become a priest, rather than one to whom it's a dampener as deadly as 'Last Orders!'. To my father, the role of the Church is neither to witness nor to challenge but simply to reassure. What greater rebuke could there be to his water-colour worship – his Christmas-card Christianity – than to have a son whose faith is carved in stone?

The call has depressed me and I turn back to the bitter consolation of Julian's letters, when I'm suddenly conscious of flashes of milky pinkness at the door. The colours coalesce into a near-naked Lyndon Brooks. But his body is so skinny, with pin-prick nipples and a concave chest which drops straight down to his scraggy hips, that it lacks all eroticism. His underpants hold no more allure than a sample stretched out on a stand.

'What on earth are you doing?'

The boldness of his appearance is belied by his lack of response.

'How did you manage to get in?' Sanity demands that I stick to trivia.

'I took the key from the drawer in the sacristy. I haven't broken anything. Honest!'

I'm aware of a faint flicker of comedy like a glimpse of another life.

'I'm sure, Lyndon. I'm not angry. But you can't stand there half-naked. You'll catch your death.' I have returned to Hanley, in spirit at least, as I seize on my mother's all-purpose prescription for covering every inch of flesh.

'I'm not cold.'

'You're quaking. There's no need to be scared. Just tell me; what are you doing here like this?'

'Waiting for you.'

His blushes emphasize his boyhood.

'I think you should put your clothes on and then we can discuss this rationally.'

'I love you.'

'No, you don't.' I snap like a pair of secateurs. In another context, the combination of ardour and frailty might be endearing; now, I see only the danger. I'm at a loss as to how to proceed. Among the placements and sermon-practice at college, they somehow failed to include a course on dealing with the sexual fantasies of adolescent boys or, for that matter, with the venal fantasies of journalists. The connection concentrates my mind.

'Get down!' I instruct him.

'What?'

'Just get down on the floor. Quickly.' I rush to the window.

'Aren't you going to kiss me first?'

I am at a loss to decide which threat takes precedence. A cursory glance reveals that the reporters remain in a gaggle at the gate. Meanwhile, Lyndon's misinterpretation takes graphic form as he curls expectantly on the floor.

'Just . . . just stay where you are for a moment!'

I draw the curtains like an admission of guilt. I turn back to Lyndon. 'Please dress yourself. We must talk.'

'After.'

'We can't talk . . . we can't do anything with you lying there like that.'

'We can make love.'

This has to be a foretaste of dementia.

'Where are your clothes?' I ask. 'I'm not joking. If you don't tell me, I shall ring your parents and insist that they come here at once.' For a moment, I see the scene through their eyes but, thankfully, Lyndon does not, and he directs me to the bedroom. I hurry upstairs, swallowing my revulsion at the rumpled duvet. I return to discover Lyndon sprawled on the sofa, his shoulders heaving, his face hidden in his hands.

'Here are your clothes.' I elicit no response. 'We can't solve anything with you like this.'

'Is it because I'm ugly?'

'No, of course not.'

'Well then?'

'I'm not interested in the way you look ... you or anyone else in the congregation. It's a matter of complete indifference to me.'

'I don't believe that. What about Mrs Hewitt? She's so fat, she makes noises. Or Bertha Mallott with her moustache.'

My only concern is with the lack of hair on his own upper lip. 'I don't judge by appearances.'

To my horror, I see that my presence has aroused him. I lose control and start to shout. 'Look, I've had an exhausting day. Either put your clothes on or leave the house in your underwear.' My bluff works. 'That's better.' I flinch as he levers on his laced-up shoes. 'Now we can have a sensible conversation.'

'You mean we can lie. The minute people put on their clothes, they begin to lie.'

'How can you say that? You who are always so helpful in the vestry.'

'I love you.'

'Please don't say it again.'

'It's true.'

'What's brought this on? Last week you were the same old Lyndon we all know and ... admire.'

'I watched the Maundy service on television; I promised Mrs Timson. I saw you attack the Queen.'

'I didn't attack her; I just made my point. I still fail to see the connection.'

'I saw how brave you were. And I knew at once that I had to be the same. I love you.'

'That's enough!' The quiver of his lower lip warns me not to underestimate his feelings. 'You're so young.'

'So was Romeo.'

'He's a character in a play.'

'Then what about King John? ... I'm doing him for GCSE. He married Queen Isabella when she was only twelve. Are you laughing at me?'

'Not at all, I promise. It's just you know what people say about buses: how you can wait for hours and then three come along at once. Well, I've had that with King John. But it's not the same. Think how much shorter life-expectancy was in the Middle Ages.' I feel a pang as the thought backfires.

'I might be struck by lightning tomorrow. Where's my life-expectancy then?'

'If you're keen to experiment –'

'I'm not.'

'Then you should find someone your own age.'

He turns sulkily away. I move to grab his shoulders but think better of it and, instead, plant myself in his line of vision.

'On Monday, you said that sexuality was a good thing,' he asserts, 'and that I could do anything I wanted so long as it was done with love.'

'But the love has to be reciprocal. Don't you think you're being a tad presumptuous? I may not love you.'

'Why not?'

'Because ... just don't interrupt. It's not only that you're far too young for me – though you most certainly are – but I'm a priest.'

'So? You haven't taken a vow of celibacy.'

'No. But I have taken one to abide by the teaching and practice of the Church. And that rules you out.'

'Have you ever broken it?'

'That's none of your business.'

'Then it's nothing to do with the vow; it's because of me. You think I'm a slag.'

'On the contrary, I think you've shown great courage. It takes guts to reveal such vulnerability.'

'So?' He suddenly looks expectant.

'So, I feel honoured ... and humbled. But now you really must leave. We have an important service this evening, and I need time to prepare.'

He takes hold of my arm and stares at me through eyes as round as chalices. 'If you'll just go to bed with me once, then I'll never ask again. I'll never speak to you again ... unless you want me to.'

'Have you had sex education at school?'

'Of course. I'm not a kid!'

'Then you know about AIDS?'

'Who doesn't?'

'Well, even if I wanted to ... to take up your offer, it wouldn't be possible. I don't have any condoms.'

'That doesn't matter.'

'You just said you knew about AIDS.'

'But not with you. I'd be safe with you. You're a priest.'

'Really? Ten years ago, people thought they'd be safe so long as they kept away from Americans.'

'But you're so clean and pure and strong. Everyone can see.'

'It doesn't work like that.'

'It'd be the next safest thing to sleeping with Jesus.'

The analogy appalls me and I can no longer hold myself back. 'I have HIV,' I tell him ... I know that Brandon would license my disclosure for the sake of safeguarding someone else.

'That's a shitty thing to say!'

'It isn't that much fun to live with either.'

'You're just saying it to get rid of me.'

'Lyndon, it's true.'

'Look me in the eyes and tell me.' He grabs a crucifix from the table. 'No, swear on the body of Christ.'

I seize his shoulders and hold him at arm's length. I gaze straight at the fleck on his right iris. 'I swear, Lyndon; I'm HIV positive. I found out today.' He bursts into tears and squirms free. I follow him round the room. 'I must have been infected years ago, long before I came to St Mary's.'

'You bastard!'

'I've told you something that nobody else knows. You must prove yourself worthy of my trust.'

'You're filthy.' He wipes his streaming nose on a knuckle. 'You're perverted.'

'Calm down; you'll do yourself no good.'

'I'm perfectly calm. You're the one who's trembling.'

To my surprise, I find that he's right.

'I've had quite a nerve-wracking day. What do you say I pour us both a shot of Judith Shellard's whisky? To Hell with Lent!'

I fill two glasses and pass one to him. He knocks it from my hand, adding an autumnal tinge to the floral carpet.

'I'm not a fool,' he says. 'Who knows what you've spiked it with. I lied; I never loved you. It was a trick to make you confess. Now I'm the one with the upper hand, and you better watch out.'

He stands still, trying to decide his next move which, it turns out, is to spit in my face. But his mouth is too dry and all that emerges is a splutter of air. Unable even to emit the intended insult, he runs from the room, wrenches open the front door and races down the garden path. I'm too tired to worry about his impression on the journalists and drag myself upstairs to strip the bed.

Sentimentality films my eyes as I assess the room like an executor, mentally assigning keepsakes to friends. Is my only legacy to be knick-knacks? I should have stuck to acting ... the BBC would pay tribute with an episode of *Locums*; my colleagues would establish a memorial fund. But, to the Church, I'm an embarrassment. My Saturday night-life will be exposed to the glare of Sunday morning scrutiny. The Archdeacon's 'I told you so' will ring out like an amplified Amen.

In the light of recent medical breakthroughs, I grant myself a reprieve, commuting my death sentence to life imprisonment, subject to a rigid regime of drugs and therapies. Never has capital punishment appeared more humane. My life is the Church, but I've betrayed it. My fears about revealing my sexuality pale beside those of revealing my status. I may have compromised myself but I have no right to compromise my congregation. Instead of helping people to Christ, I'll be a sideshow diverting attention ... 'Are those marks on his neck love-bites or lesions?' The scandal of my tainted blood will obscure the mystery of the wine.

I fall back on the pillow. The badge on my bedside table catches my eye: *The Body of Christ has AIDS*. It was so easy to wear when it was merely a metaphor, designed to shock the parish out of complacency. The we're-all-in-it-together shorthand reads very differently now that I am in it more than most. I examine the lumps on my hand. I was honoured when I thought that they might be a stigmata ... when I imagined (what arrogance!) that I might be awarded a sign of special favour; I am ashamed now that they'll be seen as a stigma ... the sign of my fallible flesh. Nothing could demonstrate more clearly the limits of my life in Christ. When the cock crows, I stand beside Peter, the original fairweather priest.

And yet it is neither Peter nor Christ but Cain, the fratricide not the disciple or the saviour, who holds out his hand to welcome me. As I recognize the mark on his forehead, I picture it spreading over my entire skin and wonder how many of my brothers I have killed. Ten years, first of fidelity and then of chastity, cannot disguise the death which has been incubating inside me. I am Cain, whose desire for God's favour was betrayed by his passions. I am Cain, exiled from Eden and sheltering in a shop doorway, clutching a makeshift placard with a spidery plea: HIV and Homeless. Please help.

We will now sing the offertory hymn *I was born under a wandering star*, omitting the third chorus ... I mean verse.

Christ's death redeems Cain's murder. And yet His command to 'love one another' glints like a dagger in my mouth. I once appalled my spiritual director by arguing that Christ's chastity would amount to promiscuity in anyone else since, by assuming our flesh,

He enjoys that unique relationship with the whole of humanity which the rest of us have only with a lover. Paradox aside, I believe 'the word was made flesh' to be the most telling phrase in the Bible and a damning rebuke to those who would like to see Him as a piece of animated calligraphy. To deny the flesh is to disincarnate Christ, not to follow Him. Nevertheless, it is hard to proclaim the sanctity of flesh – even to myself – when it will soon be eaten away, leaving me all sin and bone.

The St Mary's bell cuts through my meditation but not my despair. I have never felt so unfit for service. What right have I to wash anyone's feet when my basin is just a prop and my humility a pose? I resolve to make my way to the church and explain my position to Huxley. But I have reckoned without my retinue of reporters. Men whose love of their country is confined to the coins in their pockets jostle and josh me on behalf of the Queen. They pursue me through the churchyard to the porch, only to abandon me as abruptly as at Traitor's Gate. I hurry inside, scanning the nave until I spot Huxley in the Lady Chapel, the picture of uncompromised devotion. I am reluctant to intrude but my predicament is pressing, as the arrival of an irate Hugh Snape confirms.

With his customary selflessness, Huxley grants me leave and I escape through the sacristy. I have my own private vigil to keep, not at the Altar of Repose but at Julian's grave. We still have so much to settle. The funeral was all formality: feelings wrapped in words like winter clothes, woolly cadences which I must now cast off, whatever the risk, in order to speak from the heart. I need to encounter the earth and the ashes and the dust and not just to mouth them ... I need to brave the shadows if I'm ever to hold them at bay ... I need to stretch out my hand in the dark and feel him beside me once more, if only beneath the canopy of a family tomb.

I circle the cemetery wall, searching for the gap in the railings like a memory of my youth. Then, as a drama student fresh to London, with a waistline as thin as my wallet, I squeezed through its limbo-like opening and entered a world of undreamt-of pleasure. No nightclub ever presented a more extraordinary décor or exotic clientèle. Now, returning though the six-inch chink, more forbidding than any doorman, I am relieved to find that, despite a decade of absence, my membership hasn't lapsed. Moreover, for all our differences, I stand hand-in-hand with that eighteen-year old, whom I can never disown since I perceive an innocence in even his most fleeting encounters. I wonder too whether Julian might rest

easier in the embrace of his ancestors for the knowledge of the
more passionate embraces being exchanged outside.

A glance at the moonlit figures of Wisdom vanquishing Folly on
a nearby monument puts paid to such speculation and I jump to
the ground. Shunning any superstitious hopscotch, I saunter down
the path, reassured by the richness of history beneath my feet. The
crumbling tombs prove to be as fragile as the bones which they
commemorate. A granite grave lies buried in ivy as though it, too,
has decomposed. I shine my torch along a row of defaced head-
stones. And yet, for all the dilapidation, there is an overwhelming
sense of stability and of a peace more palpable than in any park.

Few cities can boast such elaborate designs as this necropolis ...
a last-ditch challenge to the equality of the grave. So one Victorian
grandee has built himself a tomb to house an exiled emperor, while
another has arranged the twelve apostles like flunkeys around his
bier. Cherubs weep marble over the mortality of the Bateman family, even as their neighbours, the Watsons, are mourned by a mena-
gerie of mythical beasts. But the pinnacle of vanity is achieved by
the Davenport-Finches, who reside in a gothic chapel, crowned by a
quartet of angels, one of whom has fallen, Lucifer-like, to earth.

The Blaikie monument is similarly ornate if less fanciful, taking
the form of a frigate from the Napoleonic Wars in which the first
Admiral Blaikie served. The hull is decorated with a frieze of young
ratings, heads bared and necks bowed, escorting their comman-
der's corpse. Miniature masts and rigging rise from an alabaster
deck. The figurehead is Medusa and, according to legend, was modelled on the Admiral's wife. Julian was the first of his line to break
with the naval tradition ... although he used to claim – much to
his mother's fury – that he had kept it up in other ways.

As I approach the vault, I am surprised to find that the grille is
open. The undertaker's oversight offers me a perfect opportunity. I
make my way down the steps, only to be greeted by the unmistak-
able sound of breathing. For one desperate moment, I wonder if
Julian may have been buried too soon. My presence at his deathbed is no proof against medical error. The word Lazarus flashes
like a ray of hope across my mind. I am torn between running
for help and single-handedly prizing open his coffin, when the
rasping intensifies and merges with the words 'Fuck me! Fuck me
now!'

I stagger back. Grief and guilt are infecting my brain with porno-
graphy. I am putting words into Julian's mouth – into his coffin –
which he last spoke to me more than four years ago. I seethe with
self-loathing. Far from communing with his spirit, I am profaning

his memory. There is no time to lose ... to leave. But my resolve is undermined by the sound of a second voice, which coaxes the first with a mixture of obscenities and endearments. There can be no more doubt. To my disgust, I find that men are no longer content to prowl the cemetery; they have begun to break into the tombs. It is barely one remove from necrophilia. Determined to defend Julian, I rush headlong into the vault.

Flashing my torch onto dust and flowers, and dust and brass, and dust and shelves, I light on two young men pressed into a corner who peel away from each other with the sound of a plaster being ripped off a wound. They shield their genitals like an Expulsion From Paradise. My beam touches the tip of an erection; I withdraw it like a trapped voyeur. 'Cover yourselves,' I say, my tone as curt as my words. As the one in front, a freckle-faced man with ginger hair, bends to pull up his trousers, a condom shrivels off his penis like a slug from a leaf.

I turn aside while they stumble into their clothes. Expecting expressions of remorse, I am doubly appalled when they impute their shamelessness to me. 'This how you get your kicks then?' the freckle-faced man asks. 'Prowlin' round.'

'It's a cemetery. I'm a priest. I came to pray.'

'What's wrong with church then?' he sneers, before snapping his fingers and swaggering up the steps. Pausing only for a passing 'Pervert', his companion follows him out.

Alone in the void, I catch a hint of their lingering heat mingled with the mildewing coffins; I have never been so conscious of the link between sex and death. I walk towards Julian across a scattering of skeleton leaves which crackles in defiance of the seasons. As I close my eyes and press my lips to the wood, an image of his skin flushed with aquarium tints and flaking like a fin overwhelms me. In despair, I resolve to return to the world of the terrestrial dead. The darkness has deepened during my descent and the shadows are now indistinct from the tombs. I climb the steps as gingerly as a gangplank but lose my footing when an effigy on a neighbouring monument springs to life with a burp.

'Who's there?' I ask, no longer prepared to countenance any confusion.

'Be on your guard,' it shouts. 'I have fought for my Queen and Country.'

My heart stops. Given the setting, it might be a veteran of any campaign from Blenheim to the Crimea. I retreat into the shadows, re-emerging only when I shine my torch onto the briary beard of an inebriated tramp.

He raises his hand to his eyes. 'My good sir, is such illumination absolutely necessary?'

I begin to suspect that he may be a ghost after all. 'Who are you?'

'Do I have the honour of addressing a member of Her Majesty's constabulary?'

'Certainly not.'

'Then may I ask on what authority you inquire?'

'None ... that is my own. I just wanted to know your name.'

'I would give it you with pleasure. But I regret to say that I have temporarily mislaid my card.'

I admit defeat. 'Please, go back to sleep. I didn't mean to disturb you.'

'Sleep! A slur! I am lamenting my dear departed wife. I come here every night to lay my broken-hearted heart on her tomb.'

I pass my torch over the plinth and read aloud 'Sacred to the memory of Louisa Tallboys, 1821–1847.'

'My darling girl.'

'Beloved wife of Winston Tallboys.'

'Adulterer! Fornicator! Imposter! I spit on his grave.' He does so in earnest, while I am reading the second part of the inscription. 'And Winston Tallboys, 1817–1892 ... Look, I'll just slip away. Please, forgive the intrusion.' I fumble with the torch which, momentarily, lights up my face.

'For the love of Christ!' he shouts and drops his bottle. I see that he is confused by my collar.

'Don't worry,' I say. 'I'm not here in any official capacity.'

'Oh Lord Jesus, look kindly on me, a miserable worm ... an ant ... a stick insect!' He clambers off the tomb and falls to his knees.

'Is something troubling you? If I can be of any help...'

'Have mercy on me, Lord. Don't let me be cast into the bottomless pit.'

He crawls towards me, insensible to the gravel, and clings to my legs with a grip so desperate that I am unable to break free. I am even more concerned to dislodge the misconception which has gripped his mind. I try to raise him from his knees, but his bulk threatens to topple me and I slip down beside him, receiving the full blast of his brewery breath.

'I'm not the Lord,' I say gently. 'My name's Blair Ashley. I'm an Anglican curate. Feel.' I put my hands in his. 'Flesh and blood like yours.'

He traces my palms with his fingers and then examines them with the torch. 'The wounds from the nails!' As he presses them to his cheeks, I feel a double imposter. I hit on a plan to save us both.

'Do you know that it's Maundy Thursday? Do you remember what Jesus did two thousand years ago today?'

'Tell me, Lord, I'm listening.'

'He washed His disciples' feet. And priests throughout the world have done so ever since. Now I shall wash yours.'

'Oh no, Lord.' He falls back, grabbing hold of his shoes and pressing them together.

'Trust me. All we need is some water ... wait!' I run over to the Blaikie monument, certain that Julian will forgive me as I throw out a bunch of wilting lilies and appropriate a plastic urn. 'Will you permit me to wash your feet?'

'I'm yours to command, Lord.' He laboriously unlaces his shoes. I move upwind of his socks. He starts to untie his belt with all the misplaced zeal of Peter at the Last Supper.

'No, it's only your feet.'

'I know, Lord.' He looks perturbed at this lapse of omniscience, as he removes his socks to reveal trousers with jodhpur-like bottoms. He slips them off, oblivious to his lack of underclothes until he sits back on the stone-cold plinth. I avert my gaze from the patch of darkness between his legs and kneel to take his feet in my hand. Bruised and scarred, they resemble a map of his travels. And yet, far from feeling revulsed, I am exhilarated by the authenticity of the ingrowing toenails and ingrained dirt. These aren't the perfect pedicures of a symbolic ceremony but the roadworn feet of humanity. As I pour the turbid water over them, a stray petal sticks between his toes. He chuckles and flicks it away before bursting into song.

'And did those feet in ancient time
Walk upon England's mountains green?
And was the holy Lamb of God –'

A shaft of light dazzles my eyes and, for a moment, I am caught up in the man's transcendent vision. But the rumble of engines and the screech of brakes make an unlikely accompaniment for the Heavenly Host. Having identified the vehicles as police cars, I stand, foolishly fearless, in the glare of the headlamps, while several officers pile out. One runs towards me. Two dash into the distance. A fourth escorts Lyndon and his father.

'Is this the man?'

'That's him,' Lyndon's father says with disgust. Lyndon breaks away from the group and flings himself at me, kissing me frantically on both cheeks.

'I never meant to tell them anything. Honest!'

'Lyndon, get back over here!' His father drags him away by the neck.

'They forced me!'

'Don't you know he's sick?' Lyndon sits sobbing on a stone, while his father snarls at me. 'If I find you've laid a single finger on my boy, I swear I'll break every bone in your body.'

'That won't be necessary, sir,' the Sergeant says. 'Leave it to us.'

'It's worse than we thought, Sarge,' the Constable says. 'He's got himself an old dosser. We've caught them doing the business.'

The idea is so ludicrous that I laugh out loud.

'So you think it's funny?' the Sergeant asks.

'I scorn your insults,' my fellow suspect declares. 'I have a friend in Jesus.' He crosses his legs with dignity, folding his shirt-tails over his genitals.

'I was washing his feet,' I explain.

'Isn't it a little late to be worrying about hygiene?'

'In celebration of Maundy Thursday.'

'So where's the punters? All I see is a rancid, half-naked old tramp . . . Wilkins, help him get dressed.'

'I'd rather not, Sarge. Look!' The Constable points to the trousers which lie like a dead rodent, crawling with lice, in the glare of the headlights.

'Flaming Norah! What do they teach you at Hendon these days? Macramé?' The Sergeant picks up the offending item and throws it at the old man. 'You, grandad, make yourself decent . . . if it isn't too much to ask.'

'Would I be correct in thinking that I am addressing a member of the Metropolitan Police?'

'Spot on, grandad.'

'Then who might you be?' the old man asks me.

'I've told you already. The curate of St-Mary-in-the-Vale.'

'You lie, sir. You told me that you were Jesus Christ.'

'What?' The Sergeant is incredulous.

'He told me that he was Jesus Christ and ordered me to take down my trousers.'

'Ten out of ten for originality,' the Sergeant says, 'if not for taste.'

'This is quite absurd. You can see how befuddled he is.'

'Officer, you have saved me from infamy. Be assured of my undying gratitude. I shall recommend you for a medal.'

'One more word out of you and I'll do you for drunk and disorderly.'

'Quite right. I know my duty. I'm ready to perform a citizen's arrest.'

'One more word!' the Sergeant threatens. The Constable holds up the old man's trousers, which he hobbles into like an amputee.

The remaining policemen approach with two men: one young, shaved and metallic; the other, older, gaunt and bearded.

'No sign of your man, Sarge,' the first policeman says.

'That's all right, Davies. He's here.'

'But we did find these two playing hide-the-sausage in the bushes.'

'Point of fact, there was three,' his colleague says. 'But one shot away before we could nab him, bollock-naked except for his boots.'

'Hear that?' Lyndon's father asks him. 'Do you want to end up like this? Catching diseases off gravestones?'

'Have you nothing better to do?' the bearded man addresses the officers. 'Are your arrest figures so low that you need to round up some queers?'

'Belt it, will you?'

'You have to show what big, butch men you are. Well you're not the only ones.' He pulls a knife from his pocket, flicks it open, and waves it at his escort's ear.

'Jesus!' one of the other officers exclaims.

'Please! Put it away. Don't be stupid!' I shout.

'Who are you?' the man with the knife asks.

'Father Blair Ashley.'

'You mean they're even bringing priests?' He tosses the knife to the ground. 'Now I know we can never win.'

One policeman handcuffs him, while the Sergeant previews his charge. 'Resisting arrest. Carrying an offensive weapon...'

'Wouldn't you carry something if you'd been queerbashed three times in the past six months?'

'How about a donor card?' The Constable chortles.

The Sergeant considers the logistics of transporting us to the station. A few moments later, I am sitting beside him in the back of the first car, speeding towards the cemetery gates. As the driver steps out to unlock them, a flash-bulb explodes in my face.

'How did the press find out where we were?'

'How the hell should I know?' the Sergeant replies, taking un-disguised pleasure in my exposure. 'Perhaps they heard your young friend and his father when they called us from the church.'

He says 'young friend' as if it were already an item on the charge-sheet, but, on reaching the station, I find that it has been jettisoned in favour of assault on the old man (whom I can hear providing a rambling but compliant statement), criminal damage to Julian's tomb and making a disturbance in a churchyard. Incredulity numbs me. I am in the darkness-before-dawn world of the stag-night strip-per; any minute now, my best man is going to jump out with a silly hat and a pixilated grin to rescue me. Until then, I try to focus on the Duty Officer who is reading me my rights and permitting me one phone call. As I don't have a solicitor, I phone the vicarage, only to hear that 'Jessica and Huxley Grieve are unavailable'. I leave them a message and prepare for a night in the cells.

Uniforms take over from people and I respond to the function rather than the face. My current interrogator asks me if I take any medication for my condition. 'What condition?' I ask, and she tells me not to be clever. It is only then that I recall the three letters which are now stamped on me as indelibly as a tattoo. Yes, I want to say, I take fresh air and long walks and loving kindness. 'No,' I say, 'I'm asymptomatic. My condition is to wait.'

The stark white tiles of the blue-lit cell come as a shock. On one wall, a patch of smears provides a solitary dash of colour, the source betrayed by the smell. As I test one of the catacomb-like ledges which pass for beds, I try to picture myself as a mediaeval anchor-ite. The door opens and I tell myself that it's a pilgrim arriving from town. But it's the Duty Officer, exuding contempt like halito-sis, as he hands me a mug of tepid tea.

I try to make sense of the sequence of events but bump into too many imponderables. I cannot understand what Lyndon was doing in the cemetery or why Huxley should have disclosed where I was. Questions buffet my brain. I lie down in an effort to evade them, but there is nowhere to lay my head. The pillow is richer in stains than in stuffing, while the niggardly blanket provides neither com-fort nor warmth. An attempt to make a cushion of my shoes is thwarted by the graveyard smell clinging to the soles. So I fall back on the technique perfected at college to see me through morning prayers of sleeping, eyes open, sitting up.

It must work for, the next minute, I'm walking through Hampstead, past a launderette where I see Huxley at a machine, washing what I know, even before looking, are my clothes. I rush in and pull him away.

'Have you forgotten?' he says. 'It's Laundry Thursday. Besides, your time is much too precious to waste. Here.' He hands me a prayerbook which turns out to be a wad of banknotes. 'Go out somewhere and unwind. Put all this to one side. See some friends.'

The restaurant is full, but the *maître d'* immediately offers me the best table, ousting a party of bankers, who change into shirt-sleeves and aprons and gather around me. I ask to see a menu, only to be told that I have already placed my order. A procession of chefs lines up the dishes in front of me. I watch aghast as the lids are whipped off to reveal a human foot laid out like a pig's trotter, a calf like veal, and a thigh like a ham. I thrust them aside, but the food keeps coming ... liver and kidneys, tripe and ribs and chops. Finally, the *maître d'* brings in the *pièce de résistance*: a head, flambéed like a Christmas pudding and garnished with a sprig of holly, which spreads rapidly into a crown of thorns. What is worse, as the face comes into focus, I recognize the Archbishop of Canterbury.

I try to break free, but I am tied to my seat. 'Have a slice of tongue,' the *maître d'* says. 'It's particularly tender. Or perhaps you'd prefer the parson's nose?'

'You're insane!' I shout.

'You're the one who ordered it,' he replies. 'You asked for his head on a plate.' He plucks out the Archbishop's eyes. 'There. Now you can gorge your fill. He won't see a thing.'

'I'm not a cannibal!'

He pierces one of the sockets with a fork and holds my glass to the gush of gore.

'The blood of Carey,' he proclaims. I dash it to the ground.

'Sacrilege!' he shouts. 'Grab him!'

My shoulders are wrenched from behind but, on looking round, I discover that it is not by a waiter but by a policeman.

'Put a sock in it, can't you? You'll wake the entire block.'

'I'm sorry. It must have been a bad dream.'

'Guilty conscience,' he says, with the air of one for whom guilt only arises at night. 'You have a visitor ... Barry, get in here. You two should have a lot in common.'

My hope that the visitor might be a solicitor sent by Huxley is dashed by the sight of Barry, a sallow, surly man in his late twenties, as compact as a Swiss Army knife. Even in person, his face has the look of a mug shot, with a flat forehead, snub nose and pop-eyes. The muscles which bulge through his nylon shirt seem to have been honed with home-made barbells rather than the custom-built work-out of a gym. The ill-fitting trousers testify to both a lack of concern about his appearance and a confidence about his appeal. As the officer slams the door behind him, I wonder what on earth he thinks we may have in common. This is not company but isolation with threats.

Barry pads the cell heavily. I say nothing. Until he acknowledges me, I judge it wiser not to draw attention to my presence. He examines the room as if trying to commit it to memory and then suddenly darts at me. I freeze as he shoves me aside and pulls my blanket away. 'There it is,' he says, pointing triumphantly at a scratch on the board.

'What?' I wonder if he is on drugs.

'B.F. Barry Farson. Yeah!' He lifts his arm as in a Wembley salute, and I realize that I am in a cell with a hardened criminal. 'They can't ever wipe us out.'

'Have you been here before?' I try to make my concern sound conversational.

'Did you say summet?' He takes me in.

'I was asking whether you'd been here before.'

'What's it to you? Are you a journalist?'

'I'm a priest,' I reply, gambling on the respect which sees me safely through estates which policemen only enter in pairs.

'You having me on?'

'I assure you it's the truth.'

'What you here for then? Fiddling the collection money? Vicar's perks?'

'No, nothing like that.'

'Here. You ain't a shit-stabber, are you? No arsing around with the choirboys. I warn you.' He thrusts out his fist, although I note that it is his left hand with 'Love' inscribed on the knuckles, rather than the right with the more appropriate 'Hate'.

'I was arrested in a cemetery. The police claim that I was performing some sort of satanic rite.'

'Fuck me!' he says and instantly tenses all his muscles in case I take it for an invitation. 'Were you?'

'No,' I say, at the risk of forfeiting his esteem. 'I was just praying by a tomb.'

'And they done you for that?'

'It was late at night.'

'It's your job, ain't it? Might as well nick an MP for graft.' He laughs and shouts through the grille. 'Rozzers – tossers!' He moves to sit on the edge of his bed. 'We had a vicar near us when I was a kid. He was all right. He had a snake called Lucy. It was short for summet. The name not the snake. The snake was a bloody great thing. Six foot ... more. He used to bring it with him to Sunday school.'

'Unorthodox ... but each to his own.'

'He used it in sermons. You know, like the Garden of Eden, where God created women.'

'And man too.'

'Yeah, but it was woman who was tempted: woman who made him steal the apple.'

'And man who wrote the story.'

'Filth, that's what they are! And thick. They have smaller brains than us ... that's a fact. By rights, they should be extinct. Like dinosaurs. I said to her "If you get any fatter, you won't be able to see your knees, let alone move them." Her tits ... I'm sorry, vicar, but I'm sure you've heard worse ... her tits spread like a lorry had run over them. Everything she touched she left a mark. It was like living in a chip-pan. She just sat all day on her great greasy arse: sat behind the till at Safeway's; sat in front of the box at home. What sort of life was that for anyone? I tell you, she was better off dead.'

'You killed your wife?'

His forehead furrows. 'Why do you say that? I ain't never said that.'

'I'm sorry. I didn't mean to interrupt.'

'The bitch ... the bleeding, blubbery bitch. And that other bitch, her sister. She shopped me.' He moves to my bed and squeezes beside me. I feel the heat like an unexploded firework. 'A mate of mine – yeah, the best sort –' His thin lips curl. 'Showed me a way how, instead of her costing me, I could make something back. He knew a bloke who knew a bloke who was a photographer. Fat birds were in demand. Sickos! First off, she said "no" straight out. Hollered at me, spouting crumbs all over the shop. But I made her; I mean she fucking owed me. Soon, it seemed like they couldn't get enough of her. My mates took the piss. But I was laughing ... I was made! What I didn't see – what I didn't see until it was too bleeding late – was that the bitch was starting to get thin.'

We have barely met, but the ending of his story is as predictable as a daily prayer.

'They put her in films – don't get me wrong, she wasn't aner-what'sit, but she weren't just for the sickos any more. She started to forget who she was. She'd give me lip. And, when I slapped her, she'd scream "not my face", on account of the films. She said that the money coming in was hers. No loyalty. No gratitude. No thought for the bloke who got her into it in the first place. I said to her ... I said "I'm the brains. You're just the fucking fat body." "Fat," she said. "Have you looked at me lately? Or are you blind as well as dumb?" It was when she came to, that she told me she was leaving. That's when I made up my mind. Food. She had to start eating again. I got in all her favourites. *Penguins.* Crisps. *Wagon-wheels.* But she wouldn't touch them. Said she had to think of her figure. So I locked her in the bathroom, with the radio blasting out to drown her bawling.'

'Did none of the neighbours complain?'

'What, them coons? Most of them's booming out jungle-music like they were still there ... Morning and night, I'd check up on the food, but she never touched it. She'd just lay in the tub in her own stink. Slut! If I'd locked her in the bedroom, I could understand ... there'd be some excuse; but the khazi was right under her nose. She stayed there for weeks, while her face went dark and the bones started sticking out everywhere. And it was obvious. The bitch was trying to die just to spite me. She was out to stitch me up. But she married the wrong bloke if she thought she could walk on top of me. So I crumbled the crisps and the biscuits and shoved them down her like medicine. Then, when she puked them back up, I pressed her jaws together so she had to swallow. But the filthy slag went and snotted it out through her nose ... That's what I can't get through their thick skulls. If I wanted to snuff her, I wouldn't have gone to all that trouble crumbling stuff, would I? Or else I'd have mixed it with glass. I bust a gut trying to get her to eat. I put a peg on her nose to keep it closed. And I took this funnel thing that she used for her hair-dye and I stuck it in her mouth. And I piled the food in, so she'd have to chew or else she wouldn't breathe. But nothing happened. Only her eyes moved.' He laughs. 'Rolling round and round like little hamsters. "Eat," I shouted. "Eat." And then she let out this great fart ... like as if we was being invaded. The funnel flew out of her mouth and the peg blew off her nose. And this green slime poured out of everywhere – her cunt, her ears, her arse, even under her nails. The whole room was covered in it. It stank so rotten that I had to leg it out the flat to get some air. And, when I went back, she was lying like she was on a police slab. There was more of her guts in the bath than in her body. Now they're saying I killed her. And they'll bang me up for fifteen years.'

As he beats his fists on his head, I picture him caught in the clash of their rival emotions.

'Was I wrong? You're a vicar; you be my judge.'

'I'm afraid that's the one thing I can never be.'

'But you got to. Or what'll it be like when I'm dead? I tell you she'll be up there now, filling them in on her side of the story.' The desperation in his eyes reveals that this is no mere figure of speech.

'That's nonsense.' He bristles. 'I don't mean to be rude, but it's important to set one thing straight. I said that I won't play God; well, more to the point, God won't either ... at least not in that sense. He isn't some hard-line Home Secretary, stretching "life means life" to last eternity.'

'What then? Parole for good behaviour after a hundred million years?'

'Paradise, irrespective of behaviour, from the moment we die. It may be difficult to grasp. The peace of God passes all understanding ... whether it's yours or mine or the Archbishop of Canterbury's.' I stumble over the memory of the dream. 'The closest we come is by analogy. Take the most common one of all: God the Father. You know – everyone knows – how a father will visit his son in jail.'

'What's he in for?'

'Robbery. Rape. Even murder. It makes no difference.'

'It bleeding does if you're the one inside.'

'I mean that it makes no difference to the argument. Let's say murder.' I feel his muscles tense. 'If a father can stand by even the most abandoned criminal, should we expect any less of God?'

'My old man never come near me once when I was in the nick.'

'Really?' I refuse to be thrown. 'Well, I promise you that God will keep faith with us come what may.'

'Then why go to all the hassle of trying to be good? Why not just have a good time while you can?'

'That supposes that doing good and having a good time are at odds. That supposes that doing bad makes you feel good. Two serious fallacies.' He looks blank. 'Do you ever wonder why it is we're all here?'

'I don't know why half the world's here – bleeding waste of space, most of them.'

'That's a bit harsh. I believe that God created us with one over-riding aim: that we should experience his world to the full, learn-ing to be whole human beings ... not perfect – if He'd wanted that, He'd have kept us with Him – but whole. To be whole is to be holy ... though the link goes way beyond words. Doing wrong will only satisfy you –' He glares. '– that's to say any of us, if we sup-press our better natures. Which is the opposite of that wholeness and a punishment in itself.'

'You mean it's like when you're a kid and you do summet spite-ful and the teacher says you're only hurting yourself?'

'Exactly.' The power of my theme allows me to forget my predica-ment. 'And there can be no surer guide to those better natures than children, since, unlike the rest of us, they haven't bought into any book-based morality. For instance, do you remember, as a boy, ever doing something which you knew to be wrong – even though no one had told you – and then being found out?'

'I was always found out, me. Couldn't breathe without some-thing breaking.'

'Let's say, for the sake of argument, that you were punished.'

'There were no argument about it, mate. I saw more of my old man's belt than he did.'

'But which was the real punishment? The belts and the early-to-beds and the lost privileges, or the feeling that you'd let people down: your parents, your friends, your teachers and, most important of all, yourself?'

'No contest. The beltings.'

'Don't you think you may be muddling two sorts of pain? The belt may have smarted more for a short while –'

'With my old man, you couldn't sit down for a week.'

'But it's the spiritual hurt – call it guilt or disgust or disillusion – which is the real killer ... so much so that we bury it deep within ourselves, where it festers for the rest of our lives.'

He stares at me as keenly as if I were proposing a plan to break out of the cell. Then he stands up and, much to my relief, moves to his own bed.

'If you ever feel like packing in the preaching, Vicar, I wouldn't half mind having you as my brief.' He lies on the ledge, pulling the threadbare blanket over him. It exposes his body like a parcel torn in the post.

'Would you like to swap places?' I venture, as he tosses and turns.

'You what?'

'Since you've been here before. It's sometimes easier to sleep in a familiar bed.'

'You take the biscuit, you do.' I am unable to tell whether he is amused or angry. 'Vicar or not, you wouldn't last five minutes down our way.'

The offer dismissed ... the discussion over, he pulls the blanket around him and stares at the wall. I cast covert glances at his coil-like body, taking heart from his presence rather as a naughty child is reassured by a naughtier friend. So much for all my fine phrases! In the last resort, I clasp at the same sodden straws as everyone else.

I wake up from a fractured sleep full of fervid images. Far from feeling refreshed by the nightly Feast of Fools, I am as stale as though I had sat through a four-hour sermon. Barry is perched on the makeshift lavatory. He clearly fails to share my qualms about either noises or smells. I am grateful for my constipation and decide that, as an added precaution, I shall refuse all food ... a resolution which is strengthened by the arrival of breakfast. Watching Barry wolfing down the sausages and bacon, I conclude that his best defence would be to invite the jury to eat with him. Anyone who sees the way he shovels the meal into his mouth must reassess his motives in making a Strasbourg goose of his wife.

In my concern for my own plight, I have forgotten Christ's. A sudden recollection of the day reinforces my abstinence: a decision which Barry takes as a personal affront.

'What's wrong? Too proud to eat with me then?'

'Not at all. It's Good Friday. I always fast before the noon service.'

'Oh yeah. Well you won't mind if I have this then.' He swaps our trays. '"Waste not want not," as the Good Lord said.' He winks as though offering me food for thought.

'Did He?' I ask, wishing that I were better versed in the Bible.

'Course.' He looks at me suspiciously. 'At the Feeding of the Five Thousand. When He give them all the scraps.'

Breakfast over, his frustration increases. He rails at 'the filth' for keeping him locked up without charge. As he fires off grievances, I find it impossible to distinguish which are aimed at me and which at the wall. So I sit as unobtrusively as possible, with a shop-window grin on my face. He begins to exercise, filling the airless cell with the violent thrust of his body and the acrid smell of his sweat. He throws himself into a punishing routine of press-ups, coupling the movements with advice on the importance of remaining fit. He orders me to keep count and then berates me for failing to keep up. I am rescued by an officer announcing visitors. I follow him out under strict instructions to 'fetch back some fucking fags'.

The labyrinth of corridors leaves no trail of memories to aid my escape. But, at last, we come to a small room where Huxley is sitting with a woman whom he introduces as his solicitor. The officer, in a voice like sifting sand, informs us that we can talk for up to half an hour. I find it hard to look Huxley in the face and am amazed when he returns my apologies ... his inadvertent disclosure of my whereabouts can hardly be compared to my breach of trust. Tears well in his eyes as he asks what sort of God can allow this to happen. His agonizing seals my guilt. No matter what the verdict on the other charges, my true crime – and one for which I can never be forgiven – is to have undermined his faith.

Time is running out and I have still to consult the solicitor. Exuding confidence in her I-know-how-to-play-the-game black suit offset by the but-don't-think-I'm-not-my-own-woman red glasses, she explains her strategy. It seems that, far from being a gamble, her demand that the police either charge me or release me is as familiar a gambit as Queen's Pawn to Queen's Pawn Four ...

although it has yet to draw any response other than that they are still conducting their inquiries. She describes how they can hold me for twenty-four hours without charge, and a further thirty-six in the case of a 'serious arrestable offence', (causing the twelve which I have already spent to pale into insignificance). At which point, I abandon hope of Easter. Christ will rise from the tomb while I remain locked in the cell.

The Duty Officer takes such pleasure in telling us our time is up that I fear for his children's welfare. He replies with a terse 'No can do' when the solicitor requests that I be held on my own. Barely muffling his ill-will, he points out that, with no Magistrates' Court sitting on Good Friday, the station is chock-a-block. He leads me back to the cell, where Barry's grim face reminds me of my forgotten mission. I proffer an excuse, which he interrupts with a torrent of abuse, forcing me to revise any notion of his inarticulacy. As he details his disgust and my perversion, I realize that some enlightened policeman has let him into the secrets of my bloodstream.

He demands an explanation. 'How can you ... a vicar? It's a fucking joke. You're supposed to be better than the rest of us.' Reluctant to enter a debate on the nature of priesthood, I put it to him that the virus is a by-product of love.

'You call that love ... that's what I shit down.'

'And that's what you piss from.' I am goaded into attack. 'I used to think that it was a fault in our design that we made love with the same organs we used for excretion.'

'You what?'

'But now I see that it's right we should transcend our bodies just where we're trapped by them. Every part of us is holy. God created us. Christ shared our natural functions.'

'Can it, can't you! Now you're really out of order. Just 'cos I don't go to church don't mean that I ain't got respect. And there's two things you never slag off: a bloke's tart and his religion.'

I think with envy of the saint – wasn't it Christopher? – who converted his fellow inmates in prison.

'Fucking weirdo! You're lucky I don't land you one,' he adds. 'But I ain't going to take the risk.'

Our breath punctuates the silence. I fear that the stertorous irregularity of mine will fuel his fears of infection, and I am relieved when the Duty Officer hauls me out for questioning. The relief is short-lived. Against all the evidence, they persist in trying to establish a connection between the cemetery and the Abbey; it is as if, in their subservience, they cannot conceive of anyone but a satanist attacking the Queen. I lead them through the chapter of accidents as emphatically as a first-time author. I insist that my only offence was to break into the cemetery and that, if they are still not satisfied, they should contact the Clerk of Works who interrogated me at the Abbey. Much to my dismay, they reply that they already have.

Ignoring the solicitor's protests, they send me back to the cell. Barry may be nowhere to be seen, but he remains in spirit or, rather, in stench, clinging to me in unwanted intimacy.

After lunch (the hour not the meal), the solicitor calls on me *in situ*. Her mask of impassivity on entering the fug is either a tribute to the rigour of her training or a pointer to the routine of such visits. I fail to find out which, for she immediately embarks on a long apology for the delay and an account of a further development. Lyndon's mother has discovered a cache of pornographic magazines under his mattress, which she is trying to link to me.

'As model or supplier?' I ask bitterly.

'It may be,' she says, in such measured tones that I know it undoubtedly is, 'that, in order to exculpate himself, he's trying to lay the blame on someone else.'

Poor Lyndon! My heart goes out to him, in spite of all that he has done to me and, what's more, seems still to be doing. His attempt to keep adolescence at arm's length has been exposed with a vengeance more public than acne. He is as stripped of modesty as a nun who wakes from surgery to find a group of students examining her remaining breast.

'Is there nothing else they'd like to pin on me while they're at it? The disappearance of that racehorse, or Lord Lucan?'

'Your only job is not to lose heart. Let me see to the rest. It may just take a little longer than we anticipated.'

'It's Good Friday. My only job ... my only place is in church.'

'I might try to rustle up a radio. There's bound to be a service or at least selected highlights on Radio Four.'

I venture to suggest that it is hardly the same and that, in any case, it is unlikely to prove acceptable to the rock-tuned ears of my cell-mate. She assures me that I need have no fears about Barry who has been released without charge. But, instead of relief, I feel outrage at such preferential treatment. They free a suspected murderer – 'pending further enquiries,' she interjects – while I, who have committed no offence – 'and have yet to be charged', she adds – remain locked up. She departs with the promise that she is right behind me. Yes, I think, like an actress kissing a soldier as she waves him off to war.

Despair grins at me like the faces at the grille. 'Take my hand,' it says, 'rest your head on my shoulder. After all, who else do you have? Not Christ. He is busy on the Cross, suffering the torments of the damned. He has no interest in you. He's banned you from the church. You've been scrubbed from the guest-list ... *persona non grata* at the Passion. And don't kid yourself that His hands are tied. Nailed perhaps.' His laugh rattles like a shower of pills. 'But not tied. Do you think that the man who raised Lazarus from the dead couldn't arrange for them to drop a few charges? It's time you learned to recognize your real friends.' He speaks the truth. I have no companion but bitterness: no consolation but pain. And I lay my head on the slippery slope of the welcoming shoulder.

'That's right,' says Despair. 'Despair.'

Mocking policemen, their faces like passport photographs, peer into the cell as though to underline the distinction between solitude and privacy. One throws in a selection of the day's papers to help me pass the time. I thank him for the first act of kindness I've encountered since my arrest ... he has gone before I have time to retract. I've been crucified – which is not a word I use lightly on this of all days. With blithe disregard for the facts, they manage to make a sustained narrative out of a series of isolated incidents. The *Sun's* headline, *AIDS Vicar Spits at Queen*, contrives to contain three inaccuracies in a single sentence (even so, I doubt that it's a record). There is equally unedifying fare inside, as I find on turning to Page Three for my *Good Friday Dish of the Day*: *Miss Hot Cross Buns*.

Other papers show more subtlety, but no less bile, in their familiar display of mean-mindedness masquerading as morality. They publish statements from Huxley which make far sorrier reading than the front-page distortions of the *Sun*. In them, he denies that he had any knowledge of my sexuality, upholds the teaching of the Church on the supremacy of marriage and insists that he would never permit the blessing of same-sex couples at St-Mary-in-the-Vale. Now I understand why he felt the need to apologize so profusely. Their stories do, however, have one virtue. The more I read, the more reconciled I grow to my detention. And I consolidate my new-found friendship with Despair.

The solicitor returns in the evening with the news that, whether off his own bat or in deference to a higher authority, the Superintendent has signed the Extension Order. As I shrug off the prospect of a prolonged ordeal, she praises me for taking it so calmly. The truth, however, lies less in tranquillity than in indifference. I have reached a state of apathy where the sunny side of the street isn't sweeter, merely sweatier, and the grass isn't greener, merely parched. As a palliative, she announces that Huxley has left my sponge bag and a change of clothing with the Cell Officer. I express surprise in view of his remarks to the reporters. She chides me for a cynic, adding that he also tried to bring me the Reserved Sacrament, but the Duty Sergeant refused permission until the wafer was analysed.

'What did he think it contained?' I ask in amazement. 'Cyanide?'

'They're paranoid about drugs.'

Time tiptoes by as though around a sick-bed. I lie on my ledge and wait for the Cell Officer's crowing to usher in the morning. In the event, I find that his manner towards me has changed. The reason becomes clear when he takes me in to see the Super-intendent, who declares that, after reviewing all the evidence, they have decided not to press charges. My initial feeling is less of relief than of affront ... as if I had queued all night for a smash-hit play only to discover that there were seats at all prices. He rejects my request for an explanation, saying simply that, had it been left to him, the outcome would have been very different. Then he hands me back to the Cell Officer who returns my property and instructs me to be at the front entrance at ten o'clock, ready for the car which is coming to collect me.

At ten past ten, with my watch newly strapped to my wrist, my shoes newly laced, and my collar snapped back into place, I stand in the fumy air of the jagged street. I feel faint and fear the worst until I remember that it is a day and a half since I ate. Counting on Huxley's chronic unpunctuality, I plan a quick dash to a nearby sandwich-bar, when a car pulls up at the kerb. 'Hop in. I couldn't park anywhere. Didn't they tell you I was coming? Some bloody policeman had the nerve to move me on.'

I stand transfixed. It isn't Huxley after all but the Diocesan Communications Officer, the Bishop's right-hand man, popularly known as Moloch. He arrives bearing a summons from his master. 'Hurry up. It's a double yellow. Pull the knob backwards. No, backwards. That's right.' I feel as though I am stepping into a tumbril.

Moloch, whose greatest coup to date is to have placed his boss as the celebrity guest on the National Lottery following a widely pub-licized scriptural defence of its principles ('Acts 1, 26: "And the lot fell upon Matthias"'), makes no effort to hide his animosity. The Bishop is a television natural and Easter should be a key event in his diary. But, during the past two days, his appearances on *Question Time, Newsnight,* and even *Richard and Judy* have been highjacked by the controversy surrounding me. Instead of putting across his – and Christ's – message, he has been thrown onto the defensive by critics who have seized on one rotten apple in order to upset the entire cart.

Blanching at the charge, I attempt to vindicate myself but he cuts me off and turns his attention to the traffic, weaving in and out of lanes to a horn accompaniment which is hardly in the spirit of his Hoot For Jesus sticker. On arrival at London House, he leads me down a dark, prelate-lined corridor into an office where the Bishop's secretary greets us with a downtrodden smile.

'Working on a Saturday?' I ask.

'No peace for the wicked,' she says and bites her lip.

Moloch asks the whereabouts of the Bishop. In reply, she points through a doorway where he can be glimpsed bounding up the stairs, dressed in a purple tracksuit embroidered with a large silver cross.

'Isn't he something?' he says. 'I must catch him while he's changing.' He turns to me. 'You wait here.'

My hovering disconcerts the secretary, who invites me to take a seat, offering me a choice of reading of the *Church of England Newspaper* or *Hello*. I immediately plump for the latter, its incongruous presence explained by the picture-spread of our third most senior bishop and Mrs Bishop in their historic London home. My hunger grows acute and, despairing of any unprompted hospitality, I ask if I might have a cup of coffee and biscuits. She recoils as though from a pass, assuming an expression of such distaste that I am forced to remind her of where I have spent the last two nights; at which she jumps up and, keeping me firmly within her sights, edges around the room towards the kettle.

'Is there any choice?' I ask, as she pulls out the plainest biscuits from the filing cabinet.

Shocked by this further proof of my unbridled appetites, she replies as though it were a tenet of canon law. 'Chocolate are for suffragans. Bourbons for archdeacons. Vicars and curates get Rich Tea.'

I accept my stipendiary ration with a semblance of gratitude. By my third bite, she seems to find my chewing even more disturbing than my speech and suggests that I might be more comfortable in the Bishop's study. Her true impulse becomes clear when she opens the door and points to a cushionless oak chair with an emphasis which is no doubt laid down in another statute ... sofas are for suffragans; armchairs for archdeacons; vicars and curates must sit on wood. Assured of my compliance, she retreats to her room, leaving me beneath the beady eye (and piggy eyes) of a sub-Holbein Henry VIII.

Ignoring her instructions not to move – and the half-open door through which she might enforce them – I raise my cup to the monarch whose marital record, however instrumental to the founding of the Church, must be a constant affront to the Bishop's family values. Venturing further, I approach the desk and am disturbed by both its extreme orderliness (even the pencils are ranged according to length) and the trinity of inscribed photographs from Billy Graham, Margaret Thatcher and the Queen. I resume my seat in time to greet the Archdeacon, who seems as surprised to see me at liberty as I am to see him at all. After confiding that the Bishop has asked for his advice, he moves to the fireplace, flapping the seat of his soutane in the draught as though to dry it. He looks dreadful. No 'Just say no' poster could paint a more graphic picture of dissipation: his face at once pasty and flushed; his eyes wild but vacant; his few sweat-streaked strands of hair sticking to his scalp; his goitre grey with stubble.

'At least there's one person who comes out well from this whole sordid affair,' he says.

'Oh yes,' I say. 'And who's that?'

'Why me, of course.' He gazes at me in genuine surprise. 'I always knew that you weren't suited to Holy Orders. That's why I couldn't keep you as my curate. You lack so many of the qualities essential to the priesthood: dignity; forbearance; self-restraint.' He rewrites history as though it were an entry in his diary.

'The reason you got rid of me was because of Julian. Our happiness drove you to despair. It threatened everything you hold dear: the hair shirt of your sexuality.'

'That's libellous! I have witnesses.' He swings round and recoils as he faces the King. 'You have no proof.'

'When Julian went – in part ... in large part, I should say, because of the strain of keeping up a front which would withstand your sniping – who was it who propositioned me and charged me with disobedience when I refused?'

'The effluence of a foetid imagination.'

'Who was it who had a spare key cut for my flat?'

'It was parish property!'

'And came bursting in on me when I was in the bath?'

'In my day, curates took one bath a week before Sunday mass. They didn't loll around all day blowing bubbles.'

'And, in your day, no doubt, the way for a vicar to greet his curate was by making a grab at his genitals. Well, for your information, times have changed.'

'You're evil,' he screeches at me. 'You're the anti-Christ.'

Before I know it, he has flung himself at me, lashing out with his elbows. As I parry his puppet-like blows, he topples onto a standard lamp, dislodging the shade which lands like a mitre on his head.

I am chilled by the glint of madness in his eyes. I know him well for a tyrant and a bully, but sheer irrationality is a side of him which I have never before encountered. I lean over his chest, breathing in the familiar smell of pear-drops and rust, and try to pull him up. He pushes me away.

'Remember,' he warns with a glassy intensity, 'the dogs who drank Jezebel's blood.'

Roused by the noise, the secretary rushes into the room. 'You've assaulted the Archdeacon,' she gasps.

'No. It's my fault. I tripped over the wire,' he says, forced to exculpate me in order to protect himself.

'But I heard you shout.'

'What are you? A spy? Does the Bishop employ you to eaves-drop?' He slaps away her hand as she tries to guide him to a chair.

'Don't fuss. I'm not four years old.'

'You must sit down.'

'Impossible,' he says. 'I'm a martyr to piles.'

'I'll try to find out what's keeping the Bishop,' she says, blushing deeply. 'He may need rescuing from his wife.'

The instant she leaves, the Archdeacon draws an imaginary line between us. He walks to the window and stares out so intently that I visualize a team of scaffolders. In a momentary respite from my own wretchedness, I contemplate the aridity of his life, locked in the vicarage with his mother, now well into her eighties but still insisting, to the horror of the parish, that she doesn't feel a day over forty. She cooks for him, cleans for him and entertains his friends, a closed circle of priests of a similar age and inclination, relics from an era of reticence, sadly unaware that a sea-change in society has rendered their secrecy as obsolete as their slang.

Misogyny is the Archdeacon's cardinal virtue. Women are a closed book to him, unless they are carrying a prayer-book, unwel-come except when they are kneeling in the nave ... or, better still, embroidering the kneelers. The sole exception – apart from his mother – is Mary, who barely functions as a woman at all, giving birth from a bloodless womb through an intact vagina. He treats her with the reverence that his lay counterparts accord to a great female star such as 'Judy'. His icons are their memorabilia. I counted sixteen Virgins in his living-room alone: the most telling, poised in triumph over the serpent which tempted Eve, stamping the slither of sexuality underfoot.

The Bishop's entrance brings my speculation to an end. He bounds into the room as though he has read in a Self-Help Manual that first impressions count, scowls at me and then turns to the Archdeacon.

'Ah Alf.' The Archdeacon shrinks from the diminutive as if from a blow. 'Good of you to come at such short notice. Your lady-mother said you'd been praying all night.'

'It's my practice on Good Friday.'

'Well, you know my three rules for a balanced life. Prayer, prayer and more prayer. But sit down. You look tired.'

'Forgive me, Bishop,' he says sanctimoniously. 'If you don't mind, I'll stand. My joints...'

The Bishop turns to me. 'Do you pray?'

'Yes, of course, every day.'

'I don't mean ten minutes here and there: that's spiritual tourism. To pray is to inhale God and to exhale self.' He makes it sound like jogging. 'Shall we pray together now, the three of us?'

'Bishop, I've no wish to interrupt,' the Archdeacon says, 'but I've been on my knees all night. I have an Easter Vigil to prepare. There are some little people I have to visit.' He swallows a laugh on the 'little'.

'Very well.' The Bishop sounds put out. He fixes me with a frown. 'I don't suppose you've ever appeared on television?'

'As a matter of fact, I have. Before I trained, I was an actor –'

'And still are,' the Archdeacon exclaims.

'I mean for real: as yourself.'

'Only on chat-shows.'

'Stop interrupting.'

'I'm sorry. I thought it was a question.'

'You're doing it again!' He regains his composure. '"Only on chat shows" ... if Our Lord ate with publicans and sinners, should I turn up my nose at *Richard and Judy*?' This time, I keep silent. 'I was left with egg on my face in front of two million viewers. And I mean yolk ... thick, sticky yolk. All I heard was "Gay Curate" ... "AIDS Vicar".'

'May I say right now that I don't have AIDS. I'm simply infected with the HIV virus.'

'There's a virus infecting the lifeblood of the church: homosexual clergy!' As he bangs his fist on the desk, he displays an alarming resemblance to the portrait of Henry VIII. 'I want to support you ... and all the rest of my team in their ministry. But I cannot condone sin. It's my duty to uphold the Biblical ideal. We all fall short – the Archdeacon and myself as much as anyone ... isn't that

so, Alf? – and yet we can be forgiven, just as you can. Only, first,
you have to repent.'

'It's not that easy.'

'Don't you believe in repentance?' The Bishop's shock is
palpable.

'Of course I do, but not in the running-up-credit-and-then-
settling-the-bill-at-the-end-of-the-month sort so prevalent in the
Church. And I'm in good company. Christ Himself laid far less
emphasis on repentance than on God's all-forgiving love.'

'He not only persists in his sin; he revels in it,' the Archdeacon
squeals.

'What sin?' I ask.

'Homosexuality,' the Bishop declares, with the assurance of one
who reads aloud the ingredients on cereal-packets, 'is against God
and against Nature.'

'I would dispute that ... may I dispute that? I presume that
you've invited me here to explain my position.'

'You have been *ordered* here to hear the Bishop's decision,' the
Archdeacon interjects.

'No, let him speak. Never let it be said that Ted Bishop refused a
man a hearing.'

'I don't believe it's against God because I believe that it comes
from God who is the source of all love.' The Archdeacon looks as if
he is being forced to sit through *The Singing Nun*. 'And, as for
Nature, we must first define terms. Do we mean some idealized
Mother Nature, as serenely unreal as an icon of the Virgin?' The
Archdeacon shifts uncomfortably. 'Or do we mean the sum total of
everything we find in Nature? In which case the charge is self-
evidently false. Nature is, first and foremost, about striking a balance, and, far from distorting that balance, homosexuals are essential to its preservation.'

'You can talk,' the Bishop says, 'but how well can you listen?
And, when you listen, are you sure it's not just to the beatings of
your own lustful heart? You've no idea how hard I've wrestled with
this issue. My wife and I lie in bed at night weeping over homosexuals.' I lose the thread of his words in the image of soggy win-
ceyette. 'I've prayed and I've sought help from Scripture, and all I
find are clear condemnations of homosexuality, and the depiction
of marriage as the fulfilment of God's plan for mankind. It's there
right from Genesis, not just in Eden but in the Flood. When God
rescued the various species, He sent them in two by two, not one
with his "significant other".'

'But that's a myth.'

'I know it's a myth; I haven't just got off the boat! But why does He give us the myth, if not to show us the deeper truth ... the story not just of one man but of every man. God created marriage so that mankind could have what's best. Anything else is a perversion of His gift of sexuality.'

I feel the weight of the Bible pressing down on me like a débutante learning deportment. I struggle to shrug it off.

'With respect, you couldn't be more wrong. My sexuality, like yours, is a gift from God. It's not an aberration or a deviation or a disorder. I fell in love ten years ago and it transformed my life. I felt taller and fuller and stronger and more alive. I grew out of myself and closer to God. When I applied for ordination, I made no secret of the relationship.'

'My predecessor had many sterling qualities, but judgement wasn't one of them. Take it from me, you'd never slip through the net today.'

'Then I believe that would be everyone's loss. My vocation was real and my love was real and each fed the other. If I'd said "I shouldn't feel like this" ... if I'd denied my sexuality, I'd have become a sour, resentful human being and I'd have turned against God.' I daren't look at the Archdeacon. 'The one thing which I wouldn't have altered was my sexual desire.'

'Which, judging by your disease,' the Bishop says, 'remains insatiable.'

'It isn't a disease; it's a diagnosis.'

'You can hardly expect ordinary people to appreciate the distinction,' the Archdeacon interjects.

'Maybe not. But I can expect bishops.'

'Don't shout at me, son!' the Bishop says. 'You forget your duty.'

'I'm sorry.'

'So where is this person now?'

'He died at the beginning of this week.'

'I see.'

I rage at the lack of even the most perfunctory expression of regret. 'Although we split up some time ago, we spent nearly six years together.'

'In the eyes of God, there's no difference between six years and six minutes. The only distinction is between temporary and permanent. My wife and I have been married for thirty-five years. We know the meaning of "till death do us part".'

'Unlike some of us who are stuck on "till society – or the Church – do us part".'

'I'm tired of all your whingeing. You people ask us to be liberal:

to sanction those in stable relationships. But how many so-called "stable relationships" last? And how many unstable relationships does it take before you become an unstable person?'

'I wouldn't know. I've only had one ... relationship, that is. And the reason that it broke up owed a great deal to the Church. Why not ask the Archdeacon to explain? After all, I was his curate.'

The Bishop looks in surprise at the Archdeacon, who turns crimson with rage and embarrassment.

'That much is true. I was the first of his victims. I did battle with him.' He emits a strange yelp-like laugh. 'But I lost. Which is why I had to send him packing. His shamelessness mocked my celibacy.'

'And exposed your deceit.'

'You evil man!'

'I refused to deny half my life.'

'You could have married,' the Bishop suggests.

'Oh yes? And what was my wife supposed to do? Curl up with the Good Book and think of the Church of England?'

'That's right: descend to smut.'

'I stopped going on Retreats when I grew fed up of fending off clergy on weekend-release from their wives.'

'You see; he even stoops to blackmail!'

The Bishop and I share a moment of bemusement at the Archdeacon's outburst.

'Are you sure you're all right, Alf?' the Bishop asks. 'You don't look yourself at all. Why not pull up a chair?'

'It's my haemorrhoids.'

'There are plenty of cushions.'

'I have an inflammation around my entrance.'

The Bishop stares at him coldly. 'Most people, Archdeacon, would call it an exit.'

The Archdeacon flounders wildly. 'I'll kneel then, shall I? Will that suit everyone?' He falls lumpily to the ground as if in prayer. The Bishop looks beleaguered, unsure whether to reason with him or to reprimand me. He opts for the latter.

'I'm now more convinced than ever that you have no future in this diocese. We've not heard one single word of contrition in all you've said. What's more, you've forfeited the authority of the Church. How can you tell other people to repress their desires when you've made no attempt to repress your own?'

'But I've no wish to tell them anything of the sort. There's quite enough repression already. The serpent occupies far too central a place in our culture.'

'He mocks the very foundations of the Church,' the Archdeacon
shrieks.

'No, not the foundations,' I reply, 'merely some later embellish-
ments which stand like a rood-screen obscuring the Cross.'

'Enough! You've left us in no doubt as to your attitude. Well
shall I tell you mine?' the Bishop asks, as if extracting a piece of
gristle from his teeth. 'Homosexuality is caused by diabolic posses-
sion. The victims are infected by demons which enter through the
anus.'

Without noticing, I have been transported back more than four
hundred years. The portrait on the wall is that of the reigning
monarch. The stake is being prepared for me on the green outside
. . . unless benefit of clergy reduces my sentence to branding.

'God has made me your bishop and called me to drive the devils
out of you. So I shan't abandon you, whatever the provocation.
What I shall do is to suspend your licence . . . Do you think, at this
point, you might make the effort to stand, Archdeacon?'

The Archdeacon tries to rise but his legs give way; which puts
me in the anomalous position of propping up one of my judges.

'The police, as you know, won't be pressing charges,' the Bishop
adds.

'They'd look pretty stupid if they did.'

'For which you can thank me. But don't imagine you're off the
hook. We shall be investigating all the claims made by the parents
of –' he glances at his notes – 'Lyndon Brooks as well as the various
irregularities of conduct. You'll have a full opportunity to state your
case before we reach a final decision. In the mean time, you have
twenty-four hours to leave the parish.'

'What?'

'You're at liberty to go where you choose, but my secretary has a
list of retreat-houses which have served the purpose in the past . . .
in your case, I strongly advise that you choose one of the convents.
We don't want to risk any problems with impressionable young
monks.'

'This is sheer vindictiveness; I've done nothing wrong.'

'That will be for the investigation to decide. Now you may go.' I
make my way to the door. 'One last thing.' He catches me at the
threshhold. 'On no account, are you to make any statement to the
media without clearing it through my office. Our Communications
Officer is on hand to advise you twenty-four hours a day.'

Consolation mocks me like an understudy . . . I should never
have left the stage. As I make my way through the secretary's
office, she bows her head as though to avoid even eye contact. I am

tempted to ask what sort of biscuits are specified for suspended curates, but I can already hear the answer: 'the crumbs'. I enter the tube and find, to my horror, that I am sitting opposite myself on the front page of the *Daily Mirror*. Further revelations are promised on Pages Six and Seven; but they remain, at least temporarily, out of view. I take some comfort when my anxious glance along the corridor is met with blankness. I suppose that I must be unrecognizable without my horns.

The yellowing air of yesterday's news clings to me as I reach my front gate unmolested by any journalists. The only sound comes from a neighbour's car, wailing like an abandoned child, its alarm invalidated by indifference. I hurry indoors to plan my future. 'Twenty-four hours to leave the parish' beats like a metronome in my brain. Where am I to go? To which of my friends should I offer the dubious privilege of housing me? I could ring a fellow priest, inviting him to show the hospitality of Christ and risk the wrath of the Bishop. Or I could contact one of my former colleagues, explaining that, after six years in London's longest-running farce, I am ready for a change of role. Or I could go back further still … 'Mum, it's Blair. Remember, I told you that I wasn't free this Easter? Well, circumstances have changed and I find myself at a loose end.' I anticipate a gulp at the other end of the line. 'Oh son!' she says, taking her cue from my father. 'You know that this is always your home. But it's such short notice. I'll have to stock up on all your favourite things: Rubber gloves; paper plates; bleach' … I despair of the cynicism with which I keep despair at bay.

Packing and preparation take second place to the attractions of my bedroom wall, which I contemplate as though it were a sacred relic. It is yet one more in this chapter of ironies that I should attain such a prayerful state when I have no further use for prayer. The only thing which distracts me is my stomach. Since I have no wish to add bodily mortification to my spiritual woes, I augment the London House biscuits with a pork pie. Then, having spent the early afternoon disproving the analogy between boredom and staring at paint, I spend the second half in front of the television. The BBC is celebrating Easter with the biblical epic, *King of Kings*. I watch listlessly as a Hollywood gloss is put on the gospel story, all complexities as carefully removed as the hair from Our Lord's armpits.

The telephone rings and the answering-machine intercepts a further torrent of abuse. For once, however, I decide to respond. I make no attempt to reason with the caller who doubtless lost his reason during the twenty years in the Territorial Army which he cites like a badge of authority. I counter with every graphic green-room epithet that I learned in my twenties. The line goes dead, but the machine whirls on, soaking up my vitriol. It is as though any obligation to forgive my enemies has been suspended along with my licence.

I am shaken by the vigour of my violence. It is as unexpected as my ability to tap for a tour of *The Boyfriend*, where my two left feet were given a solo spot. But, this time, there is no one to applaud. I stand alone to face the full force of my rejection by both God and man. I try to console myself with thoughts of the Cross, but they are no longer sustaining. Christ's despair, which once filled me with hope, now seems to be empty rhetoric, a momentary lapse brought on by His agony. If He'd truly believed that His Father had forsaken Him, He would not have promised the Penitent Thief to be with him in paradise later that day. But my despair ... were I to allow myself to despair ... were I to give way to my feelings ... would be boundless. Christ's suffering was part of God's plan, whereas mine is part of His indifference. I fall like a shaving to the carpenter's floor.

Christ transcended the Cross; His death was His triumph. I shall become my death ... it will devalue my life. Blair Ashley, the curate of St Mary-in-the-Vale? Blair Ashley whom I worked with at the Royal Court? Blair Ashley who was a pupil at St Peter's, Penkhull? Wasn't he infected with ... ? I heard he was struck down by ... Didn't he die of ... ?

Silence completes the sentences, the condition contained in the taboo. But, as I won't be here, why should I worry? 'I'm going to die ... I'm going to die ...' I break into a playground chant. But, when I try to envisage the course of my slow decay – fixing my head onto Julian's body – reality seeps through. I hear again the scratchy strings of his breath; I see the mocking standstill of his legs; I stroke the hungry contours of his flesh. I mourn for a life which is over too soon and a death which lingers too long. Meanwhile, the Church wrings its hands and covers its options. The Body of Christ has AIDS ... I wouldn't mention that on Sunday, Vicar. You'll put them right off their Easter eggs.

The Body of Christ has AIDS ... there's no need to tell me, chum; I've bought the badge, banged the drum, waved the collection box. That's what is so unfair. I'm not some Paisleyite bigot determined to Save Ulster From Sodomy ('Oh, hello there, King Billy; of course, we wouldn't be meaning you!'). Both in the pulpit and at the altar, I have made my commitment clear. But now my compassion will be compromised. Everything I say or do will be deemed to be self-interest. 'Naturally, he preaches the all-inclusive love of God,' they'll sneer. 'He has no choice.'

Dusk creeps over my deliberations. I flag as my circular arguments become elliptical. My boiler-room head is in need of fresh air and I decide to take a walk. Although my proximity to the Heath has long been a subject of mirth among my more knowing friends, the truth is that I have never ventured out there after dark. What a fellow curate, much to my surprise, once called a great natural resource (as though leather-clad men were part of the indigenous flora and fauna) has remained strictly off-limits. Nevertheless, like Gandhi sleeping beside young girls, I have been glad to have the temptation at hand to prove that I am able to resist.

Now, my feelings have changed. I am anxious to make up for lost time. In spite of all my brave words to the Bishop, I have not had a single lover since Julian. I gave up any chance of intimacy in order to stay close to God, who has nonetheless abandoned me ... I am not naïve; I know that life is unfair, but I never thought that the unfairness would be so arbitrary. My one consolation is that it is not too late to discover what I have been missing: to leave St Mary's behind and explore my primal self in the shadows of the vegetation. And so, with a shiver of excitement tinged with transgression, I slip into the chill familiarity of the garden and out of the gate.

The clang of the grille marks my rite of passage. The moon is smothered by clouds and the breeze exudes a sappy threat. Horrifying images flash through the haze as I step onto the scrub. Treacherous tree-trunks shoot up before me with beanstalk alacrity. Stinging nettles jealously guard their patch. Sagging branches stretch across the root-rutted path. I long to sing my way to confidence but, as the only tune I can remember is *Onward Christian Soldiers*, I settle for silence. Stumbling forward, I trample on an old coke tin which offers a stark reminder of the daylight world of fizzy drinks and carefree people that I leave behind.

I edge further into the darkness, away from the houses and through a hollow, past benches dedicated to the memory of Hampstead gentlewomen who would be appalled at the company that they are now being forced to keep. An icy ray from the emerging moon cheers me and catches a squirrel, all twitches and tail. Part of me longs for it to lead me into the wild wood of a children's story, where the night-time challenge to domesticity can be savoured from the safety of fleecy pyjamas and flannel sheets. But the rest of me stands firm, as I enter a world in which I have no protection and where the greatest danger comes from dawn.

The path becomes more pronounced and the landscape more formal. I stride down an avenue of trees to the main road. I know that, from here, I will have a view of the church, but I am determined to avoid the stab of its spire. Instead, I fix my gaze on the entrance to the West Heath. Cars zoom by as in an amusement arcade. Dazzled by the glare, I rush headlong through them, provoking nothing more untoward than a flurry of horns. Such devil-may-care behaviour feels appropriate to my plight. I pass Jack Straw's Castle and gaze at all the bleary faces in beery fellowship. Loneliness hits me like a cramp and leaves me more desperate than ever to make contact. I turn down a clearing into an inky morass.

Tripping over a log, I slide down a mound first on my feet and then on my bottom. With my leaf-splattered sweater and jeans, I feel like Oberon and long to enter his realm of erotic enchantment. Puck and Pan are the presiding spirits of a place far more ancient than church or temple. The tangy air is dank with passion. Creepers twist and turn in their own coition. Wind-swept bushes expose their secret doorways like a maze. The setting is perfect, but it is devoid of people. My only companions are a pair of glow-worms circling each other in a luminous mating-dance. I watch, transfixed by the ritual, until I realize, with a jolt, that they are two men, choreographing their cruising with cigarettes.

The step-puff-blow movement intrigues me, and I begin to wish that I smoked. A cigarette has so many secondary uses: to steady the nerves; to break the ice; to light the way. I am extending the list to 'to occupy the hands' when I find that I need to keep mine free as one comes out of the blue – or rather the black – and gropes me. I freeze. The knowledge that this is why I am here doesn't make the intrusion any easier to accept. I have no idea of the etiquette (or lack of it) but, in any case, my penis shows no enthusiasm for his prying. I refuse to be reduced to a zipper and make to push him off, when he saves me the trouble. Deterred by the combination of soft flesh and stiff metal, he backs away.

'Ill met by cigarette-light, proud Titania,' I think, apropos of nothing, and brush any remaining leaves from my back before they give the wrong impression. I check my fly as though returning from the Gents. I resent the blatancy of his approach. It's not that I expect white wine and red roses, but I would hope for something more than an exchange of genitals. A second man sidles up, as if to demonstrate a different technique. 'You're the best-looking bloke I've seen all night,' he says, peering through the darkness. I would like to respond but, as the most I could manage would be a reference to his striking silhouette, I stick to 'Thanks'.

He moves towards me and plants a smudgy kiss on my lips. I bristle at the beard. 'Been here long?' he asks.

'No.'

'You'll find it busy.'

'Yes.'

'I've just been at the orgy-tree. It was crawling.'

I gulp at the designation, anxious not to betray my ignorance. I have heard of the umbrella tree and the monkey-puzzle tree and the bread-and-wine tree, but never the orgy-tree. I wonder if it is a botanical term suggested by its intertwined branches or an unofficial name for a genus specific to Hampstead Heath.

'Prick-tease!' the man says and walks away.

I decide to advance deeper into the woods, which my pagan mind defines as a journey of liberation and my priestly mind as a descent into an inner circle of Hell. I pass a condom hanging limply from a twig like a pussy willow and try not to speculate on the variety of squelches underfoot. I arrive at a grove where, illuminated by a grey light which puts me in mind of an automatic car-wash, two young men are having very public sex. The six-of-the-best position of one across an ossified stump is accentuated by the slippery thwack of flesh as the other rams into him. I am mesmerized by their lack of modesty which, imperceptibly, becomes mine.

Rustles in a nearby bush attract me as keenly as any woodland animal. Guided by my blood, I make my way into the murk. Three men are at play, their faces entwined in a mutual embrace which favours symmetry rather than commitment, their hands working each other's penis with a relentless rhythm reminiscent of a milking-shed. At times, one will stroke a chest or tweak an earlobe, but the basic pattern remains unchanged. Then one of them starts to quicken, his body buckling from nipple to knee. The others focus their attention exclusively on him. I turn away to allow him a moment of privacy and am given the all-clear not by any human exclamation but by the splash of spluttered leaves.

This is passion reduced to a muscular spasm . . . *la petite mort* to *le petit mal*. The man hauls up his jeans as casually as if he had pulled them down in a doctor's surgery (just for one night, can't I forget the virus?). Then, with a gentle slap on the two still naked backs but not a single goodbye or thank you, he moves off. I suddenly feel exposed. One of the remaining men summons me with a gesture which may, equally, be sending me away.

'What are you waiting for?' he shouts.

'I don't care to be the filling in a sandwich.'

'No, you'd rather be the crust.'

His words hit home as I realize that is exactly what I am becoming: stodgy, stale and peripheral. I move towards them, pulling out my penis like a handshake. They take it in turn to greet me, and the beast with three backs revives. Love has never seemed so impersonal as in the speed with which I fill the gap. Tongues flick at me and I tentatively taste each. Their kisses are totally different: the one, heavy and herby; the other, toothpaste-fresh. I long to take things slower ... to know them better, but they are intent on exploring permutations not possibilities. This eternal equilateral triangle is the perfect expression of our semi-detached state.

My own needs are swept aside as first one and then the other shudders to a climax. At last, I feel a connection as the blood pounds through their veins. It is so long since I have experienced the force that twists limbs into spasticity and speech into incoherence that I am quite disturbed. Then, like exhausted hosts reluctantly offering drinks to their only remaining guest, they redouble their efforts on me. But the roughness of their touch brings no satisfaction. So, as a matter of courtesy, I fake an orgasm, dabbing my fingers onto their damp bellies for corroboration. 'He's still hard,' one says admiringly, as he delves into my pants.

Leaving my companions to marvel at my virility, I take myself deeper into the woods. I am angry at having made the pretence. I am supposed to have thrown off all notions of self-sacrifice. Tonight is devoted to 'Nature red in tooth and claw' not 'It is more blessed to give than to receive'.

I trudge through a coppice, tripping over tendrils, when I pass a man lying lengthwise on a log. It is not until I am by his side that I distinguish him from a fungal growth on the bark. His head is masked and his body is swathed in leather – apart from his buttocks which are exposed in all their pallid vulnerability. He makes no acknowledgement of my presence except to point to a cloth on which are laid out, with dressing-table neatness, two small bottles, several condoms and a tube of grease.

I back away, wondering how to judge a love that not only doesn't speak its name but doesn't even exchange a glance. Is it anonymity stretched to the point of indifference? Or is it an escape from the constraints of personality into an expression of the universal will? I am no nearer an answer when I see someone else approaching the log: a huge man in late middle age, with a double chin and a triple paunch, grizzled hair and glasses. He takes a sniff from the proffered bottle, a condom from the pile and liberally applies grease to the buttocks. Then he enters them and begins to thrust. The masked man remains inert except for pressing the bottle to his nose. Their contact is so tenuous that I fail to see why one doesn't use a dildo and the other a doll.

I leave them to the carnal equivalent of ironing and continue my quest for ... what? Love? Degradation? At the bottom of a mound, I reach a stream or rather a slowly oozing river of mud. I take one of the stepping-stones and sink my feet with over-rapid relief into something verminous on the opposite bank. I run through the grass, twisting and turning like a dog with ticks. Through the foliage, I catch a glimpse of a road lined with mansion-blocks and feel uncomfortably close to civilization. At first, I was worried that I wouldn't be able to find my way out of the wood; now, I am not sure that I want to. These are my people; this is where I belong. I may be in Hell, but it is here that I must look for the authentic 'me'.

Putting the shimmer of Hampstead behind me, I once again brave the chimera of the Heath. I draw back a willowy curtain to find that Easter Eve has turned into Walpurgis Night. Some forty or fifty shadows are harnessing their sexual energy in a sort of satanic ceremony ... or so it seems to a mind steeped in religion (worship, even of the Devil, is something I am able to understand). But, as I circle the group, I realize that the reality is both more basic and more banal. This is the naked pursuit of pleasure: one so jaded that it is indistinguishable from pain and so brutish that the participants have modelled themselves on animals, their heads shorn of humanity, their bodies branded and pierced.

Hands, mouths and buttocks beckon as I prowl around the human zoo, the only animal without a keeper. One man, being whipped so hard that his back must be as tough as his leather trousers, accepts his torture like a medieval flagellant, a sensual asceticism which is no longer a contradiction in terms. A few yards along, a man being drenched in a stream of stranger's urine, welcomes the moisture as ecstatically as drought-relieving rain. Next to him, someone whom I take for a vet has his forearm buried in his partner's anus. He delves as if the secrets of the heart – of the soul – were to be discovered in the bowel ... as though he had a key to the mystery of life denied to those who observe more conventional practice. I wonder where it can end. And, as if to provide an answer, the man removes his arm, unlaces his boot, and tries to enter, instead, with his foot.

I turn away in horror, struck by the bitter irony that, while they are trying to rehabilitate the traditional domain of the Devil, I have discovered the reality of Hell. I curse my folly in putting myself through such torment. Where I hoped for a joyous brotherhood which would supplant the church fellowship, I have found only incest. Where I sought a bodily ecstasy which would compensate for the body of Christ, a communion of semen to replace the communion of saints, I have encountered only a darkness which breeds on darkness: a dance of death masquerading as a rite of spring.

I shudder as a man slopes up to me and puts his hand around my neck. 'Are you into bondage?' he asks.

'Of the flesh or of the spirit?' I reply, before running up a bank of stumps. I scramble so fast that I narrowly avoid spraining my ankle and pause to nurse it at the top, where I become aware of another man staring at me. I sense the intensity of his gaze, even though it is too dark to see his face, let alone his expression. I can make out nothing about him except that he is tall and solid and on his own, not hiding from himself in a group. Hope revives. My whole body pulses with the certainty of my desire. He whistles to me; I respond with breathy enthusiasm. He calls out 'Here boy; come to daddy,' and snaps his fingers. I should have known that it was too good to be true, and yet the flame in my flesh burns so fiercely that, if he wants to play games, I am willing to indulge him. He continues to shout 'Here boy, come,' as I sink to my hands and knees and crawl through the mud, stopping only inches away from him. I am just about to fling myself at his feet when I am pushed aside by a panting, padding ball of fur. It wasn't me the man was calling but his dog. 'That's my boy,' he says. 'Enjoyed your run?' And, without giving me so much as a glance – even of scorn – he snaps the lead on the dog's collar and takes him home.

I remain on my hands and knees, rejected by both man and beast. I want to laugh, but the back of my throat is so dry that I fear it will crack. Is there anything more contemptible than a slave afraid of his freedom: a free man who voluntarily places his head in another's yoke? If Eve had offered me the apple, I would have spat out the flesh and swallowed the pips.

I put my head in my hands and my hands in the mire. I will myself to return to the material of my creation. I lose track of time until the muggy comfort of the mud takes on a metallic sting and I find my fingers pinioned by a pair of steel-capped boots. Louring over me is a futuristic chauffeur in a peaked cap and a leather jacket laced so tightly as to accentuate every chest hair ... although the reflective glasses, which ought to crown the effect, in fact detract from it by throwing back an image of trees and bushes rather than the apocalyptic urban landscape essential for the full impact.

I shake like a schoolboy who has sneaked into an X-rated film only to wish it were *Bambi*. The man bends over me and presses a bottle to my nostril. Panic-filled visions of serial-killers battle with waves of pleasure. I feel as though I am on roller-skates which, when he presses the bottle to my other nostril, sprout wings. He drags me up to penis-level; although it takes me a while to realize which of the two now poking through his flies he wants me to suck. I try to focus as he guides me towards it. My lips clamp, and I trace the intimate connections of other men's mouths. 'Good boy,' he says, as though I were a baby sucking on a teat.

Once again, he holds the bottle to my nose. It is as potent as a power-station. The heath is floodlit with a single sniff. My head is woozy, but his penis supports me. My blood converts into a stream of diamonds which glitter beneath my translucent skin. All five senses explode and coalesce into taste as he forces my mouth to his chest. I suck a spot under the illusion that it's a nipple. He grabs me by the scruff of the neck, which proves to be a mistake when, as I suspected, it extends twelve foot into the air, becoming tangled with a bird's-nest in a nearby tree.

'Pull down your fucking pants,' he orders, demonstrating that the one thing which lies outside the bottle's control is language.

'Why?' I ask.

'Why do you think? I want to fuck you.'

My neck crumples onto my shoulders. My senses separate out. I want intimacy not invasion. There has to be more to sex than this.

'Have another sniff of poppers,' he says, seeking to shortcut my emotions.

'No, thank you,' I say, with a grim return to reality. 'I think I should go.'

'What do you mean? I'm not wasting half a bottle of poppers.'

My head throbs. I feel a flush under my cheekbones. The flood-lights have dwindled to a tawdry afterglow. All I can think of to say is 'I'm sorry'.

His manner alters. Leather is transformed into silk, as he pleads with me to take him in my mouth ... to bring him off quickly. But I retch as at a rancid shrimp and back away. He lunges at me, and I break into a trot. Beads of sweat slide down my forehead and into my eyes. I am unable to tell if the pounding in my brain is the effect of the drug or the sound of his boots in hot pursuit. I tear through the gorse as though through a hostile crowd. Thorns stab at my face, piercing the skin. Brambles and briars snag me from all sides. The stinging lash of thin boughs and the heavy smack of thick ones cut into my arms and legs. I begin to fear that the Bishop was right and that this is Nature's revenge on my perversity.

I keep on running until I emerge in a small grove. The change of atmosphere is immediately apparent. It feels tranquil and self-contained and almost sacred within the circle of ancient trees. I fall shivering to the ground, hugging my knees as the closest substitute for another pair of arms. The only warmth comes from the blood trickling down my face. I tentatively dab it on my tongue. It tastes rather like caviar ... who am I trying to kid? Cod's roe. I laugh, until I remember the extra ingredient (the opposite of a preservative), which makes it lethal to anyone but me. I burst into song: 'Me and my virus'. And I laugh so much that the tears roll down my cheeks. But they are no longer tears of joy.

I have no idea what to do. I have no home even on the Heath. Am I to wrap myself up in my diagnosis and bed down on the streets? I want to shriek out my anger with a pain to pierce the skies. But all I manage is a feeble echo: 'My God, my God, why hast thou forsaken me?'

'Surely things aren't that bad?'

I start. To my horror, I find that I have spoken the words aloud. There is someone else in the grove. I rise unsteadily to my feet and attempt an explanation. 'No, of course not. I'm an actor.'

'And you're having trouble finding work?'

'Not at all. It's a part I once played. My best. I was seeing if I remembered it.'

'Would I have heard of you?'

'I doubt it.'

'Try me.'

'Blair Ashley.'

'You're right. So, Blair Ashley, are you revisiting old haunts, or just old triumphs?'

'I beg your pardon?'

'That was supposed to be a subtle twist on "Do you come here often?". You've no need to reply. Almost everyone I meet is up here for the first time, or so they say. God knows why I attract them. I must have the right sort of face.'

'You do.' I make no attempt to match his subtlety. There is something about his face which I find immensely appealing. It is as much the associations as the features. With his broad forehead, pronounced eyebrows and brown curls, he is the spitting image of Blake's Adam.

'And do you?'

'Have the right face?'

'Come here often?'

'Oh,' I reply, like a novice aching to take his vows. 'From time to time.'

'Cruising?'

'Right. Though tonight turns out to have been a dry dock.'

He smiles. His teeth gleam in the moonlight. 'So you weren't looking for me?'

I am taken aback. This is the first hint that I might find a Mr Right on the Heath rather than simply a Mr Ready.

'Should I have been?'

'I told people – and told them to tell people – to meet me here.'

I have a sneaking suspicion that I may have stumbled on the orgy-tree unawares. 'Was that for any special reason?'

'Put your hand in my pocket.'

I hesitate, half-expecting a schoolboy rip ... a way to enliven double-Latin. But, instead, I plunge my hand into autumn.

'Isn't it a little late at night to go foraging?'

'They're the ashes of my best friend; I've come to scatter them.' I jump back as though they were still smouldering. 'I'm sorry. I shouldn't have done that. But don't worry, he's quite harmless. Neil meet ... I forget your name.'

'Blair.'

'Blair, of course. Blair. Well Blair, you're the last man I shall ever introduce him to. And, believe me, it's a privilege. I wish you could have known him when he was in – shall we say? – better shape.' He laughs like a taxidermist. 'This time last year, he was up here with the best of them. And then the virus began to take hold. He was in and out of Bart's as regularly as Sainsbury's. They always gave him the same bed. On his final visit, a supermodel turned up. I don't know whether it was a fund-raising event or a fashion shoot ... not that there's much difference. "I'm so jealous of AIDS victims," she said as she blew kisses like smoke-rings across the ward; "you have such perfect cheek-bones." And, six weeks later, he had the perfect skull.'

'Did it happen so quickly?' I try to hide the note of fear.

'With a little help from his chemist. That's what gets to me.' His voice falters. 'I'm not blaming him. It was his right ... his choice. I'm blaming myself for not letting him see that there was another one.'

'If, as you say, he made his own decision...'

'I was his best friend! What good is friendship if it can't make you change your mind? Of course I argued with him. I used to hate myself for arguing with him when he was so weak. But he never played for sympathy. He just asked what was the point ... when your world shrinks from pain-filled streets to pain-filled rooms to a pain-filled bed, what is the point? The only dignity lies

in choosing your death yourself and escaping the one that comes at
you in drips and swabs and kidney-bowls.'

'He may be right. You mustn't judge him.'

'I wasn't judging him. Is that what it sounds like? I loved him.
But I'm angry ... not just that he died but that he bought into
death. There was no need. A year ago, his blood counts were nearly
normal; then they took a tumble and he thought it was the end.
"There are ways of keeping stable," I said, "mind ways and body
ways." And he knew. Of course he knew. He knew about the drugs
and the trials and the therapies. But deep down here –' He pounds
his chest like a penance. 'He felt that he didn't deserve them. That
big bright star of a man believed that he should die. And so he did.'
His shoulders shake and I want to hug him, but I am more than
ever aware of the conflicts of intimacy. 'He asked me to scatter his
ashes here. It was his constant topic of conversation – at an age
when he should have been choosing where to go on holiday. He
said it was the place he'd been happiest. So here I am. I got rid of
the urn; I thought it might look ostentatious.'

'Are you doing it alone?'

'Seems like it. I spread the word among his friends. One o'clock
in the car-park by Jack Straw's Castle or one-thirty here.'

'Perhaps they couldn't find the way.'

'Most of them could have found their way blindfold. I shouldn't
have chosen Saturday night. But then Neil would have wanted
them to enjoy themselves.'

'If you'd like some company ...'

He looks at me for a moment. 'I'd like your company.'

'Why did you choose this particular Saturday? Are you
religious?'

'That's like asking if I'm English. It's where I was born.'

'If you wish,' I suggest tentatively, 'I could say a blessing. I'm a
priest.'

He sighs.

'You don't seem surprised.'

'You said you were an actor.'

'I was, but my life took a different turn.'

'I'd call that an about-turn. Still I don't suppose you're the only
vicar up here tonight. Then tomorrow morning you'll all be fulmi-
nating against sin from your pulpits.'

'Not me, I'm afraid. I've been banned.'

He stares at me. 'I know who you are. You're the guy there's
been all the fuss about ... the one who took on the Queen.'

'You make me sound like John Knox.'

'Give me your hand.' I feel the scratch of his friend on his fingers. 'You're much better looking than your photograph.'

'Thanks.' I am grateful that, for once, I need have no fears about blushing. 'But it wouldn't be hard. The *Standard* actually doctored my photograph to make me look sick.'

'The handshake's not enough. I'd like to kiss you.'

'You've read the articles?'

'Yes.'

'Then you know about the HIV?'

'I'd like to kiss you.'

I expect a cheek, but the darkness is deceptive and throws our mouths into unexpected conjunction. His kiss is a marvel of differing sensations, as the chapped roughness of his lips gives way to the oyster-tang of his tongue. I reach into his throat as though I were leaning into a well. I wish ... I wish ... The sensation is so intense and so simple, a physical compatibility which is as mysterious as grace.

We sink to the ground on a mutual impulse. The attraction has been fast, but not mechanical as it was in my earlier encounters. We seem to be tapping the ancient authority of the trees.

'Remind me to put a pound in the plate next time I pass a church,' he says.

'Only a pound. Should I be flattered?'

'It's the claimant's mite.'

'You're out of work?'

'I'm between decisions. I repair organs,' he says. 'The musical ones that is. The others I just make rise.' He puts his hand on my crotch as if to prove it. 'See!'

'I'm impressed.'

'No, I am.' He strokes my chin. 'Kirk Douglas the second.'

'In my dreams!'

'And I also have the virus.' His words chill me. This is the one unwelcome affinity. 'I say that because I want to be straight with you, not solemn. I'm not someone who believes that the dangers of HIV are all in the mind. But I do believe that the first line of defence against them is.'

'I've only just been diagnosed.' He squeezes my hands and recoils. 'I see you've noticed.' He raises the palms to his eyes.

'These don't look like lesions to me.'

'It's too dark to see properly. Please, you're making me nervous.' I snatch my hands away.

'Don't be. It may sound perverse, but I was never really happy until my diagnosis. I suppose that, for the first time, I wasn't

worried about the happiness ending. I wasn't trying to capture it or
to build on it ... just to live it. The future lay in the moment.
Accepting my own mortality meant that I no longer had to fear it.
Of course,' he says with a laugh, 'that doesn't mean that I'm not
going to live for ever.'

'You're saying you've made it work for you?'

'Right. I saw that the key thing was not to become a victim. Just
because I had HIV didn't mean I had nothing left to offer. Quite
the reverse. Even my blood which I thought was fatal can be used
to help people with lower counts than mine.'

'What do you mean?'

'Don't ask me to explain the science. You're talking to the
Princess Di of the chemistry labs. But it seems that plasma from
the blood of people who have HIV and high immune responses
can boost the cell-count of people with HIV who have low immune
responses. What's more I'm AB Negative – highly select. So, once a
month, I go off to the clinic and donate. That's something I could
never have done before HIV.'

'Giving blood so that somebody else can live?'

'Now don't go all sacramental on me. It's a medical treatment.'

'You're a remarkable man.'

'Has it taken you this long to realize?'

'And I don't even know your name.'

'Oliver.'

'Oliver...' I savour the word in my mouth as if it were his tongue.
'Oliver, the bringer of peace.'

'Is that so?' He smiles.

'You are to me ... as clearly as if you had an olive-branch in your
hand. I was in Hell but you've led me out.'

'It's mad. When I think of how often I've come up here to score
and gone home disappointed. Tonight I came for Neil; I didn't
even change my Calvins.'

'Were you and Neil lovers?'

'We were brothers. When he wanted to bug me, he called us
sisters. But then he always said I was seriously repressed.'

I kiss him. 'If you're repressed, I wonder what that makes me.'

He flicks his tongue over my eyes, across my cheek and into my
ear. 'I'd say: infinitely open to suggestion.' Just how open becomes
clear as he slips his hand into my trousers. I try to unzip my fly,
but he prefers to keep me constrained and pushes my fingers away.
My centre of gravity shifts: I am all groin ... and armpit and
nipple. I give thanks that, throughout the love-lean years, I never
let myself run to fat. I slide my hands down his bannister-smooth

shoulders and along his chest. I explore his matted strength, following the line of hair to his navel. I toy with his scrotum. He groans and tries to unbutton his fly, but I give him a taste of his own cruelty. He sneaks a kiss and lowers my guard. Before I know it, his pants are down by his ankles. His penis bursts free like a puppy. I laugh, and he asks if I'll share the joke. I decide to risk it. He looks surprised but not offended.

'Perhaps I should call it Fido,' he says.

'That means faithful,' I reply. He is silent. 'At least it did.'

He raises his penis to my mouth. I tantalize the tip with my tongue before devouring it. He tosses back his head and emits a succession of breaths which veer between pants and yelps. His body takes on its own rhythm. I cannot believe that I am giving him as much pleasure as he is giving me. Suddenly – and far too soon – he reaches orgasm. He pulls himself out of my mouth and throws himself forward, resting his weight on his hands. As he climaxes inches away from my cheek, a few ashes slip from his pocket onto my chest. He shudders into stillness, before kissing me on and around and inside the lips. He strokes my chest and discovers the sharpness.

'Neil?' he asks.

'Don't worry. The rest is still in your pocket.'

'It's as though he's giving us his blessing.'

I am touched by his words and trace my fingers over his eyes, which are warm with tears.

'Don't ask,' he says. 'Too many emotions. And kisses inside kisses like Russian dolls.'

'So find the solid one at the core.'

'If only we'd met ten years ago.' He strokes away the harshness of his words.

'Don't say that! We must try to make life what it was ten years ago.'

'And that's possible?'

'Of course. I'll put on my red braces and my Paul Smith suit.' He kisses me again, although now the kiss becomes the preliminary to the wet and winding journey from my mouth to my penis. He takes the scenic route, with detours which drive me to distraction. By the time he reaches his destination, I'm bucking like a fettered colt. I become madness in his mouth. Screaming and gurgling and crackling with fire, I split into my constituent atoms. I recognize the approaching climax and try to push him away. 'I'm coming,' I cry both in exultation and warning, but he clamps his jaws tightly shut.

For the first time in years, there are boundaries to my orgasm which, paradoxically, allow it unlimited scope. Whereas the loneliness of masturbation leaves me lost in the face of infinity, his mouth connects me to the molten centre of the earth. I feel warm and replete and grateful and sticky and vulnerable and safe. After a few moments, he raises his head and spits out my semen so lightly that I have no sense of rejection. It lands like a patch of cuckoo-spit on the grass.

After the adult intensity of our lovemaking, we cuddle up like children. I picture us as Romulus and Remus resting on the hillside, when Rome was still a twinkle in a lupine eye. We lie in each other's arms as if the silence were answering all our unspoken questions, watching the dawn wash through the trees.

'We ought to be on our way,' he says. 'It's time for the early morning joggers and dog-walkers.' I try to blot out the memory of the man from last night. 'They, of course, will be using the Heath for the purposes which Nature and the Corporation of London intended. Heaven forbid that anyone should come here to make love.'

I start to panic. I cannot tell whether it's the moment which I don't want to lose or whether it's him. Either way, I long for the chance to find out. 'Is that it then?' I ask. 'Is that the cold-light-of-day, see-you-around-sometime, it-was-fun-while-it-lasted brush-off?'

'Just try it and I'll pin your name with the most personal details to every church notice-board in London.'

'You fool!' I laugh. But the reassurance of his folly fades as I remember the Bishop's pronouncement. 'The problem is that I don't have any address to give you.'

'Of course you do.'

'No, you don't understand. Pending the diocesan enquiry, the Bishop has ordered me to leave the parish.'

'I understand perfectly, thank you. It's only chemistry I couldn't get my head round. And, until you're settled, you can come back with me. Though I should warn you that it's not Lambeth Palace.'

'Are you sure? You know next to nothing about me.'

'If I were a romantic, I'd say think how much time we have to make up for. If I were a cynic, I'd say think how little we have left to waste. But, as I'm a realist, I'll say that all I'm offering you is somewhere to stay. We'll have to take anything else from there. Now not another word.'

'Does a kiss count as a word?' I ask.

'It depends how deep it goes.'

I kiss him passionately.

'I'd reckon that at a syllable.'

I kiss him again, lapping his mouth with my tongue.

'Better . . . no more than a letter.'

I kiss him again, my lips like a pressurized chamber.

'Did you say something?' he asks.

Before we can go anywhere, he has to keep his promise to Neil. I ask if he isn't worried that he will be leaving him where, later, people will come to have sex. 'That's precisely what I'm hoping for,' he says. 'Think. When corpses are buried, they fertilize the ground and complete the cycle of Nature. But some of us have been declared outcasts from Nature. So we must create our own cycle . . . a cycle of regeneration, with memories enriching love.'

I follow him across the Heath, which is otherwise deserted, as he drops the ashes like a fairy-tale trail. I offer to say a prayer, but he declines; so I repeat some phrases from the burial service in my head. Then, with his pockets empty, he screws up his eyes and whispers 'Kick up a storm, sister,' before taking my hand and pulling me away. As we walk with ease down paths which, only a few hours ago, were clouded in confusion, he says 'Funny; all his life Neil was looking for a man with thighs like tree-trunks. Now he can make the comparison at first hand.'

We emerge at Whitestone Pond, passing a boarded-up hot dog stand with a lingering smell of grease.

'It's Easter,' I say in wonder.

'You don't have to be the Archbishop of Canterbury to work that out.'

'I meant more than the date.'

I feel such a renewal in my heart . . . such a resurrection of my entire being that, even though Good Friday remains a part of me, constantly replicating in my blood, I am convinced I can keep it at bay.

'Will you be offended if I go to your local church this morning?'

'Not a bit. When the organ swells, you can think of me.'

My happiness is so fervent that I fear I might internally combust like a character in Dickens. We cross the main road and stare out over the Vale of Health. 'Look,' I shout, 'the sun's coming up just for us. See that pink glow through the clouds around St Mary's steeple? It's going to be a glorious day.'

Oliver squeezes my hand. As he follows my gaze across the Heath, his expression turns from elation to alarm. 'Are you sure those are clouds,' he asks, 'and not smoke?'

PART THREE

ORDER OF SERVICES

SUNDAY

    10.30 a.m.   Blessing and Procession of Palms and High Mass.

    6.30 p.m.   Stations of the Cross.

    10.30 p.m.   Laying-on of Hands with Prayer and Anointing.

MONDAY

    5.00 p.m.   Confirmation Class.

    7.30 p.m.   Service of Healing.

TUESDAY

    5.00 p.m.   Service of Affirmation and Blessing.

WEDNESDAY

    4.30 p.m.   Order for the Burial of the Dead.

THURSDAY

    10.30 a.m.   Eucharist with the Blessing of the Oils.

    6.30 p.m.   Mass of the Lord's Supper.

FRIDAY

    11.00 p.m.   Good Friday Vigil.

SATURDAY

    8.00 p.m.   Easter Vigil.

    9.00 p.m.   Easter Vigil.

SUNDAY

    11.00 a.m.   High Mass of the Resurrection.

Blessing and Procession
of Palms and High Mass

Sunday 10.30 a.m.
St Mary-in-the-Vale, Hampstead

> The people gather by Whitestone pond. The sidesman
> hands out orders of service.

Joe contemplates his image in the sedgy pond. For years a fugitive
from his own reflection, he now courts it as assiduously as a co-
quette. The fat which was once a source of shame has become a
reassurance. Vanity has been redefined as health. And yet confidence fades as quickly as a stone ruffles the water. A single spot is
magnified to film-star proportions and a frog in the throat heralds
the horrors of an Egyptian plague. He probes the contours of his
neck, only to turn the gentle squeezes into invigorating slaps as his
mother's puzzled face ripples into view.

He raises his glance and allows it to range over the congregation.
Familiar faces flit into focus: Bertha Mallot, Nancy Hewitt,
Winifred Metcalfe and Trudy England, all the old faithful (in every
sense). He is skimming over the family group around Hugh and
Petula Snape when Russell, every inch the Sunday father, walks
over, extricating a hand from his baby, and congratulates him on
his forthcoming wedding. Such are the rewards of coupledom. A
man who has shown him nothing but indifference now welcomes
him to the club.

He introduces Russell to his mother, who flutes her enthusiasm
for the sleeping baby, before asking in a tone of lubricious coyness
about the prospect of brothers and sisters. It is intolerable that
innocence should license innuendo: the cooing combination of sex
and sentimentality which prompts even the primmest of spinsters
to smile. It sometimes seems as if the true burden which humanity
bears is not original sin but original salaciousness ... the patter of
tiny feet crossed with the patter of a music hall comic:

'I say, I say, I say, who was that lady I saw you with last night?'
'That was no lady; that was the mother of my child.'

The whole world is driven by sex. Which makes it all the more
urgent to pinpoint the origin of sexual pleasure. The matter is as
crucial to him as the origin of the species was to Huxley and

Wilberforce. Like them, he is torn between creation and evolution. Is it an echo of God ... a taste of the energy – and ecstasy – at the heart of the universe? Or is it rather Nature's way to ensure propagation, as skilful as the tapestry of a peacock's tail or the mimicry of a bee-orchid? So far, he has sided with the creationists, searching for the divine (while, in practice, barely attaining the human). But, if pleasure is merely the midwife to reproduction, then his pursuit of it is truly perverse. It is no wonder that Nature has taken revenge.

He stares at the dark sweep of foliage beckoning him on either side. He feels a tremor beneath his prayer-sheet. The Heath has assumed its morning face, but he delights in the dual identity which sees daytime pets and night-time passions unleashed on the self-same paths. He grins at the prospect of Lucky, Rex and Rover (or their Hampstead equivalents) being thrown off the scent by all the redolent human scents lingering on bushes and trees.

As his gaze reaches Jack Straw's Castle, he watches a man emerge with the dazed expression of someone rescued from a kidnap. He tries to picture what can have detained him so long beyond the dawn-chorus curfew. He presses his prayer-sheet harder against his groin, embarrassed by his morning-after-the-night-before irreverence. And yet it is four years after the night before to the day, liturgically if not chronologically, that he first made the acquaintance of St Mary's and renewed his acquaintance with Christ. Now, as then, the only word that he can find for what happened is 'grace'. He was groping his way to the tube, after an encounter so exhausting that he fell asleep where he lay, when he stumbled on the Blessing of the Palms. Something moved him to take part, even though he feared that he smelt much like a donkey himself. The following week he returned, washed and groomed. He became a regular worshipper, finding the peace which had eluded him ever since adolescence directed his most intimate impulses below the belt.

His train of thought is broken by the arrival of his best man ... a phrase which he has yet to master.

'Somebody write to *The Times*,' Damian exclaims. 'I've just seen my first bare chest of the spring.' He indicates the workmen drilling the road.

Joe wants to die, until he remembers the ill-effect that negativity can have on the immune system and frantically tries to waft the thought away.

'Damian, these are my parents. Mum ... Dad, Damian, my best man.' He spits out the words as if he were kitting him out for combat.

'Thrilled to meet you,' Damian says, throwing himself into the role. 'I'd no idea you were arriving so soon.' He holds out his hand, which Maureen takes like a plate of scones and Dave like a tax demand.

'You'd have known if you'd come to lunch yesterday. Where were you?'

'Oh I was in bed with...' He spins out the pause and Joe's agony. 'Food poisoning. I swallowed an unwashed grape.'

Joe searches desperately for the donkey.

'What's so special about a bare chest?' Dave asks, sparking Joe's memory of his string vest at Scarborough.

'Well I'm ... I'm developing a project for Max Factor to protect workmen from skin cancer. It's a secret formula made up of tar and horse-sweat with just a *soupçon* of brown ale.'

'What an interesting job!' Maureen says. 'Why only the other week, I was reading about the danger of all these ultra-violent rays.'

'Right,' says Damian. 'Although ultra-violence can be fine in moderation. The danger comes when it gets too heavy.'

'Mum, Dad, we're just going to speak to a couple of friends. Dee and Alice should be here any moment.'

He propels Damian towards the boarded-up hamburger stall.

> The procession approaches, led by the Crucifer. The Acolytes follow, then the Choir, the Curate with the donkey, the Thurifer and the Vicar. A policeman brings up the rear.

The children crowd around the donkey. Femi holds onto Cherish, whose head is pulled back as if by the weight of her brightly co-loured beads, while her eyelids flutter at random. She rubs the donkey's flank, savouring the ragged softness of its flesh.

'Can I have a ride?' she asks Blair.

'Not today. This is Jesus's donkey. Listen carefully and you'll hear the story.'

'But Jesus isn't on it now.'

'In a way he is,' Blair replies. 'We just can't see him.'

'It's like the Emperor's New Clothes,' James Bentinck says.

'If we were good, would we see him?' his brother Tristram asks.

'I shan't see Jesus till I die,' Cherish says. 'I'm blind.'

> The choir sings:
> *Hosanna to the Son of David,*
> *the King of Israel.*
> *Blessed is he who comes*

> *In the name of the Lord.*
> *Hosanna in the highest.*

'We might as well be at Margate,' Eleanor says to Edith, who, as one not built for sunshine, nurses a fondness for the English coast.

'It's for the children, Eleanor,' she replies.

'Isn't it enough that the shops are full of Easter eggs?'

'I rather like Easter eggs,' Edith hints.

'That much is obvious,' Eleanor says, staring at her straining buttons. 'Look at the little coloured girl. She's so over-excited, she can't hold her head straight. Trust me, it will all end in tears.'

> The Vicar blesses the palm branches and sprinkles them with holy water.

Terry, on temporary release from his organ loft and still wearing his Romburg hat from the Saturday night HALOS rehearsal, stands beside Blair watching the choir raise its branches. 'It's like Act One of *The Desert Song.*'

> The choir sings *Pueri Hebraeorum.*

The congregation hold up its miniature crosses, with the exception of Eleanor who holds up her frond. The moment that Huxley sprinkles it, the stem snaps and hangs limply in two. Stevenson caws.

'This is surreal,' Damian says. 'I need some hallucinogenic drugs.'

'You mean you haven't already had some?' Joe asks.

'Only incense.'

Eleanor dumps the broken frond unceremoniously on Edith and attempts, in vain, to quiet Stevenson.

'Did she ask permission to bring that thing?' Damian asks. 'It's not Treasure Island.'

'The story – according to Blair – is that she told Father Huxley's predecessor she'd be bringing her parakeet. He, being somewhat deaf and completely unworldly, assumed she said the Paraclete (that's the Holy Spirit to you). So now we're stuck with it.'

'Surreal.'

'Sh-sh,' Hugh Snape rebukes them.

> The Vicar delivers his homily.

Lionel, who has spent the night beneath the stars camouflaged as rubbish, shakes the dew from his coat and gazes at the gathering. He identifies the Church, which is another word for charity, and pictures the miracle of the loaves and fishes updated into fish and chips. Brakes slam, horns blast and tyres screech as he ambles across the road, waving at the windscreen glares as though they were smiles of welcome. Once at the pond, he searches for a gap in the group, while keeping an eye fixed firmly on the policeman, the one person who seems to be ignoring the white-haired man's words, clutching his radio as if it were a hotline to God.

He squeezes his voice into a whisper, but he is so out of practice that it leaps up at him like a cat. 'Spare us some change, guv! Just a few pence for a cup of tea.' A man with curly hair on his velvet collar flicks him away like a fly. He tries again, tapping a woman on the shoulder. 'Scuse us, lady, d'you think –?' Without looking round, she hands him a prayer-sheet and returns her attention to the speech.

> Ride on! ride on in majesty!
> Hark! all the tribes Hosanna cry!

Seeing the service break up, Lionel seizes his chance to accost a couple in anoraks. He tries to steal up on them but his stomach raises the alarm.

'Spare a few coppers for a cup of tea!' he asks.

The policeman walks over and grabs his arm. 'On your way, chum.'

'I know my rights...' But he also knows his reality and puts up no resistance. At least a wrenched shoulder makes a change from aching guts.

'Is there a problem?'

He looks up to see a woman like a headmistress standing in front of him. Then she smiles as if it were her day off.

'Everything's under control, madam,' the policeman says. 'He won't disturb you again.'

'This is a church, Officer. It's our job to be disturbed.'

He wonders if the policeman will arrest her, but he just mutters under his breath and walks away.

'I'm Jessica,' the woman says. 'I'm married to the Vicar. Can I be any help?'

'I don't mean no trouble. Just a few pence.'

'I'm afraid I haven't brought my purse. But we're on our way to the church. Why not come with us and then back to the vicarage for a meal?'

He is confused. A meal was no part of his plan. A meal means sitting down with washed hands and clean clothes and bread on the side of the plate, not in the middle. 'Just a sandwich. Some chips. No trouble.'

'I'm sure we can do better than that. Do come along. It's only down the hill.'

> *Ride on! ride on in majesty!*
> *In lowly pomp ride on to die.*

Alice arrives at the pond together with Dee and Dora and the echo of her mother's 'You'd be late for your own funeral' ringing in her ears. It's a rebuke which, even to a child, lacked logic. 'Why would anyone want to be on time for her funeral?' she asked, prompting a maternal sigh and the suspicion that her question was as unlady-like as her manners. She sends the cortège packing. No thought of the past can be allowed to dim the prospect of the week ahead. Art, love and family are all to be honoured. Tonight, she is to follow her own Stations of the Cross; on Tuesday, she is to pledge her vows to her lover; and, on Saturday, she is to christen her daughter. Were she to die on Sunday, she would die happy . . . no, that's dangerous nonsense. Happiness is the reason she longs to live.

Surveying the procession as it descends the hill, she is dismayed by its sparsity. What's more, even those who have turned out betray the occasion by their drabness. She is aware that her palette of hair which, with its braids and extensions is not merely multi-coloured but multi-media, invites disapproval. But it acts as both a statement and a celebration. God did not divide the light from the dark in order to have the parishioners of St Mary-in-the-Vale muddy the distinction. Apart from Lady Blaikie, with her predatory combina-tion of fox and parrot, and the blond woman in the fur coat talking to Joe's mother, no one seems to have made any effort. To the topography of tints (Venetian red, Naples yellow and burnt sienna) which she applies to her canvas, she must now add Hampstead grey.

She is more grateful than ever for the sight of Femi, walking hand-in-hand with Cherish, whose beads disarm her criticism. She has been fascinated by Femi from her first visit to St Mary's, cour-tesy of Jessica Grieve who met her at a rally outside the South African embassy. Femi's reticence about her past only encouraged her own speculations; the impression of an African queen, inspired by her Nefertiti neck, being confirmed one Sunday at the Peace when a group of fellow Nigerians bowed to her with all the defer-ence due to the daughter of a chief. While others were appalled, she was enchanted. Indeed, when Femi's husband ran off, she half-wondered whether she might take his place. But friendship cut both ways. Femi needed a shoulder to cry on, not a breast.

Now she is with Dee and able to bathe Femi in the rosy glow of what might have been rather than the resentful gloom of what never was. She gazes at Dee walking alongside her future in-laws, laying the groundwork which will permit them to be together 'till death us do part'. The phrase brings back all the pain of the service which cannot be read over them and the sacramental subterfuge to which they are forced to resort. Never mind that Blair regards it as a 'render unto Caesar' pragmatism, she knows that the altar is one place where they must always 'render unto God'. And yet their hands are tied and their vows vetoed by people who want to reduce the diversity of creation to the easy either/or of the bride's and groom's sides of the church.

She shudders, angry that she has allowed her mood to be hijacked. She takes comfort from the sight of Dora, snugly pouched on her bosom ... she at least will be welcome on all sides of the church. But, as though in revenge at having been so long ignored, Dora emits a composty smell which requires urgent attention and proves that, if nothing else, she has inherited her mother's sense of timing. Amused, in spite of herself, she bends and kisses the furrowed head.

> *Ride on! ride on in majesty!*
> *The winged squadrons of the sky*

Femi walks from Hampstead to Jerusalem via Eastern Nigeria. She revisits the Palm Sundays of her youth, which are as bleached in her memory as bones in the tropical sun. She sees the Reverend Butterfly leading the congregation in procession around the church. She hears him pounding the piano and prodding the silent top E, which he nicknamed Judas because it always betrayed him. She sits in the Sunday school and watches the children learning to read from their illustrated bibles. Then she follows the Holy Week trail to Good Friday, covering her face with mud and ripping her clothes in lamentation, and on to Easter Sunday, where the bread and wine give way to a tribal feast and even the Reverend Butterfly is moved to dance.

It was her father who built the church and led in his people. The old gods, he explained, had been sufficient to protect them from their neighbours, but they needed a bigger god to guard against men who came in aeroplanes and jeeps. And yet, having turned to the new God, he failed to heed His warning. For, even as the Reverend Butterfly preached about the Fall, oil-pipes were slithering into their Eden. But, instead of driving them out, the people welcomed them. They grabbed at the apple, only to find that, like Adam and Eve before them, they were thrown off their land. Her father was shot while leading a protest to Lagos ... although whether by order of the government or of the company was never resolved. Her brother took up the cause and was jailed for destroying company property. He was attacked by his cell-mate and died of head-wounds. Which is why, when his body was released, there was a badly stitched bullet-hole through his heart.

Her mother insisted that Femi and her sister come to England. Dayo, who could never make sense of a country where white men emptied dustbins and roads had zebra crossings, soon returned home. But she remained, rallying support for the Evore cause. Doors opened more easily than she had anticipated. She met eminent women with voices which filled her with hope (that is until she went to her first London theatre) and powerful men who agreed to use their influence with the government, but refused to put pressure on the company (citing the distinction between legitimate diplomacy and unwarranted interference in free trade). She soon saw that, for all the Reverend Butterfly's fine words, their god was enshrined in the Bank – not the Church – of England.

She retreated into married life with a musician who believed that his synthesis of African and European sounds would be the first step towards global harmony. For seven years, she supported him – less from faith in his vision than from a reluctance to lose the only vision that she had left – teaching Geography and Art in a Kilburn comprehensive. 'What's it like to walk ten miles in the sun, Miss, carrying a water-pot on the top of your head?' ... Well, it can hardly be worse than leaving the Goldhawk Road at seven-thirty on a grey November morning, waiting for half an hour at the bus-stop, being ticked off by the Headmaster for arriving late, supervising both the dinner-hour and the afternoon break, taking thirty books home to mark, cooking, cleaning and washing up, preparing the next day's lessons, and then trying to stay awake in bed. 'Oh, for us, it's no different to nipping down to the pub for a pint of beer, Darren.'

Nelson was desperate for children. But however hard they tried – and his nights were a constant attempt to exorcize the day's frustrations – England could never be a place of fertility for her. Then she heard the news that Dayo had died, leaving a baby daughter. Nelson refused responsibility. He wanted sons of his own, not a blind, infected niece. On the day that she bought her ticket for Lagos, he issued an ultimatum ... which proved to be surprisingly easy to ignore. By the time she returned, he had left home and moved in with a rich white girl whom he had seduced with the myth of Africa, as bastardized in Shepherd's Bush.

Her own sense of loss was eased by Cherish. For reasons which she hesitates to unravel, she is sure that she feels more for her sister's child than she could ever feel for her own. But feelings carry little weight with the authorities. From the day that she brought her niece to England, they have been trying to send her back, with a callousness which has turned her battle into a crusade. She refuses to give in ... not to the officials nor to the virus nor to the most powerful weapon in their joint arsenal: despair. Instead, raising her voice in a defiant descant, she lays her fears at the foot of the Cross and gently aligns the lopsided cross in Cherish's hand.

> *Ride on! ride on in majesty!*
> *The last and fiercest strife is nigh.*

Maureen waits for her husband, son and future daughter-in-law to catch her up.

'Such a nice woman!'

'Who?'

'Her in the fur coat. Her grandson's being christened this week. We've had a lovely chat.'

'Mum!' Joe says. 'You're not at the hairdressers.'

'That's all right, love.' She indicates Femi who is greeting Jessica. 'I see you've gone multi-ethnic.'

Joe blasts out the hymn.

'Don't get me wrong. I'm all for showing the hand of friendship. Though it can go too far. My niece – Joe's cousin Suzie – wed a man from Malawi,' Maureen informs Damian. 'I told her: "I give it two years." And I was right. Do you believe in mixed marriages?'

'Do you mean between men and women?' he asks.

Joe squirms.

'It was the same summer she won Miss Bolton,' Maureen continues blithely. 'She could have had any man she wanted. She's most put-out she won't be here on Tuesday. But it's that short notice. And the operation's been booked for months.' She mouths. 'Keyhole surgery in her down-belows.'

Joe rams his elbow into the middle of Damian's guffaw and shoves him forward so fast that he almost collides with Sophie Record.

'I hope you're not feeling tired,' Dee asks rapidly.

'Me? I'm as fresh as a daisy. Oops!' Maureen laughs. 'Did you hear that, Father? I said to Daisy ... never mind.' Dave grunts. 'Though my feet could tell you a different story. I'm a martyr to corns.' She gazes down. 'Your shoes look very sturdy.'

'They're Doc Martens.'

'I see.' Maureen's relief that the boots have been medically pre-scribed vanishes in a vision of hereditary deformity. 'Oh look, the hymn's stopped. Do you suppose we sing it again?'

'I'm not sure.'

'You'd think they'd choose one with enough verses. You never know what to do with silence, do you?'

'You do,' Dave says drily.

> The procession reaches the church. The choir sings the antiphon:
> *As the Lord was entering into the holy city, the children of the Hebrews foretold the resurrection of life. With branches of palm trees, they cried out: 'Hosanna in the highest'.*

Ronan hides behind a yew tree, the lurid yellow and mauve of his shell-suit at odds with the burgeoning colours of spring. He listens to the swell of the organ and the chant of voices, which sound so much more powerful through the muffling thickness of the walls. He wraps his exclusion around him like a coat and tramples over the scattered graves, relieving his resentment on the dead.

A stubbed toe from a sharp kick at the loving memory of Eliza Rawlings gives him a satisfying sense of his own impotence. His heart is black with hatred . . . which is a phrase they've instilled into his brain, although they take care never to use it to his face. When the woman from the Council questioned him about his film, she even asked if it was in colour or monochrome. He didn't realize the difference – not that it makes any now. Bastards! Hypocrites! He hates them all but, especially, the Vicar. He arranged for the grants, found them the equipment and allowed them to shoot in the church; then, at the first sign of trouble, he washed his hands. He'd like to roast him slowly on a spit, capturing every burn – in close-up. And he whirls around in a frenzy of pain and frustration which he transforms, mid-way, into the chanting of a curse.

> The Vicar reads the notices:
> *Let us remember all the sick, especially Susan Devenish, Iris Sage, Wallace Leyland, David Fern Bassett (priest), Julian Blaikie . . .*

Eleanor prays to the Almighty to look mercifully on Julian, rather as if He were an old friend at the Foreign Office she was asking to find him a job. After all, the Blaikies have served God and country for generations. That must count for something even today. She dis-dains the blanket intercessions of the congregation. Such democracy

of concern is degrading. It is bad enough that Edith should inform
her of his daily presence in her prayers ... boasting of devotions
beyond the call of duty. When Julian is cured, it is her faith, and
hers alone, which will be the cause.

... and Cherish Akarolo.

Femi looks at Cherish's upturned head, its angle suggesting engagement even as the vacancy of her eyes denies it, and tries to
imagine her response as she hears her name. Does it make her feel
special like a prayer for a saint or the Queen? Does it bring reassurance to one who has never seen herself in a mirror? Or does it fill
her with bitterness that her only status is among the sick? In
default of an answer, she peers around the church and reflects on
what the name means in the other pews. To a few, it will conjure
up a face: a blotchy, ulcerous, radiant face. To the rest, it will just
be an exotic tag from a continent where child mortality reads like a
newspaper misprint. Either way, if they have any belief in the
power of prayer, she implores them to invoke it. Let them repeat
the name a thousand times. The pronunciation is immaterial as
long as the sentiment is true.

The Vicar proclaims the peace.

Alice turns to her lover. This is the one kiss which is sanctioned by
the Church and she is determined to savour it. It has to stand for
so many others that are denied. So she whispers Peace with the
voice of passion as she presses her lips to Dee's cheek.

The peace of the Lord be always with you.

Dee is swept up by Alice's intensity. She basks in the peace which
she has had to fly halfway across the world to discover and which
she refuses to jeopardize at the eleventh hour. So she breaks away
as lovingly as when she rolls over in bed. She longs to share her
elation with the whole world but most especially with Joe. She
leans forward, fumbles for his hand and wishes him a Peace which
will not only fill his heart but revitalize every cell.

The peace of the Lord be always with you.

Maureen is moved by the evident shyness of Joe and Daisy's greeting. Now that men kiss on rugby pitches and *This is Your Life*, it is
a joy to see such natural modesty. She waits for them to finish
before taking Daisy's hands with especial warmth. Having heard
on *Woman's Hour* that there is no more insincere phrase in the
language than 'my darling daughter-in-law', she is determined to

prove otherwise. Nobody, however, could doubt the sincerity of 'my beloved son'. And she takes advantage of the setting to give Joe a hug which, for once, he cannot rebuff as though it were a return to the days when she used to dry between his legs. She wishes him Peace out loud and so many other things under her breath that she feels quite faint and is forced to forego Dave's outstretched hand in order to sit down.

The peace of the Lord be always with you.

Joe feels uneasy, sitting in Christmas closeness with his parents in the middle of spring. Christmas is a time when being a son is his sole identity. Christmas is a standing-room-only train from Euston to childhood and a last-minute search for a smile to keep him company in the five housebound days ahead. But Easter is London and an identity of his own making, which his parents subvert like a pebble-dashed semi set down in a Regency terrace. He exchanges Peace first with one and then the other. But his own hopes are crushed as his mother clasps him in a breathy embrace, which threatens to bring on his asthma, and his father grabs him in an arm-wrestler's grip, which attests to his one and only piece of paternal advice: 'Always be sure to give a firm handshake, lad. There's no better way of showing you're a man.'

The peace of the Lord be always with you.

Lionel panics. The only services he ever sits through are at St Winifred's crypt before they dole out the food. There, they keep their hands to themselves. Here, they're all hugging and kissing and shaking and whispering Pies ... which must be a signal for the meal. But no one says anything to him. The Vicar's wife has moved to the front, leaving him at the mercy of a busybody who keeps pointing out words in books as if he were back at school. He decides to assert himself. 'Pies,' he says. She looks offended. 'Pies,' he repeats with a sudden fear that they may not have enough to go round. But, instead of taking his hand in reassurance, she thrusts yet another book at him and backs away.

The peace of the Lord be always with you.

Lyndon exchanges the Peace with two of his fellow servers, but he remains on edge. There is only one person in St Mary's who can bring him peace. And he keeps Blair squarely in his sights, watching him shake hands with the Snapes and the woman who caught her shoe in the donkey-shit. He sees Father Huxley retreat to the altar: a sign that they should all return to their places. But he refuses to be cheated of his chance. So, just as Blair is approaching the sanctuary, he intercepts him on the steps.

'The peace of the Lord be always with you, Blair.'

'And also with you, Lyndon.'

He registers Blair's surprise, which increases when he sidesteps the handshake and initiates a hug. His pleasure in the moment is made all the sweeter by the knowledge that the whole church is watching them. He resumes his seat, secure in the sense of peace which suffuses every inch of his body. It is a feeling which, else-where, he encounters only in the pages of magazines. But, with Blair, there is no residue of guilt.

The Vicar gives thanks for the gifts of bread and wine.

Rosemary, whose suspicions of the tramp were confirmed by his attempt to rob the Offertory, redoubles her vigilance now that he is hidden behind the pew. Casting a sidelong glance, she finds that he isn't even mumbling into his beard. With great forbearance, she makes a further effort to embrace him (metaphorically), holding out her prayer-book and indicating the line. He ignores her. She gives him a neighbourly nudge but, instead of thanking her, he starts to shout: 'I can't read, don't you understand? I can't read and you keep handing me a fucking library.' Then he raises a fist as if to punch her, only to pull back and pound it against a pillar, before running out of church.

The Vicar speaks the prayer of consecration.
We break this bread
to share in the body of Christ.
Though we are many, we are one body,
because we all share in one bread.

Lyndon peers at Blair and anticipates unity. In the past, he believed that nothing could be closer than the 'one flesh' of a husband and wife. Lately, he has come to see that, just as a body is more than flesh ... it is brains and bones and muscles (he sneaks a second glance at Blair), so nothing can be closer than the 'one body' of a church. No realization has made him happier since he worked out at primary school that, if the whole human race were descended from Adam and Eve, they must all be brothers and sisters and there could be no such thing as an only child. But, when he tried to explain it to the boys who were bullying him, they just laughed and called him names ... names which he refuses to remember during prayers.

Now that he is older, he concedes that they had a point, since the

story of Adam and Eve is a myth. But Christ was real . . . is real . . .
as real as Blair. And the comparison isn't blasphemous because, as
a priest, Blair stands in the person of Christ. So, in giving himself
to Blair, he will be giving himself to Christ. The prospect makes
him dizzy. And, although it is only Palm Sunday, his thoughts
stray ahead to Whit and his confirmation when, for the first time,
the sanctified body will be placed in his mouth.

> The Vicar and Curate take their leave of the congrega-
> tion at the West Door.

Femi takes Huxley's hand, curtseys, and strolls into the
churchyard.

'These are my parents.' Joe introduces Maureen and Dave to
Huxley.

'We meet at last,' Huxley says. 'Joe's talked a great deal about
you.'

'All lies, I'm sure,' Dave says.

'Don't mind my husband, Reverend. He's dyslexic.'

'Come on, mother. You're causing a bottleneck.'

Maureen, all of a dither, takes Huxley's hand and curtseys.

'Why on earth did you do that?' Joe asks, as he pulls her away.
'He's not Prince Philip.'

'I watched the woman in front.'

'She's from Nigeria. You're from Rochdale. For Heaven's sake!'

Joe leads Maureen and Dave down the path. Huxley continues
his dismissals. Moments later, a young man leaps out of the
bushes and runs towards him hurling abuse.

'You're as bad as all the rest – say you'll do something and then
you never. Why bother to get us that money if you just piss all over
us? Fucking hypocrite! Someone should set a match to this place –
with you inside.'

STATIONS OF THE CROSS

Sunday 6.30 p.m.
St Mary-in-the-Vale, Hampstead

The congregation groups around the Vicar.

Alice sits behind a pillar, happiness nestling at her breast. She luxuriates in the tender discomfort of the baby's tug and the strength of a bond which remains as close as any cord. She resolves that her next work will be a Madonna and Child: a double self-portrait. She will peel away the glazed serenity of the traditional image in which Mary wears motherhood as lightly as a halo. She will bloat the sixth-form breasts and fill them with food more substantial than stardust. She will place her, not in a field of light, but at the heart of a forest, as a sign that, far from turning her mind towards the spiritual, maternity is the most liberatingly animal sensation she has ever known.

She is forty-two. In her mother's world, she would be a grandmother. In her own, she has spent the past few years watching her options run out. Every month, the blood which had turned her adolescence against itself became her sole source of hope. How she railed against God for giving her so many gifts but not the one essential ... one which owed nothing to sensitivity, integrity or skill. Politicians and soldiers, journalists and critics, all had someone to love, whereas she had only a blank canvas. Then she met Dee. And the miracle of that meeting was confirmed by its circumstance: if her flight from Wellington hadn't been delayed for twenty-four hours, their paths would never have crossed. She unravels the divine pattern which cowards call chance.

Dee rekindled her heart like the fire at the Easter Vigil. Moreover, she revived her hopes of a child. She had long decided that she would never make her own desire the guiding factor in parenthood. This wasn't from any scruples about a child's need for a father; on the contrary, she regarded the male and female principles as such polar opposites that it was hard to see how any child could survive a conventional upbringing unscarred. She put far more faith in the efficacy of two women or even two men. Nevertheless, she was obsessed with a sense of her own mortality and her child's subsequent loss. With the advent of Dee, both their futures were secured.

She gazes down on the face of her most perfect creation ... a boast which seems justified by the nature of the conception. A friend, who had offered his services in the bathroom rather than the bedroom, provided the semen. She even felt benign towards male sexuality when she saw it contained in the jar. Dee inserted it with a turkey-baster before laying her back and massaging her stomach. With no sound but the hum of Maori fertility songs and no light but the flicker of candles, the moment felt still and holy. It was both an act of love and a religious ritual, born of their passion and separate from it, existing inside and outside their bodies. Then they held each other in the silence as the candles burnt themselves out.

Pressure is eased as Dora emits a tiny burp and slips off her nipple, falling instantly to sleep. She marvels at her daughter's freedom from the dual curse of indigestion and insomnia ... indeed the only sign of her having dined is the faint trace of the menu around her lips. She stands and adjusts the pads in her blouse, prompting Dora to evince a squirm of displeasure which stops just short of a squeal.

With a mixture of pride and trepidation, she moves to the edge of the crowd gathered at the First Station. She tries to view the paintings no longer as extensions of herself in the studio but as expressions of a common faith in the church. It comes as a shock to have to acknowledge their pain and brutality. And yet, in a world where 'the absence of God' has passed from common-room debate into common currency, she feels a compelling need to assert His presence, not in the radiant faces and luminous landscapes to which her new understanding of love has gained her access, but in the horrors and the holocausts and the sickness and the suffering which have defined twentieth-century life.

She knows that any attempt to create contemporary icons will be reviled as iconoclasm by those who regard religion as a child's comforter, with angels hovering above their heads like the mobile over Dora's cot. And yet there can be no concessions to the 'No controversies please, we're Christians' brigade, who want to keep their Saviour safely clouded in the mists and myths of time. If they shout 'scandal', then let it be in the sense that St Paul used the term of Christ. For, just as Christ broke laws and broke with traditions in order to preach His message of love, so she must prise His image from the gilded frames and silver crosses in order to reveal its significance today.

Her task is made all the harder by the unfamiliarity of the story. She sometimes feels like her old classics mistress trying to instill a passion for Virgil into girls for whom every phrase was a footnote (she clutches Dora to confirm her escape from that lonely, tweedy fate). Easter today means bonnets and bunnies as much as Gethsamene and the Last Supper, while people 'wash their hands of it' as unthinkingly as they 'touch wood'. She envies the freedom of an artist who doesn't believe in God ... who is able to play God in a world of her own creation. But for her to try to do so would be to abrogate the responsibility of her calling – an art that is not creation so much as Incarnation: the Word became flesh became paint.

The congregation gathers at the first station.
Jesus is condemned to death.

Joe looks into the face of Christ as into a crystal ball. He sees his future written in His expression. It is as though Alice has taken a Puritan's axe to the images of his childhood: shattering the radiant majesty of the Christ in triumph; turning the stony stillness of a Gothic Redeemer into its own effigy. She has replaced them by a figure with pallid skin, sunken cheeks and wild-eyed desperation, as surely as if she had employed some Orwellian device to tap into his own deepest fears.

The court has been transposed from Jerusalem to London. The judges are no longer high priests but Joe and Jane Public. Christ is not dressed in a robe but in a grubby vest and pants. He is exposed to the taunts of men and women who denounce Him for His way of life: leaving His family; living on the edge of the law; mixing with undesirables. Their position is clear: it is He that is tainted, not the virus. They abandon Him to His fate, replacing the tenderness of 'Take up thy bed and walk' with the cruelty of 'You've made your own bed; now you must lie in it'. There will be no one even to change the stinking sheets.

He surveys the crowd for a face which will support Him, but its overt hostility offers Him no hope. All the people who gravitated towards Him when He was the life and soul of the party, a fund of witty tales and pithy maxims, have disappeared. He has been betrayed by His own kind as much as any other. Joe thinks of the man he saw on his last ever visit to a night-club, tears streaming down his creviced face as he desperately banged on the door of the only cubicle in the lavatory. Then he could no longer contain himself and he lost control of his bowels. A moment later, the door opened and three crop-haired youths swaggered out. 'What a fucking stench,' one said. 'You shouldn't be allowed out in your condition. It's sick.' He sees that man again as he stares at Christ in His soiled underwear, transformed into the 'dirty queer' of popular myth.

The congregation moves to the second station.
Jesus receives His Cross.

Joe approaches the second station, unsure whether Alice will have
shared the identification among different people, until a single
glance confirms its particular application to him. He weeps for
Christ who reels in agony, as illness follows illness like the blows
raining down on His head. His face is smeared with spittle, which
carries a deadlier charge than the virus. His brow is pierced with a
crown of thorns – or rather words: medical definitions that eat into
His skull. A man whose mind teemed with poems and parables
has been reduced to a series of acronyms: CMV, PCP, KS ... and
the most acrimonious of them all, AIDS. The Cross which is
strapped to His back is made not of the usual wood but of human
bones, a symbol both of His identity and His fate. He buckles
under the burden of ignorance, intolerance and despair.

The congregation moves to the third station.
Jesus falls for the first time.

Joe is grateful that his experience which is so often marginalized
should be made universal. At the same time he feels threatened.
He hides his face like Peter at cock-crow in case anyone should
connect the picture with him.

He squints through bleary eyes as Christ crawls forward, crippled
by the Cross and forced onto all fours by the neuropathy which is
draining the motion from His feet. He acknowledges Alice's skill at
capturing the humiliations of a thirty-three-year-old three-year old,
while wriggling his own toes, as keenly as when he took them to
market in his cot, in an attempt to convince himself that the condition will never afflict him. He rests his gaze on Christ's battered
body: the lesion-like lacerations on His wafer-thin chest; the rib-
cage bulging like a broken barrel; the wormcast of ruptured veins
in the crook of His arm. He sees Him collapse, only to be hauled
up, like a man pumped full of experimental drugs which allow him
just enough respite to prepare for his next fall.

He can no longer bear to look and, while the rest of the congregation fixes its eyes on the road, he stares at the shadowy houses
beyond. The closed doors and empty windows show that 'No room
at the inn' wasn't just the circumstance of His birth but the story
of His life.

The congregation moves to the fourth station.
Jesus meets His mother.

Joe is surprised by the space between Jesus and Mary. Neither looks at the other and, although Mary's hands point obliquely towards Jesus, their only connection lies in their Bacon-like rictus of pain. The road to Calvary has grown lonelier in recent years. In the gospel, Mary sets out to support her son on His final journey. Here, she appears to have come across Him by chance as He is being led away. Joe's first thought is that Alice has defied tradition to make her the epitome of all the mothers who reject their sons, leaving them to die in a crowded ward while the hospital radio pipes out *Eleanor Rigby*. But he soon sees that, on the contrary, Mary is desperate not to add her tears to the weight of Jesus' Cross. And he wonders how Alice has managed to give her the face of his own mother even though they have only just met.

Tears well in his eyes and he is grateful that the church is lit solely by candles. He looks toward his mother who is following the service-sheet as diligently as a guidebook. The thought evokes the postcard she sent him from Oedipus' Palace, complete with the greeting 'Wish you were here, love Mum'. Her pleasure that he still keeps it on the wall and her ignorance of its near-mythic status among his friends make him feel cruel. He longs to move closer to her. But the gap between them far exceeds the distance between London and Rochdale. He almost bridged it at lunch when she picked up his glass and he grabbed it from her. 'What's wrong?' she said. 'You don't have foot and mouth disease.' But he blew his nose and the moment passed.

He takes another look at Christ whose face reveals, amid the agony, His horror that His mother should be the witness of His humiliation. There may also be a flicker of guilt as He thinks back to their previous meeting when He rejected both her and His brothers in favour of His alternative family, turning His back on small-town life in order to embrace a freedom which she could never hope to understand. And yet, if she recalls it, she offers no sign of reproach. Her sole concern is to sustain Him in His final trial, even as she will be by His side when He dies.

> The congregation moves to the fifth station.
> Simon of Cyrene helps Jesus carry His Cross.

Joe looks at Jesus and Simon, their bodies contrasted as sharply as Mapplethorpe nudes. The emaciated wax-white Christ and the rugged boot-black Simon appear to inhabit different worlds of experience, virility and health. But they must both travel the same road. And Joe needs no atlas to locate Cyrene, for he sees in Simon's skin the span of a whole continent ravaged by the virus. And he sees in Simon's eyes the pain of a man far from home, abused and exploited, valued for nothing but his muscles. Nonetheless, he has eased Jesus' burden and, because of that, his own will be removed.

He thinks of the Simons he has met in the support group and their reluctance to associate with the gay men for fear that a sexual slur should be added to the effects of the virus. To some, the greatest of all threats is that their masculinity might be impugned. But others discover that sexuality is no more black and white than race; the road to Calvary cuts through all boundaries. And they learn to bear one another's cross.

> The congregation moves to the sixth station.
> Veronica wipes the face of Jesus.

Joe looks closely at Veronica whom Alice has depicted as an elderly nun, not the hatchet-faced harridan familiar from countless memoirs (he considers the lack of a separate classification for lapsed Catholics to be one of Dewey's few failures), but the wise Mother Abbess from *The Sound of Music*, which, he is embarrassed to admit even in church, remains his favourite film.

He thinks of his own encounters with Sister Hanna, who was born a Jew in Vienna and converted in the convent which sheltered her from the Nazis. Having been a nun for nearly fifty years, she has spent the past decade working among people affected by the virus. She neither proselytizes nor judges (nor makes a show of withholding judgement) and is as ready to discuss the latest bars and boy-bands with a group of young men as to take a class of schoolgirls through the story of Noah's Ark. She gives them back their innocence through her unwavering acceptance. And yet her commitment leads her into constant conflict with the hierarchy of her Order, which prefers a less practical application of prayer.

The love with which Veronica wipes the face of Jesus puts him in mind of Sister Hanna at the deathbed of his friend Jacques. As the sheets soaked up more than his weight in water and he lay in a bandage of towels ... as his teeth chattered and his body temperature fell until the sweat froze on his skin, she pulled down the blankets and stretched out beside him, warming his racked body in her embrace.

> The congregation moves to the seventh station.
> Jesus falls for the second time.

Joe sees that the Cross is now constructed of newsprint but, rather than making it lighter, it seems to weigh Jesus down even more.

Some of the cuttings are yellow with age, while others appear to be straight off the press. Straining his eyes from the back of the group (to which both size and discretion confine him), he is able to read several of the stories. At the bottom, a country vicar with a face like Hermann Goering holds a shotgun to his son's head with the promise that 'I'd shoot him if he had AIDS'. In the middle, God hits the headlines as His representatives in Wapping credit Him with the dispatch of a contemporary plague. At the top, morality gives way to economy (a subject of far wider consensus), as pundits demand that, in a world of limited resources, money should not be wasted on a minority disease.

> The congregation moves to the eighth station.
> Jesus meets the women of Jerusalem.

Joe looks at the women who follow Jesus's journey, watching while His name becomes a statistic. They wait on the edge of the road, prepared to suffer guilt by association. They brave the jeers of a crowd that impugns their motives, attributing their concern to the latest fashion and dismissing the ribbon on their lapels as of no more consequence than one in their hair. They endure the sneers of the comedian who accuses them of spreading the virus by kissing their dying friends and then going home to embrace their husbands ... a tactic as blatant as Moses' blaming the Fall of Adam on the bond between the serpent and Eve. Nevertheless, while the men turn their backs, they stand firm, determined that the last figures Jesus sees will not be wearing uniform.

In contrast to Christ, who appears to have preferred the company of men, his own closest friendships have always been with women. He feels sure that, were his body not dislocated from his emotions, he would now be happily married ... he glances at Dee with a churchyard smile. From the first day of primary school, he made common cause with the girls, maintaining the allegiance at his comprehensive where 'cissy' was no longer just an insult but a charge. He surmounted adolescence and its latent conflicts by playing the confessor, encouraging the girls to report their romantic disasters. The more he heard of fumbled passes, cidery kisses and snapped straps, the more he knew better than to risk such humiliation. Clumsiness came all too easily to one whose flesh hung around him like a cagoule. And yet, as time went on, either the boys grew more practised or the girls more indulgent and they no longer felt the need to confess. Girls flirted with their boyfriends, giggled with their girlfriends and had no room for anyone in between. His only intimacy was with his own left hand.

The congregation moves to the ninth station.
Jesus falls for the third time.

Joe is jolted by the change of perspective as Alice paints the Cross
from behind. The sole sign of Christ is in His bloody-fingered,
white-knuckled hands clutching the bar, desperately trying to keep
it from toppling onto His head. It is as if Christ has become His
Cross just as a man is reduced to his disease . . . just as he himself
has to struggle not to disappear beneath the weight of his diagnosis.

His own favourite image of the Crucifixion, Dalí's *Christ of St
John of the Cross*, also precludes any sight of the face, focusing
instead on the straining musculature of the shoulders. He remembers the confusion it caused him in his teens when it stood above
his bed, combining the sanctity of an icon with the *frisson* of an
underpants advert. He dreamt of being carried away on a back so
broad that it would bear even his weight: by day, to the spiritual
joys of Heaven; by night, to the fleshy pits of Hell.

He longs to give Jesus a face from his own iconography: men
whom he has crossed out of his address book but kept in his heart
. . . Arthur, Barry, Carlos (would that there were only twenty-six!).
But his first choice would be Lake, so named not by environmen-
tally conscious parents but by his classmates after a humiliating
incident on a school coach. Lake was a nineteen-year-old virgin
until his stag-night when he was goaded into having sex with a
compliant stripper. She infected him . . . an infection which, it was
later discovered, he passed on to his wife and child. He was beaten
up by his wife's family, disowned by his own, and derided by his
friends who assumed that he was gay. He moved to London, lost in
a haze of prescription drugs, until he was rescued by Terry, the St
Mary's organist, who gave him a room in his home, along with no-
strings-attached support. He might be there now . . . he might be
alive now, had his parents not had a change of heart. Having made
the trip to London, they suspected Terry's middle-aged motives,
turned Lake irrevocably against him and sent him back to a bed-sit
and the twice-weekly ministrations of the district nurse. Terry only
knew that he had died when he saw the name in the hospice newsletter. For once, the lack of surnames left no room for hope. How
many Lakes could there be in Ladbroke Grove?

He turns from the faceless foreground to the highly detailed
faces in the background, which Alice has depicted in all their ugli-
ness and prejudice. This is no first-century rent-a-mob but as direct
an accusation as she can bring. Government officials, as discreet
as their suits, brush up against neo-Nazi thugs as twisted as their

insignia. Scientists, compromised by their companies' cash, rub shoulders with a Pope so pitiless that he sets the potential of what might be over the protection of what is. A documentary film crew shoots edited highlights of the scene. Meanwhile, standing discreetly in the background is a couple less familiar than the others but instantly identifiable as the ubiquitous Jack and Grace, after their trademark cries of 'I'm all right, Jack' and 'There, but for the grace of God, go I'. As they crane forward in their constant search for ersatz satisfaction, they take care to keep out of the camera's eye.

The congregation moves to the tenth station.
Jesus is stripped of His garments.

Joe shudders to see Jesus stripped of His remaining clothes by overworked healthcare assistants and pushed into regulation-issue pyjamas. Modesty has vanished along with His muscles. Once again Jesus paves the way for him, as He hobbles down hospital corridors, past the incubators for premature births into the AIDS ward for premature geriatrics, where thirty-year-old men, with skin as grey as their great-grandfathers', wait to die. A sign above their beds, Nil by Mouth, hangs in inadvertent irony, like a punch-line waiting for a joke.

He stares at the milky confusion in Christ's eyes and tries to read His mind. The conventional piety of 'He died so that we might live' is no longer enough; he needs to know what was He feeling before He died. Is He grateful to have come to the end of the road and placed Himself in others' hands? Does relief at the chance to set down the Cross outweigh the horrors in store? Or is He more afraid than ever of the prospective pain? The answers may not be visible on His face, but Alice has left her own indication at His feet, like the liquid from a leaking chalice.

The congregation moves to the eleventh station.
Jesus is nailed to the Cross.

Joe looks at Christ's limp body pleading for mercy even as His lips are too agonized to speak and he sees a man being attached to a hospital drip. Doctors pump His sludgy veins with a last dose of chemicals: a dangerous burst of toxicity with which they gamble on burning up the greater danger within. And yet, while He has been so broken by His ordeal that it would take a miracle to revive Him, His tolerance of an experimental drug, prescribed only in extremis, may lead to a miracle-cure for others. He gives the conventional piety new life.

Suddenly, his sense of unworthiness is replaced by guilt. For the first time, he identifies not with Christ, nor even with the onlookers, but with the torturers, as he wonders whether a rush of sexual excitement may have shrouded his humanity and led him to pass on the virus. His confidence about his conduct since he learned of his diagnosis does not extend to the days since he learned of safer sex.

He feels sick. Christ forgave His killers, but it was coupled with the claim that 'they know not what they do'. That would hardly apply to him. Besides, how many of his own victims would be so magnanimous? He won't ever find out. The darkness of his sexuality – the back rooms, unlit Heath and unlicensed cinemas – precludes recrimination. What's more, he may be tormenting himself for no need. And yet the suspicion has taken root. He has only been able to follow the stations on the assumption that he is walking alongside Christ: that his illness allows him that instant identification ... which is now revealed to be nothing more than condolence-card cant. And, as he gazes at the Cross, he feels the shadow of a hammer in his hand.

> The congregation moves to the twelfth station.
> Jesus dies on the Cross.

Joe looks through the glass, which is no longer just a frame but a protection, and stares at the starkness of the image. He cannot tell whether it is in response to the familiarity of the Crucifixion or to the impossibility of representing the effects of the virus – which would require a canvas over thirty million pieces long – but Alice offers no body, no background, not even any paint. The sequence is shattered. All that remains is an empty plastic bag, its very malleability a mocking reminder of human frailty, pinned to a small wooden cross which stands in a pool of blood.

His customary revulsion at the sight of blood is increased by the knowledge that this is his own. He was dubious when Alice first explained her concept and the need for some of his blood to bring out the full effect. It was not as if he were being asked to sit for a portrait. Nevertheless, he agreed to speak to the nurses at the clinic, who, unanimously, refused to co-operate (Hong even accused him of planning a crime). But, eventually, he persuaded Brandon Lynch, who was sympathetic to the claims of art if not of religion, to extract a pint. His pride was dealt a further blow when Alice announced that she would have to mix it with rat poison to prevent its coagulating. He had thought that it was poisonous enough as it was.

Now that he sees it in context, he feels reassured. Besides, the meaning is persuasive enough to override his revulsion. The Passion has been reduced to its most basic element. What counts is not its provenance – whether it is pure or impure or any of the other things that racists look for – but simply whether it is healthy. A single drop will infect the supply the way that a Jewish grand-parent did for the Nazis. He looks to the top of the Cross, where Pilate wrote INRI, and, although he is too far off to see without squinting, he is sure that Alice has written AIDS.

He feels again the identification which he lost at the last station, as his blood stands for Christ's blood just as Christ's blood was shed for his. Alice was right. Even if no one else ever knows, it is important that it should be infected blood which is put at the heart both of the Crucifixion and of the Church.

> The congregation moves to the thirteenth station.
> Jesus is taken down from the Cross.

Joe studies the numbed figures of Mary and John clinging together while the soldiers, masked and gowned like hospital porters (as though death has removed all risk of offence but none of infection), pull the mangled body of Christ from the Cross. Grief breaks down all reserve. Only a few hours earlier, in a final attempt to defeat death and recreate His most important relationships, Jesus asked them to treat each other as mother and son. And yet it may well be the first time that they have even met. They are thrust into the uneasy intimacy of strangers gathered at a hospital bed.

The greater shock must be Mary's. Her face registers the confu-sion of a woman who, until she was summoned to the hospital, had no notion of her son's sexuality, let alone his illness. But, in John (who, with his fashionable Soho crop and pink-triangle badge, repre-sents 'the disciple whom Jesus loved' at its most unequivocal), he sees someone who will help her to understand. He ponders the irony of women who have had deeper and more honest relationships with their sons' lovers or buddies than with the sons themselves and longs to know what will happen to the couple in the painting. There is no further mention of their association in the Bible ... which is one reason he knows that the gospels cannot be fiction. No novelist would leave such promising material unexplored.

A glance at the figures behind them reveals two older men, Joseph of Arimathea and Nicodemus, whom Alice portrays as if they had arrived at Golgotha straight from the crush bar at Covent Garden. Joseph kept his connection with Jesus secret for fear of the Jews, just as many prominent men feel the need to bow to public opinion even today. And yet he was brave enough to stand by Jesus in death. From his agonized expression, it would seem that his feelings have moved beyond friendship to infatuation. But he has never revealed them for fear of rejection. His reticence has been both his downfall and his salvation. And, while Mary and John give way to their emotions, he attends to the practicalities of the burial: a last act of unrequited love.

These two father-figures conjure up an absence: Joseph, not the counsellor of Arimathea, but the carpenter of Nazareth. If he's dead, it has not been mentioned ... which may, of course, reflect his insignificance in Jesus's life. And yet, in the sequence which Alice has depicted, his non-attendance carries more weight. It is as though he cannot bear the shame of seeing Jesus subjected to the most ignominious death which the Romans could devise. By staying away, he becomes the exemplar of all fathers who disown their children. Even so, he has been spared the full humiliation of his contemporary counterparts, who are forced to watch while their sons' most private acts are held up to public scorn. Mary Magdalen attests to Jesus' forgiveness and not to His lust.

> The congregation moves to the fourteenth station.
> Jesus is laid in the sepulchre.

Joe looks on as Christ's body is tossed into a pit of jumbled limbs and tangled torsos which lie like the parody of an orgy. The intimacy which He was denied in dying He discovers in death. Indignity is heaped on indignity like corpse on corpse. Identity is reduced to dental records and the hospital number still tagged to His putrefying skin. His life as a man is complete as He festers with His fellow victims. The horror that he felt as a child on hearing of Oliver Cromwell's body being dug up and hung from the gallows is as nothing compared to his disgust in the face of this barbarism.

Purists will search in vain for the empty tomb. The confusion of the plague-pit appears to invalidate all reports of the Resurrection. And yet, knowing Alice, he is convinced that she intends the exact opposite. This is not an eternal Good Friday but an alternative Easter Sunday. The mass grave will people the kingdom of Heaven. The intertwined corpses will furnish the composite soul. Christ can no longer be confined to a single body. The resurrection of one requires the resurrection of all.

He has reached the end of the road and recovered his spirits. His sense of elation forestalls the 'Meet the bishop' small talk of Huxley's party. Deciding to return home straight after the service, he joins in the final prayer.

> O Saviour of the World, who by your Cross and precious
> Blood has redeemed us.
> Save us and help us we humbly beseech you O Lord.

Laying-on of Hands
with Prayer and Anointing

Sunday 10.30 p.m.
St Philips's Hospital

> The Vicar sets up a makeshift altar on the bedside table.
> He picks up his stole, kisses it and puts it on.

Huxley hears the sound of his movements amplified in the others' silence. The cross clatters on the table and the Crucifixion itself seems to be an intrusion on their grief. He gazes around the room. Blair sits at the foot of the bed, his unblinking glance set on Julian as if fixing him on the retina of his memory. Eleanor Blaikie, as stiff as a backboard, sits to his left, staring into space a few inches above her dying son's head (with Edith perched behind her like an after-thought). Massimo, Julian's Italian friend, sits to their right, avoid-ing Eleanor's glance as resolutely as she avoids Julian's. Behind him, Julian's buddy, whose name he always forgets, stands deferen-tially against the wall. He decides to direct the prayers at him.

> The Vicar hands out the prayer-sheets and explains the
> order of service.

Massimo accepts the paper with indifference. He is neither hear-tened nor deceived by the illusion of control: the pretence that death is just another page in the prayer-book. History may be one long obituary and the music of time the band playing at the wake, but the only way he is able to bear this anguish is on the assump-tion that it is unique and that Julian's dying is as momentous as his living. Religion is merely the comfort of the commonplace, like the flowers around the Unknown Soldier's tomb.

He puts down the paper and resumes the part that Julian's mother has allotted him: the simple foreigner with pizzeria English. Her tactic is as plain as dehumanizing the enemy in a war. His grievance might be greater if the fiction didn't work to his advan-tage, allowing him to keep Julian to himself. He doesn't have to pass around his memories like afternoon tea. And he can sit mu-tely through this service without either offending the company or compromising his unbelief.

Of all the figures to whom Julian has introduced him since his arrival in England, God is the least intimidating because the least evident. The rest of Julian's former life has proved to be harder to dismiss. His initial jealousy of Lady Blaikie declined when he saw that she wanted to keep Julian so far in the past that it constituted no threat ... from the photographs displayed in her house, a stranger would suppose that he had died at the age of twelve. Instead, he reserves his resentment for Blair. He wants to shake him until he spits out his false kisses like a mouthful of gold teeth. Then he wants to melt them down and mould them in his own image. But, as Julian has exacted a promise of friendship, he can do no more than hiss Judas at him under his breath.

In Naples, he wondered if it was Julian's Englishness which attracted him: a difference of nationality to make up for the sameness of sex. Here, he knows that it is the Julianness; his origins are no more than the country stamped on the bottom of a souvenir. When he agreed to take the trip home with him, he never thought that it would end like this. But then he believed that his love would guarantee Julian's immortality ... as vainly as he once believed that cynicism would guarantee his own immunity from love.

He blames himself for underestimating Julian's illness as much as Julian for encouraging it. He even told him of his status on a boat sailing towards Capri, where the sky-blue sea seemed to be a genuine reflection of paradise and the horror of his words was countered by the shimmering unconcern of the fish. Reality returned on shore. But the onset of symptoms saw no change in his commitment. This was more than a holiday romance between a T-shirt and a chequebook. He clung to Julian through the sweating and the spewing and the hordes of the sick and dying who jostled for space in their heads. As Julian's strength collapsed, his own love grew, finding new modes of expression: the mopping sponge to the brow instead of to the genitals; the spoonful of soup to the lips in place of the kiss. What's more, it felt like a privilege rather than a sacrifice. But that, too, has been taken away from him in England, where there are others to see to the wiping and the soothing and the feeding: women who regard it as their role.

His own role has been reduced to the nurse-cum-secretary-cum-valet whom Julian hired in Italy. The humiliation is assuaged by the large cheque which he has been promised when the contract comes to an end. He has bought the future with his silence about the past. He hisses Judas at himself.

> The Vicar sprinkles the patient and those gathered at the bedside with holy water.

Julian lies supine inside his body. He tests the boundaries of awareness. He reaches to his outer limits: the finger-tips and toes which
lie beside him like splints. If he lingers too long, he is drawn back
to his old sense of self: the blistering centre and arctic extremities
like a world in miniature. But, if he moves on, he soars into an
expanded consciousness: the heaven being pumped into his veins
. . . warm and drowsy and suffused with light.

> The Vicar and those gathered at the bedside speak the
> prayers.
> *Lord Jesus, you healed the sick:*
> *Lord, have mercy.*
> *Lord, have mercy.*
> *Lord Jesus, you forgave sinners:*
> *Christ have mercy.*
> *Christ have mercy.*

Blair stares at his former lover, lost in a tangle of tubes. His body is
as cadaverous as a Cranach Christ; his skin as waxy as if it were
already embalmed. His sweat sours the sheets. His lips are swollen
and cracked. His cheeks are hollow. His vegetal breath mingles
with the pustular stench from his putrefying flesh. The flowers
bunched lavishly around the bed exude no compensatory fragrance.
They are as powerless as their human counterparts in the face of
the imminent death.

He sees his old certainties slip away. There are now three states
of being: life, death and the absence of life, which hovers sense-
lessly between the two. All that is truly Julian has disappeared and
only the peripheral remains. He longs to mark the gap between
past and present as formally as the Jews, who give their relatives
new names when they're dying; as though centuries of flight have
convinced them that even Death can be deceived by the right disguise. This is no longer Julian; it's Robert . . . Robert who applies a
javelin-thrower's force to the flicker of an eyelid . . . Robert who
expends an opera-singer's strength on a stutter of breath. Julian,
meanwhile, lives as vibrantly as ever in his memory: the golden
boy with the tuft of hair like sunlight on his chest.

> *Heavenly Father,*
> *you anointed your Son Jesus Christ with the Holy Spirit*
> *and with power to bring to man the blessings of your*
> *Kingdom. Anoint your Church with the same Holy Spirit,*
> *that we who share in his suffering and his victory may bear*
> *witness to the gospel of salvation.*

Julian emits a laugh which slides down his throat like an oyster. He is gradually becoming accustomed to the scrambling of his senses. He listens to the gentle music which is being pumped through his mask directly into his lungs, bypassing the feeble amplification of his ears. He scents the gorgeous blossoms which pour out of Huxley's mouth and pollinate every pore of his skin. He gazes through closed eyes at his mother and his friends and sees the auras surrounding them with far greater clarity than he ever saw their faces. Each one has a distinct tone: Blair is azure-blue and Massimo golden yellow; Nick is Lincoln green, his mother fiery crimson and Edith watery brown. Only Huxley eludes him: a patchwork of rainbow profligacy, as if a stream of conflicting energies were struggling for ascendance. He longs to help him find harmony, and yet to move his lips would require a Stonehenge effort. So he sidesteps words, which are themselves confused, and speaks directly with light and colour, sending him a wave of pure pink love.

> Our Lord Jesus Christ went about preaching the gospel and healing. He commanded his disciples to lay hands on the sick that they might be healed. Following his example, and in obedience to his command, we shall lay hands on Julian, praying that the Lord will grant healing and peace according to his loving and gracious will.

Huxley holds his prayer-book like a play-script ... a radio-script which he doesn't even have to learn. He takes comfort from the metaphor. If a white man can black up to play Othello, then a sceptic can present the man of God. On the other hand, a white Othello might be applauded at the Old Vic, but it would hardly pass muster in Soweto. The metaphor begins to break down along with his confidence. He is unable to detach his role from its setting and reads the service by rote, the measured tone of his voice quite at odds with his inner turmoil; a discrepancy which fuels his despair.

Christ missed out the most important beatitude: 'Blessed are the agnostics: for they shall believe in chance'. In a random world, Julian becomes merely a victim of circumstance: a virus which spread from monkeys to men in a parody of evolution. Faith, however, rejects such easy consolation. If the universe is ordered by God, then suffering must have a purpose. And yet the practice of making people physically ill and morally better, a dubious one at the best of times, is indefensible when that illness cannot be cured.

A random world is unjust by definition; an ordered one is unjust by default. A supposedly righteous God picks on his inferiors as savagely as any school bully. A stray glance at Blair calls to mind the Lent study group and his eloquent apologia for suffering on the grounds that it aligns the victim with Christ. Nevertheless, he has come to believe that Blair – and indeed the whole Church – overplays Christ's importance. If Christ really did usher in a New Testament, why is there so much of an Old Testament world left? The writing on the wall should, by now, be mere graffiti. Plagues should have been wiped out with the firstborn of Egypt. Leprosy should be in a museum and locusts in a zoo.

Such misgivings lead him to make his Holy Week journey in two directions ... not just to Christ on the Cross at Calvary but to Prometheus on the rock in the Caucasus. The pair are forever linked: both sons of God who have been abandoned by their Father. Prometheus over-identified with man and is tortured for all eternity; Christ over-identified with man and is sacrificed for all time. But, while he speaks of Christ, it is Prometheus who has come to speak more strongly to him. He shows that the gulf between God and man defies all mediation. It is at his feet that humanity learns that its aspirations can never be fulfilled. His fate reveals not the redemption of the world but God's implacable hatred. It offers a myth of our ultimate impotence rather than a message of false hope.

> Saint James writes, 'Is any among you sick? Let him call for the elders of the church, and let them pray over him, anointing him with oil in the name of the Lord'.

Nick listens to the prayers with glazed politeness, as bored as by the report of someone else's dream. He resents the Vicar for bringing a sense of time into the room. He has witnessed the passing of five of his boys (and the way that he can say 'boy' without prurience is the one saving grace). He has watched them struggle and acquiesce, rasping with pain and flying on morphine, and, in each case, the clock ceases to count. The world takes its beat from the dying man. He is told that he has sat up for two days and nights and that he must feel tired. But he feels nothing, neither tired nor hungry, just the rhythm of Julian's dying, the essence of the past-and-future present, which is now being drowned by dead saints and moribund words.

Fatigue hits him like a fistful of facts and figures. The Vicar's voice imbues him with the ache of mortality and he anticipates the aftermath of Julian's death. First, there will be the flurry of the funeral and, then, the months that the Trust will require him to take off before it assigns him to anyone else ... months whose lack of purpose already fills him with dread. 'I don't know how you do it,' says Miss Turkin, from across the hall, a woman so terrified of pain that she has never married and so repulsed by dirt that she won't even have a pet. 'A man your age. There'll be time enough for hospitals soon enough.'

It is hard to explain to someone whose greatest fear for the future is the rising cost of burials that it is only by caring for the dying that he has come to terms with life. After a middle age as estranged from his emotions as a divorced father, he has experienced an intimacy so profound that it makes the 'joy of sex' sound like an idle boast.

> Come, Lord, with your love and mercy in this ministry, and
> comfort Julian in his distress and free him from harm:
> Lord, hear our prayer.

Edith waits in the corridor, her face pressed against the bedroom door, tears misting the glass. Grief mingles with self-pity. Every visit to a hospital is infused with a deep sense of loss. Julian is dying, but it is her own youth that she mourns ... the plumply pretty nurse whom patients loved and junior doctors courted and her imperceptible transformation into the testy sister whom they feared. She left the Middlesex twenty years ago when her faded looks and soured personality (how easily she assimilates her tragedy) confirmed that her only marital prospects were 'to the job'. She joined a private agency and dreamed of a deathbed marriage to a millionaire. After several old ladies and an Anglo-Irish peer with a heart more philanthropic than lustful, she was engaged by Admiral Blaikie, whose roving hands led to nothing but laddered stockings and disillusion. So, when he died, she accepted the post of companion to his wife.

She gazes at the ramrod figure of the employer whom she hates with all the passion of her subservience, a woman whose sole joy in life is to demean all around her. It may be the gardener Tom – or rather Lionel, who, on the pretext that it is easier to remember (a blatant lie from one whose memory is as sharp as a bed of nails), she forces to answer to the same name as each of his predecessors: something second-hand to deprive him of personality and monosyllabic to deny him weight. Or it may be the cleaner, Rosa, whom she berates for indolence and bad breath.

She is the one who bears the brunt of Eleanor's attacks. Even now, she has been sent from the room because her sobbing disturbs the prayers. Unlike some, she is unable to hide her feelings; unlike some, she has feelings to hide. Julian was the one exception to the malice of the Blaikies ... the only one whose kindness wasn't compensation for having gone too far. No adopted child could have revealed a more singular nature. If Julian were her son – an 'if' which tugs at her heart like his illness – she would cradle his head: she would flood the ward ... the hospital with her pain. Whereas Eleanor chose to leave him for a whole day, because duty demanded her attendance at a family wedding in Bath.

Her only comfort is the prospect of revenge when senility reverses their roles. She enjoyed a foretaste when they were banished to the day-room during a visit from Julian's doctor on Friday. They sat beneath a poster warning of the risks of unprotected sex alongside baskets of condoms designed to reduce them. She fetched some tea. Eleanor demanded sugar, only to pre-empt her search by reaching into a basket and picking out a sachet of lubricant. She ripped it open and squeezed it into her cup, surprised by its texture but pleased by its taste. 'Not disagreeable,' she decreed as she took a sip. 'It has a different flavour from the granules. What's it called ... ? "K-Y Jelly". Remind me to order some for home.'

She wipes her eyes of today's gloom and Friday's laughter and relishes the sweetness of spite.

> The Vicar leads the General Confession.

Massimo wonders how much longer the prayers will last. His impatience feeds his guilt. He feels an overwhelming urge to tear off his clothes and jump into the sea ... but a sea made up not of waves but of bodies, naked bodies with a Mediterranean warmth ... bodies which thrash and crash on a dance-floor and then gently lap the walls of a darkened club. He wants to taste the salt and the sweat: the splashing on his limbs and the moisture in the air: the surge and the swell and the break and the roll and the spume; most especially, the spume. He longs to return to life.

The chill of death is tinged with rancour. Julian told him – at a time when illness was still academic – that, in Shakespeare's day, syphilis was known as the Neapolitan disease. He feels sure that these people hold him similarly to blame: Massimo, the open fly. He longs to disabuse them: to present his results like testimonials and challenge their insular conviction that Deviance is the capital of Abroad. 'I'm clean,' he wants to shout, 'I'm clean!' And the intensity of his emotions is such that, for a moment, he mistakes the desire for the deed.

He steals a glance at Julian's mother, who sits as if her feelings were locked in the bank. Propriety is her truth, as she attributes Julian's death to Legionnaire's Disease – the stigma of Naples having spread to its air. But then she cares less for her son than for her parrot ... a perverse choice of pet for one who sets such store by discretion. And he yearns to reveal what he heard when she visited the hospital last week. At first, he thought that it was his ear which was at fault; but it was her heart. She sat beside Julian's bedside and confided her fears about Stevenson, who was refusing to eat and showing some slight discolouration on his beak.

'Mother, I'm dying,' Julian pleaded, in a voice which left no room for doubt.

'It's no use pulling rank, dear,' she replied briskly, 'we all have our crosses to bear.'

> The Vicar lays his hands on the patient, saying:
> *In the name of our Lord Jesus Christ who laid his hands on the sick that they might be healed, I lay my hands upon you, Julian. May almighty God, Father, Son, and Holy Spirit, make you whole in body, mind, and spirit, give you light and peace, and keep you in life eternal. Amen.*

Julian lies in the chrysalis of his covers. The thrill of transformation banishes his fears. His mind is as peaceful as the dove which flutters over him, fanning him with its wings. He has broken all ties with the present. His last words lie sealed against his lips. The people he leaves behind will be coming with him. Nothing is lost.

The casting of life and death as opposites is as misguided as the belief that matter is solid or the earth flat. 'In the midst of life we are in death' is far too important a phrase to be lost in the whistle of wind-swept cypresses or the tears of grieving friends. Death has always been a part of him, however much he tried to dismiss it with ghost-train bravado or a cheque to Christian Aid. Now it takes its place at the edge of his bed like an old friend: a bosom pal, a soul mate, a partner for a gentle rubber of bridge, rather than an opponent for an apocalyptic game of chess.

Death is the apex of existence. It is the prism for the cosmic radiance which is refracting through his body. It is the forge of the molten stars which are streaming through his blood. His flesh and his spirit are imploding to form a new galaxy. He is both the creator and the crucible of the universe. He is Alpha and Omega, Genesis and Revelation. He is returning to ... he is part of ... he is God.

> The Vicar prepares the holy oil, saying:
> *God of mercy,*
> *Ease the sufferings and comfort the weakness of your servant,*
> *whom the Church anoints with this holy oil.*

On 17 April, peacefully in hospital after a short illness contracted abroad, Julian Stanford Blaikie, beloved son of Lady Eleanor Blaikie and the late Admiral Sir Dennis Blaikie GCB, sister of . . . no, she refuses to be coupled with Helena, even in *The Times*. She requires no buttress in her grief.

Eleanor composes the notice like an antiphon to Huxley's prayer. She is distracted by a muffled sniff . . . the masculine compromise with emotion. She makes no attempt to identify the source. She has dispatched Edith whose effusions were becoming an embarrassment. The others are not her concern. Strangers have to assert their credentials with tears. Hers is the deeper bond of blood.

She is no stranger to tears. In years gone by, dolour was her middle name: her middle married name; her middle maiden name was joy. She endured nothing but misery from a husband who was as absent at home as at sea. She endures nothing but misery from children who give new meaning to the word 'ingratitude'. Responsibility, to both, is a concept as remote as rationing. Helena married a 'performance artist' who vomited in public, while Julian has remained a schoolboy at heart . . . and in bed. Her quarrel is not with his sexuality (the Admiral's stories, though broad, were instructive) nor even with his taste for men with skin like freshly waxed floors . . . she glances at Massimo, who sits as maudlin as an opera. No, her quarrel is with his selfishness: his refusal to compromise between desire and duty; his abandonment of the future to the Saturday-night breeders; his adolescent contempt for a well-ordered double life.

A rattle emanating from Julian's mouth, like a cart trundling over a cattle-grid, seizes her attention – to her immediate regret. He looks so like her father that her isolation is increased. When Julian dies, her last illusion of intimacy will be destroyed. She will spend the rest of her life among strangers, whose pay-slip allegiance will leave her in permanent fear of theft. His death runs contrary to all her assumptions. Wives are supposed to outlive their husbands (that is their recompense), but sons are supposed to outlive their mothers. She pictures the notice of her own death ('mourned by Edith Sadler, her companion of thirty years') and, for the first time, wipes away a tear.

> The Vicar makes the sign of the cross on the patient's forehead, saying:
> *Julian, I anoint you with oil in the name of our Lord Jesus Christ. May our heavenly Father make you whole in body and mind and grant you the inward anointing of His Holy Spirit, the Spirit of strength and joy and peace. Amen.*

Huxley finds the prayer sticking in his throat like the unguent on his fingers. He is anointing Julian in a manner endorsed by St James, and yet his place in the Apostolic Succession, far from giving him courage, leaves him feeling like the sickly son of an inbred dynasty. He can neither respect a God of whom he is a representative nor expect it of anyone else.

He has not so much lost faith as faith has lost him. He continues to pray but it is prayer as therapy: an exercise in contemplation: the religious equivalent of Jessica's yoga. Its practical effect will be nil. If a divine master-plan exists (and that 'if' is the longest word in the language), it won't be altered by a few selective appeals. What's more, his egalitarian heart baulks at requesting special treatment. The gift of faith – which God alone can bestow – should be enough in itself without the faithful angling for further favours.

All his doubts about the power of prayer are echoed in regard to the power of healing. Nothing can be more absurd than a vicar with a vial of oil trying to effect a cure which has eluded the world's top scientists. He has reconciled Darwin and Moses ... he has integrated black holes with 'let there be light', nevertheless, watching the cross slither over Julian's forehead, he is acutely aware of the rift between his parents' world and God's. His one hope lies in his own irrelevance: that God will act through him as He is said to have done through men and women from Elijah to Rasputin ... not just prophets and saints but kings and queens, whose miracle cures belied their worldly lives. They too were the Lord's anointed, enabled to transcend their faults. God works in mysterious ways and one of those ways may be him.

> The Vicar makes the sign of the cross on the patient's hands, saying:
> *May the Lord who frees you from sin save you and raise you up. Amen.*

Brandon is steeped in death. In this clean, well-ordered hospital, he feels as though he is under fire in Sarajevo. He has spent the past two hours at the bedside of a patient who, in spite of incontinence and dementia, had to wait for his last breath to suffer the final indignity. After lying torpid for days, he jerked upright with a cry of 'I'm dying for a cup of tea!', before falling back on the pillow. A lifelong object of ridicule to those who took the mannerisms for the man, he goes to his grave with a red nose attached to his corpse. Meanwhile, his distraught lover is left with a fit of giggles to add to his guilt.

Having offered what comfort he could (his words proving as

ineffectual as his drugs), he has come to visit Julian. Alert to the imminence of his death and dreading any loss of professional composure, he has snatched every chance to be somewhere else all day. Steeling himself, he walks up to the room, only to be checked by a shout of 'You can't go in there!'. He stares with surprise at a severe but rounded woman, who puts him in mind of a French lavatory attendant guarding the door with her suspicions and her plate.

'Father Huxley's anointing Julian with oil,' she explains.

A closer inspection identifies her as Lady Blaikie's companion. 'Why aren't you inside?' he asks.

'It was too much for me. Unlike some I could mention. You could stick a pin in her and she wouldn't flinch.'

Gazing through the glass, he feels a surge of anger at the sight of the Vicar making the sign of the cross on Julian's hands. It is bad enough that he should be allowed to perform such hocus-pocus in church without his importing it into the hospital. The only consolation is that Julian is too insensible to respond. The Vicar might as well be polishing an effigy on a tomb.

> *Lord Jesus Christ, you chose to share our human nature, to redeem all people, and to heal the sick. Look with compassion upon your servant Julian, whom we have anointed in your name with this holy oil for the healing of his body and spirit. Since you have given him a share in your own Passion, help him to find hope in suffering, for you are Lord for ever and ever. Amen.*

Julian feels the oil spin around him like silk. He watches the words fly about the room like humming-birds. His mortal mind makes a final attempt to define ... to confine his sensations as he is swept up on the wings of a vast embrace. He has solved the mystery of creation. He is love. He is power. He is spirit. He is.

Confirmation Class

Monday 6.oo p.m.
Deepdene, Vale of Health

> My God, my God, why hast thou forsaken me? why art
> thou so far from helping me, and from the words of
> my roaring?

Blair kneels in prayer, reciting the twenty-second psalm. He finds
comfort in the fellowship of the forsaken: the evidence of a pain as
raw as his. He finds comfort in the extravagance of the expression:
the unrestrained imagery of despair. He finds comfort in the translation: that the ordinary Cambridge scholars who prepared the
Authorized Version should produce poetry as rich as Shakespeare's.
He finds comfort in its continuing place in worship: that, unlike
some Victorian aesthete desperate to authenticate his feelings, he
has no need to resort to classical Greece. Above all, he finds comfort in the sexuality of a great king: the poet, the soldier and the
Lord's Anointed: the lover of both men and women. He reads the
psalm as David's grief at the death of Jonathan and uses it to frame
his own mourning for Julian.

A shrill ring pierces the supple silence of David's tent. Blair
ignores it, until its persistence thrusts him back to the present. He
answers the door.

'Lyndon, I wasn't expecting you.' He looks at his watch. 'I haven't
missed server practice, have I?'

'It's confirmation class.'

'But we agreed last Monday that, with Jeremy and Celia away,
we'd give it a miss.'

'I don't remember.'

'I'm sure I said that there'd be no point with only the two of us.'

'Oh well, if you don't want me, I'll go.'

Lyndon's hurt erupts on his face like a boil.

'That's not what I meant. Come in.'

'Thank you.' He rushes past, as though afraid that the invitation
might be withdrawn. 'I've so much to tell you ... things the others
wouldn't understand.'

'I'm a bit pushed. I have to prepare for the PCC at seven. Still, that leaves an hour. Would you like a cup of coffee?'

'No, let's not waste time. Me sitting here. You watching the kettle. All that steam.'

'Sit down, Lyndon.' Lyndon sits on the edge of the couch; Blair instinctively moves to the furthest armchair. 'You seem agitated. Are you all right?'

'I'm always all right when I'm with you.'

'I only wish I had that effect on the rest of the parish.' He perches on the arm of his chair, idly swinging his leg. 'Well, as you say: we mustn't waste time. The topic for discussion is the nature of a Christian life.'

'I love this room.' Lyndon swivels round. 'If there were a *Desert Island Discs* for places, this is the one I'd take. Out of all the eight.'

'I'm flattered. Now, back to the Christian life.'

'The way you've hung all the pictures: the icons and the photos.'

'Lyndon, please ... Thank you. In a few weeks' time, you'll be confirmed. We've looked at what it means to be a full member of the Anglican Church. We've examined the place of communion. What we need to explore further is what constitutes a Christian life.'

'But it's obvious,' Lyndon replies with some irritation. 'Jesus made it quite clear. First, we must love God; then, we must love our neighbour as ourself.'

'Yes. That's fine as a basis. Do as you would be done by: the Golden Rule. But should we delve a little deeper? How do we define "love"? How do we define "neighbour"? Maybe, even, how do we define "ourself"?'

'How old were you when you knew that you wanted to be a priest?'

'Lyndon, this isn't like you; you're usually so focused.'

'Were you older than me?'

'I didn't want to be a priest. I wanted to be anything but a priest. I tried to escape my vocation for years.'

'Is that why you became an actor?'

'And a night-watchman, a dog-walker and a telephone pollster. Let's not forget the roles that really paid.'

'But you became famous as Dr Silkin. You were a great actor.'

'You're too young to remember. Now that would be one of my precepts for loving your neighbour: being honest with him.'

'They showed *The Hellfire Club* late-night on BBC2 last week.'

'I know. Judith Shellard told me. She would.'

'I videoed it. You were wonderful.'

'Thank you. It was a long time ago.'

'You were naked.'

'As I said: it was a long time ago.'

'I was amazed.'

'It wasn't that spectacular.'

'And they still let you become a priest?'

'I don't think that the previous Bishop of London, who ordained me, was a devotee of low-budget British films.'

'What if you become Archbishop of Canterbury? Someone could dig it up and plaster it on the front page of the *Sun*.'

'Let's take it a step at a time. I've yet to have my own parish.'

'I've kept the video. I'm never going to tape over it. I shall watch it again and again.'

'I'm beginning to find this distasteful.'

'No, it's wonderful. You're wonderful. You're the reason I have a vocation. I feel it here, in my body. Sometimes, when I'm standing next to you in church, it surges through me and I'm afraid that I'm going to explode. There'll be little bits of me scattered all over the altar.'

'And you're sure that this is a vocation?'

'I've never been surer of anything in my life. Shall I tell you my favourite time? Just before a service, when the choir and the servers pray with you and Father Huxley in the sacristy. There's no congregation to shuffle and make noises – sitting there like sheep. Baa baa baa. How I hate them! – taking our minds off Christ.'

Blair reassesses Lyndon's mood.

'You know that it's quite usual to experience intense emotions in adolescence.'

'You might at least come up with something original. You're as bad as my parents. They think my vocation is just a phase I'm going through . . . like spots.'

'I don't mean to offend you.'

'My mum actually blames my skin on the time I spend in church. She says it isn't healthy, what with all the dust. She even wants to have me tested for an allergy to incense! I said it was her cooking, more like. All the dead animals they force me to eat. "Get some fresh air," she says . . . as if we were living in the country. While my dad just sits there, night after night, watching his detective programmes – defective programmes, I call them. Not that he can appreciate the joke. The other night at tea, he hit me. And, when I said that it proved the weakness of his argument, he sent me up to my room. "Good," I said; "at least that means I won't have to eat any more of her food." I hate them; I hate them both.'

'You mustn't hate your parents.'

'How can you be such a hypocrite?'

'What?'

'You were the one who taught us what Jesus said about families. See, I learned it by heart: "If any man come to me, and hate not his father, and mother, and wife, and children, and brethren, and sisters, yea, and his own life also, he cannot be my disciple."'

'Lyndon, you've misunderstood me – or, rather, you've misunderstood Christ, which is worse. He was speaking metaphorically.'

'Hate was the word He used: Hate. You can't get away from it.'

'I'm beginning to think that your mother was right. Maybe you do spend too much time in church.'

'So you take me for a freak, like all the rest.'

'Of course not. I'm very –' he dismisses *fond* '– glad that you're so devout. Nevertheless, you need to find a balance . . . spend more time with your friends.'

'I don't have any friends.'

'I'm sure that's not true.'

'How do you know? You think you know all about me. I know what you think. Well you're wrong. I despise them. They're obsessed with sex: tittering in the classroom; whistling in the streets; scrawling in the lavatories. Sex, sex, sex! I never think about sex.'

Blair looks at Lyndon. He registers his clothes: the jumble-sale jacket, baggy shirt and creaseless flannel trousers, which give no more impression of his body than washing on a line.

'Please calm down.'

'The other day, some boys in my form put a picture on my desk of a woman's . . . a woman's thing, all stretched and dark. I thought it was the mouth of a cave with a stalactite hanging down. And everyone sniggered as I looked at it, even the girls. Because I didn't know what it was. I'm doing GCSE biology and I still didn't know what it was!'

Blair moves to hug him, trying to submerge the personal in the pastoral. Lyndon pushes him away.

'I can't be confirmed. I must go. I just can't.'

'There's no way I'll let you leave like this. Take a deep breath and try to tell me what's upsetting you. I promise that nothing you say will go any further than me.'

'But you're the only one I care about.'

'Would you rather talk to Father Huxley?'

'He wouldn't understand. He's too pure.'

'Thanks.' Blair laughs.

'I mean old; he's too old. And you were an actor. What do you

think Jesus meant by the "blasphemy against the Holy Ghost" ...
the one sin which can never be forgiven?'

'That's a tough one ... not least because I don't believe that
there's any sin which can't be forgiven. God is love – Universal,
Unconditional Love – and therefore Absolute Compassion. But, if
you insist on an answer, I'd say that it's not fulfilling your potential.
After all, human beings are made in God's image, so, if we squander
our talents ... if we deny our creativity, then we're not just dimin-
ishing ourselves but God. And, to me, that is the ultimate sin.'

'I always thought it was suicide. Which is why the bodies can't
be buried in churchyards.'

'Suicide is just an extreme example of wasted gifts: the scapegoat
for everything else.'

'I want to kill myself.'

'Lyndon, you're fifteen years old.'

'So? Is it like a driving licence or the right to vote? Do you have
to be over a certain age before you can have certain feelings?'

'I'm sorry. I don't mean to belittle you. Is there any particular
problem?' He responds to a series of sobs and sniffs by deciding to
risk the obvious. 'Would it have something to do with sex?'

'What do you mean?'

'You were evidently disgusted by that photograph of the woman.'

'It wasn't of a woman; it was just of her bit.'

'Is that because you're more attracted to men?' Blair puts on a
voice like a hospital visit.

'I shall be damned!'

'Oh Lyndon, trust me; you won't.'

'I've never done anything. Honest!' He grabs Blair's crucifix
from the mantelpiece. 'I've seen other boys. They ... do things,
even though they have girlfriends. They laugh like it's all a piece of
fun. But I swear. Not once. I swear.'

'I believe you. In any case, I'm not here to judge – not that
there's anything to judge; I'm here to help.' He clasps Lyndon's
shoulder and feels the clammy tweed. He knows that he must
stand back and does so literally. He is struck by the irony that, on a
day when he mourns his own lost love, he dare not reveal himself
to Lyndon. 'I know how you hurt.'

'How?'

'Because I'm older.' Blair drops the challenge like a match-
winning catch. 'I have friends. You imagine you're the only gay boy
in the world.'

'Of course I don't. I watch television: men in black with caps
and belts ... or wearing women's clothes as if their whole life was

a pantomime ... or dying of AIDS every time you turn on Channel Four.'

Blair feels the lesions burning on his hands. 'But there are others like you...' The 'and me' is as silent as the 'k' in knave. 'There are gay men and women of every sort, and many thousands of them are in the Church. Just as you are now and will be even more so come Whit. Confirmation doesn't mean conformity.'

'But it does mean reading the Bible.'

'Amongst other things.'

'And obeying the Word of God.'

'But the Word of God isn't only written down. It's carved in forests and hills and faces ... which seem to me to be far more authentic expressions of His will. How much of what you call the Word of God consists of words which have been put into God's mouth?'

'That's blasphemy.'

'We're not Moslems. God may have dictated the Koran to Mohammed, but He only dictated a few verses to Moses. The rest is a record, divinely inspired but humanly mediated. It's a map which is too often taken for a destination. To my mind, that's a form of Bible abuse.'

'You can't wriggle out of it that easily. Look at Sodom.'

'If I must.'

'God razed it to the ground because of its sin.'

'But that sin was inhospitality.'

'And mine's nail-biting!'

'If you won't take my word, take Christ's. His one reference to it comes in the context of people who don't make the disciples welcome. He clearly regards it as inhospitality ... with a capital "I".'

'There are lots of other references in the Bible.'

'I'll answer every one. Can you stay all night?'

'Oh yes.'

'No!'

'Because you're scared of being shown up. What about St Paul?'

'St Paul's main concern was to establish Christianity and to distinguish it from the various cults which practised temple prostitution. I doubt that he had the least inkling of the sort of loving feelings you experience.'

'They're not loving.'

'They would be if you didn't wall them up. I sometimes doubt whether St Paul had any normal human feelings at all.'

'But he was a saint!'

'He wasn't born with a halo. There were no hushed voices around his mother's bed: "Is it a boy or a girl?" "Neither; it's a saint." He was made a saint and by men who shared his way of thinking. The crunch comes when you remember what else he said, for instance, his endorsement of slavery. Did William Wilberforce or Abraham Lincoln think "Hang on! What are we doing? St Paul ruled that a slave should obey his master."? Of course not. They followed their consciences. If only middle England and middle America would do as much on other issues.'

'You never say anything like this in church.'

'It's not easy. Just because I stand in a pulpit doesn't always permit me to speak my mind. Which is why it's so important for you to bypass the preachers and work things out for yourself. Be sceptical, above all else, of people who tell you that they alone have access to the truth: the "my God is bigger than your God" brigade, whose creed isn't "I believe in God" but "I know God".'

Lyndon ponders the advice. 'They're just words. I can't see that it makes much difference.'

'Look at the people, not the words, and you'll see that it's all the difference in the world. "I believe in God" can be tested; "I believe in God" can be honed; "I believe in God" allows room for growth. But "I know God" is absolute; "I know God" implies that there's nothing more to be learnt ... "I know God": end of story, revelation and *Revelation*. "I know God", so I don't need to know you. "I know God", so I'm better than you. And where do they know him from? The Bible. But doesn't the Bible say that we're made in God's image? In which case, we must also be able to find Him in our hearts.'

'Then why do they condemn what we find in our hearts? Why do they throw it out and lock it up and call it names?'

'Power, to put it bluntly. Sex is the second strongest human instinct. What better way to assert your authority than to control it?'

'That's not true! There are lots of stronger instincts. Lots. We're not all Don Juan.'

'It holds true even if you're John Donne ... Look at the way the Church Fathers tried to curb all forms of sexuality. St Jerome even declared that too much pleasure in marriage was a form of adultery. It's as if, to him, sexual desire was Adam's curse in the way that the pain of childbirth was Eve's. Can you credit anything so perverse? The early Protestants made some amends by legitimizing pleasure between husband and wife, but they continued to demonize homosexuals on the grounds that all Catholic priests were gay.'

'And were they?' Lyndon's voice cracks with excitement.

'No, of course not. It was pure propaganda. Like all Jews have big noses and all blacks have big...'

'What?'

'Are fast runners ... born dancers: I don't know. It's a fantasy. They claimed that same-sex love was unnatural, but the very extent of their activities proves the opposite. It's precisely because it was both natural and widespread that they had to devote such resources to stamping it out.'

'So they're the ones who should have been burnt at the stake, since they were the ones who were doing the work of the Devil.'

'I'm not sure that it's helpful to think in those terms – even figuratively. It leads to precisely the sort of dualism which sees sex as sinful.'

'Don't you believe in the Devil?'

'Of course not. Why, do you?'

'Well not with cloven hooves and horns, any more than I believe in a God with a cotton-wool beard. But there has to be something out there. How else do you explain evil?'

'As easily as I define it. It's the collective force of all that's contrary to God.'

'But if there's no Devil, then God must have created it ... like establishing his own opposition.'

'God doesn't create evil; He accepts the necessity for it. To use one of the most fruitful ambiguities in the language, He suffers it ... He both allows it to happen and feels the pain.'

'But why? That seems far more perverse than any bigoted Church Fathers.'

'On the contrary, it's His greatest gift to humanity: the essence of being made in His image. Don't frown. It's not such a paradox. You said yourself that we have to jettison the cotton-wool beard. I believe that, just as God exists in three persons, so He's also composed of three aspects: creativity, love and moral judgement. The correspondences are clear: God the Father who created us; God the Son who shows us the pattern of perfect love; and God the Holy Spirit who embodies that love in practical morality. Evil is necessary for the exercise of moral choice which is a primary function of God.'

'But what if we're not capable of exercising it? What if God expects too much of us?'

'Isn't that better than expecting too little?'

'You say evil gives us a chance to be like God. But what about the victims of ethnic cleansing or a terrorist bomb or the children massacred at Dunblane? How much choice did they have?'

'The equation isn't that easy.'

'It doesn't have to be easy; it has to be fair.'

'I can only explain by going back to the very beginning. God created the universe. For years, I used to wonder why. But now I understand that it was inevitable. Creativity is the essence of His being. He could no more not have created it than you or I could not breathe.'

'We'd die.'

'Right. And God would cease to be: not just a physical death but a metaphysical impossibility. And what did He create it out of, if not Himself? But the moment that He moved from eternity to time: the moment that He moved from spirit to matter, there was bound to be a dilution: a diminution: an imperfection. And out of the imperfection of the natural world have come the earthquakes, the droughts, the floods and the diseases, just as out of the imperfection of human nature have come the tyrannies, the violence, the cruelties and the crimes. The first we can strive to contain; the second to eradicate. But we must always remember that if it weren't for these imperfections – this evil – then we'd be living in a world without conflicts or distinctions, in which free will would be reduced to nothing more than choosing between two flavours of toothpaste.'

'You make it sound as if evil is another word for good.'

'No. But I think that it might be described as a necessary evil.' He laughs ruefully. 'Which is why I can have no truck with the serpent in Eden. For the truth is not that we misused our free will and fell from paradise but that our separation from paradise is a prerequisite for our exercise of free will.'

'But, if there was no Fall, then there was no need for Christ to come and redeem us.'

'Perhaps He didn't ... perhaps He came not to suffer for us but to suffer with us. And to suffer with His father: to be the visible expression of His father's pain. It may be heresy, but I'm convinced that God's sacrifice in the act of creation was as great ... if not greater than Christ's on the Cross. Christ gave up His body; God gave up His spirit. He breathed His own life into Adam, animating him with a vast, cosmic kiss. And our failure to respond to His love has caused Him infinite anguish. Even so, He must believe that it's worth enduring or He would have ended the world long ago. Which is what gives me faith in the future. And why you must never despair.'

Lyndon rises from his chair and flings his arms around Blair, who suspects that his motive is not merely gratitude. He extricates himself from his grasp, abandoning the eternal verities under the pressure of time.

'It's ten past six. I'm afraid we must call it a day. I have to prepare some notes on the clergy-house for the PCC.'

SERVICE OF HEALING

Monday 7.30 p.m.
St Barnabas, Euston

> The accompanist plays mood music on the synthesizer.
> The projectionist projects biblical landscapes onto a
> screen attached to the pulpit.

Jessica slips into the cream and gold neo-classical interior, so redolent of the Age of Reason that she half-expects to hear a lecture by Voltaire. The incongruity is increased by the soupy, supermarket music and the fuzzy slides which suggest that the church has been taken over by a firm marketing time-share apartments in the Middle East. Pyramid selling? She quells her irreverence – even though it may be the only way to survive the service – and peers over the pews to find her friends. She catches sight of Cherish, or rather the beads which hang like Christmas in her hair.

She squeezes into the seat beside Femi. 'I'm so sorry. I went to call on Eleanor Blaikie. I thought it might help her to talk to someone else who'd lost a son. But she seemed more distressed about having used up all the dry sherry.'

'Perhaps it's her way of coping,' Femi replies. 'She has that age-old hearts-of-oak air. She always clears her throat before she talks to me as though she were tuning into the World Service. The other day she asked how I managed to keep Cherish so clean.'

'I am clean! I have to wash with a very especial cream.'

'Hush child. Do you want the whole world to hear you?'

'It's not the whole world. It's not even half the world. It's just a church.'

Jessica leans across Femi to give Cherish a kiss. As she brushes her upturned face, the pupils barely visible behind her eyelids and the nostrils aquiver with acute sensation, she wishes that she were wearing a more exotic perfume.

'Huxley loathes this type of service,' she says to Femi. 'He regards it as collective hysteria.'

'Huxley is the perfect English gentleman. He wants to make God in his own image. Decent. Restrained. He reminds me of the Reverend Butterfly, who was the first white man I ever met. He sat at his piano in church, pedalling hymns about "Afric's sons of colour deep, coming, coming from afar".'

'Be fair. Huxley would never do anything so insensitive. He's already in trouble with the PCC for banning several un-p.c. hymns.'

'That's not what I meant. Reverend Butterfly was a good man. He treated us exactly like his Sunday school in Norwich. To him, we were just white children who'd stayed out too long in the sun. Huxley's the same. He looks at us and he doesn't see the colour of our skin. But, sometimes, that's no different from not looking at us. It's to deny that things have happened to me because I'm black ... that things happened to Dayo because she was black ... that things have happened to Cherish because she's black. Bad things.' Her lips tremble. 'I'm sorry. I've had a hellish day. What I'm saying is that I can need more than St Mary's and Huxley's colour-blind prayers. My father believed in Jesus the way he believed in the Queen. He hung pictures of them opposite each other on the wall. But there was another world ... an older world which he knew that he must never offend. And, when one of us was ill or when the Mogube chief put the whole tribe under a curse, it wasn't to decent, restrained Reverend Butterfly with his *Church Missionary Hymn-Book* that we went, but to the old, wise woman with her scratchy smell and her bones and her dust and her berries and her words that slid like crocodiles out of the mud.'

Jessica despairs of a humanism which is irrelevant to half of humanity. She feels herself turning into her mother, with nothing to offer but a hug. 'If there's anything I can do...'

'Thanks. But there's not. I must put my faith elsewhere ... faith that mountains can remove. That may be hard for you; but, where I come from, the mountains are full of spirits. If my faith is strong enough, she can be cured.'

Jessica takes her hand as they stare at the Mount of Olives flickering on the screen.

> The slide of the mountain is taken out and replaced by the legend: Jesus Christ is Lord.

Femi squirms in the discomfort of the pew. She gazes at Cherish rubbing her mittens together and is moved by the resemblance to Dayo ... Dayo, her beloved younger sister who abandoned the safety of England to return home and compounded her folly by marrying Albert, a radical lawyer, who once defined the pursuit of justice in Lagos as trying to ensure that the guilty in prison outnumbered the innocent. He lived at permanent risk of confirming his own definition. And yet his downfall was not the result of any of his cases but of one of the women whom he frequented in between. Dayo knew of them and made no protest. But Femi raged across thousands of miles on receipt of her air-lettered pain.

Dayo paid for Albert's betrayal with more than her pride, as the bed which they had shared became a sickbed and the kisses infections. The one flesh of their marriage-vows shrank, first, to one skin-and-bone and, then, to one grave ... She refuses to dwell on her sister's agony; she has to save all her thoughts – all her prayers for Cherish: the child who was born with her mother's looks and heart but her father's virus. And, as if her paternal inheritance were not enough, she was left at the mercy of Africa, where a botched operation for cataracts robbed her of her sight. Femi swore that, from then on, her doctors would be the best in the world.

Her commitment has cost her dear ... the loss not just of her husband and job but of her whole identity, as she is forced to see herself in the distortions of a newsagent's window: immigrant; single-parent; scrounger. She lives in daily fear of the knock on the door from the suit and the smile come to send Cherish out of the country or, at the very least, away from her.

Wiping her eyes, she lightly rubs Cherish's mittens in an attempt to give her the sensation of touch without the pain.

> Three singers stand in front of the lectern and sing *Jesus Christ is the Lord* to the phrase *Jesus Christ Superstar.*

Jessica scans the church. The box pews make detection difficult, but she spots Esther Bishop sitting alone at the front, wearing a hat which appears to hover above her head as if to disarm criticism. Turning back, she is surprised to see a fellow refugee from St Mary's, Joe Beatty, and flashes him a quizzical smile. Goaded by a further round of 'Jesus Christ is the Lord', she stares at the three fresh-faced crooners with their clean-cut conviction and wonders if this endless repetition is the extent of their repertoire. Thirty years ago, during her one experience of LSD, she watched the patterns on the wallpaper move. Now, she is hearing them sing. Never has she felt more certain that the Devil has all the best tunes.

> The Minister moves to the front of the nave. He welcomes the Bishop and the congregation and announces the hymn: *Glorious things of thee are spoken, Zion, city of our God.*

Unable to find a hymn-book, Joe presumes that he must be expected to know the words by heart, until a glance at the pulpit reveals the first verse projected on the screen. He tries to sing but, without a book in his hand, he feels exposed. He resolves to persevere, conscious that he hides behind books too readily: at home, at work, even in church. For once, he can allow his heart to soar. But, focusing on the screen, he is horrified to find it invaded by an apocalyptic beast, all tentacles and antennae, which passes through 'the streams of living waters' and threatens to obliterate 'eternal love'.

Zion's city shakes, while the projectionist tries to dislodge the beetle which has crawled onto the slide. As stability is restored, several of the worshippers raise their hands, palms upwards, to the skies. Joe recalls Blair's description of evangelicals as Corkscrew Christians ... their arms lifting as they reach the spirit. But it suddenly seems sad rather than smart. He has come to the service in good faith. In the past, he shared Blair's reservations. Even last night, when the Bishop made the offer of healing, he barely gave it a thought. Then, this afternoon, everything changed. He stood beside Dee at the rehearsal and what had been a marriage of convenience became something more. As Huxley explained the procedures ... as his bride-to-be smiled puckishly ... as his parents sat proudly in their pew, he knew that he wanted it for real.

History is full of conversions. He must take his cue from St Paul (the Road to Damascus not the Epistle to the Romans). No one is set in his ways at twenty-eight. Besides, Dee is equally inexperienced. They will make love like brother and sister ... no, that's quite the wrong image. What's more, his stomach will be less of a stumbling-block with a woman; there will be no mirror-sharp comparisons. The only snag is Alice, whom he plans on betraying as casually as he might stand her up for lunch. But she is so much older than Dee and so absorbed in Dora and her career. She will probably produce far finer paintings as a result of her pain.

He must not become carried away. There remains one huge, microscopic obstacle in his blood. Even so, HIV is not incurable. He has heard of men who have rid themselves of the virus through Chinese herbs or Buddhist chanting. But, however religiously he follows them, he remains far too wedded to Western pills and Christian prayers. He tries to meditate, and his mantra becomes a laundry-list. He tries to visualize, and his meadows are filled with manure. So he must look for the healing at the heart of his own tradition. If the lamas and the yogis can cure their followers, surely the Bishop must do as much for him?

The Bishop strides into the pulpit to deliver the sermon.

'"Jesus replied, Go back and report to John what you hear and see; the blind receive sight, the lame walk, those who have leprosy are cured, the deaf hear, the dead are raised." Matthew 11 verses 4 and 5. Jesus healed people. The Bible makes it quite clear. And the Bible is the Word of God. But today there are many people – even those who call themselves Christians – who deny it. They are embarrassed by miracles because they contradict the world as they know it: a world in which God doesn't intervene. And why doesn't He intervene? Because they don't ask Him to. They reject the power which Jesus gave to His followers, to His faithful, to every Christian: to heal one another in His name.

'To such humanists – I call them humanists even if they call themselves Christians – healing is too hands-on, too crowd-pleasing. They want to strip Christ of His divinity, reducing Him to a first-century Robin Hood. So out go the Virgin Birth, the miracles and – dare I say it? – the Resurrection, leaving little more than the Sermon on the Mount and the parables. They read the gospels like a modern novel where nothing can be taken on trust. To them, Matthew, Mark, Luke and John weren't inspired by the Holy Spirit but compromised by their own agendas. They attack the very nub of the faith: the Christ who walks on water; the Christ who feeds the five thousand; the Christ who heals the sick and raises the dead; the Christ, in a word, whom I bring to you tonight.

'These atheists – humanists is too mild a name – are doubly culpable. They don't just deny Jesus; they deny Satan. They trot out their cocktail-stick arguments: the Devil is as mythical as the Loch Ness Monster; Christ's temptations were hallucinations (after forty days without food or drink in that heat, He was bound to start seeing things). And they laugh as though they've said something witty. They'll be laughing on the other side of their faces soon enough. And the rot reaches to the heart of the Church. When was the last time you heard a vicar preach a sermon on Hell or a bishop make a statement on Satan? No, they prefer single mothers or inner-city deprivation. What about inner-self deprivation? I tell you: if you mean to follow Christ, you must learn to give the Devil his due.

'Only liberals would call that a contradiction. The rest of us can see that, the moment you deny the Devil, you diminish Christ. If you reduce the forces of evil to the works of men, you make Christ no more than a social reformer. You turn "Let the little children come to me" into Lord Shaftesbury saving them from the mines. You turn "The demon has left your daughter" into Sigmund Freud putting her on a couch. What's more, you're left with a two-faced

God, like an Indian idol, sending down blessings and His son on the one hand and trials and tribulations on the other. You're forced to spell every disease in the dictionary with a "y": "why me? Why Aunt Gertie? Why little Sheila? Why does God make the innocent suffer?" Well He doesn't, but the Devil does. The Devil delights in innocent suffering and, not least, because it leads mankind to question the will of God.

'So who is more powerful? God or the Devil? Do I really need to answer? I leave it to the fathers among you to explain to the rest. You may ask: why did God create the Devil? But remember that, when God created him, he wasn't the Devil; he was Lucifer, Son of Light. God offered him a share of His bliss just as He did man. And, like man, he fell (without even the excuse of woman egging him on). So does this make God a bad judge of character? No, no, and again no. It shows that He is all benevolence and trust. God gave His creatures freedom. He waited for thousands of years – He waited through the whole of the Old Testament – for man to renounce the Devil and return to Him. And, when He gave up hope, He didn't give up on man but sent His son, the ultimate sacrifice, to defeat the Devil and redeem the world.

'The battle is won, but it's not yet over. It will continue until the last man banishes Satan from his heart and the Last Judgement banishes him into the eternal abyss. And we must arm ourselves for the fight every day. We must acknowledge that evil and suffering are not simply products of circumstance, still less are they blots on God's master-plan for mankind; they are trials sent by Satan. So let us pray to Christ to use His healing power to destroy them. Let us ask Him to cast out the devils of disease from us just as He did in Galilee. Only Christ has the power to do this. Remember that not once in the gospels is there any mention of Him falling ill. He was weary, yes; He wept, yes. But, despite the constant pressure – always on the move, always surrounded by crowds, many of whom, as we know, were riddled with infection – He never caught so much as a cold. What modern doctor could survive such a strain? Jesus was a man without sickness, just as He was a man without sin. Amen.'

> Let us pray in the words which Christ himself taught us:
> Our Father in Heaven.

Joe feels confused. With the aid of his counsellor, he has made his escape from the Victorian Foul Ward. And yet he remains in permanent danger of readmission. Like an alcoholic wary of a single whisky, he knows that the least remark can upset his equilibrium.

He tries desperately to prevent backsliding. On two evenings a week, he works as a volunteer for a community helpline. But his repeated assurance to callers that HIV doesn't discriminate suddenly seems hollow. A few words from the Bishop have restored a bloodstained morality ... an eye for an eye and a tooth for a tooth and a virus for a vice. Whether God was punishing him or the Devil is using him, the responsibility – and the guilt – amounts to the same.

> *Hallowed be your name.*

Esther remembers a family outing to a medieval morality play at the Scripture Union. The characters all had names like Goodlife or Badfaith so that, even though the language was confusing, the audience knew where it stood. Humour was supplied by a gang of devils who caused havoc by sweeping away peoples' meals and pulling their stools from under them. They were mischievous rather than malevolent – an effect enhanced by their being acted by children. For days, their own children played similar tricks, stealing each others' pens or sweets and blaming it on the Devil. The joke, as always, went on too long, but it was harmless ... that is until they hid one of her crochet hooks and Ted sat on it. Instead of accepting their apologies, he fetched his father's walking-stick and 'beat the Devil out of them'. Which seemed doubly brutal after he had roared with laughter at the play.

> *Your kingdom come, your will be done, on earth as in heaven.*

Jessica objects to the Bishop's bringing Hallowe'en into Holy Week. His mumbo-jumbo bears as much resemblance to healing as *The Exorcist* does to natural childbirth. And yet the danger cannot be easily dismissed. Both in tenor and tone, he puts her in mind of a Puritan Witchfinder General. Three hundred years ago, he would have examined a woman for lumps – the Devil's Mark – in her vagina – the Devil's Gateway. No doubt he would have been sexually aroused by the sight of her burning at the stake, even as he shrank from the odour of corruption. Duty done, he would have made his way to the neighbouring town and the next victim, having neatly passed off his own inhumanity as the will of God.

> *Give us today our daily bread. Forgive us our sins as we forgive those who sin against us.*

Femi finds the prayer as vivid a return to the landscape of her childhood as a visit to the Palm House at Kew. The Lord's Prayer is the first that she ever learned. The petitions still resonate with the richness of a world where daily bread was kneaded on stones rather than 'baked on the premises' and enemies weren't hidden in government offices but massed in rival tribes. That world was brought to an end by the coming of the oil-men. They appropriated words as easily as land. Even the Lord's Prayer was not exempt as they nailed up their notices, turning trespass from a sin to be forgiven into a crime to be punished by death. She escaped with her life but not her innocence. Now all that remains of her childhood is her faith – which may be why she continues to cling to it – and the small bag of earth which will, one day, be placed on her grave.

> *Lead us not into temptation but deliver us from evil. For the kingdom, the power, and the glory are yours, now and for ever. Amen.*

Cherish knows the prayer by heart and races through it. Sometimes she tries to say it all in one breath, but she always runs out of puff. Her best so far is 'temptation', but it made her sick. She mustn't be sick tonight or the Bishop might not want to come near. Mr Linden says that 'Our Father' are the most important words ever written and that they have been copied into every language under the sun ... and even places where there is no sun, where people live in ice-loos. And, somewhere in the world, at every second of the day, someone will be saying them. Which shows that we're all God's children whatever the colour of our skin. And he put his hand on her shoulder when he said it. Because she's blind.

Some people write out the Lord's Prayer on the back of their stamps. It seems like a waste, but Matthew Norris said that it's in the Book of Records. The most ever is thirty-four times, but Matthew Norris is going to break it. He says everybody has to break some record or else they won't go to Heaven. He's not very fast or brainy, so he's going to learn to write small. Then he'll be in the Book. She asked Aunt Femi what record she should try to break; but Aunt Femi thought it was a joke and said she was always breaking things. She hates it when grown-ups are funny. She cried and Aunt Femi took her in her arms and said that she was going to be the person to live the longest with ... the longest with ... But she wouldn't say with what – just the longest-living person in the world.

She knows that that record has already been won by Methuselah. He lived for more than nine hundred years. No one can beat that.

She's scared that, if she doesn't think of something else soon, she won't be allowed into Heaven. And her skin begins to burn.

> The Bishop invites all who wish for healing to raise their hands. He invokes the Holy Spirit: *Now Lord, I ask for the power to come; power to heal the sick; power to cause the blind to see; power to cast out demons.*

Ted is directed by a member of his team to Femi. He stops short at the sight of Jessica. 'Have you come for healing?'

'Not at all. I'm just here to support my friends.' She squirms beneath his Hammer-horror-film smile.

'Examine your conscience. We are all of us sick. We all need to be made whole.' He turns to Femi. 'So are you the one?'

'No, it's the child.'

Ted leans over Cherish. 'Tell me what's wrong.' Cherish hunches her shoulders and lowers her head.

'Look at me. There's no need to be frightened.'

'She can't look at you; she's blind.' Femi strokes the face which has taught her the distinction between perception and sight.

'And you're asking God to open her eyes?'

Femi is surprised by the need to give details. She is here for a cure not a prescription. 'Not only. She has an immune disfunction.'

'I have AIDS.'

Two women in front turn around. There is a general shuffling. Both Femi and Jessica are stunned.

'Say that again ... no! How did you know?' Femi trawls her memory for indiscretions. All her vigilance has been in vain.

'Hush now,' Ted exhorts her. 'Are you her mother?'

'I'm her aunt.' She determines to make the blood-relationship clear.

'Do you see?' Ted addresses the rest of the congregation. 'The Devil is very cunning. He works through our weakness and our wickedness ... through the wickedness of adults and the weakness of a child.'

Jessica suspects that Ted's theology may be more orthodox than she thought. As the sins of the fathers are visited on the children, God and Satan appear to be acting in accord.

'But Christ is strong,' Ted continues. 'He will drive out the Devil from this child. I call on him to enter her tainted flesh and polluted blood.' Cherish yelps as he clasps her shoulders. Femi aches for the scrofulous skin. Ted lifts his hands to Cherish's scalp.

'Please don't press too hard,' Femi begs. 'She has dermatitis.'

'Oh Lord, pour down your Holy Spirit on your daughter.' Ted

prays and Cherish starts to shake. 'Yes, I sense that this is going deep.' Cherish groans gutturally, foams at the mouth and kicks against the pew. 'I feel the battle rage.'

Sporadic hallelujahs echo through the nave like the guns of arm-chair patriots. Ted steels himself for the final assault. 'I denounce the spirit of disease in the name of Jesus. I claim authority over the Devil through Christ's precious blood. That's right, child, cough up your demons; spit them out!' Cherish emits a searing scream, arches her back, and sits bolt upright. Then she slumps, spent, on the seat.

'Thus I rebuke all devils,' Ted shouts. 'Depart from this child forever.' His eyes follow their invisible progress down the nave.

Jessica trembles as a woman behind her shrieks. 'Look! I see green slime pouring out of her stomach. I smell smoke ... burning.'

'I see a brown body, covered in hair,' another adds. 'I see dragon's eyes.'

Murmurs of sightings and fits of coughing spread through the nave. One woman collapses, overcome by the putative flames. Several people raise handkerchiefs to watery eyes. Jessica pursues Ted's gaze to the roof, where she finds nothing but a pair of plaster cherubs with penises like pimples. The connection is clear.

'Cherish, child: wake up!' Femi tries to rouse her without gripping her skin.

'Let her rest,' Ted says. 'Her body has been a battleground. Have faith and she will be cured.'

'God be praised!' Femi exclaims.

'Hallelujah!' Ted replies, as the Minister leads him back to the sanctuary.

'Has he hypnotized her?' Jessica asks Femi. 'Are you sure it's safe?'

'Look,' Femi replies. 'She's so peaceful. It's as if she has no more pain.'

'You can't believe –'

'I do.' Femi turns eyes on her as vehement as Ted's. 'It's we who are blind ... we who flounder in the dark. But I watched the air turn white around me. I saw the colour being bleached out like a bone. Help me Jessica, please. Whatever you believe, pray to God that the Bishop is right and Cherish will be well.'

> The Bishop stands on the chancel steps and proclaims:
> *Jesus said, Heal the sick who are there and tell them, The Kingdom of God is near you. He who has ears, let him hear.*

Joe's left arm pushes down his right like a Punch-and-Judy puppet-eer. But he knows that it's now or never. And it has been never too often before. He lifts his hand and his hopes to the skies. In spite of a slight wobble, he keeps both raised as the Bishop bears down on him.

'Are you in need of healing?'

'Yes, please.' He feels the hot breath blasting onto his cheek.

'You know what Jesus said: "No one can see the kingdom of God unless he is born again".'

'I do. I am.'

'Will you open your life to the Lord?'

'I have. I do.' He wishes that it sounded less like spring-cleaning.

'What is it that troubles you?'

'The same as the little girl,' he mumbles.

'Speak louder.'

'The same as the little girl.' He looks round and is relieved to find that Jessica and Femi are preoccupied with Cherish. Then he worries that such worldly considerations may jeopardize his cure.

'Are you a homosexual?'

'Yes.'

'Speak up. Don't you want God to hear you?'

'Yes, I am ... that is, I have been in the past.'

'Do you believe in the Devil?'

'I'm not sure. I've always believed in God. Even at school when it was like supporting the wrong football team ... I'm sorry; I'm nervous.'

'Can't you see that believing in God is easy? He wants us to believe in Him. He gives us His Holy Word as proof. But the Devil wants us to doubt him. It's through doubt that he's able to pass unnoticed in the world.'

'You said that he worked through sickness.'

'Sickness is a sign of sin.'

'I'm sorry. I may not be ready for this after all.'

'I see that the Devil has a stronger hold on you than I thought.' Ted places his fingers like electrodes on Joe's head. 'He won't give you up without a struggle. What else have you done to let him in? Have you ever been involved in witchcraft?'

'I'm a librarian!'

'There it is!' he exclaims in triumph. 'Do you stock books on the occult?'

'The odd Dennis Wheatley.' Joe writhes in pained embarrassment.

'Do you stock books on Ouija boards?'

'There may be something in *Beliefs*. Why?'

'Do you stock books on astrology and horoscopes?'

'I can't stand any more of this. I've made a terrible mistake.' He tries to escape from Ted's grip. 'You're the one who needs help.'

'Yes.' Ted is exultant. 'I hear the voice of Satan taunting me. But he has no power; I am protected by Christ.' He closes his eyes. 'I command the spirit of immorality to leave this body. I command the spirit of carnality to leave this body. I command the spirit of Sodom to –'

Joe finally wriggles free. 'Take your hands off me. You're mad!'

Esther stands in her pew and stares at her husband.

'Repent or you will never shake off Satan,' Ted shouts. 'I see him perched on your shoulder; I see his claws tearing into your flesh!'

Joe bolts from the church. With a quick word to Femi, Jessica makes to follow. But she is stopped by Ted who seems to single her out from the congregation. 'Remember the words of the Psalm,' he enjoins. '"The fool says in his heart, There is no God". But it's a still greater fool who denies the Devil. The message for all who wish to be healed is clear: give the Devil no flesh-room; purge your unclean spirits; repent your unnatural sexuality.'

Esther falls to the floor. A gasp runs through the nave. Ted turns to see the Minister and two of his team rushing to her aid. But she quickly revives and rebuffs their assistance with an embarrassed smile. 'My wife is overcome by the power of the spirit,' Ted proclaims. 'If someone could help her into the vestry, the rest of us will carry on God's work.'

The Minister conducts Esther like a foreign dignitary. One of the team picks up her handbag as though afraid that he will never live it down. Esther teeters on rag-doll legs, dreading a second collapse, until a benign presence at her side and gentle pressure on her arm bring reassurance. 'Put your weight on me,' Jessica says and guides her out.

The Bishop's Wife is led into the vestry.

Jessica persuades the Minister and the assistant to return to the service. She hands Esther a glass of water and draws up a chair beside her.

'Are you sure you've not hurt anything?'

'Only my pride. And it would have been a lot worse if you hadn't rescued me. Those men are such frauds. All they care about is toadying to Ted. Thank you for being here – although you're the last person I'd have expected after what you were saying last night.'

'It's a long story.'

'Does your husband know that you've come?'

'I'm a big girl; I don't have to ask his permission.'

'Don't you? That must be nice.'

'Do you want some more water?'

'No. Thank you. It tasted rusty, like it had filtered up through the crypt.'

They sit in silence which Esther finds increasingly disconcerting.

'Is your marriage happy? I'm sorry ... we scarcely know each other. Please forget I asked.'

'Of course you can ask. I'm just not sure that I can answer. Don't get me wrong. I love Huxley ... I love him so much that I spell the word with his name. I just wish that he didn't come attached to all of this.' She gestures expansively around the vestry. 'My father was a vicar and I was never one of those girls who wanted to grow up and marry daddy. Quite the reverse. But I did want to marry Huxley – despite rather than because of his calling. But my need to do my own thing hasn't always bolstered our marriage, let alone his career.'

'He seems so content in his parish.'

'Oh on one level, he is. But he has such talents. And I'm sure that they've only been overlooked on account of his impossible wife: the one who wrote those articles in favour of legalizing pot; the one who lived for months at Greenham Common; the one who was photographed whacking the verger of St-Martin-in-the-Fields across the head at a Trafalger Square rally.'

'Really?'

'Don't remind me. It was in support of the ANC. Someone handed me a placard. "You're holding it like a vicar's wife at a tea-party," he said. "I am a vicar's wife," I replied. Then, to confound expectations, I shouted "Down with oppressors everywhere," and bashed the passing verger.' Esther laughs. 'No, believe me. It isn't funny. Huxley never uttered a word of reproach. Which only made it worse. When I see the people who've been promoted in his place. Oh, there I go again...'

'Believe me, no one's more surprised by the rise of Ted Bishop than I am. But I'm afraid I wouldn't give much for your husband's prospects under Ted. On the way home last night, he described him as the opposition.'

'You'd have a hard job finding two less similar clergy.'

'Oh but there's another reason – one that's far more personal. Am I being disloyal?'

'You tell me.'

'It's his height. Ted's a small man. He always has been. But now he feels it more. He resents anyone tall.'

'You're joking?'

'Not a bit. And I'll tell you something else: he sweats. For a small man, he sweats so much. Sometimes, it soaks right through his surplice. One summer, when he was evangelizing at the Brockwell Park Lido, he came back so wet that I assumed he'd fallen in.'

'I've always thought of bishops as dry and crumbly like Wensleydale cheese.'

'Ted's more like a side of raw beef.'

Jessica studies her and then speaks very slowly. 'It seems to me, if you'll forgive my saying, that you need a life that has nothing to do with being Mrs Bishop – in either sense of the word.'

'You say that when you've only known me one day.'

'I'm sorry. I shouldn't interfere.'

'On the contrary, I'm wondering how you've caught on so fast, when it's taken me more than thirty years. But I have. At last I have. Can I trust you? No, don't answer. I can't even trust myself. But I need to tell you. It's only when I say it out loud that I can start to believe it's real ... I'm on the board of a woman's refuge. Two months ago, all the staff and volunteers went away for a week-end's training. The idea was to bond them together – although I've never known a group who needed it less. They invited me to join them. Ted raised endless objections. Battered wives are his least favourite charity ... he maintains that there are two sides to every marriage. But, in the end, he let me go. And it changed my life. I met so many women: women with ideas, not just responsibilities; young women who didn't treat me like their mother. I listened to them talk about sex and felt as left out as when my grandchildren talk about computers. People speak about the loneliness of being a widow –'

'Or a priest.'

'Or a priest. But there can be nothing as lonely as walking down draughty corridors lined with dusty bishops to a husband who never touches you except when he's scared.'

'You do still sleep together?'

'Oh we still share a bed, in spite of all my pleas. Even when I slipped a disc, he simply put a board underneath the mattress and complained about the bump. The children think it's romantic. How can I tell them the truth: that their father is afraid of the dark?'

'But he's a bishop!'

'I know. It's mad. By day, he battles against Satan, but, at night, he's terrified of every creak.'

'Is that what you told the women on the weekend?'

'No. I was frightened they'd think I was making it up. Besides, I promised him I'd never tell anyone.'

'You've broken your promise.'

'Yes. But then I've already broken my vows. I'm a wicked woman. Oh Jessica, you've no idea how wicked. But, for the first time, I can feel wicked without feeling guilty and it's the nicest feeling in the world.' Her face lights up. 'On the Saturday afternoon, we were taught to recognize each other's auras (I was so ignorant, I thought an aura was a make of car). We did exercises to prepare our hands. Then we split into pairs. One of us lay on the floor, while the other tried to feel the energy surrounding her body. And I did. Sometimes it rose and sometimes it fell and sometimes it pulsated. And the place where it was the strongest was here.' She points to her breasts. 'It was so strong that I felt my hands drawn down to touch her. They were resting on her breasts and I couldn't pull them away. It was some time before I realized that there was another pressure. She was holding them there herself.'

Jessica tries to assimilate the story. She wants to laugh but fears that Esther might mistake her delight for mockery. She is acutely aware of the masculine ethos of the vestry, as marked as a rugby-club changing-room. Even the Christ hanging limply on the wall looks as though His shoulders have been dislocated in a scrum. She can picture no more incongruous setting for a tale of Sapphic passion; but then she can picture no more incongruous heroine than a middle-aged bishop's wife.

'The facilitator explained – I'm sure mainly for my benefit – that some people think that auras are the origin of halos. "In that case," I replied, "Molly and I must be saints."'

'Forgive me, I don't usually need to have things spelled out. Huxley says that I can pick up a nuance at a hundred paces. But are you and Molly having an affair?'

'Yes. Have I shocked you?'

'No, not at all. Amazed ... stunned, but not shocked. Now I see why the Amazons were so successful. Their most powerful weapon must have been surprise.'

'I thought that with your views ...'

'But, for me, they're just views: support, solidarity, and yet not so much as an experiment. I used to think that my body must be less enlightened than my mind.'

'My body was what drove me. It was as though it was making up for years of neglect. Making love with Ted was like paying a tithe. With Molly, I experience such peace, such participation. I even feel natural taking off my clothes. There are no inhibitions about stretch-marks. Whereas I always feel Ted expects me to look as firm and flawless as Eve before the apple ... as if fat was another of woman's curses.'

'Huxley's always been the most generous of lovers ... not in that absurd, self-conscious "I love your cellulite" kind of way, but in a hundred little touches – and not just of his hands. I'm the one who punishes myself. Some days, I look in the mirror and feel like the Hanging Gardens of Babylon.'

'You're a very beautiful woman.'

'In my head I know that ageing's inevitable; but it goes back to what I said about my body being less enlightened than my mind.'

'I don't think I'm enlightened. I don't want to be. The idea frightens me. I just want to be happy ... I'm going to leave Ted.'

'To live with Molly?'

'The joke – if only it were – is that she's married too. And she loves her husband. Which makes everything harder. No, another friend, Diane, has offered to lend me a room. I'm waiting for the right moment. I used to think that God was unfair. When He spoke so often to Ted, He might have spared a few words for me. Well now He has. And He's urging me to move on.'

'How much of this do you mean to tell Ted?'

'I don't know. Part of me just wants to disappear like a missing person. Then I hear what he's saying tonight and feel that I have to speak out. If only I were a speaking-out sort of a woman. And yet I owe it to everyone, Ted included. After all, if his wife is possessed by devils, he ought to be warned.'

SERVICE OF AFFIRMATION
AND BLESSING

Tuesday 5.00 p.m.
St Mary-in-the-Vale, Hampstead

> The Curate welcomes the congregation.
> *We have come together in the presence of God to witness the*
> *celebration and blessing of the loving union which exists*
> *between Alice and Dee.*

It is the hats that Blair misses. This is the first 'wedding' that he has ever taken where the whole congregation has stood bareheaded before God. But then this is the first wedding that he has ever taken where the request for 'no confetti' has been extended to 'no organ', 'no flowers', and 'no photographs in the porch'. It is the first wedding that he has ever taken where one of the brides was married in the same church only four hours earlier and her husband sits alongside his best man in the front pew. It is the first wedding that he has ever taken where he can speak of 'one of the brides'. It is the first wedding that he has ever taken where the locked doors and the lack of entry in the parish register make him feel less like a twentieth-century curate than a recusant priest risking life and limb to celebrate mass.

> The partners stand before the altar, where the Curate
> questions them on their intent.
> *Alice, will you give yourself wholly to Dee, sharing your love*
> *and your life, your wholeness and your brokenness, your*
> *joys and sorrows, your health and sickness, your riches and*
> *poverty, your success and failure?*
> *I will.*

Alice feels the words entering her with the thrill of tongues. They touch her in the core of her being. She is in love and in love with the phrases used to sanctify her love. She no longer feels excluded by pronouns: neither the historic 'He' condemning her with two thousand years of church tradition nor the defiant 'She' turning a white-bearded Bernard Shaw into a double-chinned Margaret Rutherford. God has no gender. The all-powerful creator is closer to the humble amoeba than to the vain confusions of women and men.

'Our Mother' distances her from her childhood far more pro-
foundly than her scholarship to art school or her parents' deaths.
'Our Mother' paints her decent diplomat father in the darker colours of other women's experience. 'Our Mother' makes God as
changeable as fashion rather than as fixed as the sun. It's not that
she wants to escape the truth of imploding black holes in a universe as simple as 'Twinkle, twinkle little star', but that she doesn't
want to cut herself off from the world in which she first discovered
God, from the spirit in which Christ instructed people to approach
God, and from the genuine devotion of her parents.

She wonders whether they would have come to St Mary's today
. . . it is so much easier to mouth the formula that they are here in
spirit. The presence of her sister holding Dora (so far, so silent)
may be some indication. Vanessa is an architectural historian. Her
interest in churches is all external . . . with a feminist preference
for domes rather than spires. Her own interest is internal, in the
patina of prayers on the pillars. Which is why it has to be here, with
her friends all around and her pictures, like windows, on the walls,
that she proclaims her commitment to Dee.

She feels ashamed of the sham of the earlier service. Register
Offices were made for such marriages, where 'You may now kiss
the bride' is a matter of indifference. But she has learnt from
friends that Immigration Officers are as susceptible to photographs
of church weddings as elderly aunts. Even so, success is not assured. As they sniff around for proof of cohabitation, Dee and Joe
must be prepared to answer questions as prurient as those on a
television quiz show . . . 'So Daisy, if you were to buy Joe some
bedtime wear, would he prefer: a) silk pyjamas; b) a cotton night-
gown; or c)' (wink, wink, canned laughter) 'nothing at all?' Only
the prizes are different. The holiday in the Canaries if they win has
been replaced by a one-way ticket to Wellington if they lose.

While she has no regrets about lying to government officials or
to Maureen Beatty (now safely sipping tea in a Hampstead 'cafe-
tière'), she remains uneasy about deceiving Huxley. Blair, however,
insists that it is kinder than to compromise his position with the
Church (making it all the more bizarre that Jessica should have
brought the Bishop's wife). The only solution is to regard the first
service as a dress rehearsal, with Joe as her stand-in. Which is one
of the reasons she was determined to hold the second service this
afternoon. The other can be found lying docilely in Vanessa's arms.
Her baby is to be christened on Saturday. It is crucial that her
relationship with her godmother should first be legitimized before
God.

> *Dee, will you give yourself wholly to Alice, sharing your love and your life, your wholeness and your brokenness, your joys and sorrows, your health and sickness, your riches and poverty, your success and failure?*
> *I will.*

Much as she likes Blair, Dee would prefer to be married by a woman. Not only would it help to ring the changes on a day when she feels less like an item in the record-books than a candidate for the courts, but it would be a fitting symbol. It appeals to the same sense of solidarity which leads her to use an all-female taxi firm and a lesbian plumber: not separatism but a statement that women can do the job as well as men. Alice remains sceptical, which is odd given her recent series of paintings on Pope Joan. At least she agreed to the ceremony's taking place in the Lady Chapel rather than the chancel; in front of a portrait of a nursing mother, rather than the tortured figure on the Cross.

Christ means nothing to her, although she is prepared to make an effort with Him for Alice's sake. She is encouraged by Alice's faith – not in the way that her father liked her mother to go to church 'just in case there's something in it after all', but because Alice can seem so self-contained: on account of her art, her success, her money ... all the things, in fact, which she found so exciting when she was first attracted to her and so daunting when she later fell in love. Even now, as they stand at the altar, she is afraid that she has nothing to offer; she exists purely as a diversion. And yet the altar itself attests to Alice's vulnerability: a need for reassurance which is doubly welcome, even if it is addressed to God.

The one thing that she misses from the earlier service is the camera. She longs to supplement the U certificate video being prepared for the authorities with an X-rated version to be sent to her family in New Zealand. She tries not to let the thought translate into a scowl. And, for the first time since she slashed her Christian name to a single letter (no cosy diminutive but a product of the same despair which turned her body into a sleeping-bag and sex into self-obliteration), she is prepared to sign it in full. It was her father who insisted on giving her a floral name. As a child, she used to wish that he had chosen something more exotic: Rose, Violet or even Pansy, in preference to a common-or-garden weed. Later, his motives appeared to be more sinister. It was as though he had bred her for a single purpose: to be deflowered. Now, she feels able to reclaim a name which couldn't fit her better. For she is not some precious rose or shrinking violet but the hardiest of perennials, blooming thousands of miles away from her native soil.

Her heart fills with love and gratitude towards Alice and she promises to share with her everything, good or ill ... except for the history in her head.

> A flautist and a harpist play an extract from Delibes'
> Lakmé.

Joe looks at Dee and Alice as they listen to the music. All his hopes of wedded bliss are scorched by the radiance on their faces. But then, ever since he escaped from the Bishop last night, he has recognized the absurdity of those hopes. Instead, he feels happy for his friends and happy that he has been able to help.

His eyes stray to the Burne-Jones diptych of the Virgin and Child and fill with the tears reserved for those to whom birth remains a mystery. He thinks of his mother sitting through the wedding with her head turned to the altar and her heart set on the font. He dreads her dropped hints almost as much as her dropped aitches. Dee might be a lollipop lady for all the respect she accords her career. He berates her for her insensitivity. If her grandmaternal hopes were matched by maternal instinct, she would know the truth about him without needing to be told. He berates himself for his injustice: blaming her for the ignorance of which he alone is the cause.

He treats her like the reader who came up to the Enquiry Desk in a panic that she might catch 'the AIDS' from infected books. 'Don't worry, madam,' he assured her, 'you're quite safe with Barbara Taylor Bradford. But I'd steer clear of E.M. Forster and Oscar Wilde.'

The gentle harmonies of the music splinter into discords. He senses the unaccustomed weight on his finger. He savours the irony of the perfect fit. He acknowledges the bitter truth that the only marriage he will ever consummate is the Persian 'marriage with air'. It is a union to which he will be forever faithful: in which his right hand always knows what his left hand is doing: in which he can never be denied his conjugal rights.

> The Curate delivers the address.

'It's not often that I stand in a church full of prophets, but I'm doing so now. I see you shuffle in your seats. Why? If your image of a prophet stops at Jeremiah or John the Baptist, think again. And, to the woman at the back who's checking out the faces in the mosaics, don't bother. Instead, take a closer look at your neigh-bours: Patricia; Damian; Julia; and, of course, Alice and Dee. For, what is a prophet? First and foremost, it's someone who speaks for God ... which we all do, so long as we allow Him to speak through us. Second, it's someone who foretells the future. But I'd like to extend that to someone who lives the future – as we are now. For I believe, with every fibre of my being, that this blessing for Alice and Dee is the shape of things to come.

'A subsidiary meaning of "prophet" is poet: a person who puts the future into words. And, this afternoon, we're also doing that. The Church gives us no help. It cobbles together its opinions from newspaper columns the way that poison-pen-letter-writers chop up the print. The powers-that-be instruct us to keep silent. Even sympathetic bishops adopt a playground policy of "Tell me no secrets and I'll tell you no lies". The Prayer Book itself contains prayers for plague and famine, for rain and fair weather, for the churching of women and, of course, for the anniversary of the accession of the sovereign, but nothing to honour the commitment of lovers like Alice and Dee. So some inspired theologians have tried to redress the balance. And we're using ... we're living their liturgy today.

'Liturgy is a dialogue between past and present. Our past has been suppressed for too long. Pages have been ripped out of prayer-books and history books alike. We've been forced to dress our ceremonies in other peoples' cast-offs: ill-fitting words, as patched and stretched as a vicar's wife's husbandry. That has now changed. Pioneering scholars have shown that, although the Blessings of recent centuries have been exclusively heterosexual, the first thousand years of the Church's existence saw same-sex couples recognized in their own rites. So, as well as prophets, we're historians, restoring to the future a sense of its past.

'And, as historians, we may also cast an eye over the origins of the Church of England, an institution that has long reviled behaviour outside the "Lie back and think of England" norm. We may recollect that the only sexual practice Christ condemns is divorce, and yet that is the basis of the entire Anglican communion. A paradox? Perhaps. But I sometimes wonder what might have happened had Henry VIII been James I and fallen for George rather than Anne Boleyn. Would Leviticus have been despatched as easily as Deuteronomy? Would David and Jonathan and Ruth and Naomi have become role-models for the young? Whatever the answer, it ill behoves a Church with such shaky foundations to denounce relationships that Christ never mentions at all.

'I know that many of you here aren't church-goers. Indeed, when we were discussing this address last week, Dee asked me to go easy on God – it's too late to blush – forgetting how hard it is to teach an old hand in a dog-collar new tricks. But I make no apologies for alerting you to the singular nature of the service. This is the second union which we've celebrated at St Mary's today and, uniquely, it involves one of the same partners. This has prompted much soul-searching in us all, not least the partners. But, as I see it, this second service neither mocks nor repudiates the first but rather sets it in context. The Church of England is the state church and this afternoon's wedding served to correct a statutory injustice: the dif-fering rights of residence for Alice and Des and Alice and Dee. Just as, once, the Church offered sanctuary within its walls, so, today, it has done so within a wider society. And, although short, Dee and Joe's marriage was not without issue, for it has brought forth this.

'So, while we meet behind locked doors and in a side chapel, let's not make the mistake of thinking that the ceremony is in any way second-best. We chose to gather here both to leave behind the ear-lier service and to take advantage of the chapel's associations. And our position within the building speaks to me of our position with-in the Church ... integral yet independent. If I were wearing a badge, it would read Proud To Be Oblique. What's more, although the vows may be unauthorized, they don't lack authority. They've been validated by tradition, by example and by friends. Most impor-tantly, they will be made in the sight of God. And I'm convinced that His eyes, like all of ours, are smiling.

'In the name of the Father and of the Son and of the Holy Spirit. Amen.'

> *I, Alice, vow to you, Dee, in the sight of God and before these our chosen witnesses, that I shall love, honour and cherish you all the days of my life, until death divides us.*

To Alice, all vows are sacred. She was the despair of her schoolgirl gang when, having survived pulled hair and pinched arms, she would break down and give the game away rather than 'swear to God and hope to die'. But no vow has ever been as holy as this pledge to Dee. Her voice rings out with an authority which defies amplification. Her heart fills with a love which encompasses the entire church. Old girlfriends pack the pews behind her, their breath warming her like blessings. But they were chances not cer-tainties. They were boozy evenings and lazy mornings and rustic weekends and rumpled sheets. Whereas Dee is all day and every day; she is workaday and holiday; she is daybreak and dusk.

Dee has flown into her life like a swallow in winter. She has braved seasons and climates and continents. She has brought new hope and strength; she has brought green leaves and peace; she is a swallow doubling as a dove. She has remade her world as a painting. For, just as certain colours are never more themselves than in combination – the orangest orange is set against turquoise; the greenest green against red – so she is never more Alice than when she is with Dee.

The future unfolds like the last page of a fairy tale. They will live among children and grandchildren and canvases and cats, defying all censure, until the passing years bleach them of suspicion. But their passion will be as intense as ever and they will laugh at a world that considers their greatest intimacy to be bottling jam. Meanwhile, old age will make amends for all the slights they endured in their youth, as the men die off, leaving them as predominant as their grandmothers at the end of the First World War. Since their love lasts the longest, they will become not just the survivors but the norm.

> *I, Dee, vow to you, Alice, in the sight of God and before these our chosen witnesses, that I shall love, honour and cherish you all the days of my life, until death divides us.*

Dee does not care for 'the sight of God' which turns Our Father into Peeping Tom, an old voyeur with binoculars trained on her bedroom window, panting as she slips off her shirt . . .

She draws the curtains on the man – and on the image. She sees her grimace translate into Alice's apprehension and tries to reassure her with a grin. If there is a God and He's watching, then He must be suffering from a sense of *déjà vu*. She, however, is experiencing an excitement unlike any she has known before . . . not the airport excitement of flying to new places nor the party excitement of making new friends but the crossroads excitement of picking the right path. For the first time, she understands Joe's friend Ernst, who described himself as a great reader and then, when she attempted a literary discussion, explained that he only ever read one book. She was baffled, even outraged, on behalf of all the thousands he was rejecting. 'Freedom,' he said, 'lies in choosing, not in choice.'

Her book is Alice: a wondrous volume which defies classification. It is mystical and magical and educational and charming and earthy. It is a romance and a comedy, an adventure and a fantasy, a history and a poem. It is as personal as a diary and as sweeping as an epic. It is full of exquisite illustrations painted by the heroine herself. In spite of its richness, it is impossible to put down . . . She blushes for her flight of fancy, which she tries – but fails – to attribute to the lunchtime champagne.

Dora's cries are a reminder that the book already has a sequel: one which, at Alice's insistence, she now refers to as 'ours'. No one could ask for a stronger proof of love. Alice was prepared to deny herself her most heartfelt desire until she was sure that she had found the right partner. She put the future at the mercy of time. That, not the vows nor the rings nor the prayers, is what seals their union: a commitment made in blood.

> *We, Alice and Dee, witness before God that we have pledged ourselves to each other. We offer to you, O Lord, our souls and bodies, our thoughts and deeds, our love for each other, our hope to serve you truly.*

Even to a mistress of mixed emotions, the service is proving to be taxing. On the one hand, Jessica is moved by the women's vows, which replace the fashion statement of a conventional wedding with a genuine statement of intent. On the other, she feels wretched about deceiving Huxley – even by default. At their age, secrets are as corrosive to a marriage as infidelity. Her distress is increased by his obvious delight in Dee's and Joe's relationship. 'Joe has found himself,' he declared last week, as though it were as simple as changing jobs. But then he is hardly likely to show more insight into a stranger than he did into his own son.

Tears well as she thinks of Toby, on his final trip home, confessing his sexuality as grimly as the murder of a child. Her one consolation is the memory of her wholehearted acceptance, which, to her lasting regret, she has never been able to share with anyone else. Instead of questioning his demand for secrecy, she agreed 'not to breathe a word of it, especially to Dad'. Having kept her promise over the years with the devotion of a deathbed oath, it would be a double betrayal to break it now.

So Huxley remains safe in his sanitized recollections, while she is riddled with guilt. Her greatest fear is that there was a darkness to her son's sexuality which felt mocked by her instant approval and that, far from inadvertently straying from the route, he deliberately drove the lorry into danger. She rewrites Huxley's funeral address, turning 'self-sacrificial courage' into 'suicidal despair'.

> The Curate takes the rings from the two supporters and prays over them. *Bless, O Lord, these rings, that they who give and receive them may always have a deep faith in each other.*

Esther thrills as what has been a place of public prayer becomes one of private possibilities. Seeing the two women declare their love, she feels the same flush of emotions – wonder, fear, disbelief – as when she first saw a man on the moon. Listening to the words: measured, meaningful words with none of the varnish of the traditional service, she can barely believe what she's hearing, and, more importantly, where. She isn't at home watching a television documentary, its marbled commentary proclaiming the significance, but in a church at the heart of her husband's diocese. The incongruity seems to be overwhelming, until she remembers that the diocese may be her husband's but the church is God's.

She smiles at Jessica, who has been moved to tears by the vows. She owes her a great debt of gratitude ... not only for her sympathy last night but for inviting her here today. Under the circumstances, it feels particularly ungracious to be missing Molly, who is spending Easter on the Norfolk Broads with Dafydd, her kind, considerate husband ... she stresses his virtues to remind herself not just that they exist but that she must beware of making too many demands.

Unlike Molly, who suffers torments at deluding Dafydd, she enjoys lying to Ted. To her surprise, she finds that she is good at it ... not least because Ted assumes that she'll be bad. Today, she was due to accompany him to tea with the Bishop of Lund, but she told him that she still felt flushed after last night and he didn't insist. He attributes flushes to the change of life. When she was younger, he put any mood or dissension down to her periods; now he puts them down to the lack of them. It never strikes him as odd that he should regard his own body as little more than clothes – or, rather, armour – for the spirit and hers as a malevolent and unpredictable force.

It is clear that he has never loved her. Which hurts far less now that she realizes he has never understood what love is. He proposed to her because he was twenty-one and she was the leading light of his Bible Study Group. She accepted because she had never been further from home than Southend. She grew up and old with an emptiness of heart which she assumed was simply the condition of being an adult. She gives a shudder which, when Jessica catches her eye, she twists into a smile.

> The partners exchange the rings.
> *Dee, this ring is a symbol of the love I have for you; I give it to you as a token that, from this day forward, we two shall be as one.*

Leafing through a nineteenth-century manual, Joe read that 'care should be taken not to place books by different sexes next to each other'. He quoted it to amuse his friends; although the biggest laugh came when Damian said that it might have been written for him. Watching Alice slip the ring on Dee's finger, he sees his point. Ever since his schoolgirl confidantes, women have been a closed book to him or, rather, one with the pages still uncut. What's more, the Victorians may have saved Jane Austen and Alfred Austin from rubbing spines (while failing to protect William Beckford from the clandestine presence of Acton, Currer and Ellis Bell), but modern librarians are just as prone to absurdities, like the classification of Feminism between Etiquette and Gypsies. Whether it's a perpetual-schoolboy joke or a misogynistic theory, he can never reshelve *The Second Sex* without a qualm.

Nevertheless, women, in gaping close-up, provide the backdrop to his visits to cinemas ... the sort where he never asks the names of the films. Safe in the dark, he is able to escape the fatness which is the curse of his life, the bane of a body made but not shaped for passion. It has become his primary mode of identification: not 'I'm Joe' or 'an Anglican' or 'a librarian' or 'gay' or 'twenty-eight' but 'I'm fat'. It is often the first thing he says in the morning and always the first thing he sees in the mirror. He no longer looks for sympathy from friends, who treat it not as an affliction but as a neurosis: in a world where millions starve, he seems to compound his self-indulgence by complaining. So he waves back to the thin man wildly signalling for air and walks away.

His shame about his size was born of the school changing-room where soccer-sweaty boys lined up to wobble his breasts as a sub-stitute for the girls playing netball. Later, the lonely hearts adverts confirmed the link with their 'no fats or fems' proviso. As he gazes at Dee, almost pudding-faced alongside angular Alice, he feels a pang of resentment that women are allowed to become buxom, curvaceous and Rubensesque, whereas men are stuck with pot-bellied and paunchy. And, no matter what his counsellor may say, there is no mistaking the look of disappointment when carefully chosen clothes give way to imperfectly toned flesh. After one part-ner's crudely faked allergy to goose-down, he vowed never to un-dress in company or to have sex with the lights on again.

Alternatives are to hand and none more effective than the cine-mas. He discovered the first when reading of a football manager's arrest for importuning (as his mother always says, 'It's an ill wind that blows in nobody's sails'). While fuzzily projected couples are put through their joyless paces, the patrons go about theirs, retain-ing their clothes but not their inhibitions, indulging in a repertoire as adventurous as any on film. Paradoxically, many of the plots concern lesbians, the figures of least appeal to most of the clientèle. And yet he never questions anyone's orientation (gay, straight or self-deluding) but tries to foster an illusion of intimacy to match the illusion of eroticism on screen.

On one unaccountable – because so carefully guarded against – occasion, he must have contracted the virus. And yet, after an initial self-denying ordinance, he made a tentative return to the films. While rejecting the here-today-gone-tomorrow hedonism of so many of his fellows, he has no intention of becoming a monk. He is used to covering library books in plastic; now he can cover himself. His counsellor insists that it is essential not to give up on life just because he is HIV positive, while Damian claims more bluntly that man is a hunter and, since he is unable to satisfy his primal instincts by dodging trolleys at Sainsbury's, he is dependent on the pursuit of sex.

The irony is that, for all his concerns about weight, he has been infected by a virus which will one day pare him to the bone. But he prays that, before then, there may be a moment – one perfect moment – when the fat drops off but the flesh remains ... when he is able to strip off his shirt with the best of them ... when disease turns into desire.

> *Alice, this ring is a symbol of the love I have for you; I give it to you as a token that, from this day forward, we two shall be as one.*

Blair remembers his own exchange of rings with Julian, not at an altar surrounded by friends but on a hilltop in Wales in front of a flock of sheep. It was a dizzy day and not only because of the altitude. After a gentle snack of Dom Perignon and Kendal mintcake, Julian, revealing unsuspected powers, insisted that the sheep were trying to communicate with them and proceeded to interpret their bleats. They lay on the rock and gloried in the view. And yet the landscape, which filled them with awe, induced a sense of foreboding. For all their fine words about the presence of God, the crucial factor was the absence of people. The idyll came to an abrupt end when a baa-ing sheep alerted them to an approaching farmer. Trousers and hair were brushed; sweaters and voices lowered. The public/private seesaw of their lives had begun.

A loud howl from Alice's baby, who displays as marked a hostility towards him as Lady Blaikie's parrot, reminds him of his responsibilities. He resolves to ignore his own grief and re-enter the spirit of the occasion. But, casting his eye over the chapel, he is horrified to catch sight of Hugh Snape, who stands at the back, staring at the altar as though it were on fire. He berates himself for his stupidity: to have taken so much care locking the doors while forgetting how many other people held keys. Nevertheless, the damage is done. There is nothing to be gained by confronting Hugh ... and a great deal to be lost for Dee and Alice. He stammers through the prayers of blessing, while longing more intensely than ever for the hilltop in Wales.

> The Curate concludes the ceremony.
> *Will you, the chosen witnesses of Alice and Dee, do all in your power to support and strengthen them in the days ahead?*
> *We will.*

Blair enters the office, to find Hugh sitting, dead still, at the desk.

'I've been waiting for you,' Hugh says.

'I thought that you might.'

'To pass the time, I've been going through the diary. It's strange but I can't find any mention of a service to be held here now.'

'It must be an oversight.'

'Perhaps you'd like to look for yourself? There's a wedding at two o'clock to be conducted by the Vicar. Then nothing until mass at six-thirty.'

'Hugh, if you've something to say, please say it. I'm tired. I have to prepare for tomorrow's funeral.'

'I'm no prude – ask anyone. But there are limits. I come here, at the end of a hard day's work, to check on the belfry handrail. And what do I see? Our curate conducting some form of bastardized marriage between two...'

'Women?'

'Now I've heard everything. Last night at the PCC, you had the gall to lecture me on Christian principles ... you who wouldn't know a Christian principle if you were nailed to a cross. Is it any wonder people are turning away – ordinary, decent people who didn't go to university, who know the difference between right and wrong – when you and the rest of your breed try to stretch the words of Christ like a T-shirt: one size fits all. Well not any more, chum. The Vicar may be too scared to stand up to you, but somebody must. I've sweated blood trying to obtain the best deal for that clergy-house; and you treat me like I'm dirt. We'll see who's dirt when I've put my case to the Archdeacon. You'll be on your bike before you can say Karl Marx.'

Blair watches Hugh leave. He slumps in his seat, so drained that he is unable even to respond to the threat. In his alb but not his chasuble, he feels a hybrid, neither man nor priest. Alone and afraid, with no one to turn to but Christ, he apostrophizes the crucifix on the wall.

'Do you intend to stay up there for ever? Forgive me if I sound like a mocking soldier. I'm asking not because I think that you don't have a choice but because I know that you do. I understand why you had to suffer and to go on suffering way beyond any natural span. But it's time to call a halt. You've shown solidarity. You've demonstrated humility. You've made amends for the pain of the human condition. Now come back in triumph and help us find peace.'

The Order for the
Burial of the Dead

Wednesday 4.30 p.m.
Finsbury Park Cemetery

> The cortège drives through the cemetery gates and draws up close to the Blaikie monument.

Released from the cramping proximity of the coffin and the cloying smell of the flowers, Blair is exposed to the bitter rebuke of the open air. Accusatory voices pierce the silence as he stands with Huxley watching the official cars and waiting for the rest of the mourners. He gives vent to his self-disgust.

'I wonder how many secrets have been buried here.'

'People,' Huxley replies. 'People, not secrets. People who revealed some things and hid others. And who are we to judge?'

'I'm not judging anyone.'

'Not even me?'

'Don't forget, I'm also party to this deception: Grieves and Ashley, purveyors of fine funerals to the gentry, euphemisms and evasions a speciality.'

'Is it really that important to state how someone died? Those who know, know; those who don't, won't be hurt.'

'But it isn't just how he died; it's how he lived. Did you see *The Times*?'

'No.'

'"Donations to the Medical Research Society for research into Legionnaire's Disease". Very neat. Not the lie direct but the lie suggestive. We should have gone the whole hog and dressed him in a toga. I'm sure Lady Blaikie only picked the name for its echoes of Ancient Rome.'

'I discussed it fully with Massimo, who was happy to go along with whatever Julian's mother wished.'

'Oh Huxley.' Blair puts his head in his hands. 'Only you could be so naïve. Of course he is. She's giving him £10,000 to take back to Naples. The word "bribe" never crossed my lips; the phrase "hush money" isn't in my vocabulary. And who can blame him: a boy from the wrong side of the tracks? What's more, he's found the perfect way to regain face. All the scorn for his sexual tendencies will disappear as he converts them into lire.'

'I never took you for a cynic.'

'Mark it down to indigestion. I've had to choke back so many words.'

The mourners walk through the cemetery to the tomb.

Nick makes his way through the tumbledown tombs and sunken stones which seem not just to commemorate death but to be part of it. He disdains the 'pharaohs of all they survey' ostentation. It was graves such as these – like the first-class lifeboats on a liner – which turned him against Christianity as a child. The most moving memorials he has ever seen were at Ypres. There was no jockeying for size and position but rather a democracy of death in the rows of uniform crosses. Although, in his present mood, he wonders whether it was the cemetery itself which made such an impression on him or the corpses: the thousands of soft-featured, smooth-limbed young men lying underneath.

He walks on, carrying his feelings in front of him like a wreath. He takes comfort from the faded inscriptions of an earlier age, when death didn't swoop down on a whole generation but was wilful, arbitrary, patient. He drowns out the sound of the most hollow consolation-phrase in the language: Whom the Gods love die young. Only a fool could be cheered by it. For, if the Gods – or God (he cannot maintain a fiction made real only on a week's holiday in Rome) – take the best first, what hope is there, either in this world or the next, for everyone else?

There is some consolation in applying the phrase to Julian: a corrective to the view that God has sent down a plague to wipe out behaviour of which He disapproves. But it is the consolation of cleverness rather than conviction. Reassurance is further undermined as he passes a trio of young men whose path appears to be a premonition. Their taut skin shines with an eerie translucence in the sharp afternoon sun. They require the protection of subdued light like Old Master drawings in a gallery, instead of being left at the mercy of the elements like commemorative statues in a park.

He tries to dismiss them from his mind – and his tear-ducts. He feels like an actor crying over the death of a cat in order to cry for Juliet. He refuses to dilute his grief for Julian. Of all his boys, he is the most precious. He is the quintessential English gentleman, of a kind he has previously only encountered in films. He pictures his past in boats and boaters among friends who say 'topping' . . . and not as a substitute for cream. He remains dazzled by his beauty, that before-and-after beauty, as the sunny, sandy glow set into the crisp, hayricky chill.

'We were so vain, Nick,' he told him. 'We believed that we could be young forever and that all it took was the right moisturizer. Look now. The pictures have escaped from the attics and are lying in hospital beds.'

> The undertakers place the coffin on a catafalque in front of the tomb, while the remaining mourners make their way through the cemetery.

May walks with Neil, Smoke and Kevin past a row of graves like a hospital ward ... she trusts that her companions can't read her thoughts. Friends of Julian's from the support-group, they share the unexpected intimacy of a disaster movie, with herself as a cross between Shelley Winters and Steve McQueen. The discomfort of their formal suits – with the thumb-thick gap behind Smoke's collar a graphic reminder of his weight-loss since its last outing – is increased by the lack of welcome.

'Do you think they might invite us back for a drink?' Kevin asks.

'Stuff it,' Smoke replies. 'I'm not going anywhere with those stiffs.'

May giggles, provoking a backward glance from a woman whom she recognizes as a sister at the Royal Free.

'Look at all these graves,' Smoke says. 'It's a crying shame. They had class once, you can tell. Now, they're in a worse state than your drawers, May love.' May laughs. 'Me, I'm going up in flames. Six muscle-marys in sequinned jock-straps lifting me onto their shoulders while Elaine Paige sings *Smoke Gets In Your Eyes*.'

'That'll never be allowed.'

'Want to bet? I've checked with the crem. Anything goes so long as they keep their coats on till they're inside ... Then the curtains will open and I'll take my final bow. But May chuck, promise us one thing. That afternoon, you'll put on your *Marigolds* and give the oven a proper clean-out. I'm not making my exit in a midden.'

'Trust me,' she says quietly.

The conversation is curtailed as Neil stumbles. May lifts him to his feet and takes his arm.

'Flat on my face in a cemetery,' Neil says. 'Ironic, isn't it?'

May tries to still the quickening pulse caused by the pressure on her arm. She resolves to lighten the mood. 'If I'd known it was this far, I'd have sought sponsorship.'

'Don't expect sympathy in those heels.' Smoke says. 'Did you have to get planning permission to wear them?'

'You're just jealous.'

'Of your dress sense? I think not.'

May smiles in the conviction that her dress sense is impeccable. Her dress sense is who she is. Reg is many things: divorced husband, estranged father, sacked sales manager; but May is the black crushed velvet suit, the cream silk blouse, the smoky grey tights. May can truly claim to have been born in a trunk: the one locked behind the old room-divide in Reg's garage. Until two years ago, she lived very quietly, emerging only rarely, discreetly and insecurely, on trips to a small group of like-minded friends on the far side of Chigwell. Then, one day, unable to make his usual arrangements, Reg was forced to abandon May in Epping Forest. Despite scrupulous precautions, he was spotted going into the trees as a woman and coming out as a man, carrying a bag of clothes and a wig which, by the time that word reached the police, had been transformed into body-parts and a severed head.

He had no choice but to confess, to the amusement of the officers and the horror of his wife, to whom murder appeared the more acceptable option. Local notoriety and the subsequent domestic and professional upheavals have led to a radical shift in the time he spends as Reg and May. They remain, however, as one in their dream of finding a sympathetic woman who will share her life with Reg as husband and lover and May as sister and friend. Meanwhile, through her voluntary work at the hospice, May has found a role as fulfilling as any of Reg's. What's more, with her twice-weekly demonstrations of how to hide unsightly lesions, the make-up box which was, for so long, a guilty secret is now officially approved.

She is still finding her way around a world which, unlike her own, does not aim for respectability but revels in outrage. And she is taken aback when a young man, in a vein-revealing T-shirt and blood-restricting shorts, skateboards backwards around the graves. Having recognized Smoke by his thatch of bleached hair, he slides up to them and introduces himself as Xian, a name which comes complete with its own footnote, as he explains it as a snub to his God-fearing parents and one which, unlike the neutral option of Chris, keeps the insult constantly in sight. His anger at the presence of the mourners increases with the revelation that the only burials permitted in an otherwise closed cemetery are those in family tombs.

'Typical,' he says. 'Trust families to ruin everything. It can be a real turn-off cruising where they've just buried someone you know.'

'Cruising?' May asks, confused.

'Oh get a life, sister,' Smoke says ... which May considers to be most unfair since no one can have done as much to get a life as her.

'Day and night, darling,' Kevin says. 'The patter of tiny willies.'

'Speak for yourself,' Neil says. 'Aah!'

'Are you all right?' May asks.

'Apart from the landslide at the back of my head.'

'I wonder if the guys over by the mausoleum know what's happening,' Xian says. 'It's packed.'

'Really?' Smoke asks.

'One of this lot might see and kick up a stink.'

'The Vicar looks like he's ready to start; we'd better get our skates on,' May says. 'Oh, not literally,' she adds to Xian with a laugh.

'I'm going with Xian,' Smoke says. 'I'll catch up with you later.'

'Slut,' Neil says, with another grimace.

'Not at all. It's my duty to warn them of the danger at hand.'

'Don't you want to pay your respects to Julian?' May asks.

'Honey, I shall pay them in a way he'd appreciate far more than prayers.'

> As the Vicar recites the words *Man that is born of woman hath but a short time to live*, the undertakers lower the coffin down the steps into the vault and place it in a lead casket which is already prepared.

'We now come to the final act of committal,' Huxley announces. 'Some of you will be joining me in the vault; the rest will be able to follow the proceedings from up here. I'd ask you all to stand in silence until we return.'

> The Vicar escorts the chief mourners down the steps. He blesses the vault. *Holy Father, we ask you to rehallow this tomb as the final resting-place of Julian Blaikie. May your holy angels watch over him and bring him with us to your eternal paradise. Amen.*

Blair feels stifled in the mildewy atmosphere, surrounded by Blaikies past and present. He stares at a bunch of powdery flowers which, propped against a cobwebby casket, seem to have been plucked from Miss Havisham's wedding bouquet. He is seized with the fantasy of the tomb-ship setting sail and binding him until the end of time to Julian's mother, sister and uncle, his lover and priest, like the ghostly crew of a second Marie Celeste.

> *Forasmuch as it hath pleased Almighty God of his great*
> *mercy to take unto himself the soul of our dear brother here*
> *departed: we therefore commit his body to the ground.*

Gazing around the coffins, arranged like casks of vintage wine, Eleanor feels as though she is returning Julian to his ancestors rather than to God. The conviction grows as Huxley hands her the trowel and she weighs up the rich English earth. She pictures the generations of her own and her husband's families who have died to defend it: young men who were borne to their graves draped in Union Jacks. How she envies the women who lost their sons to the bayonet or the bullet . . . who could clasp the bloodstained uniforms to their breasts rather than consign the dressings to medical waste. But she refuses to yield to shame. She has done her duty as widow and mother. Now there is no one to mourn but herself.

> *Earth to earth, ashes to ashes, dust to dust.*

Helena watches her mother scatter the earth as though it were seed for her parrot.

The journey from cradle to grave seems so much shorter when it is bounded by the family christening-robe and the family tomb. This is the final inheritance. The Berkshire house may have been sold to an Eastern sect . . . bald men in orange robes may be chanting in the kitchen-garden, but the historic burial-place remains. One day, she will be brought here herself, the last of her line, to be sealed up in an eternal reproach. The Blaikie name will live on only in its monument: an unsinkable ship of fools.

She takes the trowel from her mother and feels her flinch . . . Julian is not the only one of her children lost to her. Death has proved to be as poor a peace-maker as Time a healer. She flicks the soil on the coffin and remembers covering Julian's body with sand – the seashore burial from which there was instant resurrection . . . the childhood idyll to which there is no return. She is suddenly aware of retaining the trowel like the loser in 'Pass the Parcel'. Protocol demands that she give it to her uncle, but devilry impels her to hand it to Massimo, who looks perturbed.

> *In sure and certain hope of the Resurrection to eternal life*
> *through our Lord Jesus Christ.*

However hard he tries, Massimo is unable to follow Julian's mother and sister. They scatter soil as if they were waiting for spring. But, to him, it appears to be a gesture not of hope but of defilement. Julian was such a clean man. Even in Naples, he managed to keep spotless, until ... but that was the illness, not him. What's more, this is English earth: the seedbed of hypocrisy and denial. If he sprinkles it, he will be giving Julian back to the country which he rejected ... he will have no more claim on him than a tourist seeking evidence of the land which once ruled the waves: the Cutty Sark at Greenwich; the Golden Hind at Southwark; the Blaikie Monument at Finsbury Park.

As he holds out the trowel, wavering between convention and defiance, a sudden realization freezes him. This will be his last ever chance to stand beside his lover. From now on, they will meet like prisoners through a grille. The shock sends the soil spilling out of the trowel and great gulps of grief surging through his chest. He tries to steady himself against the wall but recoils in horror as a layer of larval decay oozes onto his hand.

> *Who shall change our vile body, that it may be like unto his glorious body. According to the mighty working, whereby he is able to subdue all things to himself.*

Broderick takes the trowel from his nephew's valet with his usual dismay at displays of emotion. Archie Lynton's housekeeper was with him for forty years. They were as well established as any married couple. And yet she went straight home from the funeral, poured the scotch and passed around the ham sandwiches ... the model of a faithful servant. Still, this Massive fellow is an Eyetie and, no doubt, a left-footer. Melodrama is in the blood.

He taps the earth on the coffin much as if he were tapping tobacco from his pipe. He never really knew his nephew, but then he has never really known anyone. That's life and there's no point crying over it. People are a rum lot. They're born; they die; and the most they can hope for is not to make too big a hash of the bit in between. His own creed is simple: sit on the parish council; take communion once a month; open up the gardens to the public twice a year; and, most important of all, have a hobby ... something to exercise the old grey matter, something which will put him in touch with like-minded chaps. The right hobby will set up a man for life. He ought to know; he has two.

> The Vicar addresses the group in the vault: *Our Church leaves you with great blessing as we leave our departed resting here in peace.*

Huxley leads the mourners back up the steps. As the service proceeds, the undertaker hands Eleanor the key to the vault. She is unable to turn it and orders him to try. He has no more success

and passes it to an assistant. After a third failure, the undertaker
promises that he will alert the cemetery officials immediately following the ceremony.

> *I heard a voice from heaven, saying unto me, Write, From*
> *henceforth blessed are the dead which die in the Lord: Even*
> *so, saith the Spirit, for they rest from their labours.*

Edith's grief has been replaced by rage at having been left with the
crowd while Massimo and Blair have gone down into the vault. She
deliberately ruffles Stevenson's feathers in the hope that an outburst of squawking will explain her need to remain above ground.
She avoids Myrna Timson's expression of sympathy and gazes towards the mausoleum, where she is rewarded with an extraordinary
vision. Hovering by the colonnade is an angel with white hair, pink
flesh and grey wings. To the naked eye, he appears to be in ecstasy,
his head thrown back like the statue of St Theresa. What's more, to
judge from the lack of reaction, he has manifested himself to no
one but her.

In the interests of decorum, she decides against falling to her
knees but waits for Eleanor to climb up the steps and hurries to
give her her arm. And yet, far from sharing her excitement,
Eleanor dismisses her account without even putting it to the test.

'This is no time for mystical experiences. It's a funeral, not a
séance.'

> The Vicar asks the mourners to bow their heads and
> repeat the Lord's Prayer.

Smoke feels St Michael's stone-cold pectorals pressing into his
spine. He tingles as Xian rips off the rest of his clothing, thrusting
his shoulders against the spread of angelic wings. The cool breeze
carries the distant murmur of mourning. The numbingly familiar
cadences of the Lord's Prayer melt as Xian laps his groin. He fights
against the spiralling pleasure in a vain attempt to retain control
before yielding to the canine relish of his tongue. He throws back
his head in ecstasy and finds himself gazing into the vacant sockets
of the archangel's eyes. Frightened of climaxing too soon, he pulls
himself free, kneels on the plinth and skins off Xian's shorts, only
to be confronted by his baroque penis.

'They were Dougie's,' Xian explains. 'When he died, I asked the
hospital to remove all his jewellery. They were quite miffed when
they realized I didn't just mean from his hands.'

Smoke feels much the same and tries to salvage his erection.

'I had them put in as a permanent memorial. His parents have their names on his grave; I have him on my flesh. So now, every time that I fuck ... every time I enter someone's body, I take a bit of Dougie with me.'

Smoke banishes his unease at the unexpected threesome and slips back onto his knees.

> The Vicar shuts his prayer-book. *That concludes the service. I shall be waiting at the gate, should anyone need me. Please leave any flowers on the steps of the vault.*

Eleanor stands, her face as fixed as an epitaph, bidding farewell to the mourners. Broderick has begged her to spare herself this final ordeal, but he is overruled by thoughts of Julian who, had Nature lived up to its name, would be here in her stead. She accepts the dutiful sympathy of distant cousins and the routine regrets of fellow parishioners. She warms to the sight of Lennox Hayward who walks up with Jessica Grieve, even if a sprightly nonagenarian is almost as unnerving as a precocious child. And yet he too is reduced to platitudes, declaring that 'I brought him into the world,' as though in the hope of thanks.

'I trust you're not too exhausted,' she replies, cutting short any reminiscences.

'It should have been me. Julian had his whole life ahead of him. I'd gladly have taken his place.'

'That's sentimentality, Doctor. You heard what the Vicar said. Equality of life-span is as undesirable as equality of any other sort. We might as well live in Russia.'

She turns to the fumbling, hole-in-the-wall man who was Julian's home-help. He fixes his eyes on the ground, granting her a full view of his speckled pate, the few remaining hairs brilliantined by sweat. For Julian's sake, she swallows her disgust and shakes his hand, feeling the clamminess seeping through the fine mesh of her glove.

'Leslie Howard,' he says; which, for a moment, she takes as an introduction. 'That's who Julian always reminded me of.'

'Ah yes, of course.'

'They broke the mould when they made him.'

'Thank you.' She refrains from remarking that she was the mould. 'And thank you for everything you did for him ... Mick.'

'It's Nick,' he asserts with unexpected vehemence. 'Nick. In over a year, you've never once got it right. Can't you make the effort this last time? Nick: N for nobody; I for insignificant; C for colourless.'

'Thank you Mr ... Nick,' she says coldly. 'I may have lost my only son, but I can still spell.'

The mourners file back through the cemetery.

Blair tracks Brandon through the tombs and finds him leaning against a gryphon, puffing on a cigarette.

'Avoiding the receiving-line?' Blair asks.

'She's unreal,' Brandon replies.

'She lives by different rules. Kedgeree Christianity, Julian used to call it.'

'Because it smells fishy?'

'No.' Blair smiles. 'Because, as a child she used to have morning prayers at the breakfast table. The family knelt with their elbows on the chairs and their servants behind them. Her mother always ended with "for ever and ever, amen, do you want some kedgeree, dear?"'

'Unreal!'

'Everything got jumbled up in her mind: God, good form, table manners.'

'And you connive in it.'

'Me?'

'The Church.'

'I'm a person, not an organization. I don't call you the NHS.'

'But there's a difference. My first duty is to the care of my patients; yours is to the teaching of the Bible.'

'That's just where you're wrong. Mine is to the care of souls.'

'Dead people, of course. I forgot. Religion kills and I'm not talking figuratively. All those arrogantly humble priests who would rather proscribe than pray. Forget hardening of the arteries; look at how many people suffer from "hardening of the oughteries".'

'Even if that were true – and I underline "if" – then the culprit is the Church, not Christ . . . the messengers, not the message.'

'Come on, you know better than that. Institutions can't be separated from the ideologies behind them. We've declared communism dead with the collapse of the Soviet Union – and they only had seventy or eighty years; but you want me to give the Church the benefit of the doubt after nearly two thousand.'

'The Church has the problem of any institution based on love.'

'What's that? Compromise? Take a subject close to my own heart: the Church has been the most anti-gay influence throughout the ages.'

'The Church has been the most anti-everything influence. That's not a reason for giving up on it. We've a strong gay contingent at St Mary's.'

'Oh yes. What a nice cosy club: the love that dare not speak its name meeting the love that passes understanding.'

'Why must you automatically relegate anyone with faith to the C-stream of life ... the higher your "I believe" score, the lower your IQ? I can truthfully say that, if I didn't trust in Christ, I'd commit suicide.'

'Great, so it's served its purpose. Now get a life.'

'I have and one which won't end at my death but will last eternally.'

'So you say.'

'So I know.'

'That's it then.' He stubs out his cigarette on the tomb.

'Believe me, I sympathize with your predicament. Of all the inequalities in the world, the hardest to accept is faith. It's the one thing you can't beg, borrow or steal.'

'I'm perfectly happy without it, thank you. You say you'd commit suicide if you didn't believe in God. No, don't interrupt; that's what you said. I – were I to go in for such grand gestures – would do the exact opposite. I abhor all that existentialist crap about life being meaningless because God is dead. It's precisely because God is dead (rather never existed) that life has meaning ... that we have a chance to make the most of the chapter of accidents which produced us. If there were a God, the thought of how He's treated us would be unbearable.'

'You're approaching it from the wrong angle.'

'How about the Auschwitz angle. Shall we try that?'

'But surely you can see that there's no difference between Auschwitz and any other tragedy in what it says about God? Or else you'd be accepting the obscene premise that God allows a little suffering but not a lot. The problem – if it is a problem – is that God allows any suffering. The rest is simply a question of scale.'

'Well, surprisingly enough, I do find it a problem. Six million dead does give me pause for thought. But, since we know that, in God's eyes, we're nothing but grains of sand, maybe I'm being unreasonable.'

'Auschwitz was made by man not God.'

'So God – the all-knowing, all-powerful creator of man – just sat back and watched it happen? I can picture it now, the hydra-headed Trinity, like celestial channel-hoppers, flicking back and forth through history, zapping into their favourite massacres, from Attila the Hun to Pol Pot.'

'That isn't funny.'

'It's not intended to be. Or take the reason that we're here today – albeit unofficially. You argue that Auschwitz was made by men.

But what about AIDS?' He adopts a theatrical whisper. 'I think we can dismiss the theory that it was cooked up by American scientists as their contribution to germ warfare and accept it as a natural catastrophe. And, for good measure, we might throw in the other infectious diseases which kill over seventeen million people a year. How can you reconcile that with a benevolent God?'

'Because I'm not arrogant – yes, arrogant – enough to suppose that God views things the same way as me, with what I laughingly call my intelligence. Because I acknowledge that a wisdom and a creativity which could fashion the universe has a different perspective on suffering from mine.'

'Yes, it's deaf and blind to it.'

'Or maybe deafened and blinded by it? In his address this afternoon, the Vicar identified Time as God's greatest gift to us. I'd go one further; it's His greatest sacrifice. God became matter long before He became man. In creating the universe out of Himself, He's inevitably changed by it ... not in essence but in part.'

'You mean not the godhead but the god-fingers and god-toes?'

'If it helps you to think in those terms, yes. That's why I always resist singing the hymn with the phrase "naught changeth thee"; since, however uplifting it may be, it denies the fundamental truth.'

'Which is?'

'That God doesn't sanction Auschwitz or AIDS; He suffers it. He's part of it.'

'Then why doesn't He do something about it?'

'That's rich coming from the scourge of all authority. I can only repeat what I was saying to one of my confirmation candidates yesterday – no, on Monday – when he was agonizing over the nature of evil.'

'Poor kid!'

'That it's part and parcel of human freedom.'

'You mean they go together like love and marriage?'

'I mean that freedom brings suffering but suffering also brings freedom. That balance is the essence of what it is to be alive.'

'So, in layman's terms, God created us in order to suffer.'

'No, God created us in order to be free. And, as an admission that the balance had slipped, He sent His son to suffer on our behalf. I'm no etymologist but I find it remarkable that the English word for suffering and the French word for bread are the same.'

'So are the English word for present and the German word for poison. So what?'

'Because it's through that bread – that consecrated bread – that we both share in and are relieved of our pain.'

'Which surely proves my point. Christ drank of the cup so that we could replace it with the chalice. Fine. Then why do we need the drip and the blood-bank when we have the mass?'

'You know perfectly well that the balance isn't that simple.'

'You speak of "suffering" as if it's just another word like "chair" or "table". Those two young men, whose hands Julian's mother is shaking like the governor's wife at a prison function, are going to die very soon. Several lives will be shattered ... theirs literally. That's what suffering is.'

'How can you be so certain? I thought that there were new drugs ... that Julian was one of the few who couldn't tolerate them.'

'No, one of the many.'

'Even so – even in the very worst scenario – people still have the chance to grow. At a party recently, I met a man, about my age, whose mother had been prescribed Thalidomide. He had flaps of flesh – almost fins – hanging from his shoulders. I was amazed, not just that he could joke about them but that he could be serious beneath the jokes. "There's one good thing about having flippers," he said, as we hugged goodbye; "even when I try to keep people at arm's length, they're close."'

'You have to admire their spirit.'

'Don't mock me!'

'Then don't preach at me! What do you want? That I tell my patients to make a virtue out of incapacity, like a blind man smelling the music of the flowers?'

'Why are you so reluctant to admit the possibility of growth? Like me, you must have seen people in hospital, who've been totally transformed – that is, spiritually – by their illness.'

'I've seen people writhing in agony; people whose hearts beat so fast that their blood was literally boiling: people who died with a fury on their faces that no undertaker could disguise. I've yet to discover the virtue in such screeching, suppurating torment, but then I'm only a doctor. No doubt if I wore a cross around my neck instead of a stethoscope ...'

'Then you'd be privy to extraordinary acts of selflessness and courage. Of course, I wish they'd occurred in another – in any other – context. But that would be to ignore human nature. People don't change their lives on account of an ingrowing toenail. They rarely even change their shoes.'

Blair's attempt to lighten the atmosphere fails as Brandon renews his attack.

'What kind of man are you? All those fine words wouldn't last five minutes in the face of what my patients have to go through. I'd like to see you forced to cope with an HIV diagnosis. I really would.'

'You may regret saying that.'

'I already do.'

'I have these lumps on my hands.'

'Oh for God's sake! We've just buried Julian. I can't face any more posturing.'

'I feel I ought to take the test.'

'Go on then if it makes you happy.'

'Happy?'

'Degraded. At one with the sick and the sinners. But make sure to choose the right clinic. At ours, we get results back the same day. You wouldn't want to miss out on a moment's misery.'

EUCHARIST WITH THE BLESSING OF THE OILS

Thursday 10.30 a.m.
St Paul's Cathedral

> The Organist plays the recessional hymn. The Bishop
> returns to the Dean's Vestry. The Archdeacon follows
> the robed clergy down to the Crypt.

Alfred walks down to the Crypt in a fury. His favourite service of
the year, with its chance to meet old friends, gossip, and renew his
vows, has been ruined by the Bishop's sermon. Even the familiar
plaque to Ivor Novello fails to raise his spirits. He makes his way to
the temporary robing-room of the OBE chapel where, amid the
dismaying spectacle of clergy – of both sexes – in various states of
disarray, he is relieved to spot a pocket of Anglo-Catholics beside
the memorial to Sir Arthur Sullivan, their soutanes shining like
good deeds in an evangelical world, their faces swathed in shadows
as if posed in a picture of discontent.

He is welcomed by the Vicar of St Hilda's, Hampton. 'Nil desper-
andum, Alfred. At least that's over for another year.'

'With God's grace, the Bishop may not last that long,' the Vicar
of St Magnus the Martyr, Warwick Street, prays.

'Oh but he will,' Alfred replies with grim conviction.

'What on earth did he mean by that sermon?' the Rector of All
Saints, Ealing, asks. 'Instead of a discourse on the nature of priesthood, we get an entry from *Who's Who*.'

'Worse,' St Hilda's says, 'Who's married to who. All that guff
about his wife!'

'Cranmer had the right idea,' the Vicar of St Dionis, Tottenham,
says, 'he kept his wife in a chest.'

'And what about the perfunctory way in which he celebrated
Mass?' St Magnus the Martyr asks.

'Oh but it isn't Mass to him,' St Hilda's replies. 'It's the Lord's
Supper.'

'Wrong,' Alfred says tartly. 'It's the Lord's High Tea. But then
informality is the order of the day. Would you believe he actually
calls me Alf? I explained that I was christened Alfred, a good old
Anglo-Saxon name.'

'I'd have given him a good old Anglo-Saxon expletive,' St Dionis says.

'"If my name was Ethelred," I asked, "would you call me Ethel?"'

The Curate of Holy Innocents, Teddington, struggles to suppress a titter.

'He has no sense of the ancient Roman concept of decorum.' Alfred carries on, as oblivious to the young man's mirth as to a congregation's boredom.

'He has no sense of Rome at all,' St Magnus the Martyr adds.

'Charity, charity,' Alfred says, to the delight of his hearers, who anticipate the opposite. 'We have to grant the man some success. Look at how evangelical parishes are growing.'

'Bums on seats,' Holy Innocents says, anxious to prove his credentials.

'Please!' Alfred shudders with the air of someone who can barely stomach a 'posterior'.

The swift swivelling of heads in his direction convinces the Curate of Holy Innocents that he has overstepped the mark. His misery is only partially relieved by the Rector of All Saints, Ealing's leery wink.

'I no longer pray for Edward our Bishop,' Alfred says, 'He's destroying the fabric of the Church ... literally, when you see what he's done to the private chapel at London House.'

'Redecorated?' St Dionis asks.

'Desecrated,' Alfred replies. 'Out go Bishop Fabian's eau-de-nil drapes and the *capo di monte* Stations of the Cross.'

'Not those!' St Dionis says. 'They were to die for.'

'In come terracotta candlesticks on the altar and something like canvas place-mats on the walls. And there's another thing. I've no wish to speak ill of his hospitality –'

'But,' they chorus.

'But,' he admits with a smile, 'Madam Bishop offered me the smallest sherry I've ever seen. "Dost thou take me for a fairy to drink out of an acorn?" I asked.'

The Curate of Holy Innocents, Teddington, splutters. The Rector of All Saints, Ealing, who has angled himself behind him, rubs his back.

'Of course, she failed to recognize the quotation.'

'"Dost thou take me for..." No, I must write it down or I'll never remember,' St Dionis says. 'Does anyone have any paper?'

'Would you say "no" to a bit of rough?' Holy Innocents asks, taking out a scrap.

'Silly question,' St Dionis replies, gothically arching an eyebrow.

The group falls silent as two women priests walk past.

'Flossies,' All Saints snorts.

'Flossies,' St Hilda's echoes.

'One might as well be in Selfridges food hall,' Alfred says. 'All that wet, white fish laid out on the slab.'

'It's an abomination,' St Hilda's says. 'How will they be able to prostrate themselves tomorrow when they have those ... protuberances on their chests?'

'Perhaps they should lie on their backs,' Holy Innocents suggests.

Alfred glares at him. 'That would give quite the wrong impression.'

> The Diocesan Communications Officer leads the Vicar
> through the cathedral to the Dean's Vestry.

Huxley hurries through the vast recesses of the cathedral behind Moloch, who treats him with the strained servility of a porter who has abandoned hope of a tip. He speculates as to why he has been summoned twice in a single morning. One explanation is that the Bishop is so fired by the rhetoric of his sermon that he has determined not to delay his purge of liberals; another is that he means to put further pressure on him regarding the clergy-house. Moloch gives nothing away; although his carefully cultivated air of discretion may well be a cloak for ignorance – as damning to a Communications Officer as apostasy to a priest.

> The Diocesan Communications Officer knocks on the
> Dean's Vestry door.

'Come in! come in!' Ted shouts.

'The Vicar of St Mary-in-the-Vale, Bishop,' the Communications Officer announces as unctuously as an undertaker. On receipt of a curt nod from his chief, he backs out with an adroit blend of dignity and deference. Huxley finds himself alone with Ted, who is busily unrobing and whose starched purple stock sticks out in front of him like a baby's plastic bib.

'I don't expect you thought that we'd be meeting again so soon,' Ted says.

'It's a double pleasure,' Huxley replies, his toes curling at his tongue's efforts.

'I don't intend to beat about the bush,' Ted says. 'Esther and I are having lunch with the head of Saudi Arabian Airlines ... not the most exciting of invitations but, at least in Holy Week, we won't have to worry that it's dry.'

Huxley wonders whether he has ever studied the doctrine of free will.

'Tell me, what questions do you put to couples who wish to marry in your church?'

'As few as possible,' Huxley replies. 'We discuss their commitment . . . to each other, to their faith; their hopes of children; often, these days, whether they already have children.'

'And their gender?'

'We touch on sexuality in the broadest sense. I regret to say that most of them are far more knowledgeable on the subject than I am.'

'No, not their sexuality,' Ted says testily, 'their gender. I'm told that, on Tuesday, two women went through some form of perverted ceremony at St Mary's.'

'That's quite impossible.'

'Alice Leighton and Daisy Lawrence. Their names have just been given to me by the Archdeacon of Highgate, who was informed by a . . .' He looks at his paper. 'Hugh Snape.'

'Either Hugh or the Archdeacon must have misunderstood.' Huxley sighs with relief. 'I did indeed conduct a wedding at two o'clock on Tuesday afternoon, but between Daisy and a young man called Joe Beatty.'

'This was at five and was conducted by your curate.'

'I'm sorry. I'm finding this all a little hard to take in. May I sit?' He does not wait for a reply but slumps down on the only chair, narrowly missing the Bishop's mitre.

'The situation is perfectly clear. You held one service; your curate then held another.'

'But I don't understand. Why did they keep it secret from me?'

'The issue isn't secrecy but discipline!' Ted slams down his fist on the table. 'Is it any wonder that people are turning away from the Church when their leaders endorse these abhorrent, unscriptural practices?'

'I promise you I had no idea . . . none at all.'

'That's no defence. If you know so little about what happens in church, what does that say for the rest of your parish? Who knows what satanic practices may be rife?'

'I'm sure it's not as bad as that.'

'One rotten apple, that's all it takes . . . look at Adam. But, don't worry. I shall get to the bottom of it. Now you may go.'

Huxley's urge to comply is betrayed by his feet.

'I understand you're only the priest-in-charge of St Mary's?' Ted adds.

'Yes, for my sins.' Huxley gives a nervous laugh.

'You can let me be the judge of that,' Ted says coldly. 'Good day.'

Huxley's relief at reaching the door vanishes when he opens it to discover Moloch, who makes no pretence at walking past but simply smiles as he might on a Third World visit and enters the room.

> As the cathedral clock strikes noon, a verger stands in the pulpit and asks all visitors to join in two minutes of silent prayer.

Jessica notes the tourists' irritation as they are forced to make concessions to the cathedral. It is as though two minutes silence is a serious disruption of schedules into which they still have to fit the Tower of London and Tower Bridge before lunch. She gazes at the modern-day pilgrims, cameras around their necks in place of shells, the badge of twentieth century belief: I click therefore I am. Religion has been replaced by history; faith by facts. To these new worshippers, St Paul's is most notable as a feat of engineering – there is nothing like a dome. This afternoon, they will visit the Banqueting House in Whitehall ... 'This is where King Charles I lived until he was executed. Each year on the anniversary of his death, a small group of fanatical royalists gather to honour his memory.' She surveys the cathedral. 'This is where Jesus lived until He was deposed. Every year on the anniversary of His betrayal, a small group of foolhardy priests gather to devote themselves to His service...'

She breaks off from her reverie as a hubbub builds up around her. With the prayers over, the normal business of the cathedral can be resumed. When Huxley puts his hand on her arm a moment later, she wonders if the spark has so left her marriage that she does not even start at his touch.

'You look thoughtful,' he says.

'Just cynical ... you look pale.'

He describes his meeting with the Bishop.

'How did the Archdeacon know?'

'Hugh Snape lodged a complaint.'

'But how did Hugh find out? No one would have told him. The doors were locked.'

A tourist, with a stomach so pronounced that it might be a pillow in a pantomime, interrupts with a request for directions.

'Are you saying you knew about it already?' Huxley asks, as the man walks away.

'Don't be angry. I wanted to tell you. Alice wanted to tell you. Dee wanted to tell you. Blair wanted to tell you.'

'How many wants does it take?'

'But none of us wanted to compromise you.'

'Well you did a great job. The Bishop's about to launch an investigation.'

'But not into you. No one can point a finger at you.'

'Except myself. What sort of priest is blind to the services in his own church? How many more has Blair conducted?'

'None, as far as I know. None, I'm sure. But this was so important to Alice. After Dee married Joe ... or rather Joe's passport, she needed to have the true position acknowledged.'

'But not by me?'

'She was afraid you wouldn't approve. She looks up to you like a father.'

'The two aren't incompatible.'

'And you can't deny you were delighted when Joe announced he was getting married.'

'Of course I was; I have you.'

'I don't follow.'

'I've known the blessing of a happy marriage. Try as I do, I can't believe that any other relationship amounts to the same.'

She clasps his hand.

'Thank you. But if you'd been there – Sorry! – you might have thought differently. I was immensely moved by their vows. At least they have no chance to fall back on ready-made routines.'

'Are you talking about them or us?'

'Am I that obvious?'

'After thirty years, I'd like to think so.'

'Then I'd better speak out. This may not be the time or the place (God forbid we should become one of those couples who can only row in restaurants); but then when is? These last few months, you've been so distant. We rarely talk. And, at night, you keep as far away as possible.'

'I'm not eighteen any more.'

'You're not eighty either. I've even wondered if there might be someone else – some glamorous new parishioner.'

'Oh my darling, how could you?'

'I was desperate for an explanation.'

'I understand. If you felt that our relationship had changed ... that I no longer even existed in any meaningful way...'

'Are we referring to the same thing?'

'I think so. Aren't we? No, I suppose I'm talking about me and God.'

'Oh Him. You once told me I was all the world to you. It was only later I realized that, coming from you, it wasn't that great a compliment.'

'If I've fallen out of love with anyone, it's God. There's no mystery any more ... no transcendence. My one aim has been to keep it from affecting you, but I see that I've only made it worse.' She laughs. 'I'm glad you find it amusing.'

'No, it's not that.' She hugs him closely. She feels her flesh tingle as if they were starting to make love. 'But I thought that the problem lay in me and there was nothing I could do to solve it. Now, I know I can do so much.'

Jessica holds Huxley in her arms and kisses him, planting her mouth on his and filling it with life. Peace descends, only to be shattered by an outraged verger, who reminds them that a cathedral is the house of God.

MASS OF THE LORD'S SUPPER

Thursday 6.30 p.m.
St Mary-in-the-Vale, Hampstead

The Vicar and congregation prepare for the service.

Huxley stands in a huddle with Rosemary and Hugh. Winifred Metcalfe and Sophie Record come into church.

'I'd better report for sidesman duty,' Rosemary says, 'or else the Vicar will be putting me on jankers.'

'And I must go and vest!'

Huxley's departure is further delayed by the arrival of the Head Server.

'Shouldn't you be in the sacristy, Lyndon?'

'This is my father.' Lyndon twists his body as if in a noose.

'Delighted. Huxley Grieve.' His proffered hand goes unshaken. 'We'll speak later. Must scoot. Not literally.' He laughs feebly.

'Nothing would surprise me about you people.'

'Really? Oh dear. Lyndon, would you check that Willy's heated up the charcoal.'

'He's staying right here. After what we've heard today, he won't ever be setting foot in this church again.'

Colin stands his ground. He has unblocked too many vicarage pipes to be intimidated by the pulpit vowels.

'What did I tell you?' Hugh asks Huxley. 'Are you going to lose your whole congregation for the sake of your curate?'

'We better talk,' Colin says to Huxley.

'It really will have to wait. I'm late already.'

'It won't take long. Or would you rather I went straight to the pack of journalists waiting outside?'

'Very well. You'd better come to the office. Hugh, would you ask Judith to warn people that the service may be slightly delayed. And, please, remind one of the servers that we need warm – repeat, warm – water in the ewer.'

The Vicar ushers his visitor into the office.

Colin follows Huxley into the office and takes a seat opposite the desk.

'Forgive me if I appear abrupt, Mr Brooks, but this is Holy
Week; I don't need any more drama. What's more, I have a congregation waiting for me.'

'Oh yes? I've seen your congregation. If it were a football club,
the players would be transferred. And why do you think that is?'

'Is this a serious question?'

'Let me tell you why. Because of the filth and hypocrisy of the
vicars. I never wanted Lyndon to get involved. There was always
something that didn't smell right. But I let him twist my arm; and
I've lived to regret it. If he was difficult before, he's impossible
now. He comes home late of an evening. We ask him where he's
been and he says with a smile that looks like it's ready to bite you
"Didn't you know I'd be about my father's business?". "I'm your
father," I said and grabbed him. "It's a quote," his mother
screamed; "you can't blame someone for a quote." And I let him
go. He's smart. I never said he wasn't smart. Dressing his own
thoughts up in words from the Bible; making yours sound so simple. I ask you, is that Christian?'

'Maybe he's unhappy. So he seizes whatever weapons are to
hand.'

'I'll show him unhappy. I told you; he's not coming here again.'

'But he's due to be confirmed at Whitsun.'

'Do you think I'd allow any son of mine to join a church run by
men like your number two?'

'If only you'd speak to Blair yourself, he'd explain. He meant no
disrespect to the Queen.'

'I'm sure.' Colin curls his lip. 'I come home at the end of a hard
day's work.' He falters at the memory of an afternoon spent pouring concrete down an old woman's drains. 'I turn on the 5 o'clock
news and catch a report from Westminster Abbey. I recognize your
bloke from before. That's it, I think, and call Lyndon downstairs. I
tell him that he can't come here any more – quite calmly, the way
I'm telling you.' Huxley tries to find a discreet way of wiping off
the spittle. 'Which is when he starts yelling at me that he won't
listen. He loves him.'

'Who loves whom?'

'Lyndon loves your man.'

'Not the other way round?' Huxley asks in relief.

'I'm coming to that,' Colin says coldly. 'Meanwhile, his mother's
practically hysterical.'

'I honestly wouldn't worry. It's just a teenage crush. Some have
them for pop stars. Some for sportsmen. Some for clergy.' He trails
off lamely.

'It's not normal.'

'Which of us can say what's normal?'

'Me! I can. I may not be rich or famous or clever or even all that happy, but I am normal. That must count for something. I'm not ignorant; I read *Dear Deidre*. I've no quarrel with gay people ... each to his own. But then let them stick to their own. Like in a pet shop, with all the budgies and the hamsters on the ground floor and then the reptiles past a Warning notice upstairs.'

'We're talking about different sexualities, not different species!'

'Do you have any sons?'

'One: Luke. My elder son, Toby, is dead.'

'I'm sorry; I didn't ... but then you'll understand. That's why I want to protect him. I asked him if anything had – you know – happened. It was like trying to speak French. At first he wouldn't say. He just looked at me, all nostrils. And then he broke down. He said he hated him – that your man had AIDS.'

'What?'

'Or not AIDS. But the thing that comes first. And that was when I knew that I couldn't keep it to myself.'

'Lyndon's confusing Blair with a parishioner who died this week.'

'It's your curate. He was one hundred per cent clear.'

'Blair would hardly have confided in him and not me.'

'Well, I intend to see for myself. And right now. So where are you hiding him?'

'He isn't here. I'll get hold of him as soon as the service is over.'

'Join the queue. But I warn, you I'm not waiting – and I'm not bluffing either. If you won't tell me where he is, then I'll go back there now and I'll tell your people what I've heard. You may not know what's normal, but I hope you can still say what's right and wrong. Or is even that up for grabs?'

The Head Server stands outside the office.

Lyndon stands outside the office contemplating suicide, or rather Lyndon stands outside the office contemplating Lyndon contemplating suicide, since the only way that he can give his life meaning is to see himself as a character in a play. The play is invariably a tragedy, although his suffering is all too often undermined by the farcical scenes taking place around him. For once, he experiences the bitter-sweet satisfaction of feeling the rest of the world chiming with his own sense of fate.

No tragic hero can have sprung from less auspicious stock. He must contend with parents whose minds are as common as their sauce-bottles: his father, a man of no faith and only the crudest passions (the paper-thin walls of the hotel in Palma reverberate in his memory); his mother, a woman who exudes sweet nothings like a dental hygienist. Now they threaten to bar him from church and, even, to ban his confirmation. They forget that he is nearly sixteen years old and as hungry for the body and blood of Christ as his classmates are for sex. Like the boy-saints of the early church, he is condemned for his convictions: banished to his room the way that they were walled up alive.

He draws a pall over his thoughts and tries to catch what his father is saying to Father Huxley. But, as he places his ear to the door, all he can hear is the murmur of conspirators behind an arras. He makes a dramatic thrust with an imaginary dagger and grazes his knuckles. He is stung by a sense of futility. It is clear that the tragic hero whom he most resembles is Hamlet: the St Paul of suicide . . . the man who examines it from every angle and turns what might be an act of desperation into one of self-sacrifice. Hamlet gives suicide emotional and intellectual respectability. He passes the torch, and the cup, to him.

Suicide is taboo, which attests to its attraction. Without the artificial prohibitions, everyone would be doing it – like sleeping with their parents. Perish the thought! It is also, as Blair confirmed, a sin . . . but only because it is equated with despair and the fool who hath said in his heart that there is no God. It would be quite the opposite for someone who despairs because he is being kept away from God, who is killing himself to attain the very communion which he has been denied on earth.

The model of suicide in the Christian tradition is Judas, but it obviously should be Jesus. He entered Jerusalem knowing full well what dangers lay in store. He encouraged Judas to betray Him and then made no attempt to resist arrest. He even rejected Pilate's escape-clause. He was as responsible for His own death as if He had hammered the nails into His hands.

He starts to relax. He has found the perfect precedent. His parents may treat him like a child, their expressions of concern as transparent as the 'this hurts me more than it does you' of his boyhood thrashings, and yet even a child has power – if only to disrupt and destroy. Suicide is the ultimate weapon; which means that he must wield it with care. In a world where the fact of death counts for little, the manner is all. The most fitting method would be crucifixion; but it might prove to be impractical single-handed. Easier – and just as effective – would be to attach himself to a church bell, so that, at the exact moment of the Elevation, the unsuspecting ringer would dash out his brains against the rim.

> The sidesman stands by the door.

Rosemary surveys the church from a fortification of hymn-books. She sniffs at Judith, who flaps around the congregation, and glares at the journalists who have grouped in the St John chapel. It is clear that, should there be any trouble, she will have to evict them on her own – a prospect which isn't altogether displeasing. She is mapping out a plan of campaign when she catches sight of Willy Jeavons skulking in the porch.

'Willy, come here. Why aren't you with the rest of the servers?'

He approaches her with reluctance, his cherubic looks belied by the cotta which he wears like an exhibit in a tabloid exposé.

'Nothing wrong. Just checking to see if there were any more reporters. What's going on? Where's Father? This is better than Christmas.'

'It's all stuff and nonsense – editors with too much time on their hands.'

'It's Father Blair, isn't it? They're asking a whole load of questions. For cash. One wanted to know if he ever saw me privately. He had a string of snot in his nostril.'

'What?'

'A string of snot –'

'No, you chump, what did he mean by that? It's a disgrace. Are they trying to corrupt the child?'

'The child, as you put it, is thirteen. Look.' He holds up two £20 notes. 'You can get away with murder till your voice breaks.'

'Willy, you're a monster. I insist you put that money straight in the collection.'

'No way.'

'I shall speak to your parents. Now run along to the sacristy and warn the others to keep mum. They may not all have your *savoir-faire*.'

'It's not *savoir-faire*; it's perfectly legal.'

> The Churchwarden moves to the chancel steps and announces that the service will be late in starting.

'I'm sure they're all talking about us,' Dee whispers to Alice and Joe. 'Wondering if something's wrong. We've only been married two days – we should have better things to do than be stuck in a church.'

'Stuck is the word,' Alice says.

'Though I can see their point. I don't have much luck. Two weddings and not a single day's honeymoon.'

'Who knows? Perhaps Joe and I will go away and leave you to look after Dora.' Alice refuses to rise to the bait.

'At least we're able to show our support for Blair,' Joe says. 'What he did was very brave.'

'Was it really?' Dee asks. 'The Queen's such an easy target. And people need some colour in their lives.'

'There's colour and colour,' Alice says, 'and a world of difference between a pageant designed to dazzle the spectators and a painting intended to make them see.'

'Why are we waiting? Why are we waiting?' They all three look back as Bertha, wearing a plastic rain-hat and a pinafore around her coat, sets her impatience to the familiar hymn.

'Somebody told me she was once a brilliant woman,' Dee says.

'People like to believe that,' Alice says. 'It makes life seem fairer.'

'I intend to be just the same when I'm old,' Joe says. 'Wilful and eccentric. Not caring what anyone thinks.'

He breaks off, as the arbitrary approach of old age assumes graphic form in the arrival of Cherish, whose prematurely lined face makes her look like a Munchkin. Her perfectly plaited hair, pleated skirt and pulled-up socks appear unruffled by default. The electric blue of her jumper brings out the dead-wood dullness of her skin. Only her flickering eyelids show any sign of life as her aunt leads her slowly up the aisle.

He turns away. The uneasy truce which he has signed with the virus is violated by its invasion of the child.

> The Organist plays selections from *The Desert Song* in
> the style of Bach.

Femi slides Cherish into the second row, behind Jessica and Lennox Hayward. She cranes forward and whispers in Jessica's ear. 'Who are those men?' She points to the journalists. 'And why are there are cameras in the churchyard?'

'Haven't you heard?' Jessica replies. 'Blair ran amok in Westminster Abbey.'

'Was he drunk?'

'Not as far as I know.' Jessica is moved by Femi's marital projection. 'I'll explain later,' she says, indicating Lennox. 'I assume this means that we're talking again.'

'I'm sorry; I shouldn't have lost my temper. I just thought that the Bishop offered a hope – and one that I had to cling on to. I must keep faith, Jessica. If I stop, I'm afraid that . . . I'm just afraid.'

'Are you feeling any better, sweetheart?' Jessica asks Cherish.

'I have thump thump inside my head.'

'We've come straight from the doctor.'

'He said that I mustn't ought to think of it as happening inside my head but as a man making a floor next door.'

'Does that help?'

'It will when he stops.'

'He's given her so many pills, she'll start to rattle.'

Cherish shakes the bangles on her arms. 'See, I can rattle.'

'Oh Beauty!' Femi lays Cherish's head on her breast and speaks over it to Jessica. 'I wish we'd never heard of that service. She hasn't been so bad in over a year. She keeps complaining of seeing fire in front of her eyes – although the doctor said it's just her headaches. She shakes. Her teeth chatter. She doesn't sleep. I don't sleep. And yet somehow she finds time for the most violent nightmares.'

'Should she be here?'

'Oh yes, she insisted.' She stares into Cherish's eyes with an intensity which is mocked by the lack of response. 'She wants to have her feet washed by Jesus's holy water, don't you Beauty?'

'So long as it isn't cold.'

> The Vicar shows out his visitor and stands alone in the office.

Huxley remembers Blair wearing a badge declaring that *The Body of Christ has AIDS*. The metaphor was lost on Myrna Timson and Trudy England who took it as a warning about the danger of consuming the wafers, on a par with salmonella in eggs. It required considerable effort to convince them to return to the rail. Their reluctance will be all the greater now that the words have been made flesh ... now that the racked and lacerated body of Christ has stepped down from the Cross to stand at the altar, and the church is decked in its Good Friday colours the whole year round.

Anger, resentment and grief engulf him in quick succession. He is angry that Blair should have let himself be compromised (mankind always has a weak point, but at least in the myth it is only a heel), so that his blessing of Alice and Dee and his disruption of the Maundy will come to be viewed through the prism of his illness. He resents Blair's refusal to trust him with his diagnosis, much as if Toby or Luke had tried to protect him from an 'unsuitable' girlfriend. Above all, he grieves for Blair's youthful mortality. He pictures him lying in Julian's bed – a single bed with regulation linen and perfectly angled corners – his lifeless head as waxy and taut as in a reliquary, his shrivelled arm attached to a drip, while doctors strive to keep death at needle's length.

He leaves the office and walks back through the church. He cannot even pray for strength to sustain him through the service, since it is the aridity of prayer which has sapped his strength. No Holy Week has ever felt so hollow. He has to stand in the person of Christ on a night when he feels more like Judas. A braver man would have resisted Colin Brooks's threats and refused to reveal Blair's whereabouts – and yet there was no other way to get rid of him. He had ... he has a duty to his congregation – as is confirmed when he enters the sacristy to the cheers of the servers and choir. But the warmth of their welcome exposes his deceit. For, while Blair keeps watch in the bitter chill of the Garden, he merely goes through the motions in the comfort of the Upper Room.

> The Vicar prays with the servers and choir. *Come Holy Spirit, fill our hearts with love that we may praise you in word and music.*

As Huxley invokes the power of God, he feels like the ambassador from a nation which has been annexed desperately trying to convince his allies that it still exists.

> The Organist changes chords abruptly and commences the Introit as the choir and servers enter.

Willy has spent £2 of his new-found wealth persuading Sandy Tewson to let him take over Lyndon's position as Thurifer. He censes the nave as fervently as if he were putting out a fire. He moves to the St John Chapel and censes the reporters: a symbolic purification which, even at thirteen, he deems to be in vain.

> The Vicar concludes his sermon. He descends from the pulpit, takes off his chasuble and puts on an apron. He moves into the nave, accompanied by three servers, one holding an ewer, one a bowl, and one a towel. He kneels, washes, dries and kisses the feet of each recipient, while the choir sings the antiphon *Where charity and love are found, there is God.*

Huxley fails to find the usual relief at the end of his sermon. The move from the muddled phrasing of his own speech to the confident cadences of Cranmer's (an eloquence impossible in an age of qualification), far from lending him authority, serves to emphasize his loss. He feels as detached from the words as a ventriloquist's dummy. Empty phrases turn into empty postures, as he shifts from words to action ... or rather ritual, the Church's traditional compromise, humbling himself at his congregation's feet. And yet what should be a highly charged connection – the meeting of reverence and self-abasement – is reduced to an uneasy collusion. This is not genuine intimacy so much as the licensed transgression of a Boy Bishop.

As he lays Myrna's feet in his lap, he can feel her cringe with embarrassment – not that she should be washed in the name of Christ but that she should be exposing her hard skin and corns. He longs to free her of such pettiness: to continue up her legs or to dry her feet with his hair or to do anything that would shock her with the audacity of the act. But it would simply be imposing another obstacle. So he kisses her toes and continues along the pew.

> *Where charity and love are found, there is God.*
> *The love of Christ has gathered us together into one.*

Joe is proud of his feet, which have a delicacy lacking in the rest of his body, being long and thin with gently tapering toes. While he fights to retain his shirt and pants, even in the doctor's surgery, he welcomes any chance to remove his shoes and socks. Beauty may be in the eye of the beholder, but most beholders are myopic. Cheekbones and torsos are not the be-all and end-all. He longs for lovers to set more store by feet and dreams of a world where 'well-endowed' in the contact ads would refer to shoe-size and 'librarian's foot' replace 'swimmer's body' as an object of desire. And yet, so far, the only man he has encountered with such specialized tastes turned out to be less concerned with shape than with smells, rhapsodizing over his wearing the same pair of nylon socks for a week . . . He shudders and beats a hasty retreat from the fetid cravings of the fetishist to the incense-breathing atmosphere of the church.

> *Let us rejoice and be glad in Him.*
> *Let us fear and love the living God.*
> *And love each other from the depths of our heart.*

'You will have hundreds of men at your feet,' Alice's mother assured her. 'All the better to trample on them,' she replied . . . and, nearly thirty years on, she marvels how, at twelve with no knowledge of sexuality, her words could so conclusively have pre-empted her thoughts. Now, the only man to kneel at her feet is Huxley, who puts her in mind less of a prospective suitor than of the old soldier who used to polish her father's shoes in the Burlington Arcade. Nothing in her childhood was as humiliating as watching him buffing up brogues until they gleamed to match his medals. But, when she challenged her father to give him the money without insisting on the shoe-shine, he refused, claiming that the man would regard it as an insult. Work, not charity, was the way to ensure self-respect.

She wonders now, as she did then, how anyone can maintain self-respect while grovelling at someone else's feet. It is a position to which those in the Church are dangerously prone. She yearns to raise Huxley up: to see him standing at the altar in his Easter Sunday triumph. But the liturgy must run its course.

> *Where charity and love are found, there is God.*
> *Therefore when we are together,*
> *Let us take heed not to be divided in mind.*

Dee is sensitive about her feet. Unlike men, who are said to regard them as indicative of another organ, she feels self-conscious about their size. As a girl, reading about women with large feet gave her the same sense of solidarity which she later obtained from reading about lesbians. For years, her heroine was Lady Antonia Fraser, whose feet were the subject of an article in one of her mother's magazines. Her rival in a divorce case – a famous English actress – gave an interview in which she jeered at Lady Antonia's enormous shoes. But the jibe backfired, at least in part, for it endeared Lady Antonia to her for life.

She cut out Lady Antonia's photograph and kept it among her treasures. Her beauty and title were an inspiration, for they proved that big feet were not just for peasants and Ugly Sisters, whatever her brothers might say. Her passion for Lady Antonia remained a secret, until her brothers discovered her diary and taunted her without remorse. They urged her parents to bind her feet, as if they were in China, and, on receiving a firm (but amused) rebuff, proceeded to do so themselves. The cords cut into her flesh; but, aware that her brothers were waiting for her to scream, she bit her tongue to silence. Nor would she earn their sneers by hobbling to Mother. Instead, she spent the day in a sack-race, until her tormentors were shamed into setting her free. It was her first realization that a victim could have power.

The scars from the cords may no longer be visible but they remain raw. She fights to keep herself from squirming as Huxley lifts her ankle onto his thigh.

> *Let there be an end to bitterness and quarrels, an end to strife,*
> *and, in our midst, be Christ our God.*

Judith indicates that Huxley should pass her by. Although she has slipped off her shoes and stockings *pour encourager les autres* (culture need not begin at Calais), she fears that, after the initial delay, they may be running out of time. As churchwarden, she is used to stinting herself for the sake of her fellows, having set aside more canapés and renounced more jumble-sale bargains than she cares to recall. Rosemary Trott once described her as the parish Martha (many a true word is spoken in scorn). But, at least in the gospel, Martha and Mary were evenly matched; at St Mary's, she is outnumbered by a ratio of the whole congregation to one.

Huxley ignores her signals and picks up her foot. His touch is every bit as tender as she has struggled not to imagine. She finds her heart filling with resentment towards Jessica. As an antidote, she starts to hum, lighting on *Jerusalem* – for reasons which remain opaque until she remembers the opening line. She chuckles at how the mind, even one as well-ordered as hers, establishes so many unexpected connections, only to clear her throat quickly as Huxley looks up, in case he should suspect her of irreverence. *Jerusalem* has long been her favourite hymn, not just for the words and the music but for the associations. As the theme-tune of the Women's Institute, it represents all that is best about Britain, as much of a national anthem as *God Save the Queen*.

Thoughts of the Queen remind her of Blair's protest, provoking her to such fury that she almost kicks Huxley in the face. She may not be a flag-waver, but her loyalty remains unswerving . . . witness the names of her cats. It is not something which she will allow Blair to threaten. He may claim to speak in the name of Christ, but he knows full well how much of what Christ said is contradictory. He also knows that that is precisely to prevent His being appropriated by any one faction. Christ stands above politics, just like Her Majesty. If Blair intends to remain at St Mary's, he must start to learn humility (she beams at Huxley, a male Martha if ever there were one): a little less shouting in temples and a little more kneeling at feet.

> *Where charity and love are found, there is God.*
> *And in company with the blessed may we see*
> *Your face in glory, Christ our God.*

Femi is proud of her feet. Their hardness is honed rather than calloused. They are as comfortable as the softest slippers and as resilient as the toughest boots. For years, they trod unencumbered through a country where 'sole' and 'soul' are connected by far more than sound, and the foot is the outward expression of the link between walker and world. They strode through a country where divinity is not confined to the sky nor wisdom to the head and where the pulse of the earth is so powerful that it seems only natural for God to have made man out of mud.

She is proud of her feet in the way that her father was proud of his ancestors; their strength is sapped in a country of cars and queues. She has no chance to walk barefoot through streets paved with dirt. If they were anywhere but church, she would challenge Huxley with the need to wash the country rather than the feet. This is a country where women take pride in their shoes. And the most precious come from animals found in Africa. They have crocodile shoes and lizard shoes and snake shoes. And yet they get nothing from the skins but their scarcity. They sever the bond with the earth as they balance on heels and toes, leaving their soles to hover in the air.

These are the people to whom she now belongs. But, with the call of the past in her ears, she waits until Huxley has dried her feet and then drops them onto the stone, savouring the memory of freedom.

> *Pure and unbounded joy*
> *For ever and ever.*

Cherish is used to people touching her feet . . . she's used to people touching her all over, as she lies on a bed in a back-to-front dress. She can't see them but she makes pictures of them from their voices: the doctor who talks as if his tongue was made of toffee; the nurse who talks as if her mouth was full of pins. But she doesn't think about them too hard because she knows they won't let her touch them and she's only interested in faces which she can trace for herself.

She knows that Huxley lets her touch him, so she rubs her fingers on the top of his head, which feels like the donkey from Sunday. She's surprised when Aunt Femi takes her hands and pulls them away. It must be because of church. But while the bad part of church is having to sit still and not touch things, it's made up for by the good part, which is the singing and the smell, and by the best part, which is making pictures of the angels who fly round and round the ceiling on wings that beat as fast as a headache before a pill. And although no human person can see them, they're not invisible. They're like whistles that can only be heard by dogs. So church is the one place where having eyes is no help, since everyone is as blind as her.

Huxley is taking care not to hurt her lumps; which means that he hurts something else instead. She knows that the lumps are part of being ill, even though Aunt Femi says they're getting better . . . her voice always goes gluey when she says something kind that's trying to be true. She heard one nurse call the lumps crimson, which was scary until she found out that it was a colour. She has to work extra hard to picture colours. She knows that black is hot because she and Aunt Femi are black and they come from Africa where the black sun shines all day ... and white is cold because English people are white – although sometimes they're grey ... and blue is wet because the sea is blue and people are blue when they cry. And yellow is shivery because Matthew Norris went yellow when he was a coward. But crimson is more difficult. Crimson is sharp and itchy and burning ... until it is washed in the cool blue water and dried in the warm black towel.

She starts to shiver, as she senses something hard and brown moving behind her and breath like gravel on her neck.

Where charity and love are found, there is God.

'What's wrong with her then?' Bertha asks, leaning forward.

'Nothing,' Jessica says, leaning back. 'What do you mean?'

'There – on her foot.'

'It's just a rash. Huxley, put Cherish's sock on.'

'I'll do it,' Femi says. 'Beauty, you sit still.'

'That's no rash,' Bertha says. 'I've had rash. That's lumps. That's infectious. You're a doctor.' Stretching across the pews, she taps Lennox on the shoulder. 'You look.'

'I've nothing to say. I know nothing about it.' Lennox stares ahead.

'It's all right, Lennox,' Jessica whispers. 'She isn't asking about the Maundy.'

'If you have a problem, Bertha,' Huxley says, 'we'll talk about it after the service.' He smiles wanly at a reporter who has left his seat to investigate the noise.

'Oh yes,' Bertha mutters to a self which encompasses the whole congregation. 'Everyone else can have their say but not me. I shall write to the Bishop.'

She breaks off just as the choir concludes the antiphon. Huxley attempts to restore a devotional mood. 'Jesus said: "If I then, your Lord and Master, have washed your feet; ye also ought to wash one another's feet."' He kneels down in front of Rosemary.

'Jesus can say what he likes,' the reporter tells his colleagues in a voice unaccustomed to the echo. 'But he wasn't using that water. That kid has AIDS.'

The lights dim as the Sacrament is carried in procession to the Altar of Repose. The bell tolls as the Vicar

changes his robes from white to purple. The sanctuary
is stripped of all adornment and the church plunged
into darkness.

Prayer is the meeting of eternity and time, but Huxley is conscious
only of the latter ... the minutes which slow to the beat of his
heartache, the hours which weigh as heavy as his fears. His eyes
may have accustomed themselves to the darkness, but the rest of
him has not. Prayer has long been his private life, an escape from
the demands of family and parish; now, it has been taken from
him as painfully as by a divorce. He is utterly alone. No longer can
he banish despair with the thought of Christ deserted by His
friends in the Garden of Gethsamene, for the friend who has deserted him is Christ.

He sets aside the aches and pains – the throbbing head and the
stiff joints and the shirt which scratches like a penance – and begs
an audience of God. He bangs out his prayers like a premature
corpse pounding on the lid of a coffin. He appeals for a sign: not
for himself but for the souls in his care who may be led astray by
his misgivings. And yet, if God is listening, He sees through the
subterfuge – or, worse, mocks it; for the flutter of wings, which
descends like a ray of hope, is no angel but a bat swooping down
from the belfry, as though seeking out a creature as steeped in
darkness as itself.

His eyes smart with strain and frustration ... assuaged only by
the knowledge that his suffering is deserved. The Bishop is right
and he was wrong. Liberalism is not a creed but a quibble. All the
troubles to have afflicted St Mary's spring directly from his 'I
doubt therefore I believe' code. He has taken Jesus down from
the Cross and laid Him on a futon. He has preached the gospel
of freedom of choice beyond the bounds of responsiblity. He has
endorsed Christ's two commandments while ignoring their debt
to Moses's Ten. His only absolute has been the absence of absolutes. When his congregation asked for bread, he gave them a
scythe.

'You can't have it both ways,' as the actress said to the Bishop.

'Why not?' he replied, flipping her over. 'It is the Church of
England.'

His *mea culpa*s ring out with a mediaeval fervour. His acceptance
of blame accentuates his dilemma. His priesthood is no longer
tenable, and yet to relinquish it would be to forsake his congregation for the sake of his conscience: a return to the very liberalism
he has come to deplore. Besides, he must remain at his post in

order to guide the parish through the grief which will envelop it on learning about Blair. He must remove the question-mark from pride of place in his pulpit and proclaim a faith to which he no longer adheres, in the hope that exposure to its mysteries will, one day, restore his belief.

Hearing the scuffle at the back of the church, he turns to see two figures illuminated by the light from the porch. His mind races with dangers ranging from arrest to robbery. He attempts to stand, but fear and cramp root him to the spot. So he picks up the cross from his prie-dieu and brandishes it like a sword.

'We can't just barge in; he's praying.'

'No one prays that long. He was at it five hours ago.'

'We can tell Brian that the Church was shut – come back again tomorrow.'

'Look, if it's true what everyone's saying about this bloke Ashley...'

'Did he actually touch the Queen?'

'He yelled at her. That's saliva.'

Huxley recoils from the sensation-sated voices, as the reporters stumble through the pews by the flame of a match. He closes his eyes and intensifies his prayers, only to be roused by a tap on the back.

'Scuse us, Reverend, I can see you're busy.'

'I'm trying to pray.'

'It's for your own good, believe me. Give your side of the story.'

'What story?'

'How long have you known that your curate has AIDS?'

'That's scurrilous nonsense!'

'We've been told by one of your team.'

'I have no team but Blair.'

'The kid shaking the Aladdin's-lamp thing.'

'What? Oh, you mean Willy. He's just a child. He won't even know what AIDS is.'

'Don't you believe it! They know it all nowadays. My daughter's six. She's been taught how to put a condom on a carrot.'

'We ran the story on the front page.'

'Have you quite finished? Don't you know that this is one of the most sacred nights of the year?'

'You obviously haven't heard then?'

'Yes, I have. But it's all an absurd misunderstanding. I'm only sorry that it's reached as far as Willy.'

'He's been arrested.'

'Who?'

'Your man. Tonight.'

'How do you know?'

'We have our sources.'

'Oh yes? Another thirteen-year-old boy?'

'Our sources at the Met.'

Huxley falls silent.

'Reverend, are you all right?'

'Would one of you please help me up? I have cramp.' He accepts a hand and stumbles onto a seat.

'Watch out, you'll fall. Do you think we could have some light? It's as dark as Naomi Campbell's twat in here.'

'This is a church!'

'Sorry. Slip of the tongue.'

'Take your matches. There are candles on that pricket-stand.'

'Prick what?'

'Next to the pillar, beneath the icon of the Virgin.'

One of the reporters lights the candles. The chapel is suffused with a dusty glow.

'I'd be grateful if you'd tell me what you've found out,' Huxley says.

'Your curate's been a naughty boy. He was picked up in a notorious gay cruising-ground.'

'You mean Finsbury Park cemetery?'

'Then you know it?' The reporter tightens his grip on his tape-recorder.

'Of course I know it. I conducted a funeral there only yesterday. Blair told me he was going back to pray.'

'I suppose that's one way of putting it. "Your grave or mine?"'

'Are you saying that people go to the cemetery for sex?'

'It's no use acting the innocent. We've been told that you hold gay marriages.'

'That is absolutely untrue. It's time to set a few things straight.' Huxley fights for his credibility in default of his faith. 'Marriage is the union between a man and a woman – as the Church teaches and we practise. At the same time, we have a duty to reach out to every member of our congregation. Which may be the cause of this misunderstanding. I categorically deny that it's anything more.'

'OK, so what about his behaviour this morning in Westminster Abbey?'

'I've yet to hear a full report. Until I do, I can make no comment.'

'We can give you the gist.'

'The gist isn't the problem, thank you. All I will say is that he seems to be suffering from nervous exhaustion. It's not just me . . .

many of his friends in the parish have been worried that he's driving himself into the ground.'

'You're saying he cracked?'

'Maybe for a moment. But I utterly deny that he intended any insult or criticism of the Queen, to whom he has sworn an oath of allegiance. I can assure you that he takes that – and, indeed, all his vows – very seriously.'

'Then how do you explain the HIV?'

'I don't explain it. I don't need to explain it. I deny it. Willy has picked up the wrong end of the stick.'

'But it's not just the kid. The story has been confirmed by our source in the Met.'

'Then they're both wrong. Blair has been – is – an exemplary priest. I have unwavering faith in his character, his integrity and his adherence to the –'

'Yes, yes, let's not get sidetracked. We're talking AIDS here. And unless he's been doing drugs or is a very light-skinned Haitian –'

'Then there's only one way he could have been infected.'

'Seeing as you've already made up your minds, I'm at a loss to know why you're here. It's intolerable that a man should be condemned on the basis of unsubstantiated gossip. I can give you absolute denials on all three of your charges. Now would you please go. You've kept me quite long enough. We've a service here at noon, and I need to rest.'

A Good Friday Vigil

Friday 11.00 p.m.
St Saviour's Vicarage, Belsize Park

The Archdeacon unlocks the door to his private chapel.

Alfred descends the cellar steps and enters the familiar atmosphere of damp and devotion. He cradles a cross, its Gothic gaudiness starkly offsetting the ivory limbs of the crucified Christ. He has spent the afternoon painstakingly repainting the streams of blood flowing from the wounds. He works in nail varnish, which experience has shown to take on an added lustre in the quiver of candlelight.

He places the cross in the dead centre of the altar cloth and lights the candles. The touch of the tapering wax animates his body with a feeling part sacred, part profane. He savours the charms of a room known only to himself and a handful of initiates, before moving to the single prie-dieu set regally in the middle of the floor. He turns to the back wall dominated by an eight-foot cross hewn out of charred timbers by two young Coptic refugees. Closing his eyes and inhaling deeply, he can still sense the pungency of their presence ingrained in the knotty wood.

He begins to relax after a day in which he has harrowed himself as well as his congregation with a graphic account of Christ's tortures. At St Saviour's, the green hill far away runs red with the Redeemer's blood. He rejects any attempt to tone down the gore as part of an insidious trend to Disney-fy the Church and reduce Christ to a cross between Mowgli and Merlin. A full understanding of Christ's suffering is essential to a true appreciation of human debt. But, these days, even clergy are intent on sparing themselves pain. He has heard of men who say their night-time prayers in the comfort of their beds, while their lumpish wives, like cows in the manger, lie listlessly beside them.

He has always been drawn to the mortification of the flesh. As a boy, his spirituality was so intense that he feared that, unless he was constantly reminded of his body through pain, it would evaporate. Then, as a young man, he discovered a more intimate form of chastisement. He had long revered St Sebastian and, on a visit to

Rome, resolved to make a night-time pilgrimage to the site of his burial on the Appian Way. A chance encounter with a latter-day centurion led him to the brink of martyrdom. He still treasures the memory – and bears the scars.

Now, in his private chapel, he continues to offer up his pain for God's greater glory. He surveys the instruments of correction, which are as closely linked to his favourite saints' days as the different liturgical colours: the blindfold for St Paul; the spikes for St Conon; the nipple-clamps for St Agatha; the birch for St Bartholomew. But, of all his red-letter days, none is as full-blooded as Good Friday. Imaginatively, if not spiritually, even Easter Sunday amounts to an anti-climax. Christ has cast off the flesh and returned to His Father. But, on Good Friday, He remains at the mercy of men, who strip Him, spit on Him and flog Him, before nailing him to the Cross, where His immaculate body is defiled ... He blacks out the image. He has no wish to reach the Sanctus of his devotions too soon.

The Archdeacon is roused by the doorbell.

The doorbell rings like the angelus to alert the faithful. The soft pad of footsteps overhead warns Alfred that his mother is not yet in bed. What's worse, she appears to be opening the door in her slippers – as though they lived in a street. He laments the onslaught of old age which destroys a sense of propriety as ruthlessly as it blurs distinctions of sex. The thought sends his hands in an involuntary movement to his chest, where the portent of his mother's thinning hair and briery kisses is confirmed by folds of mockingly maternal flab.

He hurries upstairs to forestall any damage. Just as he feared, he finds her standing at the door in her housecoat. He rescues Harry Wainwright from her clutches. Harry was his first-ever server at St Saviour's, a ginger-haired boy, snub-nosed and scrawny, until adolescence and maturity (so rarely concurrent) gained him entrance to the private chapel, where he carried out his duties with a genuine relish ... the unique way in which he extinguished a candle still sends a shiver through his bowels.

Having greeted the friend who, though disqualified by age and familiarity from active participation in the offices, runs the agency which supplies his successors, he turns to appraise his latest protégé. Harry has teased him with possibilities: a northern lad with a whippety chest; a Cockney who smells like cement. But he has kept back the still more desirable prospect now present: a boy as black as the night in which he stands. He suppresses a smile, although he knows that Harry can read him as clearly as the Bishop can his bible (the promise of pleasure allows his irreverence free rein). He beckons the boy into the light. The waistband of skin beneath the cheap High Street top possesses an incalculable allure. He seethes with desire to sink his tongue into the salty (please God!) flesh.

Awash with anticipation, he dispatches his mother to bed. He is worried that her prejudices, as Empire-made as her towels, might transmit themselves to the boy. He warns her that Harry has brought his friend for an evening of private prayer and that they must, on no account, be disturbed. The boy looks relieved – as though he had feared that she might be joining them. The thought of his mother's coffin-cheating pallor alongside the boy's burnished blackness fills him with disgust.

'This is Ronan, Father,' Harry says, as soon as they are free. 'I think you'll find him to your taste.' His laughter sizzles like fat.

'Thank you.' Alfred is as saddened by the coarsening of Harry's mind as by the thickening of his waist. 'I'm very grateful for all your trouble. But we mustn't keep you.'

'Nothing's too much for our number one client,' Harry replies. Alfred acknowledges the compliment while trusting that Ronan won't be misled. 'Still, I'd best get back to base. Good Friday's always one of our busiest nights.'

Alfred clasps Harry's hand like a rosary and closes the door, before leading Ronan down the cellar steps.

The Archdeacon and his server enter the chapel.

Alfred leers at Ronan ... or so Ronan, as yet unaccustomed to the gloom, deduces from the gust of acrid breath.

'I understand Harry has told you what will be required.'

'He said that I'd be –'

'There's no need to put it into words. We're here to celebrate a mystery. You'll be well-paid. Although, by rights, it should be thirty pieces of silver.'

Unsure how to respond, Ronan keeps silent. If he were the one who was paying, he'd want to hear nothing but 'yes'; and yet he has learnt from his first few punters that other people prefer 'no' ... and, from what he has gathered from Harry, Alfred is someone who likes his 'no' spelt out hard. He feels nervous at finding himself alone with a man whom even Harry regards as 'tricky', one to whom he would never be sent so soon after joining the Agency if he weren't the only black boy on the books. And his shame in the face of his family, his friends and his future is compounded by a sense of betraying his race. Whoring is the one job for which his skin is an asset. He has found his niche in an off-white world.

He tries to concentrate on his work. So far, he has only had sex in bedrooms. The cellar makes him feel like a piece of coal.

The Archdeacon arranges the instruments on the altar.

As Alfred prepares for the celebration, he turns to Ronan, allowing his imagination to linger in places as yet out of bounds to his hands. The boy's cocksure expectancy confirms both his daytime reading that all men are full of sin and his bedtime reading that young men are full of smut. His own adolescent chastity was simply the exception to the rule.

'Harry should have introduced us before. But then I'm a martyr to Lent. You did bring the poppers?'

'Here.' Ronan takes out a small bottle from his top pocket. He resolves to clarify his position. 'I won't be in this game long, I can tell you. Harry and I got to talking in a club. I done one or two jobs, just to help him out. But I'm no regular. This is in the way of a special favour, 'cos he said you like them black.'

'Like them black?' The force of Alfred's scorn scares Ronan.

'What I'm saying is I'm no whore.'

'Then you stand alone. You remember what our Lord said: "He that is without sin among you, let him first cast a stone." Where you differ from the rest of us is that you sin openly while we cover it up. Take off your clothes.'

Ronan is shocked by Alfred's abruptness. There is no offer of a drink ... no small talk ... no talk of any sort ... that might create an illusion of intimacy. He feels as if every garment he removes is in front of a jeering crowd on a tawdry stage.

'No, leave on your b ... briefs.' Alfred stutters, as though he can hardly bear to part with a word so imbued with both the poignancy of vanished youth and the thrill of new discovery. For years, he attempted to reconcile his celibacy and his desires by watching – but never touching – while accommodating lads pleasured themselves as painlessly as Adam before the creation of Eve. But his guard was shattered when a particularly forceful emission landed on his cheek. It was a sure sign of the vanity of trying to escape the concupiscent world. From then on, he abandoned his prie-dieu and became an increasingly active participant.

Now he moves to the boy, slides his hands down his body and buries his face in his groin, savouring the swampy smell.

'All the odours of Eden. Youth. Heat. Sexuality.'

'They were clean on this morning.'

Alfred ignores Ronan's protest as he feels an encouraging pressure against his nose. Ronan is dismayed by his own reflexes.

'I can't help it. It's got nothing to do with how I feel. It used to happen during maths.'

'Oh sinful man born to a lifetime of lust. This is what it is to have lost all self-control.'

Ronan wonders, as Alfred pulls down his pants with his teeth, to which of them he is referring.

'See how futile it is for Adam to resist the lure of the forbidden fruit.'

As the ugly old man starts to devour him, Ronan fights to blot out the picture of pissing into a scummy sink. Then Alfred spits him out as abruptly as he engorged him.

'Is there no limit to mankind's disobedience? Is there no end to the ways in which we defile God's image?'

Ronan wishes that his erection were not so emphatic – like an arrow pointing to the guilty spot.

'I can always split now if you want.'

'No, of course not. We have to admit our evil. We have to stare it in the face, so that we can truly repent.'

Alfred reluctantly tears himself away from the evil at which he is staring. It stands like the half-raised drawbridge to a fortress he longs to possess. He lifts himself from his knees, moves to the altar and reverently turns the cross to the wall.

Ronan shudders as he remembers how his father always turned his wedding photograph to the wall before he walloped him.

Alfred picks up one of the candlesticks and makes a wavering return to Ronan. He examines the workmanlike qualities of his body beneath its shifting light, treasuring the treacherous no man's land of the teenager: the wisps of adolescence under his arms; the whorls of maturity on his groin. He traces a fossil-like scar with his finger.

'What's this? A stab wound?'

'Leave it out. It's from my appendix.'

'Don't lie to me. You've been in a fight – run through by a member of a rival gang.'

'You're fucking my head in!'

'I can absolve you. Don't you understand? I have the power. I shall wipe away all your sins before you leave. Unbutton my soutane.'

'What?'

'My gown.'

Ronan fumbles with the buttons. As he pulls off the sleeves, he recoils from contact with the soggy shirt. He takes hold of the candlestick, while Alfred strips off his pants to reveal a stubby penis, which sprouts in the undergrowth beneath his belly like fungus on a blighted tree.

'What are you waiting for?' Alfred says. 'Take it in your hands ... your mouth.'

Ronan concludes that, sometimes, having to go without a meal is a blessing.

Alfred looks down at the sinuous body coiling around him. 'Christ came down to save you – you personally,' he says. 'And this is how you repay Him.'

'You asked for it,' Ronan says desperately.

'You could have refused.'

Ronan no longer knows what to think. Nothing Harry said has prepared him for such perversity. He needs to assert who he is, not just to Alfred but to himself. 'Do you think I want do this? I'm telling you I'm skint, man. I'm going mad stuck in three rooms with my mum and my sisters.'

'This is no concern of mine.' Alfred feels the interruption like a breach of faith.

'It's my life! I want to make films. Ha ha. Big joke. You can laugh like everyone else. He only got three GSCEs and he thinks he's Quentin Tarrantino. But I did make a film. Last summer. With my mates. The Vicar across from the Estate helped us. He found us the equipment. He let us film in the church. He got the Council to put up money from some "keep the muggers off the streets" scheme. But when we showed them what we shot, they went spare. They were expecting something like "My beautiful Hampstead"; instead, they got it like the truth. But what no one told us was, because they gave us the money, they owned the film. They kept the only copy. Now we can't even show it to our mates. Some of them don't believe we ever made it. They look at me like I'm a complete dork. And I am – I fucking am. That's why I'm here.'

'This is neither the time nor the place.' Alfred has spent the past week listening to confessions. 'I'm not a careers officer. You're no longer an unemployed youth; you're one of Pilate's paid thugs. You see the broken, bruised, bloody body in front of you; so what do you want to do to it?'

'Cover it up?'

'No, you fool: flog it! Don't you know the gospel story?'

'Course I do. But in church. Not like this.'

'No, that's where you're wrong. For most people, the story has lost its edge. But you and I have cut to the very heart of its meaning – to the vileness of men who, when faced with true innocence, let

loose all their sadistic fantasies. They want to punish it ... to torture it. There!'

'What?'

'The cane. Go on, pick it up.'

Ronan fetches the cane, while Alfred crawls over to the altar and
kneels in front of it, spreading his arms.

'Now whip me. Hard. Put some beef into it.'

Ronan approaches Alfred gingerly. He feels about as tough as a
temporary tattoo. He brings the cane down lightly on Alfred's back,
increasing the force in line with his commands.

'Harder! Harder! Beat me for everyone who's ever hurt you ...
beat me for the council who suppressed your film.'

Ronan can no longer restrain himself and lashes out wildly.

'Harder! Harder! Remember the gospel: "And they smote him
on the head with a reed."'

Ronan thwacks Alfred across the crown of his head. Alfred
screams. 'Are you mad?' He looks at him aghast. Ronan drops the
cane.

'You said to hit you on the head.'

'That was Christ, not me.' He rubs his skull and examines his
hand. 'You've drawn blood.'

'Do you need a cloth?' Ronan casts his eye over the room but
can see nothing suitable.

'No. Don't waste time. Having scourged me, you must defile
me: "And they spit upon him".'

'You want me to spit on you?' Ronan asks, with a dry mouth.

'Not on me – in me. You must take me on the altar.'

'But you're a vicar!'

'Exactly. I must sin as a man but I must take on my enemies'
sins like Christ. I'm doing God's work as much in this chapel as in
church.'

'That's mental.'

'Who are you to question the mystery of priesthood?' Ronan
rummages in his trouser pocket. 'What are you looking for?'

'I can't find my condoms.'

'I drink the blood of Christ every day; I need no further protection. So fill me full of your blackness.'

'My spunk is as white as yours.'

'Fill me full of your sin.'

Ronan bolsters his erection with fantasy and moves towards
Alfred. He feels the same revulsion on plunging into his bowels as
when his bare feet sank into the muddy bed of Kenwood Lake.

Alfred yelps as Ronan presses against his body, pinning back his arms in a stranglehold of sex. He senses the bestial passion goring him like the lance that pierced Jesus's side. He gasps as Ronan rams into him with a force which he knows to be independent of them both, beating with the primal rhythm of a sinful earth.

'My pain is my penance,' he splutters, as Ronan gags his mouth with his hand. He longs to bite into the succulent palm but fears to dislodge his dentures. All too soon, he feels Ronan's thrusts quickening and his heart pounding against his shoulder. He tries to break away but is as powerless to resist the boy's frenzy as Pharaoh's army was to escape the surge of the Red Sea.

His bowels burn as he waits for Ronan to worm out of him. But, on shrugging him off his back, he finds, to his surprise, that there has been no such metamorphosis.

'You're still hard.'

'So?'

'You see. You can't escape your sin.'

'I'm seventeen!'

'That's why we must pray to Christ. Without Him, we can never control the beast within. Kneel down and pray with me.'

'Forget it. My Mum'd ... How can I pray like this, all bare-arsed and sweaty?'

'What do you suppose Adam was like when he emerged from the mud?'

'I'm Ronan, not Adam ... Ronan Johnson.'

'The same sin comes with many labels.'

> The Archdeacon thrusts his assistant to his knees and recites a portion of the Fifty-first Psalm.

'Now we must move on,' Alfred says. 'It's time to abandon the foothills and make our way to Calvary.' He switches on a cassette recorder, flooding the room with the St Matthew Passion. 'See.' He points to cords placed as prominently among the props as a gun in a melodrama. 'When I give the signal, you begin to tie.' He clambers onto the cross and eases his feet onto a strategically placed ledge. He stretches out his limbs as avidly as a bridegroom.

'Harder! Can't you pull them harder?'

'I'm doing my best.'

'Ow! That's more like it. Now my feet.'

Alfred's voluntary constriction has sent a rush of energy through the one organ which remains free. He longs for Ronan to finish the preparations and subject him to the humiliations of the crowd.

'There, you won't get out of that in a hurry.' Ronan takes pride in his handiwork. 'What do you want me to do now?' He grasps Alfred's penis in the hope that a few tugs will bring the task to a rapid conclusion.

'No!' Alfred shouts. '"Noli me tangere".'

'What?'

'Wait. Take your cue from me. "I thirst".'

'I could do with a beer myself.'

'You said you knew the gospel. "They filled a sponge with vinegar, and put it upon hyssop, and put it to his mouth."'

'You mean you want to drink vinegar?'

'Show some imagination. Where's the bottle of poppers?'

'You can't drink that!'

'Hold it under my nose.'

'Oh, of course.' He lifts up the bottle, while Alfred takes an exultant sniff.

'Now you can spit on me,' Alfred splutters.

Ronan pines for the not-so-distant days when he thought kissing with an open mouth disgusting. All the years of yearning to be grown-up merge in mockery, as he stands in front of the blubbery old man, rolling a ball of spittle.

'No, with wax,' Alfred says testily. 'Bring over the candlesticks. Both of them.'

Ronan's relief is short-lived as he grabs the candlesticks from the altar, wincing when a drop of wax drips onto his arm. Under Alfred's guidance, he tips each in turn, allowing the wax to fall like lava onto the alert nipples and down the mountainous chest.

'More vinegar!'

He juggles bottle and candlesticks to meet Alfred's demands. He follows instructions and pours the wax on his penis. His own contracts in sympathy, but Alfred's, now sporting an elaborate ruff, remains horribly hard.

Suddenly, Alfred's entire body contorts with such violence that it threatens to pull the cross off the wall. With a shriek of '"It is finished"', his head slumps against his chest. Ronan detects a dribble on the tip of his penis, which merges in colour and consistency with the wax.

'I bet you feel better for that, don't you?' Ronan asks in an attempt at levity. 'Say something then.' He panics at the lack of response and grabs his clothes. He slips into his shell-suit and recovers the identity which has been stolen from his skin. He forces on his shoes and moves back to Alfred, squeezing his clammy flesh in an effort to rouse him.

'Kneel!'

'Oh shit, you frightened me.' And yet any clear-cut emotion is welcome after the evening's perplexities.

'On your knees and beg my forgiveness ... beg Christ's forgiveness.'

'Look you've come now. You said yourself: it's finished.'

'On your knees, I said. Pray that Christ who put His body into the hands of men will now raise them up in His spirit.'

'You're completely round the twist. I don't care if you're a vicar ... I don't care if you're the fucking Archbishop of Canterbury! I'm not staying here.'

He dashes out, knocking over the candlesticks and plunging the cellar into darkness. He bounds up the stairs, ignoring all impediments in his desperation to escape the mad-making calls for forgiveness. He wrenches open the front door and slams it behind him, before sprinting down the road. He prays that he might move fast enough to shake off his body – the one hope of absolution left in a world where he can never again trust a priest.

> The Archdeacon hangs on the cross.

Alfred holds his breath as he strains to follow the sound of footsteps. There is no mistaking the slam of the front door. He waits for his eyes to adjust to the gloom; but there is nothing to see except for the fears which insinuate themselves into his brain. The reminder that 'there was darkness over all the land' brings little comfort now that his own Passion is spent. He tugs at the cords in a vain gesture which he pretends is tactics. He berates Ronan for tying them so tight and himself for submitting to a novice. A cold sweat breaks out on his forehead to mock his former ardour. The chafing heat around his wrists and ankles contrasts with the bitter chill on his chest, where the rivers of wax have formed into sheets of ice.

He feels utterly alone. There are no women standing at the foot of his cross. He screams for his mother, but she is two floors up, asleep and deaf. Never has he felt so conscious of his inability to whistle. He has no way to keep up his spirits, let alone to raise the alarm. He is terrified that he might suffer a stroke. He tries to take deep breaths but he has sniffed too many poppers. He wonders how long it will be before anyone finds him and wishes that he had not imposed such a strict veto on his mother's coming down the stairs. He echoes the words of his Saviour: 'My God, my God, why hast thou forsaken me?'

> The Archdeacon's mother stands at the entrance to the chapel.

Henrietta hovers at the cellar door, blinking in the darkness. The Bishop's instructions were clear, but Alfred's are clearer. He has surrounded his private chapel with as many prohibitions as the ancient Holy of Holies. In twenty years as his housekeeper, she has never once set foot inside. Fearful that her voice alone might constitute a violation, she calls his name softly, only starting to shout when he fails to reply. Risking all, she edges her way down the steps.

A pungent smell, midway between the laundry basket and the compost heap, hits her. She switches on the light. Her vision is blurred, but she is able to make out the mess: the altar-cloth awry; the prie-dieu up-ended; the candlesticks tipped onto the floor. She edges into the room, convinced that it has been ransacked by thieves, when a backward glance brings her face to face with the cross. She cannot move or think or feel anything but panic as she identifies the ivory figure hanging from its beam as her son.

Her fears are relieved by his stertorous breathing (his skin is the colour of purity not death) and her blushes spared by his wispy loin-cloth. She gazes at him with unrestrained adoration. There needs no dove to fly in, voice to thunder nor bush to burn to show that he is marked by God's special favour. The equation so often made in her mind is made concrete, as he takes Christ's place not just at the altar but on the Cross. Her heart brims with love and she is gripped by an overwhelming urge to kiss his feet.

The Archdeacon wakes on the cross.

Alfred wakes, with a head that seems to have been grafted onto his knees. Feeling a gentle tug on his left leg, he looks down to find his mother. He assumes that he must be in Hell, until a glimmer of truth hits him ... and he realizes that his assumption was right. He tries to cover his nakedness, but his hands flail against their bonds. His penis alone has room for manoeuvre and a slab of wax slips off as it swings.

'Mother, what are you doing?' A flash-bulb from the *Sun* would be as welcome. 'Whatever you're thinking, I can explain.'

'Forgive me, Alfred; I don't want to interrupt your prayer.'

He breathes again as he realizes that she is wearing her reading-glasses. God is subjecting him to a trial not to a punishment.

'You must help me down. Harry and his friend had to leave early.'

'I know, dear. I would never have intruded, only there was a phone call from the Bishop. I wasn't at all friendly – just like you said.'

'I feel sick.'

'He asks if you can be at London House for an emergency meeting at ten-thirty.'

'How do you expect me to get there? Fly?'

Henrietta is tempted to suggest that he try. Flying should come as naturally to him as walking to lesser mortals . . . but then even Jesus refused to jump off the Cross when He was taunted by the crowd.

'If I were you, I'd come down and put some clothes on. It's still only April. There's a nip in the air.'

'Mother . . .' He enunciates as though he were pronouncing an anathema. 'Look at me. No, not too close! I need you to give me a hand. No! Watch out!' He vomits down his chest.

'Oh Alfie. Is it something you've eaten? Don't move. I'll fetch a cloth.'

'Later. We can clean everything later. Just help me down.'

'I can't reach, dear.' Her words are confirmed by cracks. 'I'll pop across to the Harrises. I promised to find Donald a bob-a-job.'

'You're insane, totally insane,' Alfred shrieks. He tries to control himself, as flecks of vomit sour every breath. 'This is my private chapel. You can't bring in strangers.'

'But I'm too short.'

'Then stand on something. The prie-dieu. Bring it over.'

'Yes, of course' She tries to pull it. 'I can't . . . it's so heavy.'

'Put your back into it, you stupid, bloody woman!'

Henrietta is stunned. 'How can you speak to me like that? I'm eighty-four.' She starts to weep.

'Mother, I'm sorry. I'm desperate. This is an emergency. Try pushing instead of pulling. Just edge it along with your hip. There's no rush. We've all the time in the world. That's wonderful. Little pushes.' As he listens to each wheeze and snort, he swears that, should he ever escape from this cross, he will have her in sheltered housing by Ascensiontide.

Disobeying every doctor's order, Henrietta pushes the prie-dieu towards the cross. The pain stabs through her vertebrae, but she refuses to complain. She must suffer for Alfred, just as he suffers for Christ.

'Well done. You're almost there. Take a minute's rest.' He has to fight not to count the seconds.

'I'm almost there. Just a little step.'

He turns away from her tentative climb on the seat, frightened that one false move will destroy them both and, in years to come, they will be discovered calcified in the cellar. He shrieks with delight as she makes contact with the cord and with pain as her jointy fingers fail to untie it.

'Don't give up now, mother.'

'It's my arthritis.'

'It's all in your mind.'

'And my hands.'

Finally – after he has exhibited enough patience to earmark him for sainthood – his mother succeeds in loosening the cord to the point where he can pull his left arm free. As he swings it in triumph, he almost knocks her off the seat.

'Sit down, mother. You've done very well. I can manage the rest.' He twists his trunk in order to reach the right-hand knot, releasing a shower of chest-wax. Then, in terror of toppling head-first and clinging precariously to the wood, he bends to untie the knots at his feet.

'Your back, Alfred!' Henrietta screams. 'It's all red.'

'It's just the imprint of the wood. Don't fuss. It'll disappear in the bath.'

Having loosened the cords, he levers himself to the ground and hobbles, skin blistering, feet numb – but free – to his soutane. Recovering his modesty, he asks his mother to look the other way while he dresses.

'Thank you, mother. You've been a great help. I should never have told Harry and his friend to go. I got so caught up in the ritual.'

'You're too good for this world, Alfie.'

'Some might say you were prejudiced.'

'Then they can't know you. I'll go and make breakfast. Then, while you're off with the Bishop, I'll give this room a thorough clean.'

'No, mother!' He hastily pockets Ronan's abandoned underpants. 'I must do it myself. It's part of my penance.'

'But there's such a peculiar smell. I can't place it.'

'Incense . . . *rosa mystica*. Now let me help you up the steps.'

'I can't say I care for it. But are you sure you're all right, dear? You have a strange look in your eyes.'

'It's happiness, mother. Last night, God granted me a vision. He showed me how to save the church. We need a new congregation – one that won't succumb to the sins of the flesh. And I know just where to find it. You'll see. This evening, St Saviour's will be full of saints.'

THE EASTER VIGIL

Saturday 8.oo p.m.
St Mary-in-the-Vale, Hampstead

> The congregation gathers in the churchyard. The
> Bishop, robed in white and gold, attempts to light the
> Easter Fire.

Dressed in a grey suit and raincoat, his clerical collar the only con-
cession to his calling, Huxley stands uneasily among his parishioners like a managing director at a works outing. Nobody meets
his eye, apart from Rosemary Trott who looks ready to spit in it.
She settles for a muttered 'skrimshanker' as she hands him his
service-sheet ... he is relieved not to find a white feather tucked
inside. He turns back to Ted, who is rearranging the kindling as
desperately as a priest of Baal in the battle with Elijah. But his
hopes of a burst of flames – a smoke-screen to cover his confusions
– soon fizzle out. As he watches the fire flare up, only to splutter
and fade in the wind, he sees the symbol of Christ's new life
become a symbol of his own flickering faith.

> The Bishop douses the wood in paraffin, sets a match
> to it, and blesses the fire.

Huxley notes Ted's irritation as he grabs the can like an admission
of defeat and drenches the wood. He ponders the validity of an
Easter Vigil in a church where the Vicar has stood down, the
Curate been suspended and the Head Server withdrawn. He examines the congregation from his new perspective. Several stalwart
figures are missing: Lennox is in hospital; Eleanor and Edith have
defected after yesterday's service; Myrna and Trudy are nowhere to
be seen. Surrounded by visitors to the christening (along with the
remnant of Thursday's reporters), he feels like a host who makes
up in gate-crashers for what he lacks in friends.

He stares at the fire and is strangely warmed. He fears that concentration on the ritual elements of bread and wine has blinded
him to the significance of the natural elements of earth, air, fire
and water: the mysteries at the heart of creation. Now he has the
opportunity to redress the balance. Shakespeare found sermons in

stones; he will find prayers in parks, meditations in meadows and hymns on the heath. And yet, in spite of his resolution, there remains something in the liturgy to which he is drawn: a unique truth in the coming together of priest and people which he can recognize more clearly from outside.

Hope breaks through the gloom as boldly as a Christmas rose. He smiles as he greets the Bishop's wife.

> The Bishop carves a cross into the Paschal Candle, marking it with the letters alpha and omega and the numerals of the year.

Alice, Dee and Joe stand in a group of friends to the right of the fire.

'All this business with candles is disgustingly phallic,' Patricia says.

'Wait till you see him plunge it into the font,' Dee says. 'It's enough to give you cramps.'

'Who's that woman covered in dead animals?' Julia asks. 'Didn't Jesus say something about anyone who offended these little ones might as well jump into the sea?'

'I think you'll find that he was referring to children, not foxes,' Alice replies, flinching at the thought of her mother's moth-balled mink.

'What's the difference? Neither can speak for themselves.'

'Animals can't speak at all,' says Damian, who has little patience with the lesbian conscience.

'She's the other child's grandmother,' Dee says.

'Don't I recognize the woman she's talking to?' Patricia asks.

'Lady Stafford,' Alice says, eager to move onto less contentious ground. 'You probably saw her on TV last year, flashing her eternity ring alongside her errant husband, earning the undying gratitude of adulterous politicians and editors everywhere.'

'He's the other baby's godfather,' Joe adds.

'I'd as soon ask Jack the Ripper,' Julia replies.

> The church is in darkness as the people enter. The Bishop places the Paschal Candle in the sanctuary, where the Thurifer censes it. The people move to their pews and stand with lighted candles, as a chorister sings the *Exultet*.

Settling into the pew generally occupied by Lady Blaikie, Alice feels a pang of guilt, as though she had sneaked into the private apartments of a stately home. Dee and Joe sit to her left, offering godparental support which she trusts will allay any lingering suspicions about their delayed honeymoon.

She peeps at the baby asleep in her arms, her personality as yet more intensely expressed when dreaming than awake, her miniature hands brushing her face as if to shield it from nightmares. She breathes in the lemony, lineny smell of her clothes and the buttery-sweet smell of her skin and longs to be able to hold her this close forever: not so as to keep her dependent but to keep her safe. Her one overriding fear is that her sexuality will rebound on Dora. Children can be so cruel. Henry and Tree terrified her with their tale of Ralph's being taunted at school because Grove Lane lacked carpets. Priceless Persian rugs counted for nothing when all that his friends could see were bare boards. Dora's singular parenthood will offer an even greater challenge to their two-times-table minds.

It would help if she could call on sympathetic relatives: hordes of aunts and uncles like the sagging boughs of a Victorian family tree. But there is only her sister, standing in the row behind, smiling nobly at Julia's jokes about shotgun weddings ... Dee's brothers live at once eleven thousand miles away and somewhere unmentionable in the past. So it is all the more important that Dora should take her place in the family of the church. And yet that place is threatened. All her hopes of fostering a friendship between Dora and Lloyd, which would replace the 'milk brother' of historical novels and the 'blood brother' of adventure stories with the 'water brother' of a shared baptism, have been shattered by Huxley's revelation that, having sneaked into the Service of Blessing, Hugh has tried to block Dora's christening.

The exultant voice of the chorister belies her apprehension. This is far from the joyous occasion she had imagined. She feels angry with Huxley for putting doubt before duty and with herself for having contributed to that doubt. A relationship of great value has been soured by distrust. Moreover, since Huxley has ceded his place to the Bishop, Dora is to be welcomed into the church by a man who would exclude her mother. But then he has yet to discover the truth in his own double bed.

Her thoughts are distracted by a disturbance in the opposite pew, where Lloyd's maternal grandfather is trying with ever worse grace to keep his candle lit (the flashes of flame mirror her own desperate SOS). Suddenly, Petula Snape, usually the most unassuming of people, adds an inadvertent descant to the *Exultet* and strides from church.

> The people extinguish their candles as the *Exultet* ends.
> The Bishop reads an Old Testament lesson.

Esther listens to the lesson with an unspecific anticipation, as if
she were watching the trailer of a film. She feels distinctly nervous
about returning with Ted to the church where she was so happy on
Tuesday. It is as though the two sides of her life can no longer be
kept apart. She takes comfort from the presence of Huxley, like a
great St Bernard in the pew alongside her. As he smiles encoura-
gingly, she wonders how much he knows of her previous visit. If
he has been told, his silence is the silence of the perfect gentleman.
But then it is easy to give other women's husbands the benefit of
the doubt.

A strange sense of *déja vu* shifts her attention from the clandestine visit which she made on Tuesday to the imaginary one which
she made last night. She had a most disconcerting dream. Ted was
preaching in an unnamed church ... although the distinctive decoration no longer leaves room for doubt. The worshippers looked
rapt; but, on second glance, she realized that they were engrossed in
the Sunday papers. They read them quite openly as though they
were as integral to the service as the prayer-book. The next moment,
Christ stepped down from the Cross – contriving to appear at once
as an eighteen-inch carving and a six-foot man – and held up the
front-page headline, prompting an outburst of Alleluias and Amens.

To her intense frustration, the wording, which last night was
quite distinct, is now blurred. She is seized by an overwhelming
belief that, if she could only remember it, she would find the key to
the rest of her life.

> The Acolyte leads the congregation in procession to the
> font, where the Bishop blesses the baptismal water.

Joe stands beside Alice while Dee holds Dora. He relishes the prospect of his new role. Godfather: it is not just the prefix which fills
him with confidence. For Alice and Dee to have chosen him
amounts to an act of faith, not only in his character and memory
but in his longevity. After all, should anything happen to them, he
would be left to bring up Dora. He has never been responsible for
anyone before ... he has never known such a powerful motive to
keep well.

At moments like these he is convinced that he is beating the
virus. The tingle in his blood is a sign that the new plasma treatment is taking effect. Others may trust to drugs but, as soon as he
read of this experimental therapy, he felt in his bones – no, in his
cells – that it would be the answer. He kept faith during the pro-
tracted search for a donor (an AB Negative blood-group was no
longer such an enviable distinction). Then, last autumn, a match

was found. He has no idea who it is and no wish to know. Speculation lends intimacy even to the largest crowd. It is enough to be aware that somewhere in London there is a man, or a woman, whose gift of blood may save his life. It is not just because he is in church that he thinks of Christ.

To his alarm, Dee hands him Dora. He must learn to be more self-confident, or, rather, less self-critical; which is not the same. He gazes at Dora Rose Marjorie Leighton nestling in the crook of his arm, oblivious of the ceremony taking place around her. Should she ever object to her names (a complaint with which any Joe Soap must sympathize), she need only consider the ones that she has been spared. Having dispatched the alternatives with murderous abandon, Dee proposed Bernarda – after the turkey-farmer. Alice was outraged, until a rich Antipodean cackle apprised her of the joke. And yet he cherishes the hope that Dora's conception, far removed from any sweaty fervour, will define her character. While others seek to recreate the heat of the embryonic moment, she will remain free from all taint of primal lust.

It may seem a pipe dream but he is convinced that if, in time, more women choose to conceive in this way, it will effect an evolutionary change in human behaviour. Masculine aggression will disappear and there will be no further threat from sexually transmitted viruses. Peoples' sex lives will become as placid as those of battery hens.

> The Bishop asks the parents and god-parents to come forward.

'Are you the child's father?'

Dee's thumb pressing in his kidneys alerts Joe to the Bishop's question.

'I'm her godfather.'

'Then where's her father?'

'He can't be here today,' Alice says. He's disappeared.'

'Disappeared?'

Alice feels as vulnerable as a schoolgirl in an Irish village.

'I can vouch that they've prepared themselves fully for baptism,' Huxley interjects.

'Very well,' Ted says in a tone which suggests quite the opposite. 'Shall we proceed?'

> The Bishop addresses the godparents of the children to be baptized. *Dost thou, in the name of these children, renounce the devil and all his works, the vain pomp and*

glory of the world, with all covetous desires of the same, and
the carnal desires of the flesh, so that thou wilt not follow
nor be led by them?
The godparents reply: *I renounce them all.*

'No,' Jeffrey shouts, to the general amazement. 'You can't baptize that child.'

'Jeffrey, what's the matter?' his wife asks.

'She is.' Jeffrey points at Alice. 'You ask where the father is, Bishop. I'll tell you. In some recycled yoghurt-pot or jamjar.'

'What is it?' Thea puts her hand to his forehead. He brushes it aside.

'I don't want to spell it out. There are certain words that shouldn't be spoken in church.'

'Like what?' Alice asks. 'Love, truth, tolerance?'

'Like deviance, like perversion,' Jeffrey replies. 'I won't have my grandson dipped in the same water as her child.'

Lloyd's howl expresses Alice's horror.

'We're here to welcome this child into the Christian family. What sort of family is that?' Jeffrey points to Alice and Dora.

'My sort,' Alice says. 'The sort which doesn't spring straight from a Persil ad.'

'Would you all please return to your seats,' Ted asks. No one responds.

'You must do something,' Esther says to Huxley. 'They're your parishioners.'

'They lied to me,' Huxley says. 'They made a mockery of their vows.'

'Look at her,' Jeffrey says. 'Look at her friends. Look at her pictures.' He indicates the Stations of the Cross. 'Look at her Christ.'

'Yes, my Christ. Mine as much as yours.'

'He isn't even human.' Jeffrey grabs hold of the Twelfth Station. 'Just an empty colostomy bag full of blood.' He pulls the picture off the wall and staggers under its unexpected weight.

'Put that back!' Alice shouts.

'Order!' David Stafford shouts.

'You should respect the house of God,' Huxley says to Jeffrey.

'That's rich, coming from a man who, only yesterday, preached a sermon denying His very existence.'

'If you think that, then you seriously misunderstood.'

'Will somebody please explain to me what's been going on in this church?' Ted asks.

Judith begins to sob.

'I was expressing doubts ... uncertainties concerning the Resurrection.'

'On Good Friday?' Ted asks.

'Precisely,' Huxley replies. 'I see now that they were honest doubts. Faith can never be a *fait accompli*. Anyone who follows Christ will have doubts. After all, He did. To live in total certainty seems to me to be the definition of madness – like the men who think they're Napoleon.'

Ted draws himself up to his full height. 'Have you any idea where you are?' he asks.

'Yes, in a church where we read the Scriptures critically, rather than quoting them like the thoughts of Chairman Mao.'

'Now we see who's responsible for the rot at the heart of this church,' Jeffrey shouts.

Petula pushes her way to the front. 'Would you all please listen to me for a moment. Please!'

'Petula,' Hugh pleads.

'Yes, that's my name. Pet ... Petal. Not any more.'

Alice listens in mounting horror as Petula reveals the details of Jeffrey and Hugh's plot to swindle St Mary's. She is roused to such fury by Hugh's attempts to exculpate himself that she interrupts, addressing her challenge to his accomplice.

'You dare to tell me that I have no place in the church! You're the one who wants to defraud it.'

'You defile it,' Jeffrey says.

'I try to live a Christian life.' She ignores his hollow laugh. 'With love and creativity.'

'Creativity: this?' He lifts up the Twelfth Station.

'Yes.'

He drops it. The glass shatters. Alice shrieks.

'You bastard!'

'It's blasphemy, not art.' He hurls himself at the wall and wrenches off another picture, throwing it onto the floor. He makes a lunge for a third but is held back by three of his friends. Alice keens over her damaged pictures, her room for revenge restricted by Dora. As blood from the Crucifixion trickles onto the tiles, Dee tries to prevent anyone touching it. 'No, please, leave it to us!'

Both babies are bawling, resistant to their mother's reassurance. Two children are crying. Judith and Rosemary are arguing over who should fetch a cloth. Ted sinks to his knees.

'This is the Devil's work. I feel his presence among us. His breath is burning the back of my neck. I ask you to pray with me

... all you who hope for salvation – that we may cast the spirit of Satan from this church.'

Esther turns to Huxley.

'You must take over.'

'I can't.'

'Then at least ask your organist to play something ... a hymn to bring us together. *Jesus Christ is risen today!*'

'Is He? I don't believe that I'll ever know the risen Christ again.'

'A moment ago you said doubt was an essential element of faith.'

'But not when that doubt is itself the subject of doubt ... when every thought is liable to endless qualification.'

He bends to pick up the broken glass. Sylvia Stafford moves to Thea.

'My dear, I'm so sorry for you. Come and sit down.'

'I'm perfectly fine, thank you.' Thea pushes her away. 'I'm sure that all Jeffrey's friends know him well enough not to be swayed by the ravings of a hysterical nurse.'

David Stafford approaches Ted. 'You must say a prayer.'

Ted responds by mouthing a verse of the psalm. '"My God, my God, why have you forsaken me? Why are you so far from saving me, so far from the words of my groaning?"'

David attempts to lift him to his feet, only to be thwarted by the dead weight. Exasperated, he moves away. His practised eye is drawn to two reporters scribbling on the backs of their Orders of Service. 'Come on guys,' he appeals to them. 'You can see this is a family affair – women and babies. Happy Easter, eh?' The reporters match him smile for smile and continue to write.

Alice assesses the damage to her pictures. Two frames are smashed but the only major casualty appears to be Christ on the Cross. The blood lies splattered on the floor.

'I shall sue you for this,' she says to Jeffrey.

'Oh yes, you and whose lawyers?' he asks smoothly.

Dee who has succeeded in pacifying Dora now tries to do the same for her mother.

Rosemary, having won the battle of the bucket, returns with a cloth. 'We'll have this cleared up in no time.'

'Don't!' Alice thrusts out her hand to stop her. 'Not without gloves.'

'What?'

'The blood. It may be contaminated.'

'I'm lost,' Rosemary says.

'Oh but I'm not,' Hugh says, seeing the chance to regain ground.

'It's AIDS, isn't it? You've brought AIDS blood into the church.' The bystanders draw back as from a brawl. Joyce Bentinck cups her hand over Tristram's mouth.

'What powers of deduction!' Alice says contemptuously.

'It's a health hazard,' Hugh replies.

'Not until your partner-in-crime broke it.'

'But why,' asks Thea, a longstanding Friend of the Tate, 'when no one but you could know?'

'There are some truths which exist of themselves.'

'And where else should that blood be but at the heart of the Church?' Huxley asks.

'Yes, you have to say that,' Hugh says, 'with your curate a prime offender.'

'It's my blood,' Joe says. Judith looks at him as though he had dropped his trousers.

'Not you too, Joe?' Huxley whispers.

'But I was at your wedding,' Sophie Record says. 'I gave you a fish-slice.'

'I thought you looked familiar,' Ted says. 'You came to my Service of Healing.'

'And left because I hope to be healed.'

'You're sick,' Jeffrey says.

'No, you're sick,' Joe rounds on him. 'I'm just infected with a virus.' He trembles at his daring. 'Sorry, folks, that's the end of the public announcement. Still, at least it means I've no need to worry about gloves. Thank you Rosemary.' He takes the cloth from her unresisting hands and proceeds to mop up the mess.

He attacks the blood with a passion which barely conceals his pain. He feels Damian's hand on his shoulder but shrugs it off before it reduces him to tears.

Ted rouses himself and moves to Alice. 'I refuse to baptize your child now or ever in the future.'

'But why?'

'Why do you think? First you make a mockery of the marriage vows; next, you turn the church into a cradle of disease; and, finally, you lie to my face. You...' he points to Dee. 'And you...' he points to Joe. 'Are this wretched child's godparents. You swore to renounce the Devil and carnal desires, but the plain truth is you revel in them.'

'That's not true,' Joe says.

'We love each other,' Dee says.

'No, you love only yourselves ... your own lusts. Love is a gift of God.'

'Please Ted ... Bishop.' Esther wavers between intimacy and deference like a child on the cusp between Daddy and Father. 'Think of the baby.'

'Don't interfere, Esther.'

'Did Christ ask for marriage certificates before he fed the five thousand?'

Esther's surprise at her audacity is echoed by Ted. 'What's the matter? Are you ill? You're on dangerous ground.'

'I thought that I was on holy ground.' She breaks away. 'For my sake, won't you reconsider?' Ted snorts. 'Last night, I had a dream.'

'Who do you think you are? Pilate's wife?'

'You were preaching, but no one was listening. They were all reading newspapers.'

'My wife is ill.' He calls to his chaplain. 'Brian, would you help Mrs Bishop to the car.'

Esther brushes away the offered hand.

'Then Jesus appeared and pointed to the headline ... only it wasn't a news story but a gospel text. I remember it now.' Her face lights up. 'Every word. "At the resurrection people will neither marry nor be given in marriage; they will be like the angels in heaven." Then I knew that, at least in death, we'd be free. And, when I turned back to the choir, you were standing in the corner, like a schoolboy in a dunce's cap.'

'Why is she telling me her dreams?' Ted asks, baffled. 'She's never told me a dream in her life. Esther, let Brian take you home.'

'"People will neither marry nor be given in marriage." Salvation does lie in the Bible, after all.'

'Very well,' Ted says, choking back his fury. 'There will be no lesbian "marriages" on earth. And certainly not in the diocese of London.'

'I'm a lesbian.'

'Don't be ridiculous.'

'I'm a lesbian.'

'You're fifty-three years old. It must be the change of life.'

'Oh I do hope so.'

'Is this some bizarre notion of female solidarity?' He tries to shift attention onto Huxley. 'She gets it from your wife.'

'She barely knows my wife.'

'Thank you, Ted,' Esther says. 'I didn't know how I'd tell you. But, as always, you've taken the lead.'

'We're leaving right now,' Ted says. 'This is a shambles.'

'But the christening...' Thea pleads.

'I wash my hands of it. Next week, I'll decide how best to deal with this church. For the moment, my first duty is to my wife.' He approaches Esther.

'I'm staying here,' Esther says, searching for a serviceable pillar.

'I'm not going to force you,' Ted says, in a tone which belies his words.

'I know you're not,' Esther says.

'How can you do this to me?' He changes tack. 'A few hours before Easter.'

'That may be how I can.'

'"Now as the Church submits to Christ, so also wives should submit to their husbands in everything." *Ephesians* Chapter 5, Verse 24.'

Esther takes heart from the audible hiss. 'The thoughts of Chairman Mao ... if only I'd heard that years ago.'

'I shall pray for you, Esther.'

'And I for you, Ted.'

The Bishop and his Chaplain leave the church.

'If we're ever invited to another christening and I say I'd rather go clubbing, remind me of this,' Patricia whispers to Julia.

Rosemary moves to Esther who is slumped in a pew. 'Chin up, old girl,' she urges.

'I'm fine ... just a little wobbly,' Esther replies. Her heart appears to be giving her chest the punch that her husband withheld. 'I'm afraid I'm going to be sick.'

'Half a tick! I'll fetch a bucket.' Rosemary casts a horrified glance at Joe's and dashes into the sacristy.

'You ought to run after Ted,' Sylvia tells David. 'He looked crushed.'

'If you say so.'

'No, you mustn't leave yet,' Thea says.

'Ted – the Bishop – may need us.' Sylvia remonstrates lightly. 'Goodbye Thea dear.' She kisses her as though on a doorstep. 'I'm so terribly sorry.' As she walks out, she snaps at Esther. 'I could teach you a few things about loyalty.'

'Not now!' David squirms.

Joe finishes wiping the floor. He wrings out the cloth in the scummy, sudsy water and watches the viscous liquid swirl around the bucket.

Thea hears a murmur of discontent, which she desperately tries to quash. 'What about the christening?' she asks. 'I have sixty vol-au-vents – that is guests – expected in Stockwell.'

'What christening?' Jeffrey asks. 'There's no one left to take it.'

'Says who?' Huxley asks.

'You've been suspended,' Jeffrey replies.

'That's the first I've heard of it,' Huxley says. 'I'm not the one accused of fraud. I simply asked the Bishop to relieve me of my Easter duties. But all that's changed. If others can assert themselves, so can I. Just give me a moment to robe.'

'Wait one second,' Jeffrey says. 'Do you still intend to baptize this woman's child?'

'I most certainly do.'

'Then you won't be baptizing my grandson.'

'Isn't that up to Russell and Laura?' Petula asks.

'Haven't you done enough harm?' Hugh interjects.

'I can't let Lloyd be christened here now, Mum. Every time I heard his name, I'd think of all this.'

'I always knew we should hold the ceremony in the country,' Thea says. 'We have the best vicar. He used to keep wicket for Kent.' She breaks off as she finds herself addressing the Virgin.

'It's your decision,' Huxley says, making his way to the sacristy.

'We're going, Thea,' Jeffrey says, reeling from the rebuff. 'Pronto.'

'Yes, of course,' Thea says, putting on the bravest face ... and most natural smile, for the sake of her friends. 'Come on everyone. The wild-christening chase is over. Would the Finch-Buller party please make their way to their cars.'

Even Petula has to admire the way that Thea strolls to the door as though the whole débâcle was deliberate. Watching her friends brace themselves to follow her, she wonders how many of them will make it to Stockwell for the wake and how many manage to lose their way. She reaches out a hand to Russell, but he spurns it more cruelly than at any time since her trouncing in the mother's race at his primary school. She is gripped by a violent fear that she will never see Lloyd again.

'Hugh, where are you going?' She watches her husband following her son.

'To the party. Where else?'

'But you can't.'

'Someone has to try to repair the damage. Any case, there's nothing to keep me here.' He turns to Judith. 'Believe me, I gave you a fair survey.'

'Oh Hugh,' Petula says.

'You know nothing!' He turns back to Judith. 'Call in someone else if you like. Throw your money away. He'll tell you exactly the same. Are you coming?' he asks Petula.

Petula replies in the spirit of the question. 'No, Hugh.' As she watches him walk out of church, she tries to blink the sting from her eyes. 'I really couldn't bear to go back home after this, Mum. May I stay the night with you?'

Myrna adjusts to feeling needed.

'You made me buy the couch for all the visitors who'd be coming down. You'll be the first.'

'Then I'll christen it,' Petula says, biting her tongue.

> The Organist plays selections from *The Merry Widow* in the style of César Franck.

Terry, whose disappointment at missing the regular Saturday night HALOS rehearsal, has been offset by the drama in the nave, pulls out all the stops.

> The Churchwarden announces that the Vicar is on his way.

Alice leaves her pictures propped against the wall and rejoins the congregation at the font. She is relieved to find Joe in the thick of it, surrounded not just by friends but by several of the parish ladies. She is saddened to see Esther alone, holding the empty bucket like an accusation. She approaches her.

'I hope you won't mind my asking, but where are you going after the service? To your friend?'

'It's not quite that simple. She has a family. A husband like ... not like me.'

'You're very welcome to stay with Dee and me. We have two spare rooms.'

'But you barely know me.'

'I know what you said. That's enough.'

> The Vicar, wearing his gold chasuble, leaves the sacristy and moves to the font.

'My friends, I crave your indulgence one last time before I baptize Dora. After everything that's happened tonight, I feel that we need to remind ourselves of who we are and why we're here. So I'd like us to renew our baptismal vows once again.'

> *Do you turn to Christ?*
> *I turn to Christ.*
> *Do you repent of your sins?*
> *I repent of my sins.*
> *Do you renounce evil?*
> *I renounce evil.*

Alice is delighted to find that, despite the halving of the congregation, the responses ring louder than before. She notices that several of her friends who previously kept silent now speak up. She feels a double lightness as she places Dora in the hands of Huxley and the Church.

> *Dora, Rose, Marjorie Leighton: I baptize you in the name of the Father, and of the Son, and of the Holy Spirit.*

As he lifts her up, Huxley sees Dora smile at him ... as though in greeting from one newborn to another. Then he cups his hand in the font and wets her forehead, and the smile is usurped by an affronted howl.

The Easter Vigil

Saturday 9.00 p.m.
St Saviour's, Belsize Park

> The Archdeacon stands in the churchyard, beside a brazier in which the Easter Fire is carefully contained. He addresses the people: *Let us each throw a piece of rubbish: a symbol of our sin, our resentment and our pain, onto the fire.*

Jessica is surprised to see Alfred tossing a pair of pants onto the fire, not least because they are patently too small to be his. She discounts the thought – even though twenty years of buying her sons' underwear clamour to confirm it. It must be some arcane Anglo-Catholic ritual: a piece of cloth retained from an earlier service ... the Easter Vigil equivalent of the Ash Wednesday burnt palms.

Keeping a discreet distance from Eleanor Blaikie and Edith Sadler, who have defected from St Mary's, she scans the churchyard for Lyndon. His absence is instantly apparent in a congregation whose age and gender conform to the broadest stereotype. The only exceptions are an etiolated server, with a face like a new moon, and a ginger-haired man, wearing a black leather-jacket and jeans more perfectly pressed than trousers. She watches as the latter follows the old ladies to the fire, on which, in place of their carefully selected and scrupulously clean handfuls of rubbish, he flings a ten – or maybe a twenty – pound note. The chorus of tutting which greets this Greed-is-Good ostentation dwindles beside her own disgust. But, when the flames catch his face, the racked expression in his eyes suggests that the money may be a genuine symbol of sin.

She makes her way to the fire. While rejecting the Archdeacon's emphasis on sin, she yearns to rid herself of resentment and pain. She rummages through her handbag in search of something symbolic to discard and discovers Thursday's Order of Service from St Paul's. She rolls it into a ball and feeds it to the flames, relishing every sizzle and crack.

> *Let us give thanks to Almighty God as our sins and suffering are consumed in the glorious fire of His unquenchable love.*

Eleanor glowers at the young man who has mistaken the brazier for the collection plate. The sight of his red hair, accentuated by the flames, revives all her suspicions of Celts. She stands back from the fire, waiting for the others to take their turn, since she is loath to have her (venial) sins confused with theirs. A blue rinse and a Hampstead address are no guarantees of virtue. She gives a particularly wide berth to Edith, whose delicately brooched breast conceals a heart full of Gluttony, Envy, Sloth and, no doubt, even Lust. The thought is too repulsive to contemplate ... In her case, a mere symbolic burning may not be enough.

When the coughing and spluttering brought on by the smoke brook no further delay, she demands her neatly bound bundle of twigs from Edith and casts it into the fire, only to find that a gust of wind causes it to fall short. She is left with an uneasy sense of rejection, which is exacerbated when Edith offers to pick it up so that she can try again.

'Certainly not,' she snaps. 'Who do you take me for? Genghis Khan?'

> The Archdeacon carves a cross into the Paschal Candle, marking it with the letters alpha and omega and the numerals of the year.

Eleanor, more exercised by protocol than prayer, acknowledges Jessica with the same curt nod that she gives to the former wife of her second cousin.

Jessica, interpreting the nod as a summons, reluctantly moves over to her. 'I'm surprised to see you here, Lady Blaikie.'

'I can't see why after the way your husband treated me. I trust he hasn't insulted you too.'

'Good Lord, no!' She tries to blame her shiver on the breeze. 'Good evening, Edith.' She is taken aback when Edith, with new-found impunity, contrives to make her greeting even more brusque than her employer's. 'I came to find Lyndon Brooks – our head server.'

'I've seen him here somewhere,' Eleanor says. 'Lurking in the shadows. He always was a lurker.'

'Is he another refugee from St Mary's?' Edith asks eagerly.

'He's been forbidden to come by his parents.'

'There'll be no congregation left,' says the old lady standing beside Eleanor, who contemplates Jessica from behind a net of tulle.

'Well, I'm sure you're grateful for everyone you can lure here.' Jessica is stung into a display of loyalty.

'Do you know our vicar's wife ... that is the wife of the vicar of St Mary-in-the-Vale?' Eleanor asks her friend, whose shrug conveys not only ignorance but indifference. 'Sybil Lincoln ... Jessica Grieve. Sybil is a stalwart of St Saviour's.'

'It was I who suggested that Eleanor and Edith —'

'And Stevenson,' Eleanor interjects.

'Yes, of course. That they came here this evening. When I visited Vale Lodge yesterday afternoon, I found Eleanor in a dreadful state. Such behaviour from a priest.'

'Please excuse me,' Jessica says, spotting Lyndon. 'That priest is my husband. Still, don't let that stop you tearing him apart.'

She walks towards a clump of trees.

'She's as bad as the Vicar,' Edith says.

'Worse,' Eleanor says. 'She once sent back some tins I donated to Famine Relief on the grounds that they were out of date. I ask you, are people who wash in the Ganges the sort to quibble about over-ripe corned beef?'

'You'll be far happier here, Eleanor,' Sybil says. 'Father Alfred is the model of respect. He likes his ladies to wear a veil. And there's no nonsense about the kiss of peace.'

'Very wise,' says Eleanor, who has never forgiven Hugh Snape for taking the injunction literally one Christmas.

'There's only one problem: I'm not sure he will approve of Stevenson.'

'But he's as quiet as a mouse.'

'He wouldn't allow Hermione Tattersly to bring in her guide-dog. And he'd been trained.'

'Then he'll have to stay outside with Edith.'

'No, I can't, Eleanor. Not the whole service. I'll catch my death.'

'There's a fire.'

'It isn't Christian.'

'And should it start to rain,' Sybil coos a compromise, 'you can shelter in the porch.'

> The Archdeacon inserts five grains of incense into the candle.

Jessica moves to Lyndon, who stands, clutching a ball of rubbish, as far away from the group as possible.

'What are you doing here?' he asks with agonized brusqueness.

'I've come to find you.'

'Can't they survive without me? Are Willy and Sandy forgetting when to hand Father the cruets?'

'Don't worry. Everyone's rising to the occasion.'

'Oh, I see.' He sounds disappointed. 'Is he ... is Father Blair back?'

'I'm afraid that Blair has disappeared.'

'It's all my fault.' His voice cracks.

'That's nonsense.'

'I suppose you think it was just an accident, like a drunk driver running over a child.'

'You haven't killed anyone.'

'How do you know? You said Blair's disappeared. He may have committed suicide.'

'He hasn't. That's one thing I can say for sure. And, besides, you can put it all to rights.'

'Really? Is it that easy? Just say you're sorry; throw your sins on the fire and come back next year.' He flings the rubbish into the bushes.

'The Bishop has ordered an investigation. Your mother is claiming that Blair behaved indecently towards you.'

'He lied to me.'

'She means sexually.'

'I never accused him of anything, I swear. When they asked me all their questions, I couldn't even speak.'

'Well now you can. There'll be no permanent damage, so long as you tell the truth.'

'Did you know that one in five gay teenagers commits suicide?'

'Tries to ... they don't succeed.' She is wary of the turn in the conversation.

'One of the girls in my form read it out from her magazine. And Jason Heald laughed and shouted "One down, four to go". And they all banged their desks and pointed at me.'

'I work for the Citizens' Advice Bureau. I can find out about groups ... people who'll help.'

'Second Class Citizen: that's what I am. Unless I can change. If it isn't really me but what Blair did to me. Then my mum and dad will love me.'

'They're your parents. They'll love you, come what may.'

'It's easy to see you live in a vicarage.' He starts to whimper. She puts her arms around him, negotiating the bony cavities of his shoulders. 'Blair's the most decent man I've ever met in my entire life. And I betrayed him: I told them that he had AIDS. Now they're saying that he tried to give it to the Queen.'

'Then you must write to the Bishop and put them right.'

'He has AIDS! It's a letter I'd be writing, not a cure ... You know, it was because of Blair I started going to St Mary's. I met him when he was curate here. Then, when he fell out with Father Alfred, I followed him up the road.'

'And we're very glad you did.' She gulps.

'Now I'm back. My dad says it's St Saviour's or nothing. Look around. It's so dismal. Muck everywhere. Even the sign has been been defaced: *Please Respect These Clowns. Do Not Throw Glitter*. A churchyard with nothing but some half-dead bushes and a couple of gnarled trees.'

'Judas-trees.'

'What?'

'That's what they're called. Legend has it that it was from a tree like this that Judas hanged himself.'

Lyndon staggers back as though the corpse were still stuck in the branches.

'They should call in the tree-surgeons to cut them down! They should get rid of every last one like the snakes in Ireland!'

'Then we'd all lose out. In a few weeks' time, they'll be covered in the most exquisite lilac flowers.'

'I don't care.' He pounds his fist against the trunk.

'Watch out, you'll hurt yourself. Look, you've grazed the skin.' She fumbles in her handbag. 'I don't even have a tissue.'

'Please don't fuss. Why do people always think that just because something bleeds, it hurts?'

'The tree isn't evil. No tree is evil. It's part of nature ... as was the man who gave it his name.'

'It's all right for you. You've never betrayed anyone.'

'And you're too old to reduce the world to black and white. Besides, if there were no Judas, there'd be no Christ. There'd have been a Jesus; but that's only a tiny part of the story. It's too easy – and dangerous – to demonize Judas: to condemn a part of human nature, giving it no chance to change. We can all change, even if we've done something which, for want of a better word, we call evil.'

'Judas couldn't.'

'Oh no? You know the gospel story: how when he realized what he'd done, he was filled with remorse. So he threw away the money and hanged himself.'

'And you think that redeemed him?'

'Yes. Yes, I do. I know that we're taught to see it as an act of despair – the greatest of sins. But, to my mind, it's quite the opposite: an act of faith in which he throws himself on the mercy of God.'

'You mean if he'd really despaired, he'd have tried to keep alive as long as possible to postpone God's judgement?'

'Possibly. But that's Judas; we're talking about you.'

Lyndon smiles, as though refusing to admit the distinction.

'Thank you,' he says. 'I think we should make a move. Everyone's going into the church.'

'So you'll talk to your parents and write to the Bishop?'

'A letter, yes: I'll set everything to rights.'

> The Archdeacon holds up the candle and leads the people into church. He pauses in the porch for the proclamation *Christ our light* and the response *Thanks be to God.*

Walking down the path, Harry Wainwright feels the same sense of security as he does in the company of an elderly aunt. He is scrupulous about observing festivals ... a practice which began in adolescence, along with daily masturbation and smoking. Perverse as it may seem, it is the Church's very archaism which attracts him, particularly at St Saviour's where the rituals, rather than the Commandments, are set in stone. He is cheered by the sight of the ancient – yet ageless – congregation: the ladies who look just as they did on his first visit fifteen years ago and, no doubt, fifteen years before that. He deplores the priests who strain to follow fashion. It is essential for his peace of mind that the liturgy be left in the past.

He is not unaware of the irony that the church which now restores his innocence is the very place where he lost it; but it remains an irony, nothing more. One part of him is still locked in the sacristy, where Father Alfred confirmed him into a very different mystery from the one which he had celebrated only moments before. And yet, unlike the media moralists, he sees no contradiction. Anyone living with a spirituality as intense as Father Alfred's needs a release. And it soon became clear that providing it was where his own talent – in this setting, he hesitates to think of it as a vocation – lay. He and the Archdeacon are two of a kind. They each cater to people's deepest needs: one focusing on the sacred; the other on the profane. Their worlds are intimately connected. Only someone with a mind like a pair of scales could disagree.

> Within the church, the Archdeacon again proclaims *Christ our light.* The people reply *Thanks be to God.*

Edith contemplates the exclusion which has become her permanent fate. It is as if she is having to make up for the primness of her schooldays by an extended stay in the corridor. And yet, in spite of being paired with a parrot in the fellowship of the enchained, she remains determined to take part in the service and responds to the muffled proclamation with a defiant 'Thanks be to God'.

'Be quiet!' Stevenson orders in a voice so like his mistress's that, for a moment, she fears she will faint. He flaps his wings as if applauding the joke, leaving her to curse the injustice of a world in which a human being counts for less than a bird. 'Fetch and carry; fetch and carry,' he squawks, mocking her servility in tones which have now come to echo her own. She suspects him of the worst malevolence, purposely supplying Eleanor with the means of her humiliation. And yet she hesitates even to think ill of him in his presence, since he is less like a pet than a witch's familiar, with the power not just to repeat words but to read minds.

> The Cantor sings the *Exultet*.

Eleanor recoils from a pillar which is as infused with scents as a spice-rack. 'Is there no choir?' she asks Sybil.

'Only Monica Charteris. In her day, she was known as the King's Lynn Nightingale. Whenever a boat went missing, she would stand on the shore and sing.'

'Did her voice carry that far?' Eleanor asks, amazed.

'No,' Sybil replies in some irritation. "For those in peril on the sea". To comfort those waiting for news.'

'Oh yes, of course.' Faced with the fluttering eyelids and heaving bosom, Eleanor begins to feel queasy herself.

> The Acolyte leads the people in procession to the font, where the Archdeacon recites the Litany of the Saints.

Jessica stands in a stunned congregation staring at the twenty or so garden gnomes grouped around the font. She has heard of a service for clowns ... but they are flesh and blood. She wonders if the Archdeacon has taken the Bishop's message to heart and sought sponsorship. 'This year's Easter Vigil is brought to you courtesy of Walt Disney.'

She remains stock-still as he reels off the names like a roll-call. She couldn't be more surprised if the gnomes began to reply. One old lady asks in a hoarse whisper if it's the nursery school ... 'They're very good; very lifelike.' Another becomes quite distraught, flapping her coat as at a flock of chickens and shouting 'Shoo! Shoo!'

> The Archdeacon asks the people to renew their baptismal vows.

Alfred is blind to his congregation's distress. His sole concern is to integrate the newcomers. He appreciates their reticence. The ritual, so meaningful to the initiated, can seem overwhelming to the neophyte. So he guides them along, not only asking the questions but speaking the responses, and not only speaking but standing in their place, dashing from pillar to font like a comedian holding a conversation with himself.

> The Archdeacon sprinkles the people with baptismal water.

Alfred splashes the congregation, slapping his hand in the font like a child in a paddling pool.

'Is this what you call respect?' Eleanor hisses at Sybil.

'Please stop it!' Sybil shouts at Alfred, as her dripping skirt revives all her worst fears.

'It's Easter. Christ is risen. It's a time for joy,' Alfred says. 'And, at St Saviour's, that joy is magnified by our new members. What's more, they're not just here for high days and holidays. They'll be regular attenders ... present at every mass.' He turns on his congregation. 'Can you say as much? Or you? Or you? At last, I've a congregation worthy of me.'

'Alfred dear,' Henrietta entreats him. 'Perhaps this isn't the best time.'

'When better, mother? Come and introduce yourself.' He grabs her by the elbow and thrusts her among the gnomes. 'This is Peter; you'll recognize him by his fishing rod. The one in the glasses is Paul ... too many late nights writing letters. This is Luke ... see the stethoscope. And Lazarus ... he's the dozy one.'

'Alfred, you're twisting my arm.'

'Your vicar's even worse than ours,' Eleanor tells Sybil.

'Is no one else going to make them welcome?'

'But they're dwarves!' one old lady exclaims.

'So? Do you think Our Lord sets any store by height? When you stand in front of St Peter, it won't be a ruler he takes out but the Book of Life. Then we'll see who measures up: the rest of you with your sticky, sweaty desires, or these men who are impervious to sin.'

'Please Alfred,' Henrietta sobs. 'You're overwrought.' She appeals to the others. 'He works so hard and with so little support. When he finishes in church, he comes home and spends the whole night praying.'

'Nonsense, mother. I feel a new man.'

> *Let us now offer one another a sign of peace.*

Eleanor's glare makes it clear to Sybil that this is the ultimate betrayal.

'But we don't do that at St Saviour's,' Sybil says in desperation.

'Ah, but we do at St Saviour's and St Gnome's,' Alfred replies. 'Yes, as we renew our baptismal vows, I've decided to rename the Church: to make it more inclusive.'

> The Archdeacon proclaims: *The risen Christ came and stood among His disciples and said, 'Peace be with you.' Then were they glad when they saw the Lord. Christ is risen.* The congregation is silent.

'Come on! Come on!' Alfred rages. 'Christ is risen.'

Harry, worried that Alfred's derangement may be linked to Ronan's visit, leads the desultory response. 'He is risen indeed.'

'Why are you all ignoring our newcomers?' Alfred asks. 'Is this the fellowship of Christ? Remember what Our Lord said: "It is not the will of your Father which is in heaven, that one of these little ones should perish."' He laughs and runs over to the font, grabs Peter and presents him to an elderly lady. 'Christ is risen.' When she fails to respond, he presses the plaster lips to her cheek. She bursts into tears. 'What's wrong? Never kissed a beard before?' With the gnome under his arm, he moves through the scattering congregation. 'Right; that's enough of that. Back to your pews. Chop chop!'

> The people return to their pews. The Archdeacon and servers move to the altar.

Jessica mulls over the turn of events, while Alfred prepares for the Eucharist and the King's Lynn Nightingale trills the Sanctus. She speculates whether the gnomes might be an attempt to convey the surreal drama of the Resurrection. If so, it hasn't worked. A cursory glance at her fellow worshippers suggests that they would even prefer the Easter Vigil at the church in Devon where the vicar burst out of the papier-mâché egg. She has rarely felt so nostalgic for tradition. Nevertheless, along with the rest of the congregation, she remains transfixed.

> *Draw near with faith. Receive the body of our Lord Jesus Christ which he gave for you, and his blood which he shed for you.*

Eleanor resolves that she will go up to the altar. Not only is the Archdeacon unaware of her arthritis, but, if she keeps to her pew, she may be forced to give precedence to a gnome. She joins the dozen communicants who are easily accommodated around the sanctuary steps. No one kneels; although she cannot decide whether this is a liturgical preference or simply a reflection of age.

> *The Body of our Lord Jesus Christ, which was given unto thee, preserve thy body and soul unto everlasting life.*

Jessica watches Alfred giving the Host to the first old lady, like a doctor pressing a pill on a reluctant tongue. As he moves to a second old lady, the first begins to cough violently. He proceeds down the line, pressing wafers on tongues, ignoring the gulping and the hacking and even a piercing scream. Seeing him approach, she stands with her jaws clenched and her hand outstretched. He scowls at her and places the wafer on her palm. On lifting it, she sees that he has given her a quarter of a *Kit-Kat*. It isn't Easter Saturday but April Fool's Day. She can no longer keep silent.

'This is a chocolate biscuit.'

'It's the body of Christ.'

'But it's melting.'

'So you must consume it right away.'

He continues the distribution.

She looks, first, at the *Kit-Kat* sticking to her hand and, then, at Lyndon who has put his in his mouth and, finally, at Henrietta Courtney who is desperately chewing as if to dislodge crumbs from her plate. She decides that, for the sake of convenience, she will eat the biscuit. But she can no longer maintain the fiction of an alternative liturgy. The man is quite mad.

> *The Blood of Our Lord Jesus Christ, which was shed for thee, preserve thy body and soul unto everlasting life.*

Watching Alfred move down from the altar, Jessica fails to understand why he should be carrying two chalices for such a small congregation. The reason becomes clear as soon as he approaches the first communicant.

'Red or white?'

'I beg your pardon?'

'Do you want red or white?'

'Is there a choice?' she asks, bemused.

'Why else would I be asking? Red or white?'

The old lady looks to her neighbour for help, which is not forthcoming.

'Red, I suppose.'

'Very wise.' He raises the chalice to her lips. 'Red always goes better with lamb.'

Drink this in remembrance that Christ's Blood was –

'This is outrageous!' Eleanor backs away from the steps. 'Come Sybil, I refuse to be a party to blasphemy.' She takes her friend's arm, triggering a general exodus.

'You must do something,' a parishioner urges Harry.

'Why me?' Harry asks, afraid that she suspects his complicity.

In the midst of the pandemonium, Henrietta keels over.

'Please . . . give her some air,' Jessica says, crouching by her side. 'Someone fetch a kneeler.'

'She's bleeding,' an old lady shouts, pointing to the darkening skull. She turns to Alfred. 'You ought to be ashamed of yourself.'

Alfred is oblivious to everything but his abortive Eucharist. 'You may refuse the Sacrament, but there are those who'll be grateful.' He takes his chalices to the font.

'She seems to be out cold,' Jessica says, placing the kneeler beneath Henrietta's head. 'We must call an ambulance. Lyndon, run to the nearest phone.'

Lyndon stands locked in despair. 'It's all my fault,' he mutters. 'I'm damned.'

'Hurry, Lyndon please!'

'No need. I have a phone here,' Harry says, pressing the numbers on his mobile. 'Ambulance,' he replies to the operator's question.

'Two ambulances,' Eleanor calls, looking at Alfred who has continued to administer the Chalice, pouring the Blood of Christ down the lifeless lips of the gnomes.

'And the police,' Sybil adds, not to be outdone.

The Blood of Our Lord Jesus Christ, which was shed for thee, preserve thy body and soul unto everlasting life.

Edith stands in the porch gazing out into the gloom, with Stevenson the permanent chip on her shoulder. She has abandoned all attempt to conceal her hatred. 'When she dies,' she informs the parrot quietly, 'I shall boil up your carcass for a soup. I shall grind down your bones for a paste. I shall use your beak as an ashtray. And I shall pin your feathers in my hair.'

HIGH MASS OF THE RESURRECTION

Sunday 11.00 a.m.
St Mary-in-the-Vale, Hampstead

> The Vicar stands outside the smouldering church. He addresses the people: *As we gather outside our ravaged church, as empty now as Our Lord's tomb, let us remember that it was in a garden that Jesus first appeared to Mary Magdalen after his wondrous resurrection.*

Huxley is tossed on conflicting waves of heartbreak and elation. The church that has stood at the centre of his life for twenty years has been reduced to a burnt-out shell. As in some apocalyptic vision, fire has been followed by flood: anything that survived the flames has been drenched by the hoses. But the incorporeal church has not been broken; it has been fortified. From the neighbours in nightclothes forming a chain to rescue the treasures to the offers of help which have been pouring in all morning, it is clear that, far from being an irrelevance, St Mary's counts for something even to those who never enter it from one carol service to the next.

A week ago – almost to the minute – he remembers asking the congregation at Whitestone pond to draw closer to each other. The sight of the distance between them made him despair. Watching them cluster together now, his faith in their unity is restored.

He shifts his attention to the man across the tomb from him and wonders whether it is merely his singed eyebrows and bandaged neck that make him look older. For the source of his greatest happiness is that his curate has been restored to him. Whatever the challenge of health or prejudice or bureaucracy, they will rise to it. Like Mary Magdalen, he knows the joy of welcoming someone back from the dead.

> *We will now sing the first hymn on your sheet: Jesus Christ is risen today.*

Huxley hears the choir let rip as if song were its mother tongue, while the congregation joins in more tentatively, fearful that the lack of accompaniment will leave it exposed. He pictures the mangled organ pipes in the church behind him. With their music-making days over, they may have an afterlife as a sculpture. He toys with a possible title. Armageddon? Symbiosis One? Journey to the Centre of the Earth? There remains, however, the question of attribution. Should the artist be identified as Anonymous, A.R. Son, or God?

> *Hymns of praise then let us sing,*
> *Alleluia!*
> *Unto Christ, our heavenly King,*
> *Alleluia!*

Oliver takes his bearings. It's not unknown for him to wake up in unexpected places. Once, years ago, he found himself in Dover after a night in which he hadn't even dreamt of speed. But never has the morning after felt quite so distant from the night before. He gazes at Blair in his golden robes and shivers. The man who was so responsive in his arms seems to have passed out of reach.

He respects Blair for wearing his heroism lightly. Anyone would think that storming into a burning bell-tower was as much in a day's work as writing a sermon or visiting the sick. He tries to find a way of telling the story which will be acceptable to his anti-clerical friends. 'Are you saying he's a vicar?' 'No, he's a sprinter; he's a climber; he's a life-saver . . .' A stitch in his side takes him back to his dash down the hill and his desperate attempt to keep up with Blair, who was running like a man possessed. He was starting to lag behind, when a sudden fork to the left led them to a strange, Hallowe'en-like building which glowed eerily from within.

The surprise was that there was no sound . . . inside, the flames were cackling with fearsome intensity, but nothing penetrated beyond the walls. The smoke which poured from the steeple might have been painted onto the sky. It was as if the fire were intended as a private revelation for the two of them: a mystic emblem of their meeting. Then Blair broke the spell by rushing to the door where he fumbled desperately with his keys. He shouted instructions to run to the vicarage and raise the alarm – without giving any indication as to where it was. On being asked what he was doing, he gibbered about saving a pixie.

Standing among the bleary-eyed congregation, Oliver finds it hard to credit that the blazing intensity of dawn has been replaced by watery sunlight and a jolly hymn . . . although his involuntary surge of emotion is a testament to the composer's skill. Last night, as he followed Blair into the church, he was granted a vision of Hell. Tongues of flame spewed out gusts of halitosis. Funnels of smoke grabbed at his throat with the consistency of tar, showering him with sparks which scorched his eyes and pierced his skin. Fire roared down one side of the nave as though it were a foundry. But the green-golden, blue-golden, red-golden radiance was deceptive. He longed to be back in the comforting darkness of the Heath.

He felt helpless. He was determined to salvage something but, with Blair vanished into the inferno, he had no idea where to begin. A sharp image of the cross led him to battle through the buffeting smoke to the choir. Stumbling up steps as treacherous as trip-wire, he reached the altar. But, as he swept his hand across the top, he found that, in spite of having escaped the flames, the metal was red-hot. Whisking off the cloth, he gathered everything on it into a bundle and staggered back to the porch, where he met Blair who had emerged, carrying the pyx (a double reassurance), wrapped up in the vestments which both he and the Vicar now wear.

Selfish as it may seem, he had hoped for a word of praise: some small recognition of the risk he had taken on behalf of a symbol which meant little to him – and a man who was starting to mean a lot. In his head, he could hear a voice commanding him to 'Arise, Sir Oliver of the burning cross,' but it was promptly buried in Blair's cries of 'Raise the alarm!'. His departure was checked by the clang of the church-bell; which was so sinister that he wet himself (a detail to be excised from the authorized version). But, while he panicked, Blair saw that somebody was trapped, screamed at him to fetch help and rushed back inside.

He raced down the road, ringing bells and shouting at windows. He jumped from garden to garden so fast that, by the time the first door opened, he was already two houses away. After that, the sequence grows blurred; he will need to sit down in peace – with Blair – to restore its logic. His memory is a montage made up of screaming neighbours; a man in pyjamas – whom he later identified as the Vicar – having to be restrained from running into the flames; fire-engines pulling up outside the gate, their sirens wailing; and Blair appearing from the church carrying the boy in his arms ... boy! he was in his mid-teens and tall, and yet Blair (a moment to relish) did not even lurch.

While the others flocked around their curate (the kisses and hugs and handshakes surely dispelling his fears of rejection), his own relief was marred by Blair's desire to accompany the boy to hospital. He pictured his future disappearing in the back of the ambulance. It was recovered, at least temporarily, when a woman with a soft but insistent voice convinced Blair that he needed to rest and must return to the vicarage. It was then – at last – that his own presence was acknowledged, as she extended the invitation to 'your friend'. So he tagged along, clutching hold of his bundle, as though to prove that, while he may not have saved a life, he had still retrieved something of value. And, when he opened it to reveal the letter, he found that he genuinely had.

Maybe he should have left then, bowing out with a 'thanks for everything; tonight has been a real eye-opener; see you around sometime'. But, from the moment he entered the vicarage, he had as little control of his fate as if he'd joined a cult. He sat quietly on the fringes of the conversation while Blair gave them a brief (and selective) account of where he had been and Jessica told them about some weird service she'd attended and, more sombrely, about the death of a friend. After that, Huxley tackled Blair on church matters and insisted that, come what may, they would celebrate mass together this morning ... this makeshift service proves him to be as good as his word.

Then, while Huxley went to talk to the firemen, Blair took him home for a bath and a change of clothes. He learned that the joy in Blair's return was not universal when a red-eyed old woman, wrapped in a man's plaid dressing-gown, accompanied by a dumpy woman with a bread-roll plait, accosted them outside the church.

'This comes of your wickedness, Blair Ashley,' she boomed. 'God is not mocked.'

Blair, a model of forbearance, replied with a smile: 'You should go home now, Lady Blaikie. You'll catch cold; you're not dressed.'

The memory reassures him that he has nothing to fear from the robes.

> The Churchwarden reads the Lesson, from the Acts of
> the Apostles, Chapter Ten.

Brandon has not been to mass on Easter Sunday since he left the novitiate. Standing here now, he recalls the childhood celebrations which, while nothing compared to the ordeal of Christmas morning, formed a tedious prologue to the egg-hunt through his grandmother's garden. In recent years, the frustrations have been of a different order. Nevertheless, he is bound to make allowances today.

After the frantic messages left on Blair's machine and the futile visits to the house in case he was hiding, he was quite unprepared for the man himself to pick up the phone at eight thirty this morning. Pausing only to secure his promise not to go out, he drove straight over and found another of his patients, Oliver Lambert, sitting in the lounge. His first fear – that the truth was out and Blair had summoned Oliver as a witness – was banished by Blair's assertion that they had met that night on the Heath. He longed to learn the secret of Blair's change of heart, but any questions would have to wait on his own disclosures. So he asked Oliver if he would mind giving him a few minutes alone with Blair. 'Not at all,' he replied without conviction. 'It sounds like the perfect cue for a bath.'

He began by explaining that he knew that what he had done was against all ethics, medical and otherwise. The only excuse – no, not an excuse but a mitigation – lay in his anger after Julian's death, both with Blair himself and with everything he represented. He detested his blind faith in a benign God and was determined to shatter his complacency. It was only when Blair broke in and asked whether he was trying to say that he wasn't HIV Positive that he realized he was fudging the issue. Yes, he replied, adding that he had only intended to keep up the pretence for a few days, which was why he had insisted that he told no one. Then, on Friday morning, he saw it splashed all over the papers. He started to panic as he found no way to contact him, convinced that he had given way to despair.

He expected to receive a punch or a sermon (the impulse being interchangeable), but he met with silence. He promised to issue an immediate statement, setting the record straight. He could cite either a confusion of lab results (which had been his original intention) or medical malpractice ... the choice was Blair's. And he was struck by the irony that, while he babbled on like a patient trying to defy his diagnosis, Blair appeared to be struggling to adjust to his clean bill of health. He demanded repetition and reassurance. Then he held out his palms and asked where that left the lumps, which were redder and more pronounced than ever. He could only reply that 'Your guess – or faith – is as good as mine.'

Blair needed time to himself and went out to make coffee, only to return ten minutes later without any cups. As he sat down, he gave a pledge that he would lodge no complaint, on the proviso that the hospital issued no retraction. He was determined to maintain the illusion that he had HIV. It wasn't, he added quickly, that he dreamt of a martyr's crown (or was the kind of man who went in for unnecessary operations) but rather that, having understood so much more of the mystery of Christ over the past three days, he wanted to give others the same opportunity. That meant challenging them not just by his words but by his blood.

Shaking Blair's hand – as though they were their fathers – he felt a twinge of unease as he brushed against the lump ... But, if there is no one more conscious that medical science has yet to discover all the answers, then there is no one more confident that, one day, it will. He is a humanist not by default but by conviction. While he has every reason to be grateful to the Christian ethic of forgiveness, he stands here in communion with the man, not with the priest.

The Vicar reads the notices.

'As we come to the altar today, let us give thanks to Our Lord Jesus Christ who has called us out of darkness into His marvellous light. Amen.

'First, I'd like to welcome you all on this Easter Sunday morning to this somewhat unorthodox setting. I don't intend to say anything at this point about the fire, except to offer my heartfelt thanks to everyone who took part in the rescue operation. Last night's events will no doubt form the topic of much discussion in the months – maybe even the years – to come. For now, we can only look on with a mixture of sorrow and disbelief. All I would ask is that you dismiss the rather fanciful explanations which are already being bandied about. Let's leave the authorities to seek out the cause of the blaze and concentrate our own energies on the task of restoring the church.

'Until further notice, our regular services will take place in the crypt which, I'm happy to report, has escaped damage. Masses this week will be at the usual time of 10.30 on Tuesday and Thursday mornings. In addition, the monthly requiem will be on Thursday at 6.30. This provides an opportunity to remember all those whose anniversaries fall this month. Should you have any names which you wish to be included, please contact me at the vicarage.

'It seems safe to assume that the National Youth Orchestra of Romania will not now be performing next Saturday in church. Anyone who has purchased tickets should speak to Judith Shellard after the service and she will be in touch as soon as alternative arrangements have been made.

'Two places still remain for next month's parish pilgrimage to the Holy Land, where we will be visiting many of the sites in person which we have visited in our prayers over the past week.

'Let us remember in love and tenderness all the sick, especially Susan Devenish, Iris Sage, Wallace Leyland, David Fern-Bassett (priest), Cherish Akarolo, Lyndon Brooks, Henrietta Courtney and Alfred Courtney (priest). And, of your love, please pray for the souls of the faithful departed, especially Julian Blaikie who was laid to his rest last week and Lennox Hayward who died in the early hours of this morning. On them, and on all Christian souls, may our Lord Jesus Christ have mercy.

'Finally – and on a happier note, may I say how overjoyed I am –

and I'm sure that goes for all of you – to have Father Blair back among us this morning. His troubles have been widely – and wildly – reported over the past few days. And I'm delighted to say that the accusations against him have been unconditionally withdrawn. I trust that he will play his unique role in the life and worship of St Mary's for many years to come. Speaking selfishly, I admit that I'm particularly glad to see him at this service since it means that I can now ask him to deliver the sermon.'

The Curate moves to the front.

Terry, the organist, no longer aloft, turns to Blair with a slightly charred grin.

'Knock 'em dead in the grass, Father.'

The Curate climbs onto a tomb.

'If there's anyone who can't hear me, please shout out. No one? Good. My old voice teacher didn't live in vain.'

Sophie Record waves at him.

'Is there a problem, Miss Record?' he asks. 'Can't you hear me?'

As she mouths 'Junior Church', her attempt to minimize the distraction turns out to have the opposite effect.

'I'm afraid that now I'm the one who can't hear.'

'Junior Church,' she shouts and wriggles her neck in self-effacement.

'Of course,' Blair says. 'In all the excitement, Father Huxley forgot to release the children, who are meeting across the road in the vicarage. So, if they'd like to follow Miss Record...'

He watches the children shuffle through the churchyard, before catching sight of Cherish who has stayed behind.

'Aren't you going with the others, Cherish?' He fails to identify the tremor which runs through the congregation. 'Don't you want to hear the story of the risen Jesus?'

Femi is outraged that Blair, of all people, should be so insensitive.

'I do,' Cherish says, 'but they don't want me 'cos I might fall over.'

Femi longs to yell that, contrary to Huxley's belief, not everyone is thrilled by Blair's return. But she clutches Cherish in silence.

'Robin! Tristram!' Blair calls to two boys who have lagged behind the group. 'Come here a moment.'

They slink back with a show of resistance.

'You want Cherish to go to Junior Church with you, don't you?' They nod. 'Then you must each take her by the hand. That way, she won't just have two eyes, she'll have four.'

They laugh.

'Go on then. One hand each. That's right.'

Femi looks at the two mothers. But, whatever their objection, it spreads no further than their faces. She can only suppose that they have been shamed into acquiescence by Blair.

The children make their way down the path and, almost at once, Cherish stumbles. Femi jerks forward. Jessica puts a restraining hand on her arm. Cherish turns round and says through a gappy grin.

'I'm not hurt. I only slipped.'

The children walk out of the gate.

The Curate delivers the sermon.

'I hardly need to say how happy I am to be back at St Mary's. It's been quite a week. I trust you'll bear with me if I begin on a personal note. During my recent spell behind bars, I longed for nothing more than to be out in the fresh air ... I never expected my wish to be granted like this. Even so, I hope that we'll come to see the fire as a new opportunity – and one which offers us a chance to live out the truth of the Resurrection: to be transformed both as individuals and as a church.

'Like the church, I feel that I've been broken in order to be re-born (a true baptism of fire). Some of you might be uneasy with the way in which it has taken place. You might wish that I'd been struck down by something cleaner – multiple sclerosis, say, like that nice Jacqueline du Pré. If so, then I'm afraid that you have failed to grasp the reality of the Crucifixion ... far from being nice and clean, Jesus's death was exceptionally sordid: He was stripped, scorned and scourged, spat on by His torturers and spurned by the crowd, before being strung up like a common criminal. What's more, you have failed to grasp the reality of the Resurrection, when God turned the criminal into the Christ.

'Nevertheless, I know that I've offended many of you and the deferential side of me – the manners-maketh-man side – says that I should ask your forgiveness. That way, I could bask in the warmth of your magnanimity and you in the joy of my gratitude. We could all consider ourselves good people. But it would be a mistake – or, at any rate, too easy. What I ask instead is your acceptance: of me with all my failings ... of me in all my humanity. This way, we may, in time, become genuinely good people, just as I believe that, after the events of the past week, I have the chance to become a genuinely good priest, able to stand before you in the person of both the crucified and the resurrected Christ.

'My own faith has been strengthened by everything that has occurred over the past week, but I'm aware that, for some of you, the
process has been less happy. As Father Huxley said, there are various rumours already circulating from people keen to turn an act of
God (see your insurance claims) into an Act of God (see your Old
Testament). The most predictable portray it as a judgement on the
wickedness of the parish. After all – so the reasoning goes – if
lightning could strike York Minster a few days after the consecration of a Bishop who denied the literal truth of the Resurrection,
then surely flames can engulf a church where the Vicar expressed
similar doubts? Moreover, if God sent down a fire to consume the
city of Sodom, then why shouldn't He send a more localized one
where the Curate is accused of the same sin?

'But do these rumour-mongers seriously believe that, if God were
seeking out the depths of human depravity, He would start in the
Lady Chapel of St Mary-in-the-Vale rather than the killing-fields of
Rwanda or the torture-chambers of Iraq? I'm as grieved as anyone
that our beautiful church has been burnt; but it hasn't been burnt
to the ground. It's still standing, just as we're still worshipping. If
need be, we'll worship elsewhere. We must each think of ourselves,
in the Old Testament phrase, as "a brand plucked out of the fire".
Above all, we must never forget that one boy was plucked out
literally. If it weren't for the fire, he'd have hanged himself on the
bell-rope. And that's what counts for me – and I trust for everyone
else – not the destruction but the salvation. There's no stronger
Easter message than that life triumphs over death.

'So I have news for those people, both inside and outside the
Church, who treat God as their personal hitman: the Old
Testament God is dead. What's more, He never existed except in
their minds. To respond to the Easter message, we must give up
our obsession with sin – and, in particular, Original Sin – which is
a libel both on us and Our Creator. We must renounce the myth of
the Fall which, by spreading a gospel of despair, gives rise to the
very evil it purports to explain. If we are to take a leaf out of
Genesis, then let it the one on which "God saw everything that he
had made, and behold it was very good". Good, mind, not perfect.
Perfection is impossible in world which exists in time.

'Those of you who attended Julian Blaikie's funeral on Tuesday
will remember Father Huxley's address in which he spoke of time
as a mixed blessing: the source at once of our freedom and our
discontent. It is our fate, as the creatures closest to God, to be the
ones most aware of the distance. Which is why, when Christ came
to earth, it was as a man. By becoming one with us, He reminded

us that we are one with God. And, although in our liturgy, we speak
of Christ as perfect, what we're actually celebrating is His imperfection: that, in Him (as in us), perfection and imperfection are one.
God's greatest gift to humanity is not that He gave us perfection
but that He gave up His own. God personified Himself in Jesus
and, by extension, in you and me. And it's essential that we accept
this not just with our minds but with our whole beings. We must
stop tormenting ourselves with our faults and see that humanity –
even the messy bits – is a thing to honour not to revile. After all,
the Word became flesh, not light or music or even bread or wine (at
least not at first). Can there be any surer stamp of divine approval?

'The truth is that Christ became incarnate not in order to redeem
a sinful people who had cut themselves off from salvation but to
reassure a suffering people of their unity with God. Or, to put it
another way, the world was not in a state of sin waiting for Christ
to rescue it; the world is in a state of grace, waiting for us to
recognize it.

'So I ask that, as you come up to take the Eucharist, you acknowledge not just the Son's sacrifice but the Father's: not just the
Crucifixion, when "eternity redeemed time" (I hope you can hear
the inverted commas), but the Creation, when eternity subjected
itself to time. That is the Spirit from which we are born and that is
the Spirit to which we will be restored. For, in God, there is no
death but only an everlasting life in which we will be free of all the
defects of our bodies and all the constraints of our personalities, as
we return in a state of perfect energy to become one with eternal
bliss. Amen.'

> The Vicar leads the prayers of intercession.
> *Father, we praise you for the resurrection of your son Jesus*
> *Christ from the dead.*
> *Shed his glorious light on all Christian people that we may*
> *live as those who believe in the triumph of the Cross.*
> *Lord hear us.*
> *Lord, graciously hear us.*

Huxley affirms the triumph of the Cross after a week in which he
was caught in its shadow. Reflecting on all the doubt and despair,
the anguish and the mourning, he wonders if God decided that,
after twenty-eight years as a priest – not to mention his constant
complaint that he spends more time at the photocopier than at
prayer – he was growing stale and needed a refresher-course in the
meaning of Easter. Whatever its purpose, the stratagem has worked.
The moment he touched the font, he felt a life-giving energy surge

through his hands like a pianist in a come-back concert. Every inch of his body thrilled with faith, in clear confirmation of the double baptism.

His faith has returned and Blair has returned and the two seem closely connected, although he would be hard-pressed to say how. Blair has shown that the sermon can be as holy as the Sacrament, involving its own form of transubstantiation: from words into truth. Meanwhile, in the letter snatched up from the altar, he has the conclusive answer to anyone who believes that the fire was fuelled by God. It was a suicide-note from Lyndon, which, with all the melodrama of youth, he had placed like a calling-card at the foot of the cross. With its rescue, more than one life was saved for, in it, Lyndon confessed that Blair's behaviour towards him had been perfectly proper and that the offence had been wholly his.

This was the point he himself emphasized to the Bishop's Chaplain, when he rang London House to report on the fire and to request that the Bishop withdraw Blair's suspension. But the Chaplain's only comment was to do as he thought fit. The Bishop was suffering from nervous exhaustion and spending Easter Day in bed.

> *We pray for those who at this season are receiving in baptism your Son's new life by water and the Spirit.*
> *Dying with Christ, may they know the power of his resurrection.*
> *Lord, hear us.*
> *Lord, graciously hear us.*

Petula prays for Lloyd, whom she fears will never now be baptized, and certainly not at St Mary's. The ravaged church rules out any imminent ceremony, even if his grandparents were to relent – a prospect which seems particularly remote, given her own theory about the genesis of the blaze. Rather than look to some supernatural power, she finds her suspect close at hand. She names no name, but it is double-barrelled. Lest she be accused – not least by herself – of being swayed by her emotions, she cites his two guiding principles: profit and pride. Both will be endorsed if the church is finally forced to sell the clergy-house to pay for its under-insurance and the pyre of Alice's paintings makes up for his humiliation last night. A quick call on his mobile phone is all that he would have needed. No one has an address book filled with so many conscienceless people, neatly filed under 'B' for block or 'C' for concrete or 'D' for drains.

She glances at Trudy, whom she has had no chance to speak to since Good Friday, and is reassured by her air of resilience. Turning away, she is aware of Hugh, pressed tightly against her and yet somehow more distant than he ever was in a pew. She is confused by his return. One part of her is relieved that he has chosen Tufnell Park over some jerry-built, Jeffrey-financed development in Spain. Another is suspicious that he should have abandoned his hopes in the middle of Thea's party. She is unable to escape the fear that his penitence is part of a secret plan. Nevertheless, it seems heartfelt. And, if it took courage for him to confront her in the privacy of her mother's flat, it takes even more to brave the entire congregation. She wants to signal her support, but mistrust is less easy to rub from her eyes than sleep.

She has no choice but to forgive him ... or, if she does, it is the sort to read about under the hair-dryer not to exercise for herself. When she woke at first light, cramped on her mother's couch, she could not be sure that she still had a husband. She tried to imagine what it would be like to spend the rest of her life alone. Then she looked at her mother and knew.

> We pray for all whom we know and love, both near and far.
> May their eyes be opened to see the glory of the risen Lord.
> Lord, hear us.
> Lord, graciously hear us.

Esther prays for Alice and Dee; she scarcely knows them but she already knows that she loves them. There can be no clearer proof of their good hearts than that, in the middle of last night's chaos, they still found the time to think of her. They put her in a bedroom full of ancient maps. She curled up against a background of strangely shaped and brightly coloured places. Confounding expectations, she slept as soundly as a child. Then, after thirty-six years of lying next to Ted – with no escape but the labour ward – she awoke to the inestimable luxury of being single in a double bed. She savoured the freedom surrounding her in all directions: her own sheets; her own blankets; her own pillows; her own skin.

Thirty-six years: the echoes of a prison sentence are deafening. But she will put them behind her – even her prayers are liberating this morning. Thirty-six years: it is a gross miscarriage of justice. People should write to *The Times*: petition Lambeth Palace: protest outside London House. Thirty-six years for a crime she did not commit ... or did she? Doubts rise up, along with the gravelly voice of the Clerk.

'Esther Bishop, you are charged with the murder of ·Esther Harris. What do you plead?'

'Not guilty of murder but guilty of manslaughter, on the grounds of diminished responsibility.'

Diminished responsibility: is there any better definition of love?

She did once love Ted; now she doesn't even pity him. Their relationship has gone the same way as their Christmas trees. First, they put up a fresh one every year. Next, they tried to save money by planting the old one in the garden. Finally, after the children left home, they chose a synthetic one. It was cheaper, more practical and created less mess. Besides, as Ted never failed to remind her, they had the real thing in church.

She wonders how he'll cope. She pictures him trying to cook. He won't even know where to find the pans. Perhaps he'll extend his chaplain's duties to the kitchen; or perhaps some of his predecessor's female helpers will return . . . a divorced bishop being the next best thing to a celibate. She marvels at her own daring: slipping in 'divorced' as easily as 'Anglican' or 'bald'. She teases the word as though she were testing the waters. It is far too soon to know if she will ever speak it out loud, but, at least, it's no longer taboo.

So whether or not her future is with Molly, one thing is certain; it will be with Esther . . . Esther, 'named after the only book in the Bible in which God doesn't appear'. Nevertheless, He has reappeared in her life. For the first time in years, Easter will be more than a word.

> *We pray for those who suffer pain and anguish.*
> *Grant them the faith to reach out towards the healing*
> *wounds of Christ and be filled with His peace.*
> *Lord, hear us.*
> *Lord, graciously hear us.*

The thought of pain shoots straight to Myrna's legs. She has stood all the way through the sermon as though it were the gospel; now she has to stand through the prayers. Huxley wanted her to perch on a grave, but she was brought up in a house where it was an affront even to sit on somebody else's chair.

Everything is going up in flames. It seems only yesterday that it was Windsor Castle. Her aches and pains are compounded by a pang of conscience as she remembers that she has still to write to the Queen . . . She forces her mind back to the prayers, trying to separate the onset of cramp from the Vicar's 'anguish'. She focuses instead on Petula and Hugh. Her heart went out to Hugh when he arrived after breakfast, looking as though he had found his winning pools coupon still in his pocket. She almost broke down when he coupled his apology with a promise to let her move in with them.

And yet, although there is nothing she would like more, she intends to refuse. They need space for themselves if they are ever to
rebuild their lives.

What they can do is help her to move into a new home ... one
where she won't be in the way, or, at least, no more so than any of
the other residents. What has long seemed an admission of defeat
– as macabre as an actress sleeping in a coffin – now reveals its
attractions. *The Fortunes of Myrna*, she fantasizes, with a nod to the
boarding-school stories of her youth. The trick is to look on the
bright side. 'I'm H-A-P-P-Y; I'm H-A-P-P-Y': if she sings it often
enough, she is bound to believe it. With so many activities on offer,
the right home will be as jolly as taking a cruise – only without the
sickness. At eighty-six, her independence is as expendable as the
rest of her belongings. She will give up everything, entering the
Lent of her life in readiness for the exultant Easter of her end.

> *We remember before you those who have died in the hope of*
> *the resurrection.*
> *Unite us with them in your undying love.*
> *Lord, hear us.*
> *Lord, graciously hear us.*

Jessica remembers Lennox: a father-figure to whom she felt closer
than she did to her own father; but then she didn't know him so
well. He died at the right time. Before the service, Rosemary Trott
accosted her with a Sunday paper. Amid all the royal stories (the
Divorce Court Circular), it devotes a two-page spread to Lennox,
whom it dubs 'the red doctor', reporting his pre-war activism as
though it had a direct bearing on Blair's protest. Moreover, it prints
a picture of his wife which is the very one that was stolen from his
flat. Stifling her fury, she wonders whether she can sue them. 'No
flowers, but donations are required to mount a private prosecu-
tion...' No, too much energy has already been wasted. Even so,
nothing makes her regret the demise of old-fashioned fire and
brimstone more than the lesser fate awaiting tabloid journalists.

'What do you intend to do about it?' Rosemary asked, as affronted as if she had discovered Trotsky dining at Claridges.

'Bury him,' she replied wearily. 'Lennox died during the night.'

At least she was with him. For that, if for nothing else, she must
thank the Archdeacon. If she hadn't had to take Henrietta
Courtney to Casualty (where her injuries turned out to be less severe than her shock at finding that her son had been detained –
forcibly – elsewhere), she would not have had the chance to visit
Lennox. The Sister's warning that his condition had deteriorated

rapidly was confirmed when he did not so much as open his eyes to acknowledge her presence. The sole sign of life was the strange sewing motion of his right hand. Then, as his arm sagged, she realized that he hadn't been sewing but writing. She desperately tried to retrace the words, as if deciphering them would reveal the answer to everything. But they had vanished into air.

Now Huxley must conduct another funeral. It is just as well that he believes in the Resurrection when he has to bury so many of his friends. If she thanks God for nothing else, she thanks Him for restoring her husband's faith. For her own part, she can only continue the quest for meaning, even if it proves to be as elusive as the pattern in a dying man's phantom phrase.

> *Join our voices, we pray, Lord our God, to the songs of all*
> *your saints in proclaiming that you give us the victory*
> *through Jesus Christ our Lord.*
> *Amen.*

Blair has returned from three days in Hell. Although any official victory celebration will have to wait for the Bishop's withdrawal of his suspension, he has been immensely heartened to see how many of his parishioners are already waving flags. The Vicarage bunting was only to be expected, but he worried about the welcome he would receive elsewhere. And yet so far, apart from Lady Blaikie and Edith who are boycotting the service, it has been entirely favourable. Judith and Rosemary even gritted their teeth to greet him together. The most moving gesture, however, came from young Fiona Hayden who, with one leg twisted round the other, handed him an Easter egg. 'A curate's egg,' he said to her bemusement. Whereupon her mother, who was with her, smiled and said 'Like life'.

His own life now demands a far more positive assessment than the mere 'excellent in parts'. He feels an excitement about adopting his new identity, reminiscent of rehearsing for a new role. The urge to assume an HIV status, when so many are at pains to conceal it, is yet another of the paradoxes of priesthood. There can be no surer way to present the reality of the Cross.

The one person for whom he must resume his own flesh is Oliver, who (a more worrying paradox) is the one person who may turn away, spurning him in favour of another man who measures his mortality in his blood. He can only trust that their intimacy will render all such distinctions invalid ... that, incarnate in one another, they will be able to overcome every obstacle, however minute. And he could not be living in a more auspicious parish. The Vale of Health took its name from the refuge it offered to Londoners who were fleeing the ravages of the Great Plague. It will offer just such a refuge again.

> The Vicar proclaims the Peace.
> *The peace of the risen Christ be always with you.*
> *And also with you. Alleluia!*
> *Let us offer one another a sign of peace.*

Huxley is determined to greet the entire congregation. The expression of peace must be as inclusive as Thursday's Washing of Feet. He hugs and shakes hands with his friends and neighbours, allowing no variation in the rigour of his grip or the firmness of his voice. Having presented his cheek for Judith's peck, he is both amazed and delighted to see his younger daughter standing with her husband and twin sons next to Jessica. The setting isn't conducive to long embraces, but he makes an exception for the boys, scooping them into his arms. On announcing to Tim that 'Christ is risen', he learns in return that 'Roly, Alison, Uncle Luke and Aunty Helen are coming too, but it's supposed to be a surprise.' Laughing, he shields Tim from his parents' rebukes. 'Thank you,' he says to Jessica and continues on his round.

> *Christ is risen!*
> *He is risen indeed!*

Blair moves through the congregation in an opposite circle to Huxley. He tries to shake off the image of the Queen and Prince Philip dividing the guests at a Palace garden party, but the proximity of Myrna Timson prints it firmly on his brain. He walks up to her, taking her right hand in both of his, as though to make a double point: Christ is risen, and he has returned; the one triumphant, the other contrite. She adds her left hand and kisses him. To complete the reconciliation, he approaches her daughter, which is easy, and her son-in-law, which is hard. Nevertheless, the intensity of Hugh's gaze as they exchange greetings gives him grounds for hope.

He seeks out Oliver, afraid that he may be feeling excluded as friends and neighbours offer the first fruits of peace to each other, leaving strangers to pick up the scraps. And yet, whether as a result of the informal setting or a more considered reaction to the Easter message, people have reached wide and Oliver's hand is warm. 'Christ is risen!' he proclaims, hoping that the tenderness of his smile and the intensity of his touch will relieve any stiffness in the phrase. And, while it may be as routine as standing for the National

Anthem, Oliver's emphatic response, in both word and gesture, leaves him deeply moved.

He walks on to Femi.

> *Christ is risen!*
> *He is risen indeed!*

Femi can shake Blair's hand, but she cannot forgive him. She looks at his face and sees it livid with Cherish's lesions. Gender, age and colour are minor distinctions; all that really counts is blood. She refuses to share in the rejoicing at his return, not least because it is led by the very women who rejected Cherish. They may be taken in, but she knows him for a hypocrite and a coward, who has been charting the course of his own illness under the guise of pastoral concern.

He offers her the peace of Christ, when he has forfeited all right to it. He has made as many sacrifices to his animal nature as if he were worshipping the Golden Calf. He has raised up the body of Christ with the smell of other men's bodies still stale on his skin. He has thrust his deviance in peoples' faces like a picket's banner. No cassock and stole can compensate for such exposure.

As if he can read her mind, he keeps hold of her hand for far longer than necessary. She feels doubly compromised to find people looking at her as though she were especially favoured. What's worse is that there is no one to whom she can acknowledge the truth. She can hardly criticize him to Alice, when it was the disclosure of her affair with Dee which soured their own friendship. And Jessica would laugh and attribute her objections to Africa ... the same tribal culture that shaped the ancient Jews. Then she'd insist on the need for minorities to stick together, forging a spurious connection between those victimized on account of their sexuality and those victimized on account of their skin.

She feels an urgent need to shake more hands – to shake off her bitterness and to restore the spirit of Easter. But the first person to approach her is Joe.

> *Christ is risen!*
> *He is risen indeed!*

As Joe exchanges the Peace with Femi, and by extension with Cherish, he feels a lightening in his load of guilt. The removal of responsibility (however indirect ... however irrational), which has long eluded his counsellor, has finally occurred. And yet, as he turns to greet Blair, he credits the process not to Easter Sunday but rather to Good Friday, when he discovered that Blair had HIV. It was the knowledge of their common status which gave him the strength to speak out last night. Others may relieve his symptoms (he nods to Brandon), but no one else could erase the stigma. Ever his own worst critic, even he must hold fire now that they are travelling down the same road.

He is pleased that Blair should want to introduce him to his friend, and yet quite unprepared for the effect of taking his hand. A single touch sends the blood racing through his body. And yet the attraction lies far deeper than sex. They have never met before, but it is as if they are already linked on some primal level. Their liquid selves affirm the bond. Far from feeling threatened, he enjoys an extraordinary sense of peace.

With great reluctance, he breaks away to face Dee.

> *Christ is risen!*
> *He is risen indeed!*

Dee kisses Joe on the lips, as a signal to anyone watching that, although their marriage may be only in name, their affection is real. Her greatest fear – far greater than failing to identify his favourite breakfast cereal for the Immigration Officers – is of being summoned to identify his body. She wishes him the peace of a world in which 'virus' has become a metaphor for the past. A tremor of mortality runs through her and she hurries to Alice. Kissing her (also on the lips, but with a very different emphasis), she wishes her the peace of a world in which her life can be as bold as her art. She leans over to kiss Dora, who is sleeping so soundly that any expression of peace appears to be superfluous. So, instead, she prays that she will never forfeit the security of her mother's arms.

Having exhausted the people with whom her peace is already secured, she moves on to those in whom she has always detected disapproval, starting with Judith.

> *Christ is risen!*
> *He is risen indeed!*

Judith distrusts the free-for-all of this alfresco Peace, preferring the more measured exchanges of the pews. Her practice, whenever possible, is to single out people she dislikes, thereby ensuring that her greeting is disinterested. Today, she heads first for Rosemary, steeling her wrist in advance. Fears confirmed (and fingers crushed), she moves to Hugh, whom she is astounded to see at the service so soon after his unmasking. He responds with a gruff voice but a grateful gesture, revealing an unexpected softness in the calloused palm.

Bracing herself, she advances on Bertha, who looks at her proffered hand as though at a sandwich, tentatively lifting a finger to
see what's spread inside.

> *Christ is risen!*
> *He is risen indeed!*

Bertha clutches her arm as closely to her side as if it were valuable.
She wasn't born yesterday. When people who usually shun her like
a bad smell suddenly crowd around her, she knows that they are
after something. It's a disgrace. Just because it's church, perfect
strangers think that they have the right to fondle her. If they behaved this way anywhere else, they'd be arrested. Now the German
woman who claims that she comes from Austria is walking towards
her, and she will have to take her hand to show that she has forgotten the war. 'Peace be with you, Bertha,' she says; as though
she doesn't know it's Easter. 'It's no use; you won't be getting a
penny,' she replies; which shuts her up. She knows what's behind
everything. They want to steal all her money to rebuild the
church.

> *Christ is risen!*
> *He is risen indeed!*

Trudy is no longer afraid of the Peace, having found a peace in
herself. She is grateful for all the hands that are offered and holds
out her own in return, but she can no longer hold out her heart.
She had not intended to come to church this morning, but, when
she opened her curtains and saw the flames, she knew that she
must. And yet it is not the real her ... she found that at last night's
Seder, and she will be returning to it this afternoon. The strange
thing about the service is that, although she has been able to follow
every word, it has no meaning for her – rather like hearing
German after she moved to England. But, this time, she knows
better than to tear up her past. So, when people speak to her of
Christ, she resorts to a careful compromise, replying with a more
general expression of Peace.

She looks for Jessica, the one person whom she can trust to wish
her Peace without its personification.

> *Peace be with you.*
> *And also with you.*

The Peace is the part of the service which Jessica always enters
most fully, being the part more concerned with people than with
words. This morning she makes straight for Lionel, fearful that her

fellow worshippers' squeamishness might compromise the universal welcome. And yet his help in rescuing the treasures, all the more heroic in view of the rebuff he'd received on Palm Sunday, ought to persuade even the most rigid of them to unbend.

She clasps his hand, taking care not to squeeze the grubbily bandaged knuckles. 'Christ is risen,' she proclaims, which seems to confuse him. But then, to someone sleeping rough on the Heath, the liturgical calender must be even more remote than the secular.

'You've been chucked out too,' he said, as he watched them prepare for the service.

'In a way,' she said.

He laughed and pointed at Rosemary busily placing service-sheets on strategic tombs. 'Then I can tell that stuck-up cow, she's no better than me after all.'

'No one's better than anyone,' she replied. Then, conscious of last week's confusion, she pointed to the vicarage and extracted his promise to join them for a family lunch.

> The Vicar announces the offertory hymn:
> *Love's redeeming work is done.*

Judith passes round the collection plate. Unlike her fellow sidesman who affects indifference (transferring the attention to the trees which she used to pay to the walls), she considers it her duty to assess every contribution: smiling at the notes, weighing up the freewill envelopes, and glaring at anyone over the age of a paper-round who slips in less than a pound. It is not that she is mercenary by nature – she would far rather let herself be overcharged than query the items on a bill – but she cannot afford such delicacy when it comes to the church. Here, shortfalls in generosity must be made up in shame.

Her powers of persuasion will soon be put to the test. The sight of the devastated church is seared on her brain: the Moses window melted; the Eden mosaic scorched; the Lady Chapel smouldering like an argument. It will take a Herculean effort to restore it: auctions, tombolas and concerts; jumble-sales, jamborees and jam. And, as churchwarden, it will be her responsibility to give a lead. But she will not falter. St Mary's is her home. Poets and politicians have plaques put on their houses; she has left money for one to be placed on the transept wall ... 'Judith Shellard, who "of her want did cast in all that she had". Erected in her memory by her friends.'

> *Vain the stone, the watch, the seal!*
> *Christ has burst the gates of hell;*

> *Death in vain forbids his rise;*
> *Christ has opened Paradise.*

As he picks up the collection plate, Hugh feels Judith watching him like a probation officer. She may have offered him Christ's peace, but she is far more guarded with her own. He will need all his ingenuity if he is to win back her trust. Nevertheless, the fire may turn out to his advantage. Instead of resigning from the PCC and leaving decisions about the restoration work to a bunch of Sunday School teachers and flower-arrangers who'll be easy pickings for every cowboy in London (he stops short with a jolt), he will volunteer his services to the Vicar. Blair is not the only one who deserves a second chance.

> *Lives again our glorious King;*
> *Where, O death, is now thy sting?*
> *Dying once, he all doth save;*
> *Where thy victory, O grave?*

Alice's cheque is only a part of her offering. As well as money for the restoration, she will present her work. Never too proud to as- cribe her own good fortune to a higher power, she sees the survival of her paintings when so much else has been burnt as a sure sign that they have found favour. In addition, the two closest to the baptistery – and in the direct path of the flames – were the two which Jeffrey Finch-Buller tore off the wall. So the man who had most objected to them is the man responsible for their rescue. Which proves, according to Dee, that God has a healthy sense of irony as well as a genuine love of art.

She has been inspired to create a replacement for the triptych on the Lady Chapel altar. She will depict a new image of motherhood which draws on all the women in the Bible: not only Mary, but Sarah and Hagar and Rachel and Leah and Naomi and Ruth. Moreover, now that Blair has demolished the old view of Eden (and the fire has scorched its representation on the chancel floor), she will devote the centrepiece to Eve.

The Curate elevates the Host.

Although Trudy no longer feels able to take the Sacrament, she still feels a part of the communion. On the way to church, she bumped into Jessica rushing down the path in search of bread for the Host. She thought of the box of *Matzah* which her friends had given her to take home and which she had kept in her bag for luck. Dismissing the fear that it might be sacrilegious, she produced it for Jessica, who pronounced it perfect. So, although she won't be going up to the rail (or rather the railing around the tomb of Curtis and Deborah Fitton), she is cheered to find that, in her own way, she remains one with them and that the passover bread of the Jews is again serving for the body of Christ.

> *Behold the lamb of God, who takes away the sins of the*
> *world! Happy are those called to his supper.*
> *Lord, I am not worthy to receive you, but only say the word*
> *and I shall be healed.*

Blair trembles at his audacity, as he extends the message of the sermon to the heart of the liturgy and replaces the prayer book's expression of unworthiness with a ringing declaration of faith: 'Lord, I am worthy to receive you.' The change fails to elicit the slightest response from the congregation, who are either too rapt or too inattentive to notice. But Huxley, who is sharing the celebration, catches his eye and smiles. He alone has grasped both the words and the meaning: Christ proved us worthy when He took on our skin, not our sin.

> The Vicar announces the closing hymn:
> *Jesus lives! thy terrors now*
> *Can no more, Oh death, appal us*

'I wonder if I might butt in,' Blair says. 'You've held your own brilliantly against the passing aircraft, but may I ask you to sing this final hymn with particular gusto. As most of you know, Lyndon Brooks suffered minor injuries in the fire. He's currently under observation at the Royal Free. When I called to see him before the service, he promised me that he'd be here in spirit. I told him we could do better than that. So let's raise our voices so high that he'll hear them halfway down the hill.'

> *Jesus lives! henceforth is death*
> *But the gate of life immortal.*

As the congregation responds to his request, Blair recalls his visit to Lyndon, who marked his approach by pulling the sheet over his head, thereby transforming the ward into the morgue that had been his intended destination. The presence of his parents, by turn reproachful and apologetic, created further tension, which was only relieved when he persuaded them to go down to the café for a drink. Then, acutely conscious of the other two patients (whose eavesdropping was, in part, impeded by their earphones), he gently but firmly drew down the sheet, to be confronted by Lyndon's flushed face.

'How are you?' he asked.

'Can't complain; mustn't grumble,' he reeled off as though by rote. 'I must be all right; they're only keeping me here for tests. They think that the rope may have damaged my throat. Every word I speak feels like there's an old bottle-top stuck down it.'

'Then perhaps we shouldn't talk.'

'It feels just as bad when I breathe.'

'You do realize that that was a very stupid thing to do.'

Lyndon tried to burrow back beneath the sheet, but he was too quick for him. 'What else could I do after all the trouble I'd caused?'

'You might have tried saying sorry.'

'Sorry's what you say when you stand on someone's toe.'

'Then find some other word ... but don't bury it in a suicide note. Quite apart from the waste of your own life and the blight of your parents', it would have caused a lot more trouble – not least to me.'

'And, if I did find the word, would you forgive me?'

'Try me.'

'I mean you – not Father Blair but Blair Ashley.'

'As I said: try me.'

Lyndon gazed at him with a glimmer of hope.

'No, I couldn't. I've done the worst thing anyone's ever done to you.'

'If you talked to me, you'd find that that isn't true. If anything, it's quite the opposite. The events you caused – or rather, set in motion – have helped to empower me. They've led me to find more strength in myself – and other people – than I'd have ever thought possible. Strange as it may sound, this has been the most profound and passionate Holy Week of my life.'

'You're not just saying that like a Get Well Soon card?'

'Cross my heart.'

'And hope to die?'

'No, not for a long time ... Now I must go. I've a sermon to preach in an hour. I'll come back for a longer visit this afternoon. I just wanted to check how you were, so I'd be able to reassure all your friends.'

'What friends?'

'Do you want me to read out the parish register?'

Lyndon allowed himself a brief smile.

'Tell them I'll be there in spirit.'

'I think we can do better than that. We're holding the service in the churchyard. Are you allowed out of bed?' Lyndon nodded.

'Then stand by the window around noon. I'll ask them to sing the final hymn especially for you.'

Blair grins as he pictures the glow of reassurance on Lyndon's cheek and roars out the final Alleluia.

The Vicar pronounces the blessing.
You have mourned for Christ's sufferings; now you celebrate his resurrection. May you come with joy to the everlasting feast.
Amen.

The Curate speaks the dismissal.
Go in peace to love and serve the Lord.
In the name of Christ. Amen.

Author's Note

I am indebted to many people for their assistance in my researches, among them the Revd. Willie Booth; William Coley; the Revd. Tom Devonshire-Jones; Ernest David, the Association of Jewish Refugees; the Revd. David Fudger; the Revd. Joe Hawes; the Revd. Andrew Henderson; the Revd. Malcolm Johnson; the Revd. Richard Kirker; Canon Peter Larkin; Dr Louise London; the Revd. Bernard Lynch SMA; the late Right Revd. Brian Masters; the Very Revd. Michael Mayne; Revd. Mark Oakley; the Revd. Graham Oliver; the Revd. Rob Pearson; Rabbi Mark Solomon; the Revd. Brian Thewlis; the Revd. Mike Way; the Revd. Alan West; the Right Revd. Roy Williamson; Julie Woodland and the staff of the Wiener Library; Michael Zimmerman.

My heartfelt thanks to Hilary Sage and Penelope Hoare for their help with the text.

I gratefully acknowledge the financial support of the Society of Authors during the writing of the novel.